A KISS FOR A LADY

"Enough!" Frederica snapped. "I like to keep busy."

"Busy, I understand," Blackthorn said dryly, "but running off your legs I do *not*."

Frederica's chin rose. "Since you've no *need* to understand, there's an end of it, is there not?" she asked, her temper rising.

"Why," he asked, on a rueful note, "do you fall into a snippy-fit when all I ask, and that innocently, is that you have a care for yourself?"

"Is that what you did?" she retorted. "It sounded like more of your bullying, my lord, and I'll not have you thinking you know best when you *don't*."

"Cat." He grinned at her reference to an earlier conversation. "Sheathe those claws and promise you'll come to Seymour Court for Christmas."

"I won't promise." She raised her eyes and met the warmth in his. Unable to resist his silent pleading, she added, "But, I'll think about it." She gave him her hand. "Good-bye, my lord."

Instead of shaking it in conventional fashion, Blackthorn lifted it toward his lips and then, almost as if he could not help himself, he turned it, raising it to place a real kiss to Frederica's wrist, his eyes never leaving hers . . .

Books by Jeanne Savery

THE WIDOW AND THE RAKE

A REFORMED RAKE

A CHRISTMAS TREASURE

A LADY'S DECEPTION

CUPID'S CHALLENGE

LADY STEPHANIE

A TIMELESS LOVE

A LADY'S LESSON

Published by Zebra Books

A LADY'S LESSON

Jeanne Savery

Zebra Books
Kensington Publishing Corp.

http://www.zebrabooks.com

ZEBRA BOOKS are published by

Kensington Publishing Corp.
850 Third Avenue
New York, NY 10022

First Printing: September, 1997
10 9 8 7 6 5 4 3 2 1

Printed in the United States of America

Chapter One

"You are a brute, my lord. A monster of insensitivity," raged the red-haired termagant facing His Lordship.

Spencer James Matthew Seymour, Earl of Blackthorn, blinked. "A monster of insensitivity?"

"You don't *deserve* such a wonderful son!" Frederica MacKivern held her own squirming and grimacing boy by one ear. Her other hand touched his arms, patted his face, unconsciously checking that he was all in one piece. "Such an intelligent lad. So polite!" she stormed.

Surprise had had Blackthorn off stride, but now, brows drawing together, his own temper roused a notch. "And *healthy* I hope!" he said coldly. "Don't forget healthy. If my heir has not been well cared for I'll know the reason why!"

"Servants!" Rickie sneered, "Oh, your servants have always done their duty. The boy, my lord, is a healthy lad—" Her expression clouded. "—but he's *unhappy*." Almost under her breath she added, "I cannot bear to see a child unhappy."

"I know of no reason my son should be unhappy," retorted Lord Blackthorn.

He looked at the scowling face of the lad he'd just returned at much inconvenience to himself to the widowed Mrs. Mac-Kivern and, for the first time, he wondered why, at the beginning of their long vacation from school, the boys had managed, thanks to a great deal of luck and no little ingenuity, the complicated exchange of homes. "Besides, if we are to speak of unhappy sons, then what of your own?"

Frederica glanced down at the twelve-year-old she could not bear to release. He was home. After months away at that awful school where she could not see him, check on him, scold him, love him, he was *home!*

But, as His despicable Lordship suggested, it was also true her son wasn't exactly happy about it.

Frederica put that thought aside for later cogitation. She was calmer, having lost steam in the contemplation of her son's rebellion. Much more quietly she said, "Stewart, your friend Matthew is with your cousins up at the Hall. Please bring him here. His father may—" Her scowl returned and she glared at His Lordship. "*—although I doubt it,* wish to see that his son is in good spirits."

"Good spirits, hmm?"

Now that he knew his heir was safe, exactly where he'd been told the lad would be, and *not* the victim of a plot so twisted he couldn't fathom its aim, Blackthorn felt an unworthy desire to prod this wild beauty into a further show of passion. Juniper! That hair . . . ! That alone was enough to tempt the man, but the spirit and energy and the striking looks . . . Oh, yes, he wanted to see much more of this one!

So, in pursuance of his goal he quirked a brow, stared at the clouds scudding across the sky and, in a voice meant to be overheard, muttered, "How can he possibly be in good spirits if he's unhappy?"

Frederica quickly obliged him, firing up and storming at him. "Matthew *is* unhappy! Any boy needs his father, but does poor Matthew ever receive a word, either praise or scold, from the one person who should have only his best interest at heart? No, he does not! To never even *see* the man who means everything in the world to him! To never know if he is doing well or ill, or right or wrong, or . . ."

"Now wait just one moment here!" Blackthorn, suddenly finding himself on the defensive, didn't like it one bit. He ran splayed fingers through his hair, releasing the firmly controlled waves into curls almost as wild as his tormenter's. "I'd know at once if he were doing badly in his studies, or if he were sick or . . ."

"At once?" Frederica MacKivern asked, her brows rising in scornful arcs. "Then why did it take *a very long week* before you knew he was missing from his home?"

In this at least he was on safe ground and Blackthorn relaxed slightly, although not much. "It didn't," he said.

Frederica's exceptionally expressive eyebrows twisted into a pattern indicating skepticism.

"It is merely," continued His Lordship, "that I could not leave London for a day or two—"

Blackthorn scowled when the woman's lips twisted to match the brows.

"—I've duties in the government, Mrs. MacKivern," he added in an icy tone, "of which you can have no under-standing."

Was that astonishment he now saw? Her words revealed it was.

"Not understand?" she exclaimed. "That you are occupied in the attempt to discover a means by which Prinny will not turn your friends out of power, putting in the other side the instant he's confirmed as Regent? What is so difficult in that to understand!" She sent him a mocking look. "But *of course* such plans are *far* more important than that one small boy know his father loves him!"

"You scorn my responsibilities, but perhaps the state of the nation, which those others to whom you refer would casually set to ruin, *is* more important than one small boy!"

"Mad. You are *mad!* Nothing is more important than that we raise our children in such a way they'll be good leaders for the *next* generation."

Unable to counter that point, His Lordship was thankful he needn't—especially when there really wasn't anything one *could* say—nothing which would be a proper set down to the woman before him, anyway. He turned, a young voice calling to another having caught his attention.

His son. Unexpectedly, Blackthorn felt his heart fill.

His heir was a well-looking boy, healthy as the termagant had said, and with such a hopeful look on his boyish features. What, wondered His Lordship, did one say to one's son and heir at such a delicate age? What was there to speak of? Ah, if only the years would pass and the boy become a man, a companion, rather than a duty!

"Well, sir, I've brought him," said MacKivern. In an aside, he added, "Make your bow, stupid. You mustn't just eat him with your eyes, you know!"

Instantly Matthew Spencer James Seymour blushed red. He bowed. "Good day to you, my lord Father. I hope you had a pleasant journey?"

Lord Blackthorn felt the scornful woman beside him silently prodding him on, but he'd never held the boy, never taken him into his arms . . . and didn't know how to start now.

"Well, Matthew . . ." He cleared his throat. "A long and *unexpected* journey, of course—"

Junipers! He called me my lord, thought Blackthorn, a sudden sharp pain hitting him a frightful emotional blow. *Is he frightened of me?*

"—but not unpleasant," he added quickly and a trifle loudly. He cleared his throat. "You need not move to defend my son, young MacKivern," he added, when, adopting a belligerent stance, Stewart John MacKivern, as his mother had called him on their arrival, stepped nearer his friend. "However, now I've the both of you together, I would like to know the whys and wherefores of this imbroglio."

From the corner of his eye he noticed Mrs. MacKivern relax, her shoulders lowering and her hands unclenching. Had she too been about to jump to his son's defense? What had he done that they all felt him such a beast the boy would *need* defense?

Stewart straightened his shoulders, sent one wary glance toward his mother and said, "It was my idea. I thought . . ."

Matthew tugged Stu's sleeve, whispering, "You'd not have if I'd not . . ."

"Yes I would," hissed Stu. "Now let me tell it!"

"Not if you think to take all the blame," insisted Matthew, but his skin was white with tension and his gaze flickered warily between the two adults before returning to look at his shoes.

"Boys, the roadside is not exactly the place for explanations," said Mrs. MacKivern mildly, "I've ordered a hearty meal for which I'm sure Matthew at least is ready. The two of you can make your explanations after we've eased our hunger."

Blackthorn felt his brows arch, realized he was revealing his surprise at the thought of sitting down with children to dine, and forced an impassive expression. Not quickly enough, he discovered.

"The boys are not old enough to join adults at dinner," explained Mrs. MacKivern, finally a touch defensive herself, "but they must learn social manners at some point. I've always believed a table set in the afternoon, when boys need a goodly morsel to keep them going, an excellent place for that particular lesson. Run along boys. Wash and brush up and return at once to the parlor."

"And," said Blackthorn with pretended meekness, as the lads disappeared up the garden path and into the house, "where may *I* run to wash and brush up before coming, at once, to the parlor?" He enjoyed the red running up into Mrs. MacKivern's neck and face and wondered if she'd turn a scold on him for mocking her.

This particular attempt at rousing her temper was foiled, however, when a very nice sorrel gelding turned out the gates some little way along the road and trotted toward them. Blackthorn wondered if his fun was over. This, he feared, must be the inevitable suitor, or *one* of them, coming to protect the widow from his evil designs.

It occurred to him that *this* defender had far more reason behind that thought than the widow had had when set to defend his son. His eyes returned to her face, the lovely planes and shallows of high forehead, wide-set eyes and high cheekbones along with a generous mouth of the sort he preferred to the currently admired smallish and rather pursed Cupid's bow . . . Ah! He'd not seen such a spirited beauty in years! Nor one who attracted him as this one did.

"Ian!" called Mrs. MacKivern, obviously relieved at the appearance of a neutral party. "You are just in time to join us at the table."

"The girls said the young twig had returned and had brought along Matt's father?" The man eyed Blackthorn.

"My son is home, yes. *Finally.* Lord Blackthorn deigned to take time from . . . Oh!" Mrs. MacKivern broke off to ask if the men knew each other and when she discovered they did not, said, "Ian, may I present you to Lord Blackthorn, Matthew's father. My Lord, this is my brother-in-law and Stewart's guardian, Lord MacKivern." She frowned. "Or did I do that the wrong way around? I can never remember such silly things."

The men shook hands, Blackthorn feeling far more genial than he'd expected he'd feel. Was it possible he'd been a trifle jealous at that wonderfully bright smile she'd given the man? Ridiculous. One could feel competitive, perhaps, but *jealous . . . ?*

"Guardian to that hellborn babe, hmm?" he said, quirking a brow. "I don't envy you."

"He is not . . . !"

"Rickie," Ian interrupted, a note of scolding in his tone, "can you not see the man is jesting?"

Frederica bit her lip, turning her eyes sideways in her face in the most intriguing of manners. But it wasn't a flirting look, Blackthorn decided. Unfortunately. Then she turned fully his way.

"The brushing and washing?" Blackthorn interrupted whatever she meant to say next which he feared might be an apology. Of all the things he was beginning to want from this woman, an apology was not one of them! His head to one side, his gaze met and held hers.

Then, involuntarily staring into her eyes with far greater intensity then he'd meant, feeling as if he'd fall, tumble deeper and more deeply still, into their bright intelligent depths . . .

Ian cleared his throat. Rickie turned toward him, her eyes following a half moment later. "Yes, Ian? You said something? I fear I wasn't attending." Her tone was bemused. "Why do you laugh?" she added when his warm chuckle brought her back to him in mind as well as body.

"Never mind, Rickie," he said with a smile but, when he turned to Blackthorn, there was a faintly wary, questioning, look to it. "At the top of the stairs, my lord, turn left. The back bedroom on the right should serve your needs. The door to the parlor will be open when you return to the ground floor." Ian frowned. "I fear the dower house is not so large as we might wish and there is no dining room."

"I have told you and told you Ian, it is more than adequate to my needs. You must not apologize for it!"

"Must not wish to see you provided for in better fashion?" said Lord MacKivern. "My brother was . . ."

"Stu was exactly as I knew him to be when we married," said Frederica hotly. "You'll not say I did not know exactly what sort of man he was! Or that I had no hint of what sort of husband he'd be!"

Ian glanced at Blackthorn, who listened with obvious interest—until he realized his interest had been noted.

"I'll just go on up, then," said His Lordship, feeling heat in his ears as he turned up the path. How irritating! He'd not felt that flush of embarrassment since . . . since he was a green young man just up on the town! Caught eavesdropping, by God, as nosy as any cit!

Ian watched His Lordship disappear. "Handsome man that," he said musingly, casting a quick glance toward Frederica. "A lot better-looking than Stu ever was."

Frederica affected a shrug. "If you like such big dark men I suppose one would say he was handsome . . ."

"Big dark broad-shouldered well-built men!" Ian frowned, stared along the path to the house toward where Blackthorn had disappeared. It occurred to him that although he'd like seeing his sister-in-law animated as he hadn't seen her since his brother died, he didn't wish her hurt! "Rickie . . ."

She glanced at him, away. "Don't . . ."

"All I want to say is, he's a town beau." Gently, he added, "Be very careful, Rickie."

"As if I need!" She tossed her curls. "Just what would a town beau see in a country mouse like me! Ian, you are absurd!" she retorted, but her cheeks colored and she knew it, feeling the heat rising in them.

"Absurd? Perhaps . . . but we'll see," said Ian.

He took her arm and led her inside, entering the parlor that looked out over the back garden just as Rickie's footman-cum-butler-cum-everything-else left it, followed by her maid-of-all-work. The two had arranged a generous number of well-laden plates in the center of a table around which four places were set. Ian raised his brow and the footman nodded his understanding that another place setting was required.

While walking inside, Frederica had time to control the unusually frenzied emotions that brief interval staring at His

Lordship had induced and also to turn her mind back to her son. "When Blackthorn asked the boys to explain their—" She frowned, searching for a word. "—prank, Stewart admitted it was his fault. What did he do? What *can* he have done? And, Ian, why?"

"If by 'it' you mean the boys changing places, I'd not be at all surprised if Stewart thought to extend his escape of your smothering care beyond the end of the term! I explained it to you when I sent him to school, did I not?"

Frederica merely looked belligerent.

"My dear, I *warned* you you'd drive the lad away with your fidgets, turning him into a rebel. If this rather mild escapade is an example, I may have waited a year or two too long as it is."

"He's just a baby!"

"He's a *boy,* Rickie. You cannot keep him a babe no matter how much you wish to do so."

"He's not learned caution. He's too adventurous. Ian Mac-Kivern—" Frederica scowled. "—don't you look at me with that wry look!"

"My brother was not exactly a placid homebody, Frederica, as you knew when the two of you wed. And as *I* remember our youth, it was *you,* as often as not, who made plans for our, hmmm, shall we call it entertainment?"

She blushed hotly. "It is *because* I know the dangers a child may get into that I am so fearful for my son!"

"Ah. Because you led the three of us into danger so often yourself, is that what you mean?"

"You are laughing at me, but it is very true that through ignorance and thoughtlessness we were often in danger. You cannot deny it."

"No, but what *I* remember is that however often you or my brother led us *into* danger, you also led us *out.*"

"But not forever," she said and added in a rush, "Stu is *dead.*"

"My brother died in a curricle race," sighed Ian. "It could have happened to anyone."

"He shouldn't have been racing in such awful weather. He shouldn't have played the fool. I'll not have my son grow up such a gudgeon!"

"Very likely he'll become a *worse* one, because he'll feel he must prove to everyone he is *not* tied to his mother's apron strings," stormed Ian, exasperated. "Rickie, you *make* the boy wild by your very fears!"

Rickie twisted her fingers. "I cannot help it. I'll not lose my son as I did my husband. I will *not.*"

"Rickie . . ."

Clattering footsteps on the stairs warned them the boys were coming. The pair burst into the room only to skid to a halt when met by Frederica at her most imperious, her nose in the air and a disappointed look on her expressive face.

"I see that this precious school of yours has not only *not* taught you manners, Stewart MacKivern. It has also allowed you to forget those you once knew!"

Stewart's face flamed under his mop of red hair. Matthew turned on his heel, tugging his friend along behind. After a moment, sedately, the boys reentered the room.

"Good afternoon, Mother. Uncle Ian," said Stewart politely.

Matthew, behind him, muttered, "Good afternoon, Mother, Uncle Ian . . ." And, then, *his* face bright red, said, "I mean Mrs. MacKivern, Lord MacKivern."

Even embarrassed, Matthew's bow was far more graceful than Stewart's impatient bob. Unlike Stu, whose eyes were on the table, Matt actually looked at his hostess and at his friend's uncle, a man he held in awe. In the few short days he'd spent with his friend's mother at the dower house, he'd been unable to determine whether the feeling was because he *feared* the gentleman who took such a lively interest in his children and, because he was there, in Matt, or if it were that he'd found his idol, his ideal, a model for what he wanted to be himself. Someday. When he was older, of course.

Stewart edged toward the table, but stopped at his mother's warning look and put his hands behind his back.

"Did you enjoy the croquet game with my nieces, Matthew?" Mrs. MacKivern asked as Blackthorn entered the room.

"It was a very agreeable afternoon," said Matthew politely with a glance toward his friend who was wrinkling his nose. "It *was,* Stu. Bitsy and Mar are not such pests as you warned they'd be."

"They always worry about getting spots on their skirts or their hair mussed. Pests, *I* say!"

"Perhaps, my son," suggested Frederica, a twinkle in her eye, "it is that you are *too* willing to muss your hair and get into dirt?"

Stewart, not perceiving the twinkle, scowled, his lower lip pushing out a trifle.

"I believe," inserted Blackthorn, adopting a lazy tone intended to smooth over a scene which appeared on the verge of escalating into a tantrum, "that young Stewart prefers more strenuous occupation, such as riding, to a game of croquet. When I arrived at Blackthorn Hall I discovered him helping my grooms exercise my hunters."

He frowned as his hostess paled, her eyes snapping to look at her son who hung his head and studied the rose pattern in the rug, running one toe along the curve of a petal.

"He was doing very well according to Gruddy," offered Blackthorn.

Still no comment.

"My head groom, you know," His Lordship continued, valiantly if without understanding, still trying to set things right. "A real stickler. He'd not give praise where it wasn't due."

"I told you!" said Frederica, both voice and eyes ice coated as she rounded on her brother-in-law. "I told you, *did I not!*"

"Mother, I am unhurt. *I am not hurt!*" Stewart went to her, shaking her arm and scowling. His chin went up. "And what is more, I had a great deal of fun!"

"I'm certain you did, lad," said Ian pacifically. "I think we would all do better for our tea. Come along Matthew, Stewart. You sit here—" He touched a chair either side of his own. "—and you, Lord Blackthorn, if you'd take that place. Rickie?" Ian moved to hold back her chair before the tea things. He stared sternly at the rigid figure of his sister-in-law, his gaze telling her she must come and play the role she was meant to play.

For a long moment she didn't move. Blackthorn watched, curious. What had he said to lead her to make such an outburst? And the boy? Why such defiance? Unsure of himself, a formerly unknown condition, His Lordship remained silent.

Tea was poured, accompanied by the usual questions of milk or sugar, and was passed along with plates of buns and crumpets, sliced cold meats and a plate of summer vegetables which the boys seemed to like but Blackthorn thought very odd: There'd been no pretense of cooking the things. They'd been cleaned, certainly, and sliced, and prettily arranged, but that was all and the carrots, for instance, made an exceedingly objectionable noise when the boys bit into them.

Sighing, wishing this farce of a meal were over, Blackthorn glanced from his hostess to her brother-in-law and wondered just when he might discover the truth behind his son's adventure. When the boys finally refused more, rubbing their tummies and groaning in a ridiculously ill-bred fashion, he frowned and cleared his throat.

"I believe the time has come . . . ?"

Blackthorn saw the boys glance at each other. Stewart, who'd been about to take a last bite of a jam-covered crumpet, set it down, sighing. He pressed his lips together, cast another look of defiance toward his mother and turned to meet Lord Blackthorn's eyes.

"It's like this, sir. M'lord, I mean . . ." Blackthorn nodded, "Matt said I wouldn't like it if no one worried about me at all, so I thought he'd *like* my mother's fussing and whatever he said, I knew I'd like it if no one bothered me like he said no one paid much attention to what *he* did . . . although it seemed to me, from what he said, he didn't take much advantage of his luck—" He grinned a slightly wicked grin, looking, if he'd known, the image of his father. "—but I thought *I'd* know how and if Mother had Matt to get into fidgets about, then I didn't think she'd worry about *me.*" He looked around. "That's all," he added, when the adults remained silent.

His uncle studied a carrot stick, holding it before him like a miniature wand. "You do not see that your mother worries about you because of *who* you are and not merely because you are *there?*" he asked mildly.

"Because I'm her son," muttered Stewart. "Yes." He sighed. "That's what Mrs. Clapper said."

"Mrs. Clapper?"

"Housekeeper," said the boys at exactly the same moment Lord Blackthorn explained, "My housekeeper. Matthew, surely it isn't true that no one worries about you. I cannot believe such a thing. It is my understanding that all the older servants at the Hall are very concerned about you at all times.''

''Are they?'' asked the boy, his eyes on his plate. ''I didn't know . . .''

''I think you did,'' said his father sternly.

Matthew raised his eyes. ''Well, I did then. But *you* don't . . .''

''Worry? Don't love you?'' More softly Blackthorn said, ''I do, you know.''

Matt's gaze, which had dropped to his plate, rose sharply. There was genuine surprise in his voice when he asked, ''You do?''

Blackthorn disliked the guilt filling him. ''If I've not let you know that, Matthew, then I'm sorry.''

Big-eyed, the boy asked, ''Can . . . Can I go to London with you, then?''

''No.''

Matt instantly seemed to shrink. He once again stared at his empty plate, his shoulders slumped.

''There is no place for you in London, Matthew. I closed the town house years ago. I live in rooms. I explained that to you when you asked before.''

The boy nodded.

''Blast it, what am I supposed to do?''

Blackthorn, hurt by his son's lack of understanding, looked across the table and met the accusing eyes of his hostess. There was fire flashing in those eyes. Eyes the deep deep blue of the most valuable sapphires . . .

Blackthorn recalled Mrs. MacKivern's response when he'd said, rather patronizingly he now admitted, that she'd not understand why he must be in London. He liked it that she did know . . .

He realized that his interest in her was more than a whim, that he truly didn't wish to lose sight of this woman who was, in an unconventional fashion, quite the most beautiful creature he'd seen in years and one whose temper matched her hair and then the added inducement, a mind he'd like to explore almost as much as he'd like to explore her lush body!

No, he definitely didn't wish to lose track of this woman . . .

''I've a notion,'' he said slowly, as an idea which might solve both the problem of his son and of keeping Mrs. Mac-

Kivern within his ken popped into his head. "It would be an imposition, however . . ." He saw her straighten slightly in her chair and look from one boy to the other. He suspected, when she raised a hand to stop him, that her quick mind was right in step with his and that she'd guessed what he wished to say.

"Boys," she said, "if you've finished, and I think you have, then I give you permission to go out into the back garden with a ball or hoops or some such thing. You are not to leave the garden, but you may have until seven when I'll call you in to get ready for bed."

The boys stood, Matt grabbing at Stewart's arm to stop him running from the room. "Thank you for the delightful meal," he said, bowing. Stu grimaced, but he too bowed, saying, "Good evening Lord Blackthorn, Uncle Ian. Thank you, Mother."

When the boys rushed out, Ian got up and went to close the door. "I think we know what you would suggest, my lord. Rickie?"

"If it is that Matthew stay here with Stewart, then that would be fine with me."

"Excellent," said Blackthorn. "But that's only half my notion. I had it in mind to suggest that, come the Christmas season, you, Mrs. MacKivern and you, your wife and children, Lord MacKivern, come to Blackthorn Hall. I host a house party every holiday season and I'd be very happy if you'd join it."

Frederica instantly shook her head, but Ian lay a gentle hand on her shoulder and she glanced at him.

"We must consider carefully," said Ian, "about such a long journey at that particular time of year, my lord, but we thank you for the invitation. May we have time to discuss it among ourselves? My wife, you see, is delicate . . ."

"She's no business journeying so far in the cold. You know she succumbs to a chest complaint at the least hint of a chill," said Frederica earnestly, reaching to grasp Ian's arm.

"But perhaps *you* might come?" inserted Blackthorn smoothly before MacKivern could reply. "I not only thought to repay your kindness to my son, but that the boys would enjoy celebrating the season together. I fear," he added, apologetically, "you may find it a somewhat more tedious group than one expects at a house party at that festive time of year, because there are certain members of Parliament whom I'll

invite so that we may continue our work even at that season. . . .'' He quirked a brow, queryingly.

"I see,'' said Frederica and seemed to relax slightly. "Even
so I must think about it. My family is here. I don't believe I've
ever been away at Christmas . . .''

"But it is a holiday which, even now, you find exceptionally
difficult, Rickie. *Not* being here might be the solution,'' said
Ian, softly. "My lord, we'll discuss it, but the more I think on
it, the more I believe that, at least for Rickie, it is a very good
notion.''

Blackthorn's brow rose.

"My younger brother died shortly before Christmas nearly
five years ago now,'' Ian explained. "Each year the season
brings back sad memories of that event.''

Blackthorn nodded his understanding and tucked away the
irritating information the widow still grieved for the man. He
didn't, he thought, not revealing his thoughts in any way, have
time to overcome such missishness!

"I sent my carriage back to that small inn in the village,''
he said, "where my driver was to engage me a room for the
night. I'll take myself off now and return early tomorrow to
say good-bye to my son if that accords with your plans, Mrs.
MacKivern?''

"Nonsense!'' contradicted Ian. "You will, of course, stay
at the manor with my wife and myself for however long you
remain in the district. And I very much hope I can convince
you to remain at least a day or two before making the return
journey to London?''

Blackthorn balanced what was happening politically against
his intense desire to better his acquaintance with this surprising
woman and, finally, he nodded. "A few days then.'' Deciding
honesty would get him farther with this pair than polite eva-
sions, he added, "I am nonplussed to discover how exceedingly
awkward I am with my son. Perhaps you, Mrs. MacKivern,
may teach me something of the way one should go on when
dealing with the young?''

"You would,'' she said, her tone dry, "do far better to follow
Ian's example.''

"I cannot believe that. I've seen how easily you handled the
boys when they came into tea like rambunctious puppies.''

Then Blackthorn bit his lip. Had he given away the fact he'd been across the hall, hoping to learn more of her character, actually *eavesdropping* again? Juniper! What he'd been reduced to by a pair of speaking eyes!

"That was nothing." She waved it away, adding, "You heard my Stewart. He thought he'd have excellent notions for using what he believed Matthew's freedom from restraint. And he *did,* if riding those great brutes was any example!" She frowned, lines of concern marring her fine broad forehead. "I *know* your hunters must be spirited animals, my lord, and he such a *little* boy. Surely he isn't strong enough to handle anything beyond his pony!" She sighed. "But, I am far too possessive of Stewart and far too fearful of losing him to some such foolishness. I *too* must learn better ways of dealing with my son, or, as Ian, blast you my old friend—" She glared. "—has said, I will lose the boy in wildness and rebellion if not in actual death! I am not," she finished on a sigh, "a good model for you, my lord."

Blackthorn watched as, obviously deeply disturbed, she removed to the French windows and where she turned her back on him, staring out into the garden. Somewhere to the back the faint sound of happy young voices could be heard, the bark of a young dog, and he could tell she strained to hear them. He watched as she pushed the fingers of both hands up into her loosely piled hair and tugged at it.

Again her fingers ran up into her hair. This time a shower of pins rained down and her hair sprang into wild curls, the long tresses alive around her head and well down over her shoulders. She, her back to him, didn't notice when Blackthorn drew in a sharp breath, but Ian did.

"Would you object to walking up to the manor, my lord?" Ian asked Lord Blackthorn.

"To walking . . . ?" Blackthorn pulled his eyes from the hair falling down Frederica's back. "The manor . . . ? Oh, the manor. I'll be happy to walk. Mild exercise after a long carriage ride is more than merely acceptable. It is necessary!" He looked again at the woman who stared out toward where the boys could occasionally be glimpsed racing back and forth.

Ian looked from one to the other. He strolled to where Frederica stood. "We're going now, my dear. You'll come up this evening once the boys are in bed. We'll walk you back after supper.''

She didn't turn, responding absently, ''Come up ... Oh I don't like ... what if ... he might wake, his first night and all ...''

''Frederica!''

For an instant she stood, rigidly straight. Then, drawing a shaking breath, she bowed her head, nodding. ''All right, Ian.'' She drew in a deeper breath, released it on a shuddering sigh. ''I'll come.''

''Good.''

Ian, motioning to Blackthorn, left the room. Blackthorn hesitated, but Frederica remained with her back to him, oblivious to the fact she was insulting His Lordship by forgetting his very existence! Lord Blackthorn was unused to being ignored by women of marriageable age. He was far too great a prize on the marriage mart for an eligible woman not to wonder, at least, if she might not manage what no other had done since his wife died. In fact, he'd wished more than once that women *would* ignore him. But this one with the fire in her eyes echoing that in her hair? *She* ignored him?

They'd see about that!

Matt and Stu ran down the long brick path, following the young dog who had found his way into the garden from Frederica's small stable. The animal was beyond puppyhood, but still in that long-legged awkward stage. Now he pretended he would not be caught and dodged first one way and then another, until finally, tongue lolling, he plopped down on a patch of well-scythed grass and panted. The boys threw themselves down on either side.

''I have liked it here,'' said Matt. ''You are such a fool, Stu, to dislike it.''

''When you see your every wish thwarted, you'll understand.''

Matt sighed. ''Perhaps my wishes are not the sort grownups wish to thwart. I liked playing with your cousins. You see, I've never had anyone with whom to play ...''

''I forgot that,'' replied Stewart gruffly and buffeted his

friend's shoulder. "Say! Do you think you might stay for a visit?"

"Stay?" asked Matt slowly. *"Here?"*

"Why not? He's already said he can't have you in London, has he not?"

"He'll expect me to go home to my tutor . . ."

Stewart grimaced. "That wet blanket! I told him not to bother with me. He'd been hired for you, you see, so I just ignored him. I don't think he minded much."

"Minded?"

"That he needn't waste his time teaching me stuff, ninny! He doesn't understand boys very well, I think . . ."

"He must have *been* one once," said Matt doubtfully and ran a finger lightly around the mutt's ear.

"I don't want to talk about him. He's not worth a thought! Shall we ask? If you can stay?"

"Do you think . . ."

"Why not? It can't hurt to *ask,* can it?"

"Can it not?" asked Matt, staring at the dog. "I don't suppose so, but I cannot remember when it's *helped* either."

Stewart, thinking of Lord Blackthorn telling Matt there was no room for him in London, nodded his understanding. "Well?" He tensed his arms, hands flat against the grass, ready to jump up.

"Well what?"

"Shall we ask?

"Maybe when we go in?" asked Matt after a moment. He patted the pup which had stretched its neck to lick the boy's chin and pushed the dog back down, wishing to avoid the wet tongue.

"Good thinking, Matt," said Stewart, relaxing. "If we go in *now,* m'mother won't let us come back *out.*"

"It wasn't that." Matt turned his eyes toward Stewart, before looking down at the dog and once again running one finger behind a silky ear. "I was just thinking that right now I can hope, but when they tell me no, then there is no hope, is there?"

"Silly. Mother will do anything she thinks will make me happy."

"Then why do you get so angry with her?"

Stewart sighed. "I guess I didn't mean *that* sort of thing.

She won't get me a decent horse. She thinks I'm too little.''
He grinned that rather wicked grin. ''Don't ever tell her, Matt,
but Uncle Ian lets me ride his occasionally.''

''Should *he* not tell her?''

''He's my guardian and makes the decisions, but he says we
shouldn't make her unhappy when we don't need to. Oh, but
I would *so* like my own horse and not just that silly pony that
wasn't young when Mother bought him for me.''

''At least she bought you one,'' retorted Matthew.

''I know.'' Stewart reached over and touched his friend's
hand. ''I always thought you'd have the best horses in the
world, an earl's son and rich and all. You could have knocked
me over with a feather when I learned you didn't even have a
pony to call your own.''

''I had a pony, but he was a sly thing and no one realized
he'd gotten out of his paddock and into ripening corn. He
foundered.'' Matt sighed. ''Gruddy told me my father meant
to look out for something at Tattersall's, but I guess he forgot . . . ''

''Some adults do that. Make promises and forget.''

''Hmm. Only I don't think Father ever actually *promised*
. . . I don't think he's ever *promised* and forgot . . .''

''Then that's another thing. We'll get him to promise to find
you something at Tattersall's!''

Matt stared, wide-eyed, at his friend. ''I never thought of
that. Making him promise!''

''You got to keep thinking, Matt,'' said the other twelve-
year-old solemnly. ''Dealing with adults, it's the only way.''

''Mrs. MacKivern is a bundle of contradictions, is she not?''
asked Blackthorn with seeming idleness as he and Ian strolled
toward the gates to the manor.

''Contradictions?'' Ian absently tugged at his horse's reins,
pulling the mare away from a tasty tidbit she attempted to reach
at the edge of the lane. He walked on, thinking. ''Perhaps it's
that I know her so well that I see none?''

''Well, there is a remarkable intelligence there, is there not?''

''Remarkable? Do you think so? I'd never thought about it,
but I suppose it is.''

"And intelligent, she is yet quite beautiful."

"Beautiful!" repeated Ian. "Do you think so?" He chuckled, continuing before Blackthorn could reply. "My brother called her Carrots which she hated, and it was not her *looks* he liked so much as her spirit. And, for myself, I've always loved her as a sister, you see, so *I* don't see beauty there either."

"It is not a peaches and cream sort of loveliness or the traditional blond, blue eyed, rosy cheeked, English beauty, that I grant, but it's there. In my experience, one never encounters beauty and intelligence in the same woman, or rarely, anyway." He chuckled. "Then too, women who are beautiful are so aware of it, always, yet *she* is not. I find *that* a contradiction as well!"

Ian glanced his way and shrugged.

"On top of that, she is so good with the boys, easily controlling their flights—yet obviously she is ridden with fear for them."

Ian nodded. "That, at least, I can explain. It may be set to my brother's death."

Ian sighed and walked a few paces before continuing. Blackthorn waited, hoping for more but not wishing to reveal the depth of his interest by probing yet again. He relaxed when Ian obliged.

"Stu and Rickie were wild as bedamned. Both of them. But once *young* Stewart was born, Rickie changed. A great deal. She was more . . . settled? She no longer looked for excitement and she lost that need to live on the edge of danger that had once been bread and meat to both of them." He paused, then, slowly, as if just thinking it out, he added, "Now I think back, it occurs to me that perhaps she resented that my brother continued to feel the need for *more* when she did *not.*"

"And then felt guilty that she'd felt such resentment when the worst happened and he died?"

Ian chuckled. "Perhaps you've hit the nail on the head, my lord. Ah. We've arrived. Welcome to MacKivern Manor, my lord," he added with an old-fashioned sort of formality.

He handed his gelding's reins to a groom who ran up to take it and led the way up a series of shallow steps to a long terrace fronting the adequately commodious manor which was not, however, so large as to be a burden. They continued up another set of steps to the front door which was thrown open by a

graying, rather bent man in very old-fashioned garb for a butler:
Powdered wig, stripped stockings, buckles on the shoes and
all.

"Blaine," said MacKivern, "His Lordship will be staying
a few days. The green room, do you think? And send someone
to the inn for his man and his traps. Where may I find Tildy?"

"My lady is in the conservatory, my lord. This way."

They followed the butler's painfully slow pace and Blackthorn was, in due course, properly and quite formally
announced. His Lordship was amused the butler knew his correct style of address with no prompting. He perceived that the
country gossips had, in the usual fashion, been at work,
informing the man well in advance of his arrival at the manor!

Matilda MacKivern turned from where she trimmed the vines
of an ancient grape which grew all around the glass-enclosed
extension to the house. Six small fruit trees were set in huge
pots at the points of a large star worked into the tessellated
floor. Between pots and vine were planters of all sizes and
shapes overflowing with blooms which added a profusion of
color. The open center of the conservatory was reserved for a
chaise longue, two small sofas and a comfortable chair or two.

Lord Blackthorn had only enough time to wonder how the
room was heated in winter when, removing her gloves as she
came, the dark haired, peaches and cream complected beauty
approached, her oval face revealing no emotion whatsoever.
If this was what Lord MacKivern admired, then Blackthorn
perceived why the man saw no beauty in Frederica's strong,
more highly colored, and exceedingly expressive features!

"My lord," said Matilda in a low musical voice. "You are
very welcome although I'm sure we are very sorry for the
reason for your visit. Young Stewart is a difficult boy. I do
not envy his mother."

"He is merely thoroughly a boy!" objected Ian. "It is simply
that you do not understand . . . No! Tildy, I did not mean . . . !"

Ian's wife had turned white, dropping onto a convenient seat.
She raised stricken eyes to Ian.

"My love," he said softly, "How may I convince you I am
satisfied with things just as they are. You must not repine . . ."

"We are embarrassing Lord Blackthorn," she muttered and

made an obvious effort to pull herself together. "My lord, we apologize."

"We lost a boy some years ago," said Ian abruptly.

"I am sorry." Blackthorn felt that uneasy inadequacy most felt in the face of such information. He swallowed. "Hmm . . . I believe you mentioned a room, my lord? My boxes should arrive shortly. I'd like to change before dinner."

Ian took the hint that his wife was correct in her assumption that they'd embarrassed their guest. Or at least, if Blackthorn was *not* embarrassed, then at the very least he wished to leave them alone with their emotional problems. He rang for Blaine.

The butler appeared so quickly Blackthorn was nearly certain the man had been waiting directly outside the door. "I will join you for dinner, then," said Lord Blackthorn and raised his hostess's hand to lay a salute in the air just above the back.

It seemed to His Lordship such a measure was appropriate in a house where the butler retained the dress of the last century when the kissing of hands was more common. Besides, he was pretty certain she'd be flattered by the action and, with luck, it might distract her from sad thoughts. But the instant Blackthorn turned his back on Lady MacKivern he forgot her, his mind retaining only a vision of his termagant.

There was half a hesitation in his step as he realized how he'd phrased that: *His* termagant? Just what did he mean by that! But that hair! Ahh . . . that hair.

He could very nearly feel what it would be like in his hands, its texture as it flowed across his body . . .

"Er, yes? You said something?" he asked.

The butler bowed. "I merely wished to inform you I shall have hot water brought up immediately, my lord. My lady prefers to dine at six which I believe is a trifle earlier than London hours?"

"It varies. Many dine early so as to be on time for a play or the opera. Besides, I don't keep town hours when in the country! Six will be fine."

The door closed and, butler, the need to change clothes, dinner, and host were instantly forgotten, Blackthorn's mind turning once again like a sailor's compass to focus on Mrs. MacKivern. He wondered exactly what sort of lover she'd be when he managed to get her into his bed and images of that much to be desired event filled his imagination as, in the normal course of things, such thoughts never occupied his attention. It didn't occur to him to think that strange . . . but of course he had not gotten her there. It was only dreaming! He only hoped . . .

"*If* I manage it," he muttered, frowning . . . and allowed his thoughts free rein once again as he crossed the room to a window which, fortuitously, looked toward the back garden of the dower house.

From what he'd seen of the unconventional Mrs. Frederica MacKivern, bedding her was no sure thing. Despite the encouragement a man found in that mass of sensuous hair! Wild and unrestrained hair like Mrs. MacKivern's would have revealed a passionate nature even if her earlier behavior had not already done so.

Chapter Two

Frederica had surprising difficulty dressing for the evening at the manor. She didn't wish to give Ian another reason to chide her about Blackthorn when there was, she assured herself, no reason at all for a scold. On the other hand, for the first time in a very long while, she also wished to look her best. Except . . . it was impossible. Staring into her armoire, Frederica wondered when she'd last gone down off the wold into Broadway and ordered a new gown. Obviously, it had been some time.

She grimaced at her old yellow satin with the dyed-to-match lace overskirt. Thank goodness that wasn't suitable for an evening spent *en famille!* But the green had been worn so often and the blue, which Tildy had urged on her, although less worn, had been a mistake. Blue was not her color despite the fact redheads usually favored it. Then there was the gown she loved but Tildy detested, wondering that anyone would wish to wear brown.

Still, it wasn't exactly *brown,* was it? Frederica pulled it out and looked at it. No, not brown. What it was she wasn't certain, but she'd liked it when she chose the material and, whatever Tildy said, she liked it yet. The style, too, was right for her tall, very slightly over-full figure, however old-fashioned it might look to a man just up from London. Frederica put it on her bed and rang for her maid who must press it, quickly, since it was very nearly time she leave.

Seated before her mirror, her arms above her head, Frederica paused, a brush halfway along a tress. Why did she feel this ... this excitement? Surely it wasn't because there'd be an unknown man there, one she found ... interesting? She pulled the brush on to the end and began again.

That must be nonsense. His paternal bungling alone made him a man she could not like. However intriguing deep set dark eyes under straight brows, and hair that fell into a multitude of shaggy curls, she *must* remember the man had no proper feeling for his son; a man who ignored a son was not one who would have a care for a wife's comfort.

Frederica blinked. Where had that thought come from? Once again she paused in her normally steady brushing. More nonsense, she thought. Not just nonsense but an absurdity so wild she couldn't even laugh at the notion. Wife indeed! Blackthorn lived in London where the ton's greatest beauties, its most interesting women, must, one and all, have stalked him!

But even if one did not think in terms of marriage her attraction to him was something to be set aside. She was not the sort who could indulge in the light behavior the ton allowed widows—so long as evidence of it was not thrust upon them. And that being so, she would, she decided, remember to keep a proper distance, remain cool and collected. And poised and ...

Oh! Bedamned to cool and collected and properly distant behavior! *Blast* and bedamned! She was *never* cool or distant. She didn't know how! Frederica scowled. Why must the first man she'd met since Stewart's death, in whom she could feel the slightest interest, why must he be so far above and beyond her she would never come close to measuring up to what he'd want in a woman? She sighed. Given she couldn't be what he'd want or need, she had no choice but to behave in such a way he'd never be in a position to embarrass her by rejecting her after discovering how much she'd like to know him better.

Which meant cool. And proper. To say nothing of distant. Poised.

All those things she was *not*. So, she shrugged, why try? She'd simply be herself since she could be no other.

Having settled that, Frederica returned her attention to her mirror and very soon had her hair arranged in its evening mass of rioting curls which cascaded down the back of her head and a short distance along her spine. Then, about to rise, she resettled herself and opened her small jewel box. It wasn't, after all, *merely* an evening with her family! She could be allowed a trifle of vanity, surely.

Tumbling the beads and pins, she freed a long comb with golden butterflies posed, open-winged, along its edge. She inserted it so that the butterflies were half hidden, flirting from among the curls.

Betsy returned with her gown just as Frederica rose from the dressing table. The maid helped lift it over her mistress's head, going around behind to do up the row of buttons below the square neckline.

The waist was wrong, thought Frederica, bending her knees a trifle to show that portion of her body in the mirror. Too low for current fashion . . .

She sighed softly, but the sigh merged with a chuckle when her maid came around, looked her up and down and let out a long, satisfied, and very expressive, "Ohhhh."

"You think I'll do then?" Frederica asked Betsy.

"Oh, yes madam. You look a fair treat. Why don't you wear that gown more often?"

"I suppose because Lady MacKivern doesn't like it. She thinks brown an odd color. Especially for the evening."

"But it isn't exactly brown, is it?" asked Betsy doubtfully.

"Whatever, *I* like it. Is Martin ready to walk me up to the manor?"

"Yes'm."

"Then I'll just look in on the boys and be off. You'll be sure to remain near? In the next room?" Frederica asked anxiously.

"You know I will," said the plump maid comfortably. "I've a bit of mending to do and then I can practice my letters on the slate, can't I?"

Frederica was teaching the girl to read and write. She nodded. "You do that. And I know I can trust you."

Frederica said that last to remind herself as well as the maid. Her son's first night home and she was going out! Even if it was only up the road to his uncle's! Frederica tiptoed into her son's bedroom and across the carpet to look down at him.

Stewart opened one eye and grinned sleepily. "Forgot!" he muttered.

"What did you forget?" she asked, whispering.

"Forgot to ask if Matt could stay for a visit."

"That's an excellent notion. Perhaps he can," said Frederica, pushing back her son's hair from his forehead.

"Matt'll be surprised."

"Why?"

"He says it never does any good to ask." Stewart yawned widely and kicked his covers away.

"Can't hurt either," said Frederica, pulling them back up under his chin. "Now don't wake him! Just go back to sleep yourself. You'll have the whole summer to convince him that it sometimes does do to ask!"

"Hmmm . . ."

Frederica tore herself from the boy's side and hurried down the stairs, knowing that if she did not leave immediately, she'd not leave at all, that she'd stand there half the night staring at the lad, her heart full and her throat tight. He'd been gone so *long!* Months!

Forgetting she'd decided it was impossible, her mind returned to the notion she must remain cool and controlled. All the way up the lane and then as she stalked up the drive at her footman's side, she silently chanted, *"Calm. Cool. Distant. Calm. Cool. Distant . . ."*

Half an hour later she wondered how one could possibly remain cool and properly remote to say nothing about calm when a man set himself to be so amusing. She'd not laughed so much in years!

". . . And so you see, the poor man has kept his poodle at his side for so long it has become his nickname: Poodle Byng." He paused thoughtfully and then, with a self-deriding chuckle, added, "Just at the moment I can't recall what his name *should* be!"

"What I see, my lord, is that you are a great bamboozler!" said Frederica, pretending to scold.

"No such thing! I swear to you!"

"Then if you are not, the society in which you spend your time must include the oddest people in creation!"

"Ah. I'll not argue that I've told stories of eccentrics among the ton, but I've *not* said I spend time with them!"

"My lord," said Lady MacKivern, who felt the evening had become far too frivolous, "you are near the center of things in London. Could you, perhaps, tell us of the king's true condition? We hear such terrible reports."

"Ah." Blackthorn sobered instantly. "The king." He shook his head. "This time, I fear, there's no hope."

"But always, after a bad spell, he's returned to being the kind ruler we've loved for so many years."

Blackthorn thought of the king's autocratic refusal to allow his daughters to wed; his idiotic arrangement with his sister, Princess Augusta of Brunswick, and her daughter, Princess Caroline, which had resulted in a totally unacceptable wife for Prinny, his son and heir: His Royal Highness's stubborn refusal for any softening toward the Catholics, a policy which would, it was believed by many, lead to serious trouble in the future . . . not to mention the growing dissatisfaction across the Atlantic among a people who had already shown themselves willing to fight for what they believed, the Royal Navy's current policy for recruiting seamen . . .

But it would do no good to explain all that to this woman whose thoughts ran in conventional paths when not in actual clichés. Besides, since the clichés were common to much of the ton, what could one do?

Frederica broke the odd little silence which followed Tildy's querulous comment. "Perhaps that's the trouble, Tildy," she said gently. "He's not young, I mean. The old haven't the stamina to battle illness as the young."

"I think," agreed Blackthorn, silently praising Mrs. Mac-Kivern's tactful tongue, "that you have it in a nutshell. You are aware, of course, that he nears his seventieth birthday."

"I suppose," mused Lady MacKivern, "I've not thought of him as a *man* who might grow *old* so much as the *king* who is a special individual. One doesn't think of kings aging like normal people, does one? One doesn't think of them doing *anything* like a person who lives an ordinary life.''

''I assure you, the king must eat and sleep and take exercise just as any other! He has his worries and his pleasures, his work and, when it is done, his play.''

''But he is king.''

Lady MacKivern said that with a simplicity that had Black-thorn turning to meet Frederica's gaze which turned toward him just as inevitably. A silent communication passed between them before Frederica realized how inappropriate their behavior would seem if observed. A moment later he too turned away and noted Lord MacKivern's indulgent smile for his wife's folly.

''He is king,'' agreed Blackthorn. After all, it was true and what else could one say? He searched his mind for another subject, wishing to avoid anything controversial.

Frederica didn't feel the same reticence and asked, ''Is the Prince so fat as we've heard?'' A quick and wicked smile revealed she knew she was being provocative making a comment which could not help but raise her hostess's hackles thwarting Blackthorn's good intentions. But her face was so blankly innocent Blackthorn suspected she was up to something.

''Frederica! You mustn't!'' Tildy lowered her voice and added, ''What will Lord Blackthorn think of such indelicacy?''

''Does it matter?'' asked Frederica pertly, her eyes gleaming with rather devilish lights. Turning back to Blackthorn, she prodded, ''Well?''

Amused, Blackthorn obliged. ''Very likely Prinny's grown even fatter!''

''What sort of Regent will he be?'' she asked, her curiosity obvious.

''No one knows, but we fear caprice.'' Lord Blackthorn paused half a moment before adding, with a glance at his disapproving hostess, ''He's sadly unsteady.''

''He should have been given occupation long ago,'' Frederica said in a scolding tone. ''Can you imagine a life with no point to it except to wait and wait and wait to do the job of work for which one was born? He's been forced to suffer idleness for decades! How can he be anything *other* than unsteady?''

Blackthorn was once again struck by the beauty's perspicacity, the way she delved to the depths of a subject in an instant. "His brothers, who have had positions of responsibility, do better, it is true, but none of them," he added with a grin, "are exactly the sort to whom you'd entrust your innermost secrets."

Tildy stiffened. "You surely do not mean to insinuate that any one of the royal family is not to be trusted!"

"Do I not?" Again Blackthorn met Frederica's eyes and almost laughed when she grimaced slightly.

"You are very innocent, my dear," said Lord MacKivern, and added when Tildy turned an insulted expression his way, "which is just as it *should* be. Frederica, did you remember to tell the boys Matthew will be staying when his father leaves?"

"They were so tired, I did not. I feared it would make them too excited to sleep so decided I'd tell them at breakfast. Stewart woke when I went in just before leaving, however, and asked if Matthew might stay. I told him I thought it likely, but I'm not certain he was truly awake, so he may forget."

"Tildy informed me, when we dressed for dinner, that she meant to arrange a small entertainment for tomorrow evening, just a few friends to dinner with cards following. If you are agreeable, my lord?"

"Quite," said Blackthorn even as he wondered how he could say anything else. He turned the subject before more could be said: "As I dressed I thought it might be pleasant to ride out with you and the boys in the morning. With Lady MacKivern and Mrs. MacKivern, as well, of course. I thought perhaps it was the sort of informal setting in which I could get reacquainted with my son?" he asked a trifle hesitantly, again looking at Frederica.

Frederica's lips tipped into an expression of amused scorn. "You must be jesting, my lord. Or you've never ridden with the younger set, which is more likely, is it not? You cannot have done, or you'd know such activity will not help you!"

When Blackthorn frowned, Ian chuckled. "The boys tend to ride off in all directions, having no patience with a staid and proper pace one keeps to with the ladies."

"It might be best if you and Ian take them out. Then I may do what little I can to help Tildy prepare for her party," said Frederica, and felt both good that she was doing the proper thing for Matthew, and exceedingly martyred that she'd not have his first morning with her son!

Matilda stiffened still again, her straight spine becoming more rigid than ever. "Really, Frederica, I can do all that is needed."

"Of course you can, but you do not *like* doing bouquets and I do. I'll come up early and consult with old Padget. And that's another thing you don't like, Tildy, arguing with him and, because you won't, he gives you only the scraggliest blooms and those which are almost too old. How could you enjoy arranging such as that?"

"I'll admit that Padget frightens me to death," said Matilda, a slight curve to her lips, but her eyes remaining cold. "I've asked Ian to replace the man with someone less fierce, but he says he cannot. He assures me the man is one of those retainers it is impossible to be rid of." Her expression became totally cold as she added, "My father had no patience with that foolish attitude."

Ian's lips compressed tightly since this was one point on which, more than once, he'd had to argue with his beloved and he very much disliked contradicting her. Even such a small flaw in his lovely wife was almost more than he could bear.

But again Frederica jumped in to smooth things over. "Padget is too young to retire and far too old to find a position elsewhere. Besides, he is a wonderful gardener. You'd find no one else who works so hard or is willing to do half so many different sorts of gardening. And I am *not* afraid of him, so I'll get you proper bouquets!"

"I sometimes think," said Matilda, a trifle waspishly, "that you fear nothing." It was not a compliment.

"I am ... perhaps ... too prone to wanting my own way which is another way of saying the same thing, is it not?" Frederica realized her sister-in-law was near to succumbing to what Ian called one of her pets and which Frederica thought nothing less than a tantrum. Knowing her presence only exasperated such a situation whenever it occurred, she rose to her feet. "I must go. It is late and the boys will be up with the sun."

"But surely you'll wait for supper," said Ian, also rising, as did Blackthorn.

"I think not."

"And I," said his lordship smoothly, he, too, noticing the signs of an aroused temper in his hostess, "ate far too much of a very good dinner. If you will not think me rude, Lady MacKivern, I'll walk Mrs. MacKivern back to her gate. After such a long day in the coach, I'd like the exercise before finding my bed." Blackthorn waved a hand when Ian made a motion that implied he'd join them. "You needn't come, MacKivern. I'll not get lost between here and the dower house!"

Ian turned a questioning look on Frederica who didn't know where to look. That Lord Blackthorn wished to be alone with her was all too obvious! But why? *Had* there been something in that look they'd exchanged when he'd first arrived? *Had* it been more than imagination on her part?

Frederica finally met Ian's gaze. "Lord Blackthorn will see to my comfort and Tildy will be glad you needn't break into your evening together simply to walk me home—not that there is ever such need! I, too, am unlikely to get lost between here and my gate!"

As they strolled down the drive to the road Blackthorn referred to his hostess's naivity concerning political things. "I do not, of course, find it surprising. The surprise is that *you* know so much," he added, glancing down at the woman at his side.

"I am interested in such things, my lord," she responded, not rising to the bait.

"But you appear to know a great deal more than one would expect of someone living so isolated, far away from the center of things. Your chiding me when I arrived about my party's reaction to the war is a case in point. But, believe me, our opponents truly do favor what can only be ruin!"

"I don't know that I agree. I'm not convinced you and your friends aren't simply going down another road toward the ruination of England. Or *worse.* You'd let that tyrant on the continent have his way with the whole of Europe, crying loudly about the cost of stopping him and how terrible it is to bear such a burden as our army in Spain costs us. And then, when the Ogre comes knocking at our door, having set the whole world against us *militarily* as, with his continental blockade of our manufacturers, he's already done *economically, then* you'd cry still harder about the cost of stopping him, would you not?''

Blackthorn didn't allow it to show, but he was amazed that a woman, living in the far north of the Cotswold, very far from the sophisticated and busy world of London, would, or even *could* know so much of the country's political and economic complications. In His Lordship's experience, women were frivolous beings and not to be taken seriously.

Well, most women. There were exceptions, nearly all of them political wives, and the larger number of those of a more elderly sort. Besides, it was a serious issue she'd just raised: If Napoleon were to find himself unoccupied elsewhere, he'd surely turn covetous eyes toward England! Again.

''You have made a telling point, Mrs. MacKivern. A telling point indeed, but I believe our policies will do less damage of the sort you predict than would those others. I must continue to do what I can to keep my party in power!''

''I would think less of you,'' she said pertly, ''if you immediately changed your coat and agreed with me!''

''As would your sister-in-law if one were to explain things to her?''

''Not exactly,'' said Frederica, dryly. ''Matilda doesn't think. She merely believes what she believes she *should* believe. So if *you* were to explain something to her, she would agree because of who you *are,* not because of what you said.''

Blackthorn chuckled but didn't respond. Finally he said, ''You are aware she is jealous of the attention Ian pays you.''

It was a statement rather than question, but Frederica, pulling her mind from thoughts of the man beside her, said, ''He will not see it. He will allow himself to see nothing but good in her and I cannot discover a tactful way of turning him away from me. It isn't that I have need of him to such a degree, but we've known each other forever. He acted the big brother when we were all children together and has never gotten out of the habit.''

''He knew Lady MacKivern as a child?''

''Oh no, I meant he, his brother Stu, and myself. The three of us ran as wild as those Indians one reads about in America. I was forever going home with my petticoats in tatters and my hair in such tangles my nanny scolded and grumbled and tried to convince my father that I *must not,* but he was far too involved with his studies to care a whit what I did or did not do.''

''A scholar?''

''Yes and lost if anyone forced him away from his books. Except once or twice. For instance, when I was eight he noticed me and instantly hired a tutor for me, saying such a great girl must not grow up unable to read and write . . .'' A reminiscent smile hovered around her lips. ''He didn't know I could already read and write, of course. I'd learned my letters with Ian and Stu.''

''Here at the manor?''

''Hmm. The late Lady MacKivern was a kindly woman who allowed me to run tame in her home. But, having acquired my own tutor, I no longer had that excuse to escape my own home. Only, once hired, my father ignored the man. It was I myself who insisted he teach me as the boys were being taught and, when he objected and went to my father for instruction, Father simply told him to do whatever it was I wished, that since I was a girl, it made no difference, did it?''

''You studied Latin?''

''Latin and later a bit of Greek and, still later, political and moral philosophy. My tutor got into the spirit of things when he realized I was truly interested and would work hard at the tasks he set me, so he introduced just a little of the science which has blossomed through the founding of the Royal Institution. He should, perhaps, have taught me more of the latter, since I got just enough that I became totally intrigued by it and exceedingly desirous to learn more.''

''Ah. I wondered if the essay I noticed on the side table was yours.''

''On electricity? Electricity is one of the things I find fascinating. I don't always understand all I read but a correspondent in London looks out for what will help me and will add to my knowledge.''

Blackthorn cast her a thoughtful look. ''Just out of curiosity, is your correspondent aware you are a woman?''

Blackthorn turned his eyes sideways, wondering if a blush darkened Frederica's wonderfully clear skin. Unfortunately, although they could determine their path, there was insufficient light to read colors. He could, however, see the flash of her white teeth when she grinned.

"I doubt the man has twigged to my sex, my lord. I sign my letters F. D. MacKivern and he has never asked for a name."

"May I know what the 'D' stands for?"

"No."

"You don't like it?"

"No."

He chuckled. "Desdemona, perhaps? Or Désirée?"

"Neither of those."

"I'll ask Lord MacKivern."

"He'll not tell."

"Is it so very bad?"

"Yes."

"Donna?"

"No."

"Deirdra?"

"Not even close."

His chuckle, this time, was warmer still. "I'll guess."

"I'll not tell you if you *are* correct."

"You need not. When I guess your name, your face will become that lovely rosy color it gets when you are embarrassed or angry! I will know by that!" After a moment he asked, "Are you blushing now?"

Frederica knew flirting with His Lordship was like walking on dangerous ice, but, feeling more alive than she'd done for a very long time, she took still another step. "I am," she admitted. "I must be angry, must I not?"

"Since I can see no reason for embarrassment, then I agree, you must be angry. Should I apologize for teasing you?"

Frederica bit her lip as she debated whether she dared go on. Dared? Had she ever been able to resist a dare? "No," she said, answering both herself and him.

"No?"

She sighed. "I've had no one to tease me since Stewart died. Except very occasionally Ian. I discover that, however angry I may be with you, I have missed it."

"Then I'll oblige you by teasing you as often as possible so long as I remain here. And," he added in a rather sly tone, "when you come to me at Christmas I'll do the same."

"I have not said I'll accept your kind invitation."

"I must believe you will."

Frederica took a quick emotional step back toward solid ground, ignoring the provocative hint in his words and tone. "The boys' friendship may fall apart before then," objected Frederica, speaking in a slightly stilted voice. "At that age it would not be at all surprising if . . ."

"I think it *would* be," interrupted Blackthorn. "Surprising, I mean." He wondered just what emotion he'd revealed which had disturbed her and he, also, pulled back from an emotional confrontation. "You've no knowledge," he continued with the more neutral topic, "of the friendships boys make while at school. Such a deep connection as I've perceived between those two will, I believe, last them all their lives. It is one of the good things about our schools, those long-lasting friendships."

"I know that every letter from Stewart was filled with information about Matt, what he'd said, what they'd done, that sort of thing. Matthew, I mean."

"Until you thought you'd scream?"

It was Frederica's turn to chuckle. The warm sound of it surrounded Blackthorn and, *almost,* he halted, wishing to take her into his arms and hold her close, to *feel* the sound of her laughter.

Someday I will, he promised himself. Someday.

They arrived at the dower house's fancy wrought-iron gate, which was as far as Blackthorn had said he'd go. Frederica entered, turned, and closed it between them. They paused, neither of them quite ready to say good-night but not quite knowing how to prolong the evening.

The boys, thought Frederica. Rather primly, she said, "I must know whether there are health problems of which I'm unaware. We must discuss whether you've rules you wish enforced concerning your son . . ."

"We'll have time . . ."

"My son spends the whole of the day in the sun," persisted Frederica, "when he escapes me, that is. Will that be a problem?"

"The *whole* day?" Blackthorn frowned slightly. "I hired a tutor for Matthew. I wonder if I shouldn't send him here. He could stay at the inn . . ."

"Perhaps Ian would house the man at the manor. If you believe he's necessary? Matt could go to him each morning? I mean Matthew, of course."

"Not just the one lad. Both should go. *Matt* and *Stu*. You know that, to my son, yours is Stu? I find myself calling him by the pet name when I think of him. But the tutoring . . . It would be unfair to penalize the one while the other ran free!"

Frederica tipped her head, frowning slightly. "You think they should *not* be free during their holiday?"

"Boys require discipline. A few hours study each day will harm neither."

Discipline . . . Just what sort of discipline did Lord Blackthorn approve? Frederica knew she lacked the will to be *too* firm with Stewart. She'd never been able to cane him, for instance. "Did you have a program of study planned for Matthew?"

"Merely to reinforce his Latin, to see he's grounded in Greek and to check that the school is not scrimping his study of mathematics."

"It seems a very great deal for vacation time!" said Frederica.

"Perhaps it is." Blackthorn tipped his head, thoughtful. "You must recall that when I planned Matthew's summer, he'd have been alone. I believe a boy's day should be organized. He's less likely to get into mischief that way."

"I hadn't thought of that. Stewart tends to disappear up to Ian's stables on any and all occasions where I forget to watch him like a hawk. He'll have your Matthew there too," she warned.

"Ah! I'd forgotten! I must replace the boy's pony which sickened last winter and died. He's too old for a pony so I'll find him a mare, I think. One with a gentle disposition, of course, but enough spirit Matthew may practice his jumps."

Horrified, Frederica paused, staring. "You allow him to *jump?* But he is so young!"

"He's been jumping since he was five. You cannot mean you've forbidden Stewart that skill!"

"I'm so *afraid.*" Frederica clutched at the rods spiking up from the top of the garden gate. "He'll fall. He'll be hurt.

Perhaps killed. You know how many men break their necks each hunting season falling off horses at jumps!''

"Which is a very good reason," said Blackthorn firmly, "to see that our children are well trained and that their training begins at an early age. Three sorts of men fall, Mrs. MacKivern. Those who have no judgment, those who lack experience and those who will allow themselves to be cheated with bad or ill-trained stock when buying their hunters!''

"You are scolding me."

"I believe I am."

She sighed. "What is worse, you say much the same thing Ian says." She drew in a long slow breath, held it for a moment, let it out. "When you choose a horse for your son, will you choose another for mine? I'll repay you the cost, of course, whatever it may be."

Blackthorn made a mental note to ask MacKivern what she could afford for the boy. Horses at Tattersall's tended to be rather dear . . .

"I'll find two good mares of a suitable size," he said. He reached out and ran one finger down her knuckles where one hand still clutched the gate. "You'll become chilled, my dear. I'll say good-night and good dreams." He traced along her knuckles once again. "Dreams of me, may I hope?" he asked in a whimsical tone.

"You are presumptuous, my lord," she said, but the chiding held a gentle note as well.

"Presumptuous perhaps, but I *will* hope, and—" He chuckled softly, "—I'll know if you *have* when I see you again."

"How?"

"Because," he said, the humor yet more obvious in his tone, "you, my dear, will be unable to control your blushing!" After a moment, he asked, blandly, "Is that a growl I hear?"

"You, my lord, are a *worse* tease than my Stewart ever was!"

"Ah! You'll find I excel at *all* I do."

There was, Blackthorn realized, a trifle more innuendo in that than he'd meant to put there and he bit his lip, waiting for a proper, and very likely deserved, setdown.

"You even excel at boasting!"

There it was and well done too!

"So I do," he admitted, grinning.

But, had she meant her words as reproach or tease? Or was it possible she had *not* read from his voice that which any tonnish woman would have known was in his mind? Well, perhaps it would be better if she did not! Not until he was sure of her.

"Good night," he said again. This time he added, "I'll wait here until I see you safely inside your door."

Frederica had no choice but to go inside . . . although she'd *meant* to spend a few minutes alone in the garden thinking over all that had happened.

Especially, she'd wished to think about the meeting of eyes, which had occurred again and again, as if each had known and wished to share in the other's thoughts. And his teasing this evening? What had he meant by that? Was it merely a London beau's naturally flirtatious ways? Could he no more help flirting than . . . than the Misses Fraymark who were the neighborhood's most noted flirts? No man from sixteen to sixty-six was safe when Rose or Violet chose to exert themselves!

Ah, but the tremors which had run up her arm when he touched her hand. She'd not felt that goose-fleshy sensation along her spine for . . . years. Not since . . . since Stewart died and she'd assumed she laid such sensations in the grave with him, that she'd never again feel that way. So why now? Why this man?

Frederica concluded that, at twenty-eight, she must have reached some sort of dangerous age for a widow and that she must be on her guard. She would *not* become some man's plaything! And surely that was all a man of Blackthorn's status would ask of her.

Frederica realized she'd been standing for some time before the dimly glowing hall lamp beside which her bed candle stood. How long *had* she lingered there? How foolish . . .

She checked and discovered that, without thinking, she'd bolted the door when she'd come in. She certainly didn't remember doing it. So now, why not light her candle and go to her bed?

Why not indeed! Frederica lit her candle and went up the stairs.

* * *

Lord Blackthorn watched Mrs. MacKivern close her door. He moved along the garden wall which was constructed of golden Cotswold stone and leaned his elbows on it, staring at the cottage. Along each side of the front door were narrow windows, one pane set above the last, and framed in one was a woman's queenly figure, a lamp haloing her form and drawing glints of fire from the red-gold tresses which were her crowning glory.

Why did he find this woman so intriguing? It was nothing like he'd felt when first married, the mystery of the young and virginal girl which, in his wife, had briefly trapped him. Not that this woman wasn't innocent compared to a London widow, but she wasn't a virgin! Nor was she young. Nor classically beautiful, which was something else his wife had been. Since her death he'd met many women the ton would say were far more beautiful than Mrs. MacKivern and they'd not roused a twinge of interest, but Mrs. MacKiv- . . . No! In his *mind,* at least, he'd call her by her name!

Frederica wouldn't be called beautiful. Very likely the matrons would say she was handsome. But whatever she was called, her expressive features drew his eyes again and again. The broad forehead and straight nose. The planes of her cheeks and that forceful chin. No, not a beauty as defined by the ton, but when that generous mouth smiled, no one would deny she was exceedingly attractive. Could it be that which drew him? Merely an interesting face . . . ?

Or had he still more interest in the mind behind it?

Had he ever met another woman who so calmly admitted interest in the science of electricity, for instance? Not that he knew much about it himself, just what any reasonably well-educated man might know, but a *woman?* And a woman who'd been taught Latin and Greek, had had moral and political philosophy in her course of study. How strange. Yet it meant she listened intelligently when he spoke of political problems and had opinions she was not afraid to voice . . .

And, besides that, she'd shown a great deal of sense and diplomacy when soothing Lady MacKivern's incipient tantrums. That art was something else he admired in her. So *was* it the mind?

Or was it the teasing but unflirtatious personality?

Blackthorn, never taking his eyes from the still figure framed by the window, sighed. He didn't know. It was a mystery why this particular woman intrigued him when none of the sophisticated women of the ton, who had pursued him since his wife's death, had done so. Or was that it? Mere *perversity* on his part!

She did *not* pursue him, so was he determined she would? But why did she *not?* Had she no notion what a catch he was? Surely she must know ...

Blackthorn's reverie was interrupted when Frederica abruptly reached for a candlestick, lit her candle, and leaned to blow out the lamp. The candle's lesser light gradually disappeared as she went, gracefully, up the stairs. It reappeared, a gentle glow, in a window to one side and then, again, disappeared.

Blackthorn tipped his head, frowning and searching his mind for an explanation. Ah! She'd checked on the boys. Was her bedroom, then, to the back? No! A warm rose color appeared in the other front window and gradually deepened. The drapery covering her windows which overlooked the front garden glowed from the growing light beyond as Frederica lit one lamp and then another. So *that* was her room.

Blackthorn realized he was staring hungrily at the closed drapes, hoping for another glimpse of the woman who must be disrobing beyond them. He felt heat in his throat and ears as he visualized the removal of each item of clothing—just as a very young man might, one suffering his first infatuation.

What nonsense! He was a fully adult male creature and he had no need to merely *fantasize* about anyone! Angry with himself, Blackthorn was about to turn away when the drapes were pulled aside and, silhouetted against the light behind, was the object of his fantasy. Her floating robe, made of some fine material, was quite fragile enough so he could see the muted outline of her body beneath it ... but the body—bless the woman, he muttered, chuckling softly—was clothed in a far more sensible nightshift, the curves barely hinted at!

For a moment he continued staring and, much to his surprise, discovered Frederica's hidden body more titillating than the revealing gowns he'd seen in this or that bedroom over the years! But he should not compare this woman to the ladies he'd occasionally honored with his attentions. This was not a knowing lady, an experienced woman who knew the rules, and he must remember to treat her with care or he'd find himself in a position he'd sworn to avoid! He'd no intention of remarrying and Frederica was the sort who would think only in terms of marriage . . . unless very carefully led in the way he wished her to go.

This time Blackthorn forced himself to turn and stride off up the lane, not even slowing when he'd passed into the manor's drive. As he approached the terrace before the house he looked up and discovered Ian standing there.

"I was about to come and ascertain if you'd gotten lost after all," said Ian.

"Mrs. MacKivern and I lost track of time as we discussed the boys. We wondered if you would find it an imposition to house . . . No!" Blackthorn made a chopping motion with his hand. "It *is* an imposition. I'll have the man put up at the inn and go to Mrs. MacKivern's in the mornings to tutor the boys. There is no need at all for you to be put out by him."

"A tutor? The fellow would be far more comfortable here. And I've a schoolroom he may use, since my girls no longer need it. They are, during term, at the Misses Resternol's school in Broadway as parlor boarders."

Blackthorn reached the terrace and the two men went on up the next steps to the house.

"Although my wife requires her rest and I sent her to bed, it is not all that late," continued Ian. "What I mean, well, are you quite ready for *your* bed? I thought perhaps," he added quickly, "that you'd be willing to give me a game of billiards. When Stewart lived, the four of us played, but my wife is not fond of the game, so I've few opportunities these days to indulge my passion for it!"

"I would enjoy that," lied Blackthorn.

What he really wished was to be alone so he could come to some conclusion about what it was in Frederica that had ensorcelled him. After all, it *must* be ensorcellment, must it not, for him to postpone his return to London just when he was truly needed there!

But longed-for solitude was not to be thought of. One must do one's duty by one's host. And besides, it would not do to let MacKivern become aware of just how interesting he found the man's sister-in-law. If Ian MacKivern were half so protective of her as Blackthorn suspected him to be, any suspicion of the licentious plans he was making for their future and that would be the end of *that*.

Not that he was quite certain himself just what he meant when he referred to *that*. Bedding her, of course, but beyond that . . . ?

Ah, well. Billiards. One could not play a proper game of billiards while distracted by thoughts of dalliance. There'd be another time, a more proper place, in which he could think about his Frederica.

Chapter Three

Feeling more than a trifle cross, Blackthorn watched his son's borrowed horse pound down the lane after young Stewart's pony and disappear. Just as he'd been warned. So what was he doing here?

It took some thought, but he finally discovered the irritation he felt was simple resentment. He resented sitting on the back of a mediocre horse with only his host for company. He resented the fact that Lady MacKivern, at breakfast, could talk of nothing but the people of the region who might be expected to accept her invitation at such short notice.

He especially resented Mrs. MacKivern's non-appearance before the boys, MacKivern and he himself rode off. In fact, he resented everything which kept him from pursuing his Frederica.

And *most of all*, Blackthorn resented that the blasted woman had taken over his thoughts to the point he kept thinking of her as *his!*

"My Terror would like a canter, my lord," said MacKivern, breaking into Blackthorn's moody thoughts, "and, besides—"

A chuckle was clear in his tone if not in actuality. "—if we do not step up our pace, we'll lose the boys altogether."

The touch of humor in MacKivern's voice caught Blackthorn's ear. He glanced at his host and saw a questioning look he'd no intention satisfying. Instead, politely, he agreed. "They are beyond the curve already, are they not? And, as you say, our mounts would be better for a run."

A turn or two later they discovered the boys had stopped. Quite obviously Stewart was urging something to which Matthew objected. The MacKivern lad glanced around, noticed the men approaching and, heeling his pony, took off at top speed.

Urgently, Matthew shouted, "Stu, stop!"

Lord MacKivern yelled at the top of his lungs: "Stewart! Blast you boy! Stop this instant!"

MacKivern's fluent swearing floated back to Blackthorn, since he'd been a moment late in putting spurs to his own horse as Ian had done.

"Stewart!" yelled MacKivern.

"Stu!" That was his son giving urgent voice to *his* call.

"The bridge, boy! Stewart, stop!"

Concern and worry, *fear* perhaps in that? But, bridge? His jaw set, Blackthorn urged on his mount. The younger, longer-legged gelding caught up with MacKivern's favorite but aging hack. Next he passed his son, pounded at a dead run around another curve . . . and pulled up just too late.

Throwing his reins over a branch, he slid to the ground and ran to the edge of a gully the bridge spanned. Or was *supposed* to span.

Would span again, once it was finished . . .

He glanced back and saw MacKivern catch Matthew's reins, pulling the boy to a halt. Even as Blackthorn half scrambled, half slid, toward the boy lying, deadly still, at the bottom of the cut, he heard his son's shrill voice, arguing . . .

"Let me go!" Matt, trying to dismount, was held firmly in the saddle. "Stu . . . ! I must go to him!"

"Lad," said MacKivern grimly, "I know you want to go to him because you fear Stewart may be badly hurt, but you can and must help him in another way."

"Help?" Matthew turned terror-stricken eyes from the edge of the ravine. Somewhere below, where he couldn't see, but could plainly *hear*, the pony was in great distress. "How, my lord?"

"You must ride back the way we came. You are to find Hansard—my coachman, remember?—who will be in the stable yard or the coach house. Tell him I need the small cart, a stretcher, men, and that he's to order a groom out on our fastest horse to find and bring back Dr. Milltown. Wherever the doctor is, he must come at once. Have you all that?" The boy nodded and tried to collect his reins, but MacKivern hadn't finished. "Matthew, do you understand you are *not* to go by way of the cottage? Until we know exactly what is the matter with Stewart, we will *not* upset his mother."

Matthew tugged to free his reins. "If only Stu's pony . . ."

"Ah yes. That's another thing." MacKivern caught the boy's eyes. "Maybe the hardest thing of all. You are to tell Hansard he's to bring a horse pistol."

White-faced, the boy gulped. Shakily, he nodded—and then, finally released from MacKivern's hard hand, he raced back down the lane, leaning into his mount's neck and clutching her mane with one hand as he urged the animal on. MacKivern wondered if he asked too much of the boy. Belatedly, he hoped the boy wouldn't take a tumble of his own.

Dismounting, Ian left Terror standing and he too half climbed and half slid down the rough bank which, over many years, spring rains had made rather deep, as water, rushing toward the valley, left the wold for lower land.

"How is he?" he asked, ignoring the animal he couldn't help.

"I don't know. His wrist is either broken or very badly sprained, but if that were all he suffered I'd be ringing a peal over him. It's the blow to the head which worries me." Blackthorn finished tying a strip torn from his cravat around Stewart's head, holding a pad of the same material tightly against a gash which bled freely.

"All that blood!"

"Head wounds always bleed," said Blackthorn sharply. "You *know* that."

MacKivern nodded. "I've sent Matthew for my coachman

who is to send for the doctor. It will be twenty minutes or so before a cart can arrive. They are to bring a stretcher so we may lift him out of here without bundling him around too much. Drat it, why did this have to happen just now?''

''Why any time at all? Why is *just now* so important?'' Blackthorn folded his coat and, gently raising Stewart's shoulders, he placed it under the boy's head.

''What?''

''Why *not* now? It seems to me the very definition of an accident is that one cannot time them for occasions when they'd be more convenient.''

''Oh.'' MacKivern's eyes glanced across Blackthorn's face and back to his nephew. ''Um. Well, it's just that Rickie was beginning to recover a bit from my brother's death. She didn't like it when I sent the boy to school, but she accepted it as necessary, which she'd not have done without a good fight even a year earlier! If something happens to young Stewart now . . . well, there'll be hell to pay.'' Ian sighed gustily, again. ''Frankly, my lord, I won't speak for her sanity.''

''She is the sanest woman I've ever met!''

''You didn't see her when Stewart died. Hysterics all over the place.''

''I'd have thought, rather, that she'd have been angry,'' said Blackthorn thoughtfully.

''She *was*. She ranted and raved and I feared she'd shock the doctor out of his skin with her language, but all he said, and that far more tolerantly than I'd have thought possible, was to let her get it all out, that she'd feel better.''

''You call that hysterics?'' Blackthorn surreptitiously felt the boy's good wrist, hunting and finding a faint but reasonably steady pulse. ''I'd call it temper.''

''Perhaps I've never encountered what are generally considered hysterics and only think what she did should be called that.'' MacKivern sighed. ''Now that you mention it, I recall she'd a terribly uncontrolled temper when a mere girl. My brother could tease her out of her tantrums and she grew out of them, of course, but I never did have the knack of overcoming them. Stewart is . . . alive?''

Obviously I wasn't as sly about checking that pulse as I meant to be, thought Blackthorn. ''I think he'll do. The beat is a trifle weaker than I like, but it's steady. I wish he'd wake, though. Very likely he's suffering concussion and the longer he's out the worse it is."

"How do you know?"

Blackthorn flushed slightly. "I wished to become a doctor. It wasn't to be, but I've read and I've friends who have been kind enough to teach me some of the more basic things. Your local doctor isn't the sort who applies leeches for each and every problem from gout to a broken head, is he?"

"To the contrary." MacKivern smiled wryly. "Dr. Milltown was trained in Edinburgh. He's still a youngish man and, frankly, some of his more elderly patients insist he resort to the leech more often than he likes! Except for the fact he was raised locally and returned to help in his father's practice some would refuse to have anything to do with him and his newfangled notions."

Blackthorn chuckled. "Yes. They don't understand how much has been learned. We've better ways now, although there is a very great deal yet to be discovered! I wonder if we'll ever know everything."

"A very boring world if we did!"

"I meant concerning the human physique. It is exceedingly complicated. If we haven't a notion what some of those things inside one *do,* how then can we heal them when something is wrong with them?"

Just then a burly man half tumbled down into the gorge and went directly to the stricken pony. A single shot and, finally, the horse's dreadful suffering was over.

"Young Stu been into mischief already, has he, then?" asked the coachman approaching. "Ah now then, lad. How is it with you?"

"You had to shoot her?" The words were a mere thread of sound.

"Aye lad. Next time you're let on the back of one of my lord's animals, I may just ride you out on a leading string!"

The boy chuckled weakly. "You wouldn't then," he said . . . and passed out again.

"Boy should know he couldn't jump that!" scolded the old coachman as he frowned down at the unconscious lad.

"It was my fault, Hansard," admitted MacKivern. "I forgot

to warn him the bridge was out and not yet replaced. We must put up a barrier *beyond* the curve where it will be a warning far enough in advance even a fast-paced rider can stop!''

The coachman nodded. ''I'll see it's done proper-like. And I'll just see what's keeping those laggards with the cart!'' He scrambled back up the side of the cut.

''That's a good sign,'' said Blackthorn softly.

''That the boy spoke to Hansard?''

''Hmm. I wonder if the sound of the shot jarred him from his swoon or if he'd been lying there, at least partly conscious, for some time.''

MacKivern smiled slightly. ''If so, perhaps he was dreading a scold.''

''Or regretting the horse's pain. It was his first thought, which is good. I mean the fact he thought of someone or something other than himself. I understand that is considered a prime quality in our officers in the Peninsula.''

''It is what he dreams of. A commission. Rickie won't hear of it of course.''

''Mrs. MacKivern should remarry and fill her nursery so that this poor lad isn't burdened with all her love and the totality of her fears.''

''She should, but there's no one in the neighborhood who would interest her and she won't go elsewhere.''

A muscle jumped in the side of Blackthorn's jaw. ''I'll convince her she must come to Seymour Court for Christmas.'' He paused and then said what he knew MacKivern would want to hear. ''She'll meet a variety of men there, although they'll be mostly from government circles and many will be married. But all of them are far more up to her weight than your local men, I'd guess!''

Blackthorn found himself wondering how he might exclude one or two bachelors from his guest list. Men he'd normally invite to a house party. He wanted no competition when he . . .

Stewart groaned. His eyes fluttered.

''Blast,'' muttered MacKivern. ''I'd rather hoped he'd stay out of it until we got him to bed!''

''Stewart, can you hear me,'' said Blackthorn calmly. ''Do you know what happened to you?''

After a moment the lad said, "Bridge out." Another moment and he added, "Head hurts."

"Yes. Like the very devil, I'd think. You've also damaged your wrist, but so far as I'm able to determine, nothing else. Do you have specific hurts."

"All over . . . Diana?"

"Your pony? You don't remember?" asked Blackthorn softly.

"Hurt."

"Yes."

A long silence and Blackthorn thought the boy might have passed out again. Then, on a thread of sound, he said, "Shot."

"Hansard did the necessary, Stewart."

A tear slid under Stewart's lid and streaked through the blood staining his cheek. "My fault."

"You didn't know the bridge was out."

"Heard you shout." He paused, collecting himself. "Was angry," he added. "Should have stopped."

"Then you *were* at fault," inserted Blackthorn briskly, speaking over MacKivern's soothing words. "We all make mistakes, lad. The thing is, we must learn from them."

"My temper."

"Just like your mother's, m'boy," said MacKivern.

He stood as the sound of the men arriving with the cart could be heard. He stood on tiptoe, stretching to look over the rim of the eroded land, and by doing so, didn't see Stewart raise his eyelids and look after him, bemused. His lordship climbed up to the road to organize his men.

Blackthorn asked, "You didn't know your mother had a temper?"

Stewart started to shake his head, winced and responded silently, his mouth forming the word no.

"Your uncle was telling me it was very bad when she was young. She learned to control it and so can you. If you will."

"Diana. Temper killed her."

"Yes."

Suddenly Stewart tried to turn to his side. Blackthorn raised and held him firmly, especially his head, as he cast up his accounts.

"Feel better?" he asked the lad, sympathetically, when the sickness had passed.

"No."

"Very likely not. You'll feel very sorry for yourself for some few days to come, I fear." He heard the men sliding down to them. "And now, lad, you must brace yourself. We must move you from this most uncomfortable ground to a much more suitable bed. It will not be easy for you."

". . . deserve it."

"Perhaps, although I've never agreed with that particular philosophy. Ready?" he asked as two men approached. "That's right. Spread it taut and I'll lift the boy. Good," he added a moment or two later. "Now lift the stretcher. A bit higher if you can manage? And if you'd lean into the wall . . . Careful now!"

The transfer was made with a minimum of jouncing. Having passed the boy on, MacKivern's two tallest grooms shrugged their shoulders, loosening tense muscles which they'd strained to get the stretcher high enough so it could be taken, safely, by those above.

"Well done, men," Blackthorn complimented them, and climbed up.

He found that the boy, stretcher and all, was to be placed into the back of a small cart. Carts of this sort rarely had springs. This one didn't, nor had anyone thought to bring blankets to pad against the inevitable jarring. Sighing, Blackthorn crawled in and seated himself. Then he asked MacKivern to help position Stewart so that the boy would be held steady in the most comfortable possible position.

The trip home to the manor, slow as it was, was stressful for both Stewart and Blackthorn, who had known the position he adopted wouldn't be easy. With the lad between his legs, the boy's back and head held against his half reclining body, there was no support for his own back. Keeping his shoulders steady while maintaining the slant to his chest, so Stewart was tilted but not overly so, caused a great deal of strain to back and shoulder muscles.

They'd covered nearly half the distance when MacKivern, seeing Blackthorn wince at a particularly rough jolt, realized the problem. He stopped the procession, had one of the horses unsaddled and the saddle put behind Blackthorn's back. The rest of the slow journey was better if still not exactly comfortable.

Nor was their arrival at all comfortable.

The doctor was before them, but he'd met Frederica as she walked up from the cottage to confront Ian's gardener. She'd rather looked forward to the battle which would be necessary before she could wrest the necessary blooms for several bouquets from the curmudgeonly man, but Dr. Milltown, jovially asking what mischief young MacKivern had been up to that his presence was instantly required, put all that from her mind.

Frederica stared at the doctor for all of half a minute and then, without responding, changed course for the stables, assuming that, if her son were not there, at least it would be known what had happened. The doctor strolled along behind. She was waiting, fretting, when the cart arrived and moved instantly to its side.

Her son groaned as the horse shifted its weight, moving the poles and jerking the cart a trifle. She realized the sound meant he lived. That settled, Frederica looked up and met Blackthorn's eyes straightly.

"What happened?"

Her bluntly spoken question required an equally blunt response. "He didn't know the bridge was out."

Her eyes flew back to the bandage which didn't hide the dried blood which had flowed down cheek and neck before the pad's pressure stopped it. She bit her lip, her eyes darker and seemingly deeper set, turning to stare into Blackthorn's, wanting, but not asking for reassurance.

"He's awakened more than once," he said, understanding her unspoken need, "and he was sensible in his speech. He's also thrown up his breakfast in a most distressing manner. Given that, I suspect concussion, but not a bad one."

"You a doctor, then?" asked Milltown from the other side of the cart where he was taking Stewart's pulse.

"No. But Mrs. MacKivern needed to know the extent of her son's hurts. Beyond the wrist I could find nothing obvious."

"We'll see. We'll see," muttered the doctor. "The wrist broken or just sprained?"

"I think it a sprain," responded Blackthorn, "but the wrist is a difficult joint to check."

"So it is, so it is . . . Well?" The doctor glared. "Why is everyone standing around with their tongue between their teeth? Let's get the lad to his bed so we can see what's what?"

"But his bed is at the cottage. Blast you, Ian, you should have taken him there at once. Now he must endure all that much more jolting . . ."

Her words were abruptly halted, her old friend's hand covering her lips. "The boy remains here, Frederica. You will wish to remove yourself from the dower house to a nearby room and of course you may. But his requirements will be such that he'll be far more comfortable under my roof while he recovers. No arguments, Rickie," he added when she opened her mouth, "or I'll have to remind you I'm his guardian and my decision is final. And you know you hate it when I do that!"

She glared. "He'd be more comfortable in his own bed."

"A narrow bed. A very narrow bed, if I recall?"

"Drat." Turning on one heel, she stormed away, stalking toward the house where she tracked her sister-in-law to the dining room. "Has anyone been kind enough to inform you that you are to have a sick boy, his mother, and a well boy thrust upon you and that a bed for Stewart must be prepared instantly?"

"What?" Tildy swung around from the beautifully set table which she'd been contemplating while fingering a stack of place cards. "What has happened?" she asked.

"Stewart fell at the cut where the bridge is out. He's concussed."

Tildy's eyes narrowed. "And my husband insisted he remain here?"

"*You* argue with him. I wanted to take him home."

"Has he forgotten we've company to dinner this evening?" asked Tildy coldly.

"I've no notion what he's remembered or forgotten," said Frederica dispiritedly. She didn't need to deal with Tildy's relationship with Ian when her unconscious son had yet to be thoroughly checked by the doctor. "A room?"

"The . . . blue, I suppose," said Matilda, grudgingly. "It is near the back stairs and will be less trouble for the maids."

"Excellent. It will also be as far as possible from the evening's festivities so that the noise will not bother him." She knew that hadn't crossed Tildy's mind, but, even knowing, she added, "Thank you for the thought."

A crew of men trooped in just then, carrying the stretcher. Stewart's forehead creased with pain. Matilda immediately snapped an order that the house servants take over from the grooms so that no more dirt be tracked along the halls.

MacKivern calmly told her he knew she was worried about Stewart, but she shouldn't take her fear out in trivial fussing about such a minor problem as a trifling amount of dirt.

Luckily, thought Blackthorn, MacKivern didn't see how his wife glared at him!

The men and Frederica ignored her, too. Leading the way to the stairs, Rickie ordered them to be very careful not to tip the boy out and they smiled at her indulgently, handling the situation calmly, but more roughly than Frederica liked. Nevertheless Stewart was soon settled in the blue room and the men pointed toward the back stairs where they might not insult Tildy yet again by tracking through her house in all their dirt.

Much to her chagrin, however, Frederica was gently removed from her boy's side by Lord Blackthorn. "Let MacKivern and the doctor deal with the lad," he said. "He'll be far more comfortable if the men remove his clothing than if his mother adds embarrassment to his other problems by doing it for him."

Knowing Stewart was self-conscious when undressed in her presence although she'd repeatedly told him it was absurd, she nodded. She paced the hall, sighing deeply again and again. Taking a dozen paces one way, she'd turn, stare at the door, take a dozen more the other way and repeat the process.

"I assure you he'd not want . . ."

"You are correct," she interrupted. "It makes it no easier, knowing my baby has no use for me! He is not still unconscious, then?"

"He came to when removed from my arms."

"I don't believe I thanked you for easing his journey that way."

"It was nothing."

She fell silent, again pacing . . . staring at the door, pacing . . . staring at the door . . . which finally opened.

"Ah then," said the doctor, anticipating her demand for

information. "Boy's concussed as His Lordship here suggested. His wrist is badly sprained. He's bruised in places he'll not admit exist ... at least not to *you*," he said to Frederica, wiggling his brows suggestively. "What else? Ah. Think the elbow may have been wrenched as well. Wouldn't be at all surprised if the lad saved himself with that arm which buckled, of course, and then hit his head, but far more gently then it might have done. He'll do."

"What do I do?" asked Frederica. "Laudanum, I suppose, for the headache ..."

She looked toward Blackthorn who cleared his throat roughly at her words. He stared at the doctor, a strained look about his eyes and forehead.

"What is it?" she asked.

"Man there knows his onions," said Dr. Milltown approvingly. "Like to have a talk with you sometime, my lord, and discover just how many onions you do know! What he'd have me say, Mrs. MacKivern, is no laudanum. Not tonight, that is. Want him awakened regular-like, every hour." The doctor held up his hand. "Know your theory about sleep being important to healing, missus, but *not* in a case of concussion. You check he's sensible. Also, you look at his eyes. See that the black center is even, the same size in both eyes. When that's true again, then he can sleep all you like. By tomorrow, most like. And you get some sleep yourself. I know you, Frederica MacKivern," he growled. "Likely make yourself sick a worrit'n about the boy!"

"I'll see she rests even if she doesn't sleep," said Blackthorn. "We'll take it in turns to sit with Stu, as my son calls him—" His eyes flashed to her when she made a negative move. "—Mrs. MacKivern, he'll be fine. We," he added a trifle whimsically, "are the ones with the problem! How to keep him quiet while his head heals, as I believe the good doctor was about to recommend!" He cast an apologetic glance toward Milltown who chuckled. "Another onion, I hope?" he asked the doctor politely.

"Another it is, my lord. Such a one you are! If you keep this lady from overdoing and needing me for her own sake, then I'll go away with far less worry. She's not easy to control, though. Why, I remember ..." The doctor broke off, laughing when Frederica made a warning sound. "Well, then, I'll not tell your secrets, Mrs. MacKivern. I believe my wife accepted Her Ladyship's invitation to dinner tonight. Don't know if it's canceled or not, but, Her Ladyship—'' His brows arched. "—well, I rather doubt it. I'll come a trifle early and look in on the boy, but I don't anticipate any difficulty beyond the usual. He may vomit again, I suppose. Shouldn't eat anything much until I see him tomorrow. And, keep him quiet.''

"That's all?"

"That's all. Heads are the devil. Can't really predict what will happen, but he seems completely aware. Didn't even forget what happened which wouldn't have been at all surprising, you know. Ah well. The good Lord will have His way in this as in all things.''

"But I'm hungry," protested Stewart MacKivern for the third time. "I don't see why I cannot eat. What difference if it only comes back up? I'd like it going down!''

The door opened and Frederica swung around. She met Blackthorn's eyes. Once again, it was as if they were connected in some deep meaningful way. Which was ridiculous. Frederica forced herself to look at her clasped hands. It would *not* do to find herself seriously attracted to this man! Especially not now. Not when her son needed her.

"Already decided you've suffered enough for your sins, young MacKivern?" asked Blackthorn. His sarcastic tone drew an outraged gasp from the boy's mother, but the man ignored her, catching and holding Stewart's quick glance. "I thought you'd decided you deserved it.''

"Didn't know they meant to starve me . . .'' said the boy, scowling.

"Did the doctor say he couldn't eat?" asked Blackthorn, frowning. "I cannot recall.''

"He said not till he'd seen him tomorrow, and if he might vomit, that can't be good for him, surely.''

"I'm trying to remember. I think his exact words were *anything much.* Something very easy to digest, perhaps? A gruel or panada or . . .''

"Milk toast?''

"Ugh!"

"Boy, you be still. Of all things the doctor ordered, the most important was that you stay quiet!" said Blackthorn, a faint laugh in his voice. "Perhaps something so simple as barley water would help ease his pangs?"

In a much more quiet voice, Stu said, "Yuck."

"I'll stay with Stewart, Mrs. MacKivern," Blackthorn continued, "if you wish to see what you can do in the kitchen. When I went down to see what *I* might do, I caused such pandemonium among the staff that the cook nearly had a spasm—which would not *do*. Not with a formal dinner ordered at such short notice for this evening." He noted her soft sigh. "Yes, the dinner goes on despite my explaining that I thought it far too much with a sick boy in the house. I was politely told to go to the devil."

Frederica's chuckle was rather watery, but it was a laugh. "I doubt very much Matilda said anything of the sort. Particularly, she didn't say it to *you*, the lion of her evening."

"You've caught me out. It's *that*, above all things, I had wished to avoid, of course. I cannot like being paraded before company as part of the evening's entertainment. But surely," he said in a dry tone, "you can't have thought a mere concussion worthy of much concern on the part of the boy's aunt."

Frederica sighed. "I think I heard a touch of scorn or perhaps it was a bit of a scold, but you must understand what a burden Stewart and I are to her. If only Ian had taken Stewart to our home! I'd much prefer it . . ."

"You dislike being beholden to her as much as she resents being put out. It *is* something of a coil when MacKivern is the boy's guardian."

"And Stewart's heir," added Frederica softly. "That is the worst cut of all. Her own son died and the doctor insists she is to have no more children. She is *not* well, you know. Truly. Is it any wonder she resents us?"

"I'm hungry," complained the heir.

"You go," said Blackthorn to Frederica. "I can entertain our scamp here for half an hour or so."

"Don't give him brain fever on top of concussion!" warned Frederica, wishing she merely need ring the bell for a maid. She hated leaving Stewart for even a moment, but it seemed she must. If the kitchen staff were at sixes and sevens and in chaos, it might actually be best if she ran over to her own kitchen at the dower house. "I may be as much as an hour, since I'll have to do it myself."

"Can you?" asked Blackthorn bluntly, his brows arched.

"Oh yes." It was her turn for arched brows. "As can *any* woman who has been properly trained. How can one expect to order a household if one cannot do the work oneself? If you don't know what needs doing, you don't know what to order. And if you don't know how, how can you train your maids?"

"Perhaps that explains why my grandfather made me work one whole summer in the stables." He noticed Stewart's mild show of interest and turned more toward him. "I was about fourteen at the time and rather enjoyed it. Except for the day I was made to shoe a placid old workhorse. The first three shoes went on smoothly, but I must have done something wrong with the last. I remember the creature turned its head and booted me in the rear with his nose. I tumbled straight into a—" His eyes flicked toward Frederica as a quick grin passed across her face. "—well, a *mess* and was furious with him. I can't recall if I ever *did* get that last shoe on!"

A faint chuckle from the bed reminded Frederica of her son and she felt guilt that she'd momentarily forgotten him. Blackthorn felt a trifle guilty himself, for rousing the lad, even if it was a happy sound. He strolled to the window reminding himself sternly that he must stop flirting with Mrs. MacKivern.

At least, it must stop while the boy was ill.

"I'll come back as soon as I can. Stewart, you must try to sleep while I'm gone."

The door closed and Blackthorn turned back to look at the boy. "Can you sleep?"

"Head hurts like the devil."

"Yes, very likely it will, at least for this one night. Tomorrow you may have a dose of the poppy which will ease it."

"No!"

"No laudanum?"

"Makes me stupid. Hate the stuff."

"We'll talk with the doctor and see what he says. Perhaps some willow bark instead, although it is not so effective. Now be still. I didn't, you know, come to entertain you," he said with mock severity, "but to give your poor mother a change from fretting over you." He noted the boy's stricken look, and nodded. "You'll do, lad. But you must rest."

Blackthorn sat down and opened a book he took from the pocket in the tail of his coat. He began humming softly, a soothing and well-known ballad. Stewart, after plucking at his covers, rolling his head, and finally heaving a great sigh, slid into a troubled sleep. Blackthorn didn't stop his soft humming, but he put the book aside, unable to concentrate on it and his thoughts and his song all at the same time.

Gradually the thoughts took precedence and the humming stopped. Blackthorn frowned. Why, when he'd finally found a woman he wished to know better, had something like this interfered with his pursuit of her? Or had it? Would they not, perhaps, have a greater opportunity now and then for far deeper talk than in the formal setting of a crowded drawing room? Or at a table where, very likely just because he wished it otherwise, his hostess, perverse woman, would seat Frederica as far from him as possible?

The boy began tossing slightly and Blackthorn rose and went to him, putting aside all thoughts of the widow. He put his hand to Stu's forehead. It was cool enough, thank heaven, and the contact seemed to ease the boy. He settled and, finally, his lordship lifted his palm. It was, he feared, going to be a long and difficult convalescence. Stu—no, he must remember to call the boy Stewart as his mother preferred—Stewart was not the sort of lad to take kindly to the restrictions of a sick room.

Perhaps he should lengthen his stay a trifle. Instead of a few days, did he dare stay at least a week? *Someone* must see that Frederica did not wear herself to a thread caring for her young hellion. The door opened and he heard a gasp. Turning, he discovered Lady MacKivern staring at him.

"Did you want something?" he asked softly.

"That woman!" stormed his hostess. "How dare she ask our guest to demean himself this way?"

He crossed the room on silent feet and, literally, pushed the woman from the room. "You will not wake the boy! And if you refer to Mrs. MacKivern, by your insulting tone, *I* sent her away to prepare something invalidish for the lad who feels a trifle peckish. Which is a good sign. Not, of course, that his condition interests *you*."

For half a moment Matilda stared at him, wide-eyed, and then she gasped. "You are insulting!"

"Am I? Perhaps I am, but someone needs to tell you home-truths you don't wish to hear. You, selfish and jealous, have done nothing to make that sickroom more comfortable. You've ordered nothing to help Mrs. MacKivern care for her boy. You've not even detached *one* maid from her work to run errands for her! You, my dear, are an exceptionally cold and uncaring woman, something I sincerely hope Lord MacKivern never discovers. He is unwise enough to love you, you see."

"You can't know . . ."

"I know," said Blackthorn carefully, "that, like many women, you've lost a son. It has been intimated you can have no others. But that is not a reason to hate a boy who still lives. It is not *his* fault."

"I do *not* hate him . . ."

"Do you not?"

Matilda turned a wild look toward the sickroom door. Restraining a sob, she rushed away along the hall. Blackthorn stared after her for a moment before returning to the bedside where he looked into Stewart's wide open gaze. "Was that Aunt Tildy?"

"Yes."

Stewart sighed. "She doesn't like me."

"Did you hear our discussion?"

"Through the door? No. One can't in this house . . ."

"She is not a happy woman, Stewart."

"Why?" The boy looked truly bewildered. "When she has so much? Uncle Ian would do anything for her. And the girls are always thinking of things, bouquets and sewing samplers, ways of pleasing her. It doesn't make sense."

"No it doesn't, but needn't concern you. Put her from your mind, lad, and rest. If you are agitated when your mother returns, she'll have my head for washing and, worse, won't allow me back. Which could become a problem, since I mean to do what I can to lighten her days while she cares for you!"

Chapter Four

Much later that night the door to Stewart's room softly opened. "How is he?" asked Ian, not entering.

"Restless," said Frederica, going to him. "I wish he could sleep," she added. "But how can he when I am forced by the doctor's orders to wake him so often?"

"But he's no worse?"

"No worse."

"Good." He dropped a kiss on her forehead and patted her arm. "See you in the morning, Rickie."

Frederica, already tired from her concern for her son, glared at the closing door. Beyond Ian she saw just a glimpse of another figure but couldn't raise enough interest to care who it might have been. She returned to the bedside and fretted.

Nearly half an hour passed before the door opened again. This visitor didn't hesitate, but strode to the table in the window. Blackthorn set down the tray he carried and turned. "Am I correct? No one bothered to remember to feed you?"

"I didn't expect it, not with all that was going on. Besides, I'm not hungry."

"Cook was overset you'd not been fed. I think you'll find she did you proud."

"But I don't think I *can* eat. You should not . . ."

"Of course you can," he interrupted before she could point out the impropriety of his being there, essentially alone with her, since her sleeping son didn't count. "Or do you want to be sick too?"

Frederica met his stern gaze. She sighed. "I never eat well when something's wrong with Stewart. It's as if my stomach were all clenched up in knots."

"It may feel that way, but come take a few bites and see if there isn't more space there than you think."

"You are laughing at me."

"Perhaps. Come," he coaxed, holding back the chair. Once Frederica was seated he went to the bedside.

"Don't wake him," she whispered. "I just got him back to sleep. Sort of!"

Blackthorn nodded and began the humming which had soothed the boy when he'd sat with him earlier. It seemed to work again and he seated himself in the chair his mother had pulled closer to the bed. He stood up again when, after a few bites, he saw Frederica push back her plate.

"Come now," he sang softly to the tune he been humming. "You can do better."

She ignored his scolding words. "Why did he fall?"

"Why him and not you?" he asked, perceptively. "You cannot live the boy's life for him."

"I only want him to be happy. To be healthy. To live a good life."

"As all parents wish for their children."

"But there is only me to see he does. It is such a responsibility."

"I doubt very much there is 'only' you. There is Lord Mac-Kivern. There is my son. There is, for that matter, total strangers such as myself. Frederica, if you will not eat, then you must go to your bed. I'll sit with the boy."

She turned startled eyes his way, shaking her head. "Oh, no. I could not allow . . ."

"It is not a question of *allowing*. I *wish* to stay with him. After all, if I'd been only a few moments faster, I might have stopped him. So you see I do have responsibility for him too."

"It isn't right. You are . . ."

". . . a stranger," he finished for her. Holding her gaze, he added, "Frederica, I don't feel like a stranger."

She met his gaze with wide startled eyes. "I . . ."

". . . don't feel like one either," he finished for her. "It is very odd, is it not?" he asked with that faint touch of humor Frederica had come to like too well and to listen for. "You are, I think, to stay in the next room?" It was only half a question and he nodded toward the proper connecting wall. "I'll knock if I feel the boy needs you. Agreed?"

Despite herself Frederica yawned. "But it simply isn't

proper. No,'' she decided. ''I mustn't give in to such temptation and you mustn't tease me so, my lord.''

''I tease you *not.*'' He picked up the small glass of good port he'd had the butler add to the tray. ''Try this.''

''I'm afraid to. Wine makes me sleepy.''

''Good. Drink.'' He held the glass to her lips. She took a small sip. ''Now, a bite or two of that very good berry thing.''

She chuckled. ''You mean the raspberry fool?''

''If you say so.'' He handed her the spoon.

''Did anyone ever tell you, my lord, that you are a bully?''

''Am I? I've always felt it is only that when I know what is best I must see my will is done,'' he responded in a suspiciously bland tone.

She eyed him, sighed. ''It is too bad of you to be so provocative when I am below par and not up to arguing.''

She took a bite of the dessert. It was good. She took another. When he again handed her the wine, she drank off a portion without thinking while watching him cut up the slice of chicken breast. He lifted a bite to her mouth and she accepted it, her gaze caught by his. As she watched the look in his eyes, a glow which seemed to warm her, she felt again those tremors which had troubled her before. Very careful not to touch him, she took the fork.

''I am not a child to be hand fed,'' she scolded.

''No,'' he said, and the warmth seemed to have moved from eyes to voice, ''you are not a child.''

Frederica didn't dare look at him, but finished her meal and the last of the wine and then, bewildered, looked at the empty tray.

''I can never eat when something is wrong with Stewart!''

''It is because, on this occasion, you needn't worry enough for two.''

Frederica frowned, not understanding him.

''I am here to share that duty with you,'' he explained, speaking softly. ''Now. Off to bed with you and don't return for at least four hours.''

* * *

It was nearer six and Frederica was filled with guilt when she saw the dark circles beneath Lord Blackthorn's eyes. "Is he . . . ?"

"He's been just fine." He rose to his feet and approached her. Her attention was on the bed and Blackthorn silently laughed at himself. He'd been sitting there thinking of her and in *such* a way, it was not surprising he found it *not at all* to his satisfaction that she'd interest in no one but her son! "The difference in his eyes has abated and I've let him sleep through the last couple of hours. I'm sure he'll be just fine, Frederica."

"I don't know how to thank you."

"For bullying you unmercifully?" he teased.

"For that and for caring how my son goes on. Thank you."

"Forget it," he said gruffly. This time it was His Lordship who could not repress a yawn. "I think I'll take the advice I gave you and go find my bed." He yawned again. "Now if I can just remember . . ." He broke off on still another yawn.

". . . where it is?" she finished, a chuckle warming them both. "Was it a room stifled in deep dark red velvets and a great deal of old wood paneling and dark heavy furniture called, for reasons beyond my comprehension, the green room?"

"How did you guess?"

"Tildy saves it for important guests. Go to the head of the stairs, my lord, and it is the first door beyond on the left."

"I wonder if I should not go to your bed," he mused.

Frederica's startled look drew a smile.

"If you were to need someone, I'd be at hand," he explained and wanted, very much, to draw her near, touch her, hold her. He compromised by lifting her hand and holding it, playing with the fingers. "MacKivern should have assigned a maid to sleep near here."

"I . . . manage quite well." She couldn't take her eyes from their joined hands, felt her breathing affected by the touch. "I don't need anyone," she said, knowing it was a lie that, just then, she needed *him*. Needed him in ways she barely understood . . . and then again in ways she understood all too well!

Blackthorn wanted to argue, wanted to tell her that she did, that however much her Ian might *want* to care for her and her son, the man hadn't a notion of how to go about it, wanted to tell her . . . so much he would not, could not, *should* not say!

The discovery of the sorts of promises hovering on the tip of his tongue had Blackthorn shivering in horror. He was *not* looking for another wife. He'd tried that and found it a stifling arrangement. Far better something less permanent, less demanding . . .

Blackthorn dropped Frederica's hand, in order to cover what was, this time, a pretense-yawn—a pretense which instantly became all too jaw-crackingly real.

"You, my lord, had better leave before you curl up on a cushion like a cat and snooze away right here!"

Her words brought back the images, never far from his mind, of just how he'd like to deal with this intriguing woman. Lying with her on a cushion before a fire was a new thought, but as provocative as all the rest and he couldn't resist responding to her scolding words.

"Would you stroke my fur, Frederica, as you would the sleeping cat?" He heard that the warmth had returned to his voice. And, once again, he realized he was playing with fire when he flirted so with this woman who didn't know the rules. He cast one last look toward Stewart and, quietly and quickly, left the room.

Frederica stared at the closed door. "Would I stroke you, indeed!" she muttered, hands on hips and a glare in her eye. But the glare softened and a sigh escaped her. It would, she feared, be all too easy to succumb to the temptation to stroke him! She could almost feel her fingers running through his dark head of hair, along his shoulders and back . . . and forced herself to think of Stewart instead!

If His Lordship had let her son sleep, then perhaps it would be all right for her to do the same. And it did seem as if Stewart were less restless, more deeply asleep than he'd yet been. It was such a shame to pull him from the healing arms of Morpheus. But the doctor had said . . . what exactly had he said? Frederica berated herself for not listening more closely and then again for not asking Lord Blackthorn *why* he'd felt it all right to let Stewart sleep; what, exactly, the boy's eyes had to do with anything and how did he know anyway!

Dr. Milltown had seemed impressed by Blackthorn's medical

knowledge, had he not? So perhaps His Lordship knew what he did?

But then again, perhaps he did not?

Frederica fretted, but could not bring herself to wake her son. She was very happy when the doctor himself, followed by a very cross Matilda, entered the room.

"I don't see why you blame *me*," said Ian's wife. "She might have *asked*, you know."

"Tildy," said Frederica, her tone soothing, "please. More softly?"

"Oh." Matilda came close to stamping her foot. "You are always so *reasonable*. I do not understand you."

"If you'd only accept I've no designs on your husband, you'd understand me a whole lot better!"

Matilda gasped. "You are outrageous!"

"Ladies, will you take your argument elsewhere," said the doctor testily. "We've a sick boy here. Lady MacKivern, if you would merely do as I request and assign old Sal to attend Mrs. MacKivern here in the sick room, I'd appreciate it very much. Sal has a very good touch with a sick child. I should have thought of it yesterday."

"Really, no," exclaimed Frederica. "I do not wish to be a nuisance. And don't bother to say," said Frederica with some asperity, glancing at Tildy, "that my very existence is a nuisance to you!"

"As if I'd be so rude as to say any such thing," said Matilda in the cold voice Frederica heard all too often. "I will inform Sal she is to come to you at once."

The door closed with a bang which roused Stewart. "I'm hungry," he mumbled. "And I gotta . . ." He opened his eyes and met those of the doctor. He glanced at his mother, and back, this time a more pleading look, cast toward the man leaning over him.

"Mrs. MacKivern," said the doctor with a grin, "if you would be so kind as to step into the hall, there are a few things to which this young man and I must attend."

Frederica immediately stiffened. "He's worse?"

Milltown took her arm and bundled her toward the door. "Nothing of the sort. In fact, I think I'll find he's doing even better than I'd hoped. You just leave us be for a bit," he added, his eyes twinkling. ''The boy's problem calls for a man's help, you see.''

Enlightenment dawned. She looked at her son who glared back at her. ''Oh, of all the ridiculous ... !''

''But very natural, you'll agree,'' soothed the doctor. ''You just go off and do what you want, for ... perhaps half an hour?''

''That long?''

''I suspect you need a rest.''

''Actually I don't. I had nearly a full night's sleep. Bla- ... Someone else sat with Stewart for a time.''

''Excellent!'' The doctor cast her glowing cheeks a quick look, but refrained from teasing. He merely repeated, ''Still, half an hour, I think.''

Defeated, Frederica moved quickly toward the back stairs and down to the kitchen where she was greeted by a shower of questions concerning Stewart, who was well liked by the staff despite, or perhaps *because* of, his charmingly mischievous ways.

Frederica reassured them and then said. ''I hate to trouble you, but I've only a few minutes before the doctor will have finished and I must return. Could I have a tray for Stewart, please. You know the sort of invalidish things he'll require ... and perhaps a bit of breakfast for myself?''

''My lady had words with me and I'll take up the lad's tray in a moment,'' said the plump and roguish, though gray-haired, Sal who was busily arranging a tray even as she spoke. ''You, madam, take yourself up to the breakfast room where you belong,'' she went on in the scolding tones of an aging and indulged servant. ''And,'' she added, when she saw Frederica glance at the tray, ''you needn't worry I'll feed him the wrong things. I've nursed bumped heads before, you know.'' Another of those teasing looks and she added, ''Or you *should* know, since one was your own!''

''I'll—'' Frederica tried to think of a reason she not go up to the breakfast room but could discover no reasonable excuse. ''—go up then.''

Just before she exited through the door to a hall which led to a handful of stairs which took one to a green baize covered door, the entrance to the manor's entrance hall, she glanced back, her look begging Old Sal to take good care of Stewart.

Sal, pretending insult, shooed her on.

Even though she was almost certain Blackthorn wouldn't be there, that he'd sleep for hours yet, she entered the breakfast room cautiously. She was both pleased and chagrined to discover herself correct. Blackthorn was *not* there. Ian, however, was. He'd piled his plate with buttered eggs, bacon, a good sized portion of a large sirloin, and a couple of rolls.

"You'll grow fat if you eat like that all the time," teased Frederica. "And what will Matilda say to that?"

He ignored her final comment, referring back to the first. "*You'll* never have that problem, Rickie. You burn yourself down to a thread when you forget to take care of yourself! Something you do all too often. How's the boy?"

"I believe Stewart will be fine. I hope the doctor will tell me I may take him home."

"Nonsense. He'll be much happier here."

Ian didn't raise his eyes from his plate so didn't see her grimace. But Blackthorn, entering just then and looking as if he'd never ever have even *thought* of spending the night by a child's sick bed, did. "The boy all right?"

"The doctor is with him now," said Frederica, blushing. She hadn't a notion why she blushed, but she did.

The door opened a crack and, hesitantly, Matt peered in. "The footman said to come here?"

"Come in, Matthew," encouraged Frederica, starting to rise. "Can I help you to your breakfast?"

"You sit and I'll do it," said Blackthorn. "Matthew, I apologize that I've spent so little time with you I don't know your likes and dislikes. You'll have to tell me what to give you."

Shyly, Matthew pointed at a roll and asked, politely, for a bite of egg. His father gave him a rasher of bacon as well and set the plate near his own place. Then Blackthorn filled his plate, choosing a breakfast similar to his son's, except for several extra rashers of bacon. He was both surprised and pleased that his son waited for him to be seated before picking up his own fork. As he recalled, he'd not have been so polite at the lad's age!

He glanced across the table at Frederica. "I'm pleased you

came down," he said. "It didn't occur to me you could be torn from your son's side long enough to eat a proper breakfast." He grinned at her. "I'll admit to finding myself surprised."

"So you should be." Frederica flushed again, but this time with anger. "I'd *not* be here if Dr. Milltown hadn't thrust me from Stewart's room and said to go away!"

"Good man." Blackthorn beamed. "Excellent, in fact. And I see you are not half so tired as I feared, or you'd not have the energy to lose your temper with me!"

Frederica ground her teeth. "Ian, tell His Lordship that I've quite enough stamina to—" She glanced at Matthew who, a bite of food halfway to his mouth, watched her with great interest. "—care for my son," she finished, deflated.

Matthew sighed, as if he knew she'd not finished her original thought and was disappointed. He finished raising his fork to his mouth and chewed thoughtfully. "Is it permitted," he said after a moment, "that I ask if Stu will be all right?"

"He'll be fine," said his father, before Frederica could respond. "Unfortunately, he must remain quiet for some days. Perhaps weeks. No riding or running or jumping. I wondered if you might have any notions of how we may achieve such peace?"

"Poor Stu," said Matthew. "He won't like that at all."

"No he won't. Will you think about games he can play while lying in bed?"

The boy chewed thoughtfully for a moment. "I suppose I might teach him piquet."

Blackthorn sent his son a startled glance. Carefully, he set aside his knife and fork. "Just where," he asked a trifle ominously, "did you learn *that* particular game?"

Matthew, obviously equally startled by his father's tone, looked first at Frederica and then Ian, and finally, quickly, at his father who's glare had him turning his gaze, instantly, back to his plate. "Mr. Tenniel," he said so softly he could barely be heard.

"Tenniel! Your last tutor? Before you went to school?"

"Hmm." Matthew nodded, wondering what was the matter. "Whenever I did well. It was a reward."

"Some reward," said Blackthorn gloomily. "Did he also teach you to lay wagers?"

"Oh no." Matthew's eyes widened. "Of course not. That, he said, was an evil I should be strong enough to avoid even when I was old enough to join others my own age in such pastimes. He said," added the boy solemnly, "that there were bad people in the world who would attempt to bring me to ruin by driving me down that particular path and that I should remember and not allow it to happen when the time arrived I might go on the town by myself."

"Thank the good Lord for small favors," laughed Frederica. "What an odd tutor he must be."

"He was a *good* sort of tutor," said Matthew just a trifle belligerently. "I *liked* him."

"I think perhaps I'd have liked him, too," said Blackthorn gently. "But I suspect you and I had better have a little talk, Matthew, and discover just exactly what else this very odd tutor has taught you. Besides your Latin and maths and something of writing your letters with a reasonably decent hand . . . and *not* to lay bets although he taught you to play cards. Juniper! *I've* no notion what else. That's the problem."

"But should you dislike it if I teach Stu to play piquet?"

"Ask his mother."

Frederica controlled a smile with difficulty. "We will teach him together, Matthew. I haven't played for some years, so perhaps you'll have to remind *me* of the rules."

"Do *you* lay bets?" asked the boy innocently.

"Oh yes. The very wildest of bets. I think I lost the moon to Ian once. And then there was the time I bet the whole of Kensington Palace to Stu . . . to my husband . . . I lost that too," she finished and rose quickly from the table.

Matthew didn't catch the undertone of sadness she'd not kept from her voice at the mention of her husband. Instead he laughed. "You bet the *moon?*"

"Yes. Against Ursa Major, if I remember correctly—"

As Frederica continued, Blackthorn saw the tension drain from her.

She heaved a great pretense of a sigh and added in soulful tones, "—I did so wish to win. Just *think*. To own the whole of the great dipper with which one might dip from the Milky Way!"

"Yes," said Matthew solemnly. "That would be a very great

thing, would it not?'' He smiled and she returned it, all the while edging toward the door. Matthew's wistful voice stopped her. ''May I see Stewart today? I mean, just *see* him?''

''Matthew . . .'' began Blackthorn, warningly.

''I don't see why not so long as you are careful not to tire him,'' said Frederica, interrupting his lordship before a denial could be expressed. ''I mean to read to Stewart this afternoon. It's all I can think of to keep him quiet. I think it is still too soon for him to play games, but why don't I send someone to find you and you too may listen as I read.''

''Thank you,'' said the boy fervently. ''I know no one would lie to me. It isn't that. But I want to *see with my own eyes* that he's going to be all right.'' He looked around, his very large gray eyes begging the adults to understand. ''Do you see?''

''Of course, Matthew,'' said Frederica gently. ''It is why I suggest you come when I was reading. Neither of you will expect to talk during a story, you see, so Stewart will not be overly excited by your visit, but *you'll* have an opportunity to check on your friend.''

''You're a Trojan, Mrs. MacKivern,'' said Matthew with something of the same fervor with which he'd thanked her.

''Thank you. I think!'' Frederica cast a smile somewhere between the men and left the room.

''I'm rather surprised by how wide awake and cheerful she is,'' mused Ian a trifle absently as he cut another bite from his beefsteak. ''The lad must be in far better shape than I'd have guessed.''

''He is not at all well and will need careful nursing for some days,'' warned Blackthorn at his host's careless words.

''Really? You've seen him this morning?''

Blackthorn thought briefly of mentioning the hours he'd spent at a restless Stewart's bedside during the long, dark, early morning hours, but he merely nodded.

Ian shrugged. ''I've told the footman not to allow Dr. Milltown to leave until he's reported to me. I suspect he'll be here shortly. There is nothing wrong with the doctor's appetite and he'll eat before he leaves unless there is an emergency he must get on to . . . Will you wait?''

''I'd like to hear what the man has to say.''

Their conversation continued as Ian politely asked a few

questions about the current situation in the government and Blackthorn politely responded.

Matthew finished eating but remained quietly at the table, making himself as small and quiet as he could while listening with half an ear as the men discussed the problems of establishing a regency.

". . . but don't you agree he'd be better for his own bed?" Matilda's crisp tones came clearly from beyond the partly open breakfast room door and, hearing it, Ian rose to his feet, his brow clouding. He strode to the door, opened it.

"Dr. Milltown," he said. "I hope you've time to join me in a cup of coffee at least?"

The doctor, about to give a sharp answer to Lady Mac-Kivern's question, turned, nodded, and turned back to reply to Her Ladyship.

But Ian's hand on his arm urged the doctor into the sun-filled room and away from the woman whose compressed lips and tight features said volumes. Not that Ian read the language of that look correctly.

"You are very concerned, Tildy, as you should be," Ian said, softly. "I'll tell you exactly what the doctor has to say later. I know how much you dislike anything to interfere with your morning duties, so at luncheon, perhaps?"

"Yes, Ian. At luncheon." Matilda turned on her heel and click-clacked her way back toward the front hall.

" 'Fraid I've bad news for Her Ladyship," said the doctor who *had* correctly read Matilda's desire to be rid of the boy and, still more, to be free of his mother. Once he'd filled a plate and seated himself he added, "Don't think the boy *should* be moved yet. Concussion, you know. Keep the room dim so the sun doesn't harm his eyes. Keep him quiet. Only thing we know to do."

"Matilda had hoped Stewart was not so ill as I'd told her was the case. She doesn't like illness, you know. Hasn't since . . ." Ian frowned, heaved a sigh and added in a firm voice, "Stewart will, of course, stay here just as long as necessary."

The doctor cast Ian a questioning look. "Still mourning the boy you lost, is she? Hadn't thought of that. Apologize."

"Apologize? For what must you apologize?"

The doctor compressed his lips against a desire to tell Ian

just how mean a woman Matilda MacKivern could be when she set her mind to it. "Never you mind. Now," he went on in a less brusque tone, "I've ordered Old Sal to nurse the boy. *Your* problem is to see his mother gets exercise and sleep. Sal knows how to deal with sick lads. Won't take any nonsense. Boy'll do well with Sal. But you know Mrs. MacKivern!"

"We do indeed. I'll insist she ride out at least in the mornings and perhaps stroll in the shrubbery in the evening?" asked Ian.

The doctor harrumphed. " 'Suppose it'll do. Better than nothing." Milltown noticed the silent but big-eyed Matthew. "And you, boy. Don't want you getting ill neither. Don't you think that because Stewart can't run about, that you should *not*. In fact, lad, you just take yourself off to the stable and have a groom take you out riding now. Be good for you. Run along now!"

Matt looked at his father, silently pleading that he be allowed to remain, but once again unexpressed desires were misinterpreted, and, instead of allowing him to stay, Blackthorn shooed him off, telling him what a good notion it was and to enjoy himself!

Once the boy slipped off his chair and moved slowly toward the door, Blackthorn asked Milltown, "What more would you suggest be done with regard to Mrs. MacKivern's health?"

No one noticed when Matthew, his ears on the perk, slid into a corner by the buffet and slipped to sit on the floor with his knees pulled to his chest.

"Active woman, my lord. Not used to being boxed up in a room. Out in all weathers, after all! Boy's old enough she needn't stay there hours on end, but try to convince *her* of that."

"Are you worried she'll make herself ill?"

"Harrumph. She's that sort," growled the gruff man who was really not half so old as he sounded when concerned for his patients!

"We'll do what we can, then," soothed Blackthorn. And then realized he couldn't stay more than another few days at most. After all, it was not a fudge that he was needed in London! "At least . . ." he glanced at Ian.

"Of course we'll do what we can. *Long* rides, for instance. And my wife is planning a few tables of cards this evening.

She will join us. I'll have to put my mind to what else we can do.''

"Cards?" laughed Blackthorn. "Perhaps you should ask my son to join us!''

"Yes, I saw that news rather startled you." Ian explained to the doctor about the piquet and the betting.

"I wonder if his tutor was any good and how well he taught Matthew," mused Blackthorn and decided he'd have to find out one day soon.

"It might be amusing to play at piquet with one's son," said Ian a trifle wistfully. He breathed in deeply and let the breath go slowly. Glancing up he noticed Blackthorn's eyes upon him and, more cheerfully, he added, "A quiet time, you know, when one could discuss . . . things.''

"So it would be. I'll have to remember that as my son gets older." Blackthorn passed Ian his cup for another cup of coffee and asked the doctor if there was much illness in the region. He listened with more interest than Ian to the resulting lecture.

". . . and I want something done about those cottages or we'll have typhus amongst us again!" finished the doctor, frowning.

"Typhus!" The word caught Ian's attention as nothing else had done. "Where did you say?''

"Lord Merrick's old cottages. Those along the stream. In bad shape and in hot weather . . . well MacKivern, *you* know better than most how it can be," he finished awkwardly, remembering again that Ian's son had died of typhus. "Trouble is, can't convince Merrick.''

"You won't," said Blackthorn abruptly. "Not if it means spending his blunt!" The other two men stared at His Lordship so he added, "Rumor has it he's rolled up.''

Milltown sighed. "Blast! Been clues enough. Should have guessed." He picked up a strip of bacon and chewed thoughtfully. "Well, I'll have to go talk to those pensioners of his again. Maybe I can teach them to take care.''

"Don't count on it," chuckled Ian. "A more stubborn lot of characters I've never met. And set in their ways! Well, you know.''

"Characters. Now, that's the word for them. Right out of a play," agreed Milltown with a smile. "And I do know, of course," he said, pushing away from the table. He rose and added, "I'll be off to my thankless task, then."

"You're riding over to talk to the cottagers now?"

"Hmm. Must try, you know."

"Is there nowhere else they may live?" asked Blackthorn.

"Nowhere to which any of them will move," said the doctor a trifle testily. "I tried that once before."

"They have their cottages for life and fear that if they leave them they'll lose them," explained Ian. "At their age, they greatly fear they'd be placed in a workhouse."

"I know, MacKivern. I know. It's a problem." Glumly, the doctor removed himself from the room, Ian following to do the polite and see him off.

The boy stood and approached the table. "Typhus?" he asked. "What is that?"

"You still here? Boy, I thought you wanted to ride."

"Yes, but even more I wanted to know about Stu. What is typhus?"

"A terrible illness which kills quickly. We've no notion how to cure it. Matthew, I will discover in what direction those cottages lie and I'd appreciate if you'd avoid going anywhere near them. I would be devastated if I were to lose you, you know."

The boy nodded, solemn-eyed. "You'd have to marry again. And you don't want to."

Blackthorn swore softly. "Who told you such a stupid thing?"

"That you don't want to marry again?"

"That the only reason I think of you at all is that you are my reason it is unnecessary!"

"Oh, well, I heard Cook say it was a good thing I was a boy, since you needn't wed some featherbrained bit like my mother and be made unhappy all over again while trying to get another heir on her." After a half instant's pause, he asked, "By the way, just how *does* one get an heir?"

Blackthorn choked on a last swallow of coffee, cleared his throat and glanced at his son's big eyes. Instantly he decided the lad was too old for nursery lies. "You've seen the mares bred?"

"When the stallions are put to them?" If anything the boy's eyes grew still larger.

"Exactly. It is similar and something we can discuss in greater detail when you reach an age where it becomes important, but for the time being, I think you should put it from your mind."

"How terrible for them," mused the boy. "Perhaps that's why women are featherbrained? Like Cook said Mother was? So they needn't worry about it?"

Blackthorn grinned. "Matthew, I won't argue that your mother was a bit of a widgeon, but there are some differences between a woman and a mare. For one thing, with proper attention, a woman may enjoy the experience a great deal." He gave his son a warning look when the boy opened his mouth to ask another question. "As I said, we'll discuss it when you are older."

Hearing approaching footsteps, Matthew settled into a chair. He decided that perhaps he'd ask Mrs. MacKivern for more information. *She* didn't seem particularly featherbrained ... but she was no longer married, either, so perhaps was no longer troubled by such things? On the other hand, perhaps it would trouble her to think of it ...

Life, thought Matthew, *is a very complicated business.* He very much doubted he'd ever understand it!

Chapter Five

Two days later Lord Blackthorn quietly entered Stewart's room. In the corner, half hidden by a screen, Old Sal sat sewing. Matthew sprawled on his friend's bed, the two boys listening avidly to Frederica's soft voice. Blackthorn listened, too, and recognized that she read from Thomas Shelton's translation of *Don Quixote.*

"... 'It seems that thou wast likewise beaten,' replied Don Quixote. 'Evil befall my lineage!' quoth Sancho; 'have not I told you I was?' 'Be not grieved, friend,' replied the knight;

'for I will now compound the precious balsam, which will cure us in the twinkling of an eye' ''

She closed the book and, at Blackthorn's clapping, turned, her clear skin showed the red which came so easily to it.

"Matthew, you've been remiss," teased his lordship. "You might have told me what an excellent reader Mrs. MacKivern is. I'd no notion what I missed!"

"*Father,*" said Matthew in a disgusted tone.

"Truly, I'd have enjoyed listening to Mrs. MacKivern read." His features took on a more serious expression. "Now it's too late. A messenger has arrived from London calling for my return. I must go, so I've come to say good-bye."

He'd been looking from one boy to the other, but now his eyes were drawn to Frederica's and he was somewhat soothed by what he saw. If he interpreted her fading color correctly, she wanted him to leave as little as he wanted to go! She set aside the book and rose, turning toward him, but, avoiding her, he moved closer to the bedside, putting his back to her. If he looked at her, he'd never be able to speak to the boys.

"Papa?"

"You still wish to stay here, Matthew?"

"Oh yes. I like it here."

"Good. I'll send for you a couple of weeks before term begins." When the boy grimaced, Blackthorn smiled. "You'll need a new wardrobe and I thought you might enjoy Astley's Amphitheater."

"You mean . . . London?" asked Matthew on a breath of sound. "To stay with you?"

"We'll make arrangements so you'll have a few days there. I'll see my schedule includes enough free time that I may introduce you to my tailor."

Matthew's eyes grew larger and larger. "You are bamming me."

Blackthorn chuckled. "Perhaps a trifle. But, assuming there is a performance, we *will* go to Astley's. That I promise."

At the word "promise," the two boys looked at each other. "Go on," whispered Stewart, urgently.

Matthew bit his lip.

"Do it!" insisted Stewart.

"Don't be afraid of your father," said Frederica gently. "What is it you wish to ask of him?"

"That-he-promise-to-buy-me-my-horse," said the boy in a rush.

"I fully intend to go to Tattersall's the instant I've a free moment."

"But you must *promise*," said both boys together.

Blackthorn frowned slightly. "I don't believe I understand." There was the faintest edge of sternness to his voice and Matthew seemed to shrink. "Come, now. I'll not eat you, but I wish to understand."

Matthew's eyes begged Stewart to do the explaining. Stewart mouthed, "Baby."

Matthew scowled and his mouth compressed. He picked at a loose thread in his shirtsleeve.

Stewart heaved a sigh. "It's like this, my lord," he began. "You will never find a free moment if you do not promise."

"Of course I will."

"You didn't last time."

"What?" Blackthorn cast his mind back to when he'd talked to his head groom after his son's pony died. "I see." He forced his son's chin up so the boy would meet his eyes. "Gruddy passed on the word I meant to find you a mare at Tattersall's, did he?" Matthew nodded. "Well, I suppose it is time you learn I am merely human. I forgot."

Matthew's eyes widened again. "Forgot . . ."

"I forgot. We've been exceedingly busy in London, but that is no excuse. All right." Blackthorn glanced from one boy to the other. Solemnly, he said, "I *promise* to find what is needed as soon as may be." His eyes twinkled and his lips curved into a smile. It faded and he added, "Now, I must go."

"My lord," said Frederica, "surely it is too late. It's past lunchtime."

Blackthorn turned and looked at Frederica. "I'll not get all the way, true," he said. He glanced around. There were the boys watching him. And Sal, he recalled, sat behind the screen. He'd be *damned* if he'd tell this woman good-bye with such an audience! Taking her arm, he drew her from the room.

"See," said Stewart, once the door shut. "Tol' you all you needed was a bit of backbone."

"I don't think I'll ever be as brave as you are, Stu," said Matt wistfully. "I wish I were."

"Well, he's promised, so that's all right. And, Matt, *I* may agree I'm brave," teased Stu, "but Mama says it's merely foolhardiness."

"He said I'm to go to London," whispered Matthew, his eyes wide with excitement. It faded. "But likely he'll forget. He didn't promise about *that.*"

"He promised about Astley's and he can't keep that promise if he forgets you're to come to London." When Matt still looked doubtful, Stewart suggested, "Maybe you could run and catch him . . ."

Matthew shook his head. "I don't think I want to. I don't think I'd enjoy London so very much if you can't be there too. Maybe I don't really want to go. Alone."

"Don't be an idiot. He said *Astley's!*"

"Yeees . . ." Matthew played with the thread again. "Maybe your mother could take you and then all four of us could go. Like a family . . ."

Like a family. Stewart's eyes rounded until they nearly matched Matthew's. "Matt," he whispered, "do you know what you just said?"

"What?"

"That we'd be like a family."

"I'd like that."

"But we *could* be family! Don't you see? If your father and my mother married, then *we'd* be brothers." Stewart's eyes glowed. "Wouldn't that be something like!"

"Married . . . ?" Matthew straightened. The boys' eyes met. "Actually, since we're the same age, *we'd be twins!*" Both boys were silent for a moment, awed by the notion. "Should we ask them? Maybe I *can* catch them . . ."

Stu grabbed his friend's arm, yanking him back down onto the bed. "Don't be a ninny."

"No, my lad," said Sal, coming around the screen, "you can't just *ask.* 'Tain't the way to manage that notion, boy. Not at all."

"Oh dear," whispered Matthew who had forgotten the servant's presence, but Stewart just grinned. "You got a better idea, Sal?" he asked. "You going to help us?"

"Don't know about helping you, but we'll see." She pursed her lips, her eyes narrowing. "Still . . . seems a good notion. An all round good notion," the old woman said softly.

A wicked glint entered her eye when it occurred to her that if *Mrs. MacKivern* became the Earl of Blackthorn's countess, it would put *Lady MacKivern's* nose well and truly out of joint, since *she* was wife to a baron! In the opinion of the servants, Lady MacKivern didn't deserve her luck in having wed their very special master. They all thought she needed bringing down a peg or two!

Sal grinned from one boy to the other. "We'll just see what we can do, then, won't we . . . ?"

Out in the hall Frederica was asking, "But, my lord, will you even reach Burford?"

"With luck I'll get as far as Oxford, but even Burford would be a goodly step on my way and cut hours from tomorrow's travel."

"London's not so very far from Oxford, is it?"

"Between fifty and sixty miles." He paused, his voice more abrupt when he continued. "I very much dislike leaving you with both boys and *one* of them tied to his bed."

Frederica chuckled softly. "At least I know where they are!"

He smiled. "Yes. Stewart can't very well get himself into more trouble for the time being. Frederica . . ."

She interrupted. "You wish to tell me not to keep too tight a rein on the boys."

Diverted, Blackthorn agreed. "The tutor will be here soon. I don't want Matthew tied to the schoolroom, but do set up a reasonable schedule of study and see they stick to it."

"I will."

"And, with two boys to see to, you are not to overdo looking after other things."

"Overdo? Other things? My lord, I haven't a notion what you mean."

"Do you not?" He cast her a wry look. "I've heard you do any number of things around the estate which, rightly, should be Lady MacKivern's duty."

"As you know, she is delicate and I don't mind. In fact,

since I enjoy visiting with Ian's tenants and she never knows what to say, it is just as well I can do it.''

"And teaching two days a week in the village school? And heading the lady's group at the church? And training young girls how to go on as maids so they may get decent work either in local houses or in one of our cities? And . . ."

"Enough! I like to keep busy."

"Busy, I understand," said Blackthorn dryly, "but run off your legs I do *not*."

Frederica's chin rose. "Since you've no *need* to understand, there's an end of it, is there not?" she asked, her temper rising.

"Why," he asked, on a rueful note, "do you fall into a snippy-fit when all I ask, and that innocently, is that you have a care for yourself?"

"Is that what you did?" she retorted. "It sounded like more of your bullying, my lord, and I'll not have you thinking you know best when you *don't*."

"Cat." He grinned at her reference to an earlier conversation. "Sheathe those claws and promise you'll come to Seymour Court for Christmas."

"I won't promise." She raised her eyes and met the warmth in his. Unable to resist his silent pleading, she added, a trifle crossly, "But, I'll think about it."

"And will you write occasionally—" He saw she was set to automatically refuse such an unconventional request. "—telling me how Matthew goes on? I'd like to know your son fully recovers, as well, although I see signs he'll be up and about soon enough. Perhaps by the end of the week, even. And then you'll add keeping track of their whereabouts to your list of activities!"

Frederica still hesitated.

"If you'd feel it compromising to write me directly, I'll ask Ian to send your notes to me undercover of one from him."

"Ian? Write?" Frederica stifled a surprised chortle. "A *letter?*"

"I see." His tone edged into a dare. "Will you chance your reputation, then, by writing to me directly?"

"I see no reason why it should compromise me if I pass on word to a father about his son's health and general happiness."

"How prim you sound."

Their eyes met and she chuckled. "It does sound a bit unlike me, does it not?"

"Yes."

Frederica wasn't certain what to say to that simple response and was relieved when Ian turned into the hall from the front of the house. "I suspect that means you must go, my lord. As late as it stays light this time of year, you've a chance of reaching Oxford. But not if you linger," she warned. "Good-bye, my lord." She gave him her hand.

Instead of shaking it in conventional fashion, Blackthorn lifted it to toward his lips and then, almost as if he could not help himself, he turned it, raising it to place a real kiss to her wrist, his eyes never leaving hers. Frederica, blushing furiously, glanced at Ian, who grinned knowingly. She jerked her hand free, and turning, rushed into Stewart's room where she leaned, her eyes closed, against the door.

"You all right, Mama?"

"All right? I don't know that I am." Frederica blinked furiously. "I don't know if I'm angry, or sad, or merely hurt to the quick. Matthew, your father is the most impossible man I've ever met."

The boy's forehead creased. "What did he say to you?"

"Say? It wasn't . . ." She glanced from one interested boy to the other. "Oh, never you mind! I was reading, I think . . ."

"No. You'd finished," said Matthew politely and looked at Stewart for a lead. Stewart shrugged. Matthew sighed. "Shall we," he asked, still overly polite, "continue Stu's lessons in piquet?"

Frederica hesitated. "You deal out a hand or two between you. Sal," she said to the older woman, "I'll return shortly."

"No you won't," said the servant, severely. "You just take yourself off for a good long walk. Maybe it'll straighten out your head," grumbled the old woman, "and—" She glanced up from under her brows, a sly look in her eye. "—maybe it'll soothe the twists and twinges in your body, too!"

"Sal!"

"Well?"

Frederica sighed. "You always did know too much," she muttered and, once again, exited. The door shut, she hurried toward an empty room at the front of the house. The drapes were closed, but she easily inserted herself behind them.

She was nearly too late. Blackthorn's coach was already moving down the drive. She stared after it, wondering if she'd ever see the irritating man again. And then she wondered if she wanted to. Finally, sighing, she admitted she did. Very much.

But, *Christmas!* How could she bear . . .

The coach, and its irritating but fascinating contents, was all too soon beyond sight. Slowly, her feet dragging, Frederica returned the way she'd come and went on to the back stairs and down them into the kitchens. She nodded to Cook and the servants working on the evening meal, but didn't speak. She didn't even sniff at the good smells but continued on and out the back door into the walled kitchen garden. Near the gate was a neat knot garden made up of herbs. She seated herself on the round bench in the middle and pinched off a few leaves of an overgrown tarragon.

How very foolish of me, she thought. *At my age, too.*

"Rickie?" asked Ian from beyond the patch of lemon thyme. "Are you all right?"

"Of course I'm all right. It is just that Sal insisted I come out and take some air."

Ian nodded. "There is no resisting Sal when she puts her mind to something. Besides, I approve and would have told you to come if she hadn't. What I *cannot* like is that look on your face."

"I haven't a notion what you mean."

"I'm not certain I can explain it. Defeat, maybe? But why? Stewart hasn't had a relapse, has he?"

"No. Stewart is going to be just fine. I mean to take him home tomorrow."

"Rickie . . ."

"Don't argue, Ian. We've been more than enough of a problem for Tildy as it is."

"Tildy . . ."

"Is Tildy. Don't worry, Ian. I understand your wife."

"She has never understood how two families can be so close as yours and ours was. That we were almost like one family . . ."

"We are one family, now," said Frederica. "Ever since I married Stewart."

"Yes."

"But nevertheless I'll return to the cottage. Blackthorn said the tutor should arrive soon. I think I'd like him to come down to us in the morning. Say from nine to twelve. That should satisfy His managing Lordship!"

"Get on your bad side?"

"Blackthorn?" She sighed. "No. Not really."

"I thought perhaps you thought that kiss outside of enough the way you ran off." Ian spoke idly, but his gaze was sharply focused on her half averted face.

"It was rather presumptuous of him to tease me that way with you right there watching! He *likes* to tease, Ian. He thinks it great fun to make me blush. It is not fair of the man when there is no conceivable way I can get my own back!"

"Teasing . . . ?" Ian drew in a slow breath, then went on slowly. "Rickie, you know my belief that you should rewed. I'll admit I rather hoped . . ."

"Don't go seeing a romance where there is none!"

"But you know it is long past time you thought of remarrying. If not for yourself, Rickie, then for Stewart's sake. I think you should seriously consider attending His Lordship's Christmas party. If you cannot like *him,* you needn't think of that, but there will be others there. You might meet someone you could accept."

"What you do *not* think on, Ian," said Frederica in a dry voice, "is that a marriage is not something I may decide I want and, poof, it is done. The man must find *me* of interest as well. And why would any man look at a widow long past her first youth who has lost what looks she once had, who has a son as an impediment, no dowry worth speaking of, especially when the man may have his choice of the girls placed on the marriage mart each year, each and every one lovelier and far more wealthy?"

"You do yourself too hardly, Rickie. There is that property near Oxford which Stu bought shortly before he died."

"That's our son's inheritance, not mine."

"Still, you have the income until Stewart reaches an age

where he needs it. And I have it from Blackthorn's own lips you've a startling if unconventional beauty.''

"Nonsense." She blushed. "Now it is *you* would set my flags-a-flaming!''

"I only repeat what he said to me. He was surprised I could not see it, and I admit I don't even when I look for it, but I'm only your brother, Rickie, first by deciding it was so when you were about four, and then, later, by your marriage to my brother. It is not surprising I've never noticed. Brothers don't.''

Frederica felt the warmth in her cheeks fade slightly, but it didn't altogether go. "I think I must take a walk, Ian. Very soon I need to return to Stewart's side. And do,'' she added, ''inform Tildy we'll be leaving tomorrow. She'll be glad of it!''

Ian, confused by her sharp tone, finally decided it must be that Rickie felt embarrassed to be beholden. *Silly girl,* he thought, fondly.

"My Lord Blackthorn . . ."

Frederica lifted her pen and stared at the words. She and the boys had returned to the cottage, Sal with them, two days previously. In many ways she was glad to be back in her own home. But, whenever she entered her son's small bedroom, she wished for the generous proportions of that which he'd vacated at the manor. If only . . .

But that was a stupid wish. When her father died, Stu sold her inheritance and invested the whole in a small jewel of an estate situated much nearer London. One day, when he reached his majority, it would be Stewart's. She remembered liking the house when Stu took her to see it. They'd been preparing to move to it in the new year . . . but Stu died and she'd been in no state to object when Ian rented the place for her.

Besides, it was the sensible thing, the income paying the mortgage with some left over which she carefully saved, knowing there'd be extraordinary expenses as Stewart grew older and needed more. Like the mare Blackthorn was to buy him . . . if he did not forget!

But, however sensible it was that someone else bore the cost of maintaining the neat little manor a little east of Oxford,

Frederica suddenly wished she were there, away from the stresses Tildy caused, away from Ian's generous but rather smothering and somehow insensitive care . . . away from here and closer to the man to whom she was supposed to be writing! She dipped her pen into the ink.

"Mr. Simpson, your son's tutor, arrived yesterday," she penned *"Tomorrow the boys will, much to their often expressed disgust, have lessons from nine to twelve. Mr. Simpson had your note explaining the change in plans, so he was not surprised by the lessened lessons."*

Frederica reread that last and almost scratched it out. Lessened lessons, indeed! How infelicitous.

"We have returned to the dower house," she continued. *"Old Sal came with us, so we are a trifle crowded but not impossibly so."*

Did that, she wondered, sound like whining? She hated whiners . . .

Frederica bit the end of her pen. What else could she say? That Stewart was getting more and more impatient with his bed? But Blackthorn would know that. That his son was, rather reluctantly, taking a ride each day with a groom in attendance? Would His Lordship care? Well, that the boy was getting proper exercise, yes, but then, he'd expect she'd see to his welfare, so it was unnecessary to inform him she *was*.

On the other hand, she must say *something*. She'd barely started the page. Frederica searched her mind. Ah! *"Word has reached us that Lord Merrick is expected home in the not too distant future. I understand you know him. (You will please note I do not accuse you of being his* friend.*)"*

Would he know she teased him? Frederica decided he'd recall their conversation that first evening concerning the oddities he knew in London but with whom he would claim no friendship. He'd catch the joke. He was quick that way, having proved more than once he'd a tenacious memory.

"If rumor does not lie, His Lordship will not stay long, but will leave not merely the countryside, but the country *itself. Gossip insists he means to take up residence somewhere on the continent. It will, one must admit, be a relief to the region to have him gone. It would be a still greater relief if the estate were unentailed! It might then be sold to pay his lordship's*

debts and someone with a greater sense of responsibility take on the problem of restoring Merrick Heights to its former prosperity."

Half the page. Now what? Since she couldn't say the things she wished to say, Frederica tried to recall who else in the neighborhood, known to his lordship through Tildy's entertainments, had done something memorable enough she might write about it . . .

"You will remember the Misses Fraymark. Since you've left the neighborhood, they've the difficulty of deciding on whom they will next set their flirtatious gazes. Rose is in favor of Milltown, but Violet says she wished to try their luck with Merrick when he comes. Milltown, by the way, is muttering, Cassandra-like, about typhus. We've had none in the region for several years, but Milltown has an uncanny way of foreseeing trouble. The boys will be kept well away from any possible contamination, of course, so do not fear for them."

Should she have said that? Would he worry? Frederica dithered. Perhaps she should begin again and *not* put in that bit . . . ?

A tap at the French doors startled Frederica into twisting around to see who had arrived. She swore softly when she realize several drops of ink had spattered onto her gown and was, therefore, irritable when she went to let Ian in.

"Well?" she asked, returning to her seat.

"I hadn't seen you for a day or two and, since Milltown set me to seeing you got enough exercise, I thought I'd best check that you are. In pursuance of that, I've brought along your mare, just in case I could talk you into riding?"

The thought of a ride tempted Frederica a great deal. She'd not had one since Stewart's accident, since she hadn't liked to leave the boys so long to a servant's care. But Stewart was doing much better. The lads were occupied with several invalidish sorts of games and should not find mischief for themselves. At least they wouldn't if she only briefly indulged herself. Besides, she must change her ink spattered gown for another and set Betsy to washing this one and she might as well change into her habit.

Besides *that*, she couldn't think of another thing to say to His Lordship . . . Another *suitable and permissible* thing to say to His Lordship!

She couldn't, after all, tell him of the dreams that flirtatious kiss on her wrist had seduced her into dreaming. She didn't even dare tell him how often something occurred and she'd think of him, wishing to share it with him, yearn for him to be there so she might glance up, meet his eyes as he looked her way, know that he'd understand what she was thinking.

She wasn't even allowed by polite usage to express so simple a fact as that she missed him!

It was very difficult, she thought crossly, as she climbed the stairs to her room, this writing to a man to whom one must give not the least hint one had tumbled headlong into an untried girl's infatuation!

And why *had* she done so? She was long beyond her girlhood, when one might innocently wish for the moon and the stars or, if one were the sensible sort and knew those were out of reach, then dream that Prince Charming might ride by on a white charger, rescuing one from the indignity of finding oneself unwed and on the shelf! Nor, for that matter was she unwed and on that particularly nasty shelf kept by the polite world especially for spinster ladies . . .

Or was that it? That she'd once been wed? Was the *infatuation* no more than that she'd finally met a man who made her remember the . . . closeness. The warmth and satisfaction of making a man happy and content. Content? Well, at least *momentarily* Stewart would relax and would seem to be *hers* and wouldn't be planning his next adventure or off on one he'd already contrived or moping because there was nothing to do . . .

Frederica placed her perky little hat *just so* and, after a nod at what she could see of her reflection, she paced briskly out her door and into Stewart's room. The boys looked up with identical expressions of alarm. She paused, glanced from one to the other and frowned. *"Now* what are you plotting?"

Matthew looked at Stewart whose lower lip poked out belligerently. He sighed. "We were writing a letter to my father," explained Matthew, ending with a sigh.

"That seems an excellent notion. Assuming you are writing him nothing of which I'd disapprove."

"But that's just it. I think perhaps we are," admitted Matthew and added an ''ouch''. He glared at Stewart who had pinched him.

''I think I'd better hear the rest. Stewart?''

''Christmas. We thought it a good idea if we could spend it together.''

''And it would be only fair, would it not?'' asked Matthew hurriedly. ''I am Stu's guest this summer, so you and Stu should be our guests then, should you not?''

''And he's been telling me all the things they do.'' Stewart's eyes lit with excitement as he continued. ''Matt says I can help hand out the presents at the children's party . . . For the estate children . . . ?''

Frederica nodded, her mind churning. Should she tell the boys she'd already had such an invitation. Since she'd not yet determined whether to accept it it seemed to her she should not.

''. . . And a great huge pudding with all the tokens in it. Matt got the ring last year,'' Stewart added, casting his friend a roguish look.

Matt blushed. ''My father traded it for the horseshoe he found. He said I was a little young for a ring.''

Blackthorn had the traditional wedding ring from the pudding? Frederica told her heart to settle, that such nonsense was only for fun and meant nothing. But, the ring . . . ?

''And Matt gets to help bring in the yule log and put up the greens and . . . and I don't know what else!''

''In other words, you think it would be a far more exciting Christmas than holding it here with me?''

''Mama!''

''Well?''

The lip was again in evidence. ''We thought you'd come too,'' he muttered, with a quick look at Matthew and back at the paper.

Frederica sighed. ''You may tear up that epistle and begin another.''

''Mama!''

''I think you must write a proper letter to Lord Blackthorn in punishment for thinking you might request anything so awkward as an invitation for not only yourself but for your *mother* to another man's home. Particularly at Christmas which is a time for family." She recalled Blackthorn's description of his house party and sighed again. "I'd no intention of telling you this until I'd come to a decision—" She caught and held her son's eyes. "—And, Stewart, I have *not* come to a decision. No begging or teasing or even a single comment, do you hear me?"

"About what?"

"Did I not say? We've already received an invitation to Seymour Court for the Christmas holiday."

Both boys' faces lit up with joy and, for an instant, Frederica was tempted to agree to go just to keep them so happy, but she could not. Not until she achieved some control over her ridiculous emotions!

"I have *not* said we'll go. I think it likely we will *not*, but you are not to make my life miserable while I come to a decision, do you hear?"

Matthew calmly ripped up the pages the boys had labored over so carefully. "Yes, ma'am. We'll write another letter while you are out riding, won't we, Stu?"

"I suppose we have to. Mama ... ?"

"*No*, Stewart. I'll have no son of mine whine and nag or become a bully when it comes to wanting his own way. Sometimes one cannot have one's fondest wishes. In fact, very often in life one may not. You boys are old enough to know that."

Glumly Stewart nodded.

"I'll return soon."

"Not too soon," said Matthew, quickly and with a trifle of panic. "Not if we're to write *a whole letter* while you are gone!"

Frederica smiled. "Very well. Not too soon."

In London, his cravat untied and his vest undone, Blackthorn sat at his desk and reread the letter he'd just written Frederica. He bit the corner of his lip, wondering if he actually dared send it. She'd not yet said she'd come to the Court for Christmas. Would this tip the scales weighing her decision to the *yes* side ... or the *no?* Blast! Perhaps ...

Blackthorn lifted the heavy pressed paper and set his fingers to the edge, preparing to rip the thing into shreds . . . then he paused, laid it down, and began reading it still again:

"Dear Mrs. MacKivern, I assume this finds Stewart recovered and you well rested, once again, as beautiful as when we first met."

Perhaps she'd think he was teasing. She tended to think that when he gave her compliments, even when he was perfectly serious.

"You may tell our boys that I found time to attend a sale at Tattersall's yesterday where I discovered a pair of nice little mares with excellent manners and, I think, a decent but not excessive amount of spirit. Perhaps you should not tell them that last? I've set them on the road to you by easy stages in the charge of my groom who will return to London once he sees them settled. Since they are on the way, perhaps the boys may occupy a trifle of their time choosing names. If it is relevant to that process, the mares are chestnut in color, have slightly lighter manes and tails and each has two white stockings. The one has both front feet dipped in white. The other one front and one back. That last also has a white star above her eyes."

There was nothing in *that* to bother her!

"I anxiously await your decision concerning the Christmas holidays. My son will enjoy the festivities far more if he has Stewart at his side and I believe the same is true for your boy. I know I'd enjoy your presence. I beg you to come, my dear . . ."

Would she object to that "my dear" or would she think it merely the improper manners of a London flirt and dismiss it? Which would be almost as bad! She had that irritating habit, he thought, of thinking he could not possibly be serious, but merely flirtatious!

But *serious?*

The thought had Blackthorn putting aside the pages and settling back into his chair. *Was* he serious? He could feel his features stretching into a wide, very-likely-inane grin as he realized that *yes he was.* He wished to espouse Frederica D. MacKivern!

What began as an understandable desire to take the woman to his bed had grown to a far more complicated need to have her in his life. In every aspect of his life!

". . . You would enjoy the ball we hold just after the New Year. Besides the usual festivities, I believe you'd find friends among the women. There are two wives, for instance, who take great interest in their husbands' work. They've been invaluable over the years in bringing together, in informal situations, people who need to talk but who wish to avoid showing any sign of approaching the other publicly. I think you'll find they lead interesting lives and are knowledgeable about things which concern you . . ."

Was that an improper hint of his intentions? Just when *had* he decided she'd make him a good wife? Marriage hadn't been in his plans when he met her. And when he left her? He fiddled with his pen, holding it lightly with both sets of fingers. No. Not even then.

So, when had it happened?

He didn't know. He just knew, somewhere deep inside, she *would* make him an excellent wife, mothering his son, hostessing his parties, someone to whom he could talk . . . He nodded, the decision confirmed. Frederica MacKivern's days as a widow were numbered!

Content, he reached, again, for the letter rereading his last few words before continuing.

". . . interesting lives and are knowledgeable about things which concern you. My aunt, Lady Amelia Morningside, will write you soon, reinforcing my invitation. Aunt Amelia is kind enough to be my hostess each year, despite her increasing disabilities . . ."

Damn! That made it sound as if he were looking for a wife merely because the woman who obliged him by taking on the role of his hostess was getting beyond it. Blackthorn frowned and again debated the wisdom of tearing up of the letter but, still again, decided to send it.

". . . I would like you to see Seymour Court at its best and Christmas is one of its 'bests'! Aunt Amelia loves the place and will enjoy telling you its history if you are interested in such things."

Was that again too much of a hint? Blackthorn pursed his lips. What could he add to lighten the whole? Something teasing? Something about the boys? The mares?

Blast it all. This writing to the first woman to interest him

in far too many years had him in more of a dither than he
remembered feeling since—since he was seventeen and in love
with the new vicar's young wife! Blackthorn grinned at that
particular memory. Poor woman! He'd embarrassed her to
death, but she'd been very kind to a boy-verging-on-manhood.
It suddenly occurred to Blackthorn the vicar's wife couldn't
have been very much older than he'd been himself. Good Heavens! It must be true, what they said about girls maturing earlier
than boys! What a startling thought.

He bent again to his letter, determined to finish and send it.

*"I had hoped to think of a joke with which to end, but I
can't. I don't think I'll have much of a sense of humor between
now and when I know you'll accept my invitation to the Court.
Please, Frederica, do not deny either of us the pleasure of
continuing our all too brief association. I enjoyed it. I am
immodest enough to believe you did too. Let us discover
together if it was merely a fluke or whether it might not develop
into a life-long . . ."*

Blackthorn lifted his pen and reread what he'd just written.
A muscle jumped in his jaw. Dammital, he would *not* make
Frederica what amounted to a proposal in his very first letter
to her! He hesitated only a moment longer and wrote: ". . .
friendship."

There. It was done. Blackthorn signed it, folded it, addressed
it and sealed it with a blob of sealing wax marked with a fancy
letter B rather than with the more formal one which bore his
crest. He set the missive against his inkwell and stared at it.

Soon it would be in the hands of his future wife! He would
wed her just as soon as possible. Assuming he could overcome
her remaining grief for her first love and convince her it would
be a very good thing for her son as well as herself to wed
again. And, in particular, that she wed himself!

Again he settled back, still staring at the missive. Just what
could he offer to make her want him as he wanted her? She
wasn't mercenary, so his fortune would hold no special appeal.
Nor did she have a single ambition to shine among the ton . . .
although she *would* shine. She'd have all the men around her
like bees to the honey pot, which, come to think of it, was *not*
what he wanted! He smiled at that forewarning of the jealousy
he'd feel toward the men who would wish to bask in her fires!

They could just go away and find someone for themselves with the same fiery nature. If they could!

Ah, but she'd have the women eating out of her hand as well and, if her manner with the matrons where she lived was any example, she'd do it easily and naturally. He chuckled. It was no wonder Lady MacKivern detested her sister-in-law! Without desiring it or attempting to lure it to her, Frederica was given what Lady MacKivern craved, the attention and respect of those around her.

". . . Your servant, Frederica MacKivern."

Frederica folded the letter, addressed it, sealed it with an antique seal which her father had received from his grandfather which had the Scottish thistle on it. It was done. She set it against her inkwell.

Now . . . did she dare send it? Had she been too informal? Too . . . flippant? But the purely formal would not do. He'd done too much for her son. For *her* by helping her son. She could not treat him like a stranger.

Worse. She didn't want to treat him like a stranger.

Frederica sighed. It would have to do. She couldn't tear up still another version and begin again. It was late and she must get to bed. Stewart tended to wake at far too early an hour! It would be a very good thing for all of them when Dr. Milltown agreed the boy could begin doing things again! The exercise might wear him out enough to allow him to sleep a little later!

But, as Frederica climbed the stairs, all thought of Stewart slipped from her mind. Instead it was filled with the feel of Blackthorn's lips warm against her wrist, with wondering how they'd feel against her cheek, her mouth . . .

That night the sensation of her brush sliding through her hair was sensual in a way it had never been before. Perhaps, she decided, feeling heat rise up her throat, it was not the *brushing* but the daydreams which went with it? Daydreams about a man she barely knew? Abruptly setting down her brush, she went to her bed, determined to set aside all thought of the man who occupied her mind far more often than she thought necessary.

But sleep was elusive and, jealous, she wondered what Blackthorn did that evening in London . . . and with whom. A play?

A ball? Perhaps he visited a discreet house somewhere where he did far more intimate things than hold a lady's hand and place a kiss on a pulse where he should not? Her fingers went to her other wrist, touching the spot his mouth had touched.

Blast His Lordship! Was she going to have to accept his invitation to Seymour Court so that she'd have the opportunity to seduce him and discover just what it was she dreamed at night? Dreams she could never quite remember in the morning? Except, they had to do with *him* and that they left her feeling somehow . . . odd and more than a bit excited and . . . and needy in the way she used to feel when Stu rolled over and went to sleep at night?

Frederica sighed, punched her pillow into a new shape and berated herself for a fool. Even if she did wish to take advantage of the freedom allowed a widow, could she find the courage? And even if she did, she hadn't a notion how to go about seducing him and knew of no way she might learn at this late date!

What a failure she must be, that she didn't know such a simple thing about the way men dreamed so that she could figure out how to seduce one! Musing over that particular problem, Frederica finally went to sleep . . . and woke the next morning with her sheets once again every which way and with those curiously hot tensions she didn't quite understand. Or at least, had only had a hint of their existence when married to Stu.

She only knew that they had to do with Blackthorn and were intriguing and tempting and left her wishing the man were here so she might do something about them! Except she shouldn't *want* to do anything about them. She was the mother of a growing and impressionable son. And she was *way* beyond the age of dreaming there was more to life than . . . what there was.

But those dreams . . . !

Blast the impertinent rogue. He could, at the very least, have the courtesy to stay out of her dreams!

Chapter Six

"My Lord Blackthorn. I write this note to inform you I was correct that all was set for typhus here abouts. You must know that I have just returned from seeing my first case among those cottagers of whom we spoke; I immediately set pen to paper to suggest you send for your son. At once. All indications are that this summer will be a bad one. Your servant in all things, Merrill Milltown, Doctor of Medicine."

Blackthorn stared at the stark missive. He read it again before lifting his head and staring at his valet who was preoccupied with carefully brushing a suit of clothes proper to a morning visit.

"Browning, I want a portmanteau, my light traveling carriage, and Rufus. And not that coat," he added nodding to the blue superfine Browning was clutching next his thin chest. The valet immediately lay it aside. "I'll need clothes suitable for riding, of course."

"You'll be going out on Rufus, my lord?" The valet grabbed a set of small clothes and clutched those to his chest. "But, my lord, I was sure you said it was a breakfast meeting with Mr. Perceval." The valet's sharp pointed nose very nearly twitched.

"My plans are changed and the first minister will have to wait." Blackthorn untied the broad tie to his silk robe and shrugged out of the calf-length garment. He pulled his nightshirt over his head and let it drop. "Browning," he said, having emerged from the latter, "don't dawdle!"

"Er, yes, my lord. The small carriage and your horse. And—" The man visibly swallowed. "—will I be traveling with you, then?"

"No. You are merely a bother on the road. As you know."

Browning flushed. "I cannot help it, my lord," he said sadly. "No matter how I try, I always feel desperately ill."

Blackthorn grinned. "Don't let it concern you. I find you

too useful in the usual course of things to resent what you cannot help.''

The flush turned to a blush of pleasure. ''Thank you, my lord.''

Blackthorn was on the road no more than an hour later which was a good half hour beyond what he'd hoped. Not only had Browning insisted in his quietly fussy way that His Lordship eat a bite, but there had been a handful of notes to write, first of all excusing himself from the meeting that morning and informing those with whom he worked that he'd be out of town for some days, and secondly, excusing himself to the hostesses of one or two social occasions which would occur while he was absent, the invitations to which he'd accepted.

But, finally, he was on his way. On his way to Frederica. Blackthorn tried hard to still the more rapid tempo of his heart, but it would not be stilled. At the end of his journey was his Frederica! The thought gave him pause and he wondered, for the first time, if the attraction he'd felt would still be there. The need to cosset and help and generally watch over her . . . would that, too, have survived their separation?

But, he was to see her again and far sooner than he'd had any hope of seeing her. Perhaps . . . before the day was out?

No, it was too far. He'd arrived too late. Still, unconsciously, he urged Rufus to a quicker pace and very soon the carriage, forced to travel at a more sedate rate of speed, was far behind.

Blackthorn had eyes for nothing but the road, seeing neither the broad prospect of golden fields of ripening grain and distant trees, nor the shy red poppy growing in the hedges and grassy verges. His thoughts were too mired in plots whereby he would convince Frederica he must remove not only his son and tutor, but also herself and her son from the danger of typhus. Would the thought that Stewart might contract the dread disease be enough?

He grinned to himself as he realized what he'd unconsciously planned: He would steal her away as well as his son and hers. He meant to see she was cared for and pampered and generally spoiled to death so that when he finally admitted to her he could not live without her, she'd have another reason, the pleasing existence he'd arranged for her, to say him yes!

And if she did agree to come away? Where should he take her? Take them, that is, he thought, guiltily. *All* of them.

His town house had been left under dust covers and in the hands of a single caretaker for too many years. It couldn't be prepared for company in a brief space of time even if it had occurred to him before he left London to order it done.

His Aunt Amelia would have been the proper person to take Frederica in charge, of course. And she'd be glad to oblige him if she could, but she was no longer in London. At the end of the season, she'd left the city for Bath where, annually, she visited a friend. Blast and bedamned. What *was* he to do with them? As unconsciously as he'd picked up speed, he slowed his pace.

When he finally admitted there was no way he could have Frederica in London, at least, not in a proper and conventional fashion which would do no harm to her reputation, it occurred to him he must take them to Seymour Court. No one could say it was improper for Frederica to be there if he left immediately after he'd delivered them and went on to London, remaining not even one night under the same roof.

There was the problem that he might not be believed if it were known . . . but who was to know? For that matter, who would know if he *stayed* a night or two. To see them settled of course?

Blackthorn laughed at that wishful thinking, making Rufus's ears twitch. "It's all right boy," said His Lordship, patting the horse's neck. "Or perhaps it is not. I seem to have lost my usual good sense. As much as I wish it were not so, it is impossible that I stay at the Court." The ears twitched again. "You wonder why? The neighbors, Rufus, my boy. The neighbors. Frederica must not be touched by scandal. I'll not have it. And the servants, however loyal, can't be expected to hold their tongues if I not only take her there but then remain a few days as well."

Blackthorn searched his mind for ways and means and could find none. "No. I cannot stay. I *must* leave . . ." Recalling his work and that there seemed no end in sight for it, he sighed. "Besides, I've no choice. I am needed in London."

Seeing a small inn he'd patronized on some previous occasion, he decided to bait Rufus, rest the poor creature, who had been pushed a trifle hard, and have a proper breakfast himself, the bite he'd had earlier not at all adequate.

Later that afternoon and much to his disgust, he was forced to cut short his travel and stay the night in Burford. Just over the old humped bridge on the market town's northern edge, Rufus lost a shoe and he had to lead him back—only to discover the blacksmith had chosen that particular day to visit his sister in Little Barrington.

Seated with a tankard of good ale in the walled garden at the back of the inn, he decided it was probably just as well—however much he wished he'd gotten at least so far as Stow, or even beyond! The lengthening shadows indicated that hiring a horse to take him on, was not truly an option because he'd arrive far too late to do anything. Too late to see Frederica . . .

But would he be too late to talk to Lord MacKivern? Blackthorn grimaced at having even thought for a moment of arriving that late at anyone's home. Let alone a near stranger's. So, perhaps another notion: He'd send a message, warning MacKivern of his intentions! Blackthorn chuckled. His intentions? *Part* of them, the fact he meant to take the boys and Frederica to a safe place! The thought was no sooner in mind, then Blackthorn called for the landlord.

Ian MacKivern could, and very likely *would,* order his heir to leave the dangers of typhus. All that would be left would be to convince the heir's mother that she too must come away!

"Paper, man. A decent pen and ink. And a messenger with a fast horse. I've a message to go tonight up near Broadway."

"That road down into Broadway is treacherous, my lord," said the landlord. "Don't know if I can find someone to chance it in the dark. No moon tonight, you know."

"The manor I want is on the wold. No one need trust themselves or their horse to a dangerous road down into Broadway!"

"Ah, in that case, then. Very good, my lord." The landlord, too, cast a knowledgeable eye to the sky. "Very likely midnight before a man can arrive."

"Very likely. And the longer we are, the later he'll be?"

The landlord took the hint and trundled off.

The note to Ian was written and watched on its way, but then Blackthorn was unable to settle to anything. Hands clasped behind his back, he paced. And dreamed.

In his mind, he could see Frederica riding around his estate. He could see her enjoying his library. He could even visualize her meeting and getting to know his tenants! And then, at the end of summer when it was time to fulfill his promise to Matthew that he come to London, he'd connive at an invitation for Frederica and Stewart as well. He'd have her in London at last.

Even if only briefly.

However short, he'd have time with her under unexceptional conditions during the period before their sons returned to Winchester and Frederica removed to her dower house where she'd stay until Christmas when she *would* join his house party! He'd insist.

Still dreaming, he strolled idly down the hill, looking into shops along High Street and then, reaching the edge of town, continued on over the bridge which he'd already crossed and recrossed earlier that day. He walked on as far as the other side of Fullbrook before returning.

Then, after supper, he went up to his bed. It was early for bed. Far too early. But, if he were going to do nothing but dream of Frederica, then he might as well do so in comfort!

"But Tildy," said Frederica in exasperation, "why don't you ask him yourself?"

"Because he'll do anything for you!" Tildy sounded wild. "Just do as I wish. Ask him. I beg of you. I cannot bear to lose another child as I did our son. I will forgive you everything if only you can convince Blackthorn to take my daughters away from this evil place when he takes his son." The frantic woman fell to her knees, her hands clutching Frederica's thighs through her skirts. "Frederica, have mercy. *Please.*"

Her mouth open, Frederica stared at her sister-in-law. She didn't know what part of the woman's tirade to respond to *first.* After a moment's hesitation, she decided it was most important to discover what she'd done that required forgiveness. After demanding that Matilda let go her skirts and get to her feet, she asked. "Forgive me what?"

"Don't tease!" Tildy turned to stare into the dower house garden where her girls played with their cousin and Matthew.

"I cannot bear this," she whispered before straightening and turning back. "What must I do, Frederica? How must I humble myself further?"

"Tildy, I'd no notion you indulged such Gothic freaks. Now, sit down and explain what you believe me to have done. I'll not even discuss the girls until I've a notion of how I've sinned in your eyes!"

"But you know."

"No I do not." Frederica emphasized every word.

Tildy sighed. "I see you must have it in words. You will make me abase myself utterly."

"I do no such thing. I cannot change my ways, which obviously *must* be changed, if you will not tell me how I've erred."

"But it is obvious. How can you not know it!" Tildy rose to her feet, her color rising as well. "You've stolen Ian's . . . affection from me! You know you have."

Frederica blinked. "Ian has always loved me and I him, Tildy. You know that. He's my big brother and I'm his little sister. It has been that way since we were children."

Matilda scowled. "You are no longer children, Frederica, and no relation whatsoever . . ."

"Nevertheless," she interrupted, finally realizing the tenor of Matilda's complaint, "in our hearts, that *is* our relationship. You have been told that over and over. I do not know how else to convince you."

"He is here. Every day, he . . . comes to you."

"Rarely more than once a week! Twice perhaps, if there is some problem."

"Not . . . every day?" Matilda bit her lip, frowning. "Problem, you say? What can you mean, problem?"

"He stopped by today to discuss what he must do about this typhus scare, for instance, to protect his tenants as much as possible."

"Merely to *discuss* . . . ?" Matilda looked skeptical.

Frederica nodded.

"But, I was so certain—" Tildy's complexion paled, her hands wringing together. She stared, her eyes painfully wide. "—Then, if *not* you, where *is* he finding the woman I know he needs . . . ?" Tildy's eyes turned blank, looked inward. "I *must* know," she muttered. "I must *know* to whom he turns . . ."

Frederica thought of the barmaid in Broadway who had winked at Ian one day when they'd met at an inn after a morning's shopping—but it would not do to suggest that sort of convenient and, Frederica guessed, very occasional, connection. Frederica began to wonder if Matilda had had her mind turned by her inability to give her husband an heir.

"He came to me every night," whispered the distraught woman. "He sometimes took me to our room in midday. He cannot have given that up. It is impossible that he . . ."

Frederica cleared her throat. She knew Matilda. Ian's wife would never forgive herself for having revealed so much. "You are wrong, Tildy. A man who loves a woman as much as Ian loves you would do anything for his wife. Even to adopting a state of celibacy, if that would protect her as you must be protected."

Tildy gazed at her, hope shining in her eyes. "Do you think it possible?"

"Of course it is possible."

Now, thought Frederica, *if only I can get to Ian before she does, and warn him. He must* not *give away the fact he occasionally strays!*

Convinced, Tildy returned to the other subject agitating her. "You will beg Lord Blackthorn to take away my girls?"

Frederica frowned. She'd never been the sort to beg anyone for anything and she wasn't about to start now! "Have you discussed this with Ian?"

"No. I won't. He'd never allow it—" She turned a sly look on Frederica. "—but if his lordship were to *suggest* it, as if it were *his own idea . . . ?*"

"Tildy . . ."

"Please, Frederica. You cannot know the terror I feel whenever the word typhus is even whispered . . ."

Observing her sister-in-law's large eyes, the lids forced so wide the whites showed all around the iris, the pale skin, the wild hair where one normally never saw a strand out of place and the trembling in Tildy's hands, Frederica had to believe her. "In my opinion you should ask Ian to take you and the girls to your parents' home. They would enjoy their grandchildren and you have not seen your mother for some time, I think?"

Matilda shuddered. "I might, I suppose," she said in a dead voice. Again she stared at the children. "I have never had a close relationship with my mother, Frederica. We . . . disagree on so many things. I don't know if I could live in her house again."

Frederica had not known. Almost she pitied Matilda, but then she remembered the woman's manipulative ways and sighed. "I see. Well, I'll ask. That is all I can do."

"You could beg!"

"Could I? I've never been very good at that, Tildy. I don't think I know how."

Matilda glared. "You are despicable!"

"*Now* what have I done?"

"Why must you always show me up, make me feel ashamed, make me feel so inferior?"

"I do *what?*" Frederica stared at her. When Matilda would have spoken, she added, "I certainly don't do so consciously!"

Again the dead emotionless voice. "It is not necessary that you *think* about it. Because you *are* superior. I am merely . . . who I am. I've never known how to fight that."

"Superior?" Frederica chuckled, finally seeing some humor in this scene. "Not in *Ian's* eyes, if that's what you fear."

Tildy frowned. "But how can that be?"

"He likes *you.* Loves *you.* You and I are far different women. If he likes and loves you, then he cannot find me superior, can he?"

Tildy's frown deepened. She thought about, sending brief glances toward Frederica. Finally the logic appeared to have reach her. "I cannot change around so fast," she admitted. "I have always hated you. Ever since Ian brought me here." She studied Frederica, the frown not dissipating one iota. "I don't think I'll ever like you," she finished, "but perhaps I can truly forgive you?"

"You do that," said Frederica dryly. "And when you've forgiven me, I hope we may get along a bit better."

"But I *won't* if you don't beg His Lordship to take my girls away from here!" threatened Matilda as she stalked out the French doors. She collected her daughters and disappeared down the path to the back gate.

When Matilda was gone, Frederica dropped into a chair. Her

head thrown back, eyes closed, and her hands resting on the chair arms, she hoped she didn't have to go through too many such scenes in the future . . . !

Suddenly she felt warm lips touching her own. Her eyes closed more tightly. For a long moment she allowed the gentle touch, trying to make herself believe it was merely another of her dreams. But, finally, she had to raise her eyelids. And then she looked straight into Lord Blackthorn's gray eyes.

Gray, she thought. *I'd wondered* . . . but then she recalled Tildy's tirade.

"You heard." She closed her eyes again, this time in embarrassment.

"I heard." He stood up, away from where he'd leaned over her, hands on the arms of the chair. "If you will go with them to keep track of them and be responsible for them all, I'll take you and the four children to the Court where my servants will see to your comfort." He straightened. "If you will not come, there is no way in hell I'll have her brats."

Putting the forbidden kiss to the back of her mind, Frederica forced a chuckle. "I am to understand you'd still take Stewart?"

"Oh yes. I intended all along to take Stewart with Matthew. I wish very much to see that you are safe as well. And I *will* take MacKivern's girls *if* you are there to see to them."

She glared at him, her eyes flashing fire. "You, my lord, are as manipulative as Tildy!"

He smiled.

"It is an imposition," she continued, thinking about the work five extra, four of them children, would be to his servants.

"Yes it is," he said blandly. "Forgive me. I don't know how I had the nerve to ask you to see to her brats."

"I didn't mean that!"

"I fear," he said dryly, "that it is your *duty* to agree to come away with them, Frederica. If you *do,* just perhaps that woman will relax a trifle. She's so tense she's about to explode like one of Whinyate's rockets."

Her temper evaporated instantly in the mental picture his words induced. "You mean," she said, a gurgle of laughter coloring her tone, "that she'd fly off in all directions, totally uncontrolled, as his invention is said to do!" Still smiling Frederica nodded but the smile faded. "I hadn't noticed until today how very tense she is. I wonder now if she's been quite right ever since she was told she was to have no more children. And then her son dying . . . it would be enough to put a twist in any woman's head, perhaps.''

''Yours? I doubt it. You'd instantly bully your husband into choosing an heir and would take the lad to your bosom as if he were your own.''

Frederica eyed him. She had, more than once thought Matilda should do something of that sort. She'd hesitated to raise the point with Ian, however, her reason totally selfish. She'd feared Ian would demand her son who was the obvious and logical choice for the role.

Frederica bit her lip, attempting to force down her curiosity, but found she couldn't manage it. Meeting Blackthorn's eyes, she found herself asking, ''How do you know so well how I'd go on?''

Blackthorn shrugged. ''How do I know *anything* about you?''

That certainly didn't sooth her curiosity!

''Have you suggested such a thing to Lord MacKivern?'' he asked.

''Once and in a roundabout fashion. He says he wouldn't impose on his wife that way. I think, unconsciously, he knows she'd *not* take the boy in anything but resentment.'' She sighed. ''I cannot live his life. Nor will I open his eyes to his wife's defects. And, now I'm aware just how desperate . . . how desperately *unhappy* she is, I'll agree to your blackmail and go with my son and nieces to Seymour Court. May I ask,'' she added sweetly, ''just for the record, you know, *who else* will be there?''

''If you mean as chaperon, none will be necessary. I'll quite literally drop you at the door and immediately start on for London.'' His lips twisted in self-derision. ''I left London in something of a rush and must return as quickly as I can. If, by chance, I've an opportunity to come down for a week or so later, I'll be certain to attend to the problem of chaperonage!''

''I see.''

''You feel it will look odd, your living in my home?''

''I very much fear that it will.''

"I will set around the story of your sister-in-law's ... problem."

"I'd rather you did not."

"Because it makes her look bad?"

"More that it makes Ian look a fool. She has parents, the girls' grandparents."

"I heard. Just who are they?"

"Sir Handey was knighted for amassing such a huge fortune he has been able to help to support the war effort with loans to the government. *Not*, of course, to the degree Rothschild's bank in London supports it, but enough so it earned him a title."

"Ah. I see." He shook his head. "It is that she's ashamed that her father's a cit."

"Oh no." Wide eyed, Frederica shook her head more vigorously. *"Worse.* Far worse. He and his wife rose from cottagers who made their living spinning and weaving. He invented one or two improvements, eventually built a mill, then another. I vaguely remember something about a canal, coal mines ... I don't know what all. Her mother still speaks so broadly I cannot always make out what she says."

"They do visit, then?"

"Tildy makes up all sorts of reasons why they should not come, but Ian just laughs, thinking she jests, and invites them for holidays. Occasionally they accept."

"Ah."

"Very expressive, my lord. What *else* would you like to know?"

"I believe we've discussed your sister-in-law's foibles to a far greater extent than I ever wished to do. While you order the boys' packing and see to your own boxes, I'll go up to the manor and talk to Lord MacKivern. I'll arrange for the boys' horses, and yours of course, to be sent on with the trunks we cannot manage today. You see," he added with an apologetic and questioning look, "I'd like us to be away in an hour, if that is at all possible?"

Frederica, who had set Betsy to work on Matthew's trunk as soon as Ian came to her early that morning to tell her of Blackthorn's note, went up the stairs to begin her own and her son's packing. It would take far longer than an hour to do it

properly, but the fact needn't concern her. She'd take only what
was needed immediately and Betsy would do the rest after she
left and Ian would send it on.

So, though she must have a portmanteau or two to tide her
over until her wardrobe arrived, she'd *not* keep his lordship
waiting. But, as she folded her son's smallclothes, she wondered
if Matilda, who must pack for two daughters and had far more
conventional notions about how one went about such things,
could possibly manage it.

To her surprise they were on the way in very little over an
hour. The boys had convinced Lord Blackthorn they should
ride, so Frederica and her teary-eyed nieces, along with old
Sal, were not particularly uncomfortable in his smallish, but
very well sprung, traveling carriage. Ian had suggested they
go down into Broadway and south through Cheltenham to
Cirencester before cutting down to Swindon and on down
through Andover toward Winchester. Seymour Court, they'd
been told, was no more than two hours east of Winchester.

It had seemed a good plan, but Ian had not thought how
difficult the road into Broadway was for a loaded carriage. Or
perhaps, since he invariably rode, he had forgot! Frederica
swore silently when she heard the drag thrown out and wished
she'd put on her habit and ridden!

Sal, after one quick glance at the set of Frederica's mouth,
settled the younger girl on her lap, singing one of her country
ballads in an ancient and rather cracked voice. She calmly kept
the two girls from realizing the team pulling the carriage might,
at any moment, find itself in difficulties. Frederica glanced out
and realized Blackthorn rode to the side of the horses, soothing
and pacing them.

But where were the boys? Behind? Of course. Why had she
even wondered if His Lordship had allowed them to go on by
themselves! He must know better than *that*.

A faint frown creasing her brow, Frederica reluctantly
accepted that there was nothing she could do. Accepting it,
however, didn't make the worry go away. If anything, it made
dealing with her fears *more* difficult! How long, she wondered,
had it been since she'd ridden down the escarpment in anything
larger than a gig? Usually, if the weather was fine, she too
rode. As the road took another tight curve she swore that, if

they reached the bottom safely, she'd never again ride in a carriage on this abominable road!

When they did reach the town, Blackthorn guided the leaders into the first coaching inn they came to. He dismounted as soon as grooms came to the heads of the wild-eyed animals, the creatures' legs shaking with the strain of the long downhill route. They must be calmed and rested before they could continue. The door to the carriage swung open as he approached it and he reached in to swing Frederica to the ground.

She glanced round. Then she looked again, searching everywhere. Alarmed, she asked, ''Where are the boys?''

''They should be inside.''

''But how could they . . .''

''I sent them on ahead to ask the host for a private parlor and that he provide refreshment for four children, two adults and four servants. As soon as the horses recover, we'll be on our way.''

''You sent them on,'' she said slowly, glaring at him.

''Frederica, if an accident occurred as, at one point, I feared likely, it was better they be elsewhere! I couldn't have dealt with them as well as whatever else must be done!'' He smiled as she acknowledged that with a wry grimace. ''You'll recover when you go in and see what they've been up to.''

''I don't know if I'll ever recover,'' she muttered.

He chuckled. ''Of course you will. Take the girls in. Sal?'' he asked, turning back to the carriage. He lifted the old woman to the ground, swinging the girls down next. ''You go in with Mrs. MacKivern, please, while I see to the grooms and my coachman.''

''Forgotten just how far down it is from the wold into Broadway,'' said Old Sal. ''Thankee for your care.'' She nodded and followed Frederica into the inn, a girl held firmly on either side of her.

Blackthorn soon joined them in the parlor where he was met by Frederica, who still wore a frown. ''Is something wrong, my dear?'' he asked softly, once he'd ascertained the children were properly seated and occupied with filled plates and glasses of lemonade.

She gestured. ''If you mean to feed them like that at every

stop I think I'll ride your Rufus and *you,* my lord, may have my place in the carriage!''

His brows rose. ''You fear travel sickness?''

''Cream buns? At *this* hour? It's certainly not an impossibility!''

''Hmm.'' He eyed the buffet. ''Our sons appear to be more enterprising than I'd have thought possible!'' He grinned. When Frederica *didn't* he added, ''I merely asked that they order refreshment for everyone. I didn't say *what.*''

Frederica turned her glare toward the table. ''I might have known.''

''If that's an apology, then I forgive you.''

''You forgive me! I meant I might have known you'd allow those imps of Satan far too much liberty!''

Blackthorn's shout of laughter turned all eyes their direction. He took Frederica's arm and led her to the sideboard. ''What may I pour out for you, my dear? You've a choice it seems. I see—'' His arched brows expressed astonishment. ''—a burgundy, a lighter wine which I believe to be a canary, ale, coffee, tea, or you may have . . . lemonade, is it?''

''What? No ratafia?'' asked Frederica in mock outrage.

''Don't jest. We have also two kinds of meat pie, a cold sirloin, a plate of fruit tarts . . . ah, the boys seem to have missed one of those cream buns you mentioned, and here is a plate of plain sandwiches!'' When Blackthorn turned from the sideboard, he stared at the two boys. ''Just which of you ordered this display which might have been set out for a royal prince?''

''We didn't know exactly what to order,'' said Stewart, who had just cleared his plate and was sliding from his chair. Holding the empty plate he approached the food and looked up at Blackthorn, grinning. ''But this is something like, is it not?''

''Something like, but I don't know like *what,*'' was the dry response. ''When we resume our travels, young Stewart, you, Matthew, and I must have a little talk about finance to say nothing of the evils of greed and the tastelessness of ostentation!''

Stewart looked at the groaning board. He turned an innocent gaze back to Blackthorn. ''You mean it is too much.''

''*Far* too much. Not only can we not eat anything like that much, but if you continue such display, I'll soon outrun the carpenter! And then where would we be?''

''I've my savings with me,'' said the boy promptly, turning to carefully consider the food and what he'd have next. ''That would help.''

''Yes, that would help.''

''And I think Mama brought along the remainder of her quarterly allowance.''

''That's no good at all. It would be far better if we do not draw the bustle to such an extent that it might be necessary for me to ask. A man does not borrow from a woman, Stewart. It is not done.''

Stewart, attempting to choose between two tarts, gave up and took both. Having done so he glanced up at his mother and then again at Blackthorn. ''I do not think Mama would consider that particularly good sense, my lord. She would say that, if a loan were needed, then the source shouldn't be important.''

''Up to a point she may even be right. But I've said we'll discuss this when we are again on our way.'' He watched Stewart take a spoonful of trifle, and, overly politely, asked, ''Are you certain you've quite enough there, you disgusting child? A sandwich perhaps? Or should I cut you a slice of this very fine sirloin?''

''Would you please?'' asked Stewart. He ignored the jesting note which referred, he supposed, to his appetite; adults always seemed to find his appetite something to tease about.

The stop at the Broadway inn took longer than His Lordship anticipated. So did each and every stop thereafter. If it wasn't the boys wanting still another helping of food, it was one or other of the girls who had not yet made use of the facilities at the back of the garden, or who insisted their hair must be brushed before their hats were replaced, or . . . whatever.

Thus, it was very late in the evening when they drew up at a posting inn in Swindon at which he was all too well known. He frowned when he helped the tired girls from the coach, and Sal, and finally, a reluctant Frederica. ''We stop for the night, my lord?'' she asked, a frown to match his on her fine broad brow.

''We can go no further. There will be only a useless sliver

of moon, and besides, the children are overtired.'' He smiled.
''The boys won't admit it, but they are. I've heard nary a peep
out of them for the last hour.''

''Yes. I almost offered to have them in the carriage at our
last stop.''

''There isn't room.'' He smiled when, reluctantly, she nodded agreement. ''Tomorrow I'll hire a postchaise and Sal can
see to the girls in one carriage while you take the boys in the
other.''

''Which means you may remain safely alone on horseback!
Men!''

He chuckled. ''Selfish beasts, are we not? Come along now.
The house is excessively full, but I've managed two rooms.
The boys will have to come in with me and the girls with you.''

''Which nicely solves the problem of chaperonage, does it
not?''

''Does it soothe your sensibilities? I'm glad.'' Blackthorn
chuckled but the laughter died when he looked away from her
and met the flinty gaze of one of his more censorious neighbors.
''Ah. Mrs. Newton. How are you this fine evening?''

''Very well, my lord.'' She looked at Frederica and back to
Blackthorn.

Reluctant, although it was doubtful anyone but Frederica
realized it, he made the introduction. ''There is typhus in the
region where Mrs. MacKivern lives. She will stay at Seymour
Court with my son, her own, and her nieces, until the danger
is over.''

''You escort her yourself, my lord?'' asked the woman with
syrupy sweetness. ''How very good of you.''

''Yes, isn't it! My son has been Mrs. MacKivern's guest
since school let out. I'm sure you knew he was not at the
Court.''

''I'd heard something of the sort. I'll have to send you and
Mrs. MacKivern an invitation to dinner one evening soon,''
said the lady with a coy look at Frederica.

''I'd enjoy that, Mrs. Newton, but, since I'll be responsible
for four children, I don't know if I should accept.''

''Oh. Their governess . . .'' Mrs. Newton cast a scandalized
glance at Lord Blackthorn before turning back to Frederica
once again. She straightened, her nose elevating itself a trifle.

"I apologize," she said in a tone which contained no hint of apology, "for embarrassing you."

"Mrs. MacKivern is no such thing! And I would be pleased if you *would* introduce her to some of the neighbors, Mrs. Newton. The summer will be very long and lonely for her if she has no acquaintances."

"Lonely . . . ?" The woman turned a totally disbelieving look his way.

"Well, of course!" His brows rose and he cast her a look of great surprise. "My aunt is unavailable just now. As is usual with her, she is in Bath for a few weeks. *I* cannot stay at the Court since I must return instantly to London. Retrieving my son will have taken me from my duties for far too long as it is."

His expression of boredom and superiority very nearly threw Frederica into whoops, but she managed, somehow, to contain her laughter.

"I believe," she said, "I must find the children, my lord. It is beyond the girls' bedtime and the boys are, I fear, in that excessively tired state in which they tend to get themselves into mischief. If you'd excuse me, Mrs. Newton . . . ?"

Frederica didn't wait to see if she were or were not excused, but walked to where the inn's host stood waiting for Lord Blackthorn. "If you'd direct me, sir?" she asked with a smile.

Cornered by Mrs. Newton, who wished to satisfy herself as to *exactly* who Frederica might be, it was nearly three quarters of an hour later before Blackthorn found the private parlor. As he'd feared, it was empty. Sticky glasses and a stack of dirty plates adorned the table. He counted. Five. Now did that mean Frederica had eaten with the children . . . or had Sal? Would Frederica return . . . or not?

He was *damned* if he'd eat alone! He stalked to the bell-pull hanging to one side of the mantel. A maid appeared almost instantly. "I assume Mrs. MacKivern went to her room to see the girls settled. I wish to know when she means to return. Please find out for me." He turned his back.

"Please, my lord," said the girl softly.

Suspecting he was damned, he swore softly, leaning one arm on the mantel and staring into the empty grate. "Yes?" he encouraged, knowing he didn't really wish to know.

"The lady said to tell you, my lord, that she could not leave the girls alone in a strange place. Your servant is sitting with the boys, my lord, and the little girls, well, she, the lady, I mean, said not to say anything, but they, those girls I mean, are fussing and fretting. Wanting their mother? You see?"

"There is typhus near their home. Their aunt is taking them away until the danger is past."

Now why, he wondered, did he bother to explain? There was no need to explain anything ... even to Mrs. Newton who had wormed the whole history of Matthew and Stewart's friendship from him, including a quickly devised explanation for why Stewart had come to the Court earlier that summer *without* Matthew! Blast the woman. Perhaps he should offer her to Wellington. With her ability to talk one into telling her what she wanted to know, she'd be quite an addition to his motley crew of spies!

"Have a tray brought in then. Just a light supper. We want to get away early, so I'll take myself off to bed as soon as I eat."

Ye gods! There he went again. Explaining when it was unnecessary. Was he worried about Frederica's reputation? Was he feeling *guilty?* Did that explain why explanations tripped off his tongue at every comment? Nonsense. For what should he feel guilty?

Blackthorn's eyes lightened and the corners of his mouth tightened against a chuckle at his own expense. It was perfectly obvious to himself if to no one else, hopefully, why he should feel guilty! He'd been thinking all day of the hour or so he might spend with Frederica at the end of it. Well, he'd his comeuppance! *She,* it seemed, had had no similar notions. Which served him right, he supposed.

After all, although he'd been dreaming of her ever since he'd met his termagant at her front gate, very likely she'd not given him a single thought beyond the fact he was Matthew's father. Except ... she had kissed him, had she not? Returning that impulsively given token of his affection when he'd arrived and after he'd heard Lady MacKivern's tirade? *Surely* she did not kiss just anyone! But ... just how well *did* he know her?

Lord Blackthorn stared morosely into the well-scrubbed grate until his tray arrived. Discovering he'd no appetite, he ate little of it, and very soon, went to his room. He sent Sal to her trundle bed in Frederica's room.

Moving beside the bed by the window, he looked down at the sleeping boys, cuddled together like puppies. His depression faded as a kind of warmth spread through him. One of those tousle-headed lads was his. The other was Frederica's. And they looked so right together. Now how was he to convince his love of that fact . . . especially when he had to be in London and she at the Court and there was no possible way he could woo her!

He looked at the second bed and sighed. It was going to be, he thought, a very long night.

A long and lonely night . . .

Chapter Seven

Blackthorn's coachman stopped him when he would have followed his party into an inn for a luncheon the next day. "Yes, Murdock?"

"Weak spot in the harness, my lord. Fix it."

Blackthorn, used to his coachman's elliptical speech patterns, didn't think he himself was to do the fixing. "How long will it take you?"

"Half an hour. Check the rest."

"Another half an hour, I suppose?"

"Hmm."

"Will we reach home this evening or should I send a groom ahead to reserve rooms in Winchester?"

The grizzled man pondered. "Rooms."

"Very well. Send on the man who ordered for us last night. He'll know for what he's to ask."

"Hmm."

"Send in to the host when you're ready to leave."

"Hmm."

"Very well." As he turned from his coachman, Blackthorn was clapped heartily on the back. Too heartily. He winced.

"Trouble, Blackthorn?"

Blackthorn stiffened, his eyes closing. The last man in the world he'd have wanted to meet while traveling with Frederica. Slowly he relaxed, turned. "Quincy. What a surprise."

"What'r'ya doing here, anyway? Thought you were settled with the politicos in London. For the duration, doncha know?"

"A family emergency, Quincy."

"Settled now? All's right and tight?"

"Everything is going to be quite all right," agreed Blackthorn.

"Well then, come along now. Haven't seen you forever. Lots to talk about. Get us a heavy wet. Or two?" The burly man leaned closer in a confiding manner. "You'll get good ale here, you know. Best in the county."

"Excellent. A word with my coachman and I'll join you."

"Right you are." Lord Quincy, youngest son of the Marquis of Rowland, smiled benignly, but his eyes were exceedingly watchful. Nor did he move away.

"I'll not jabber," said the Murdoch. "Know what's what," he added when Blackthorn cast a quick look toward the inn. His coachman wasn't stupid. He too knew it was necessary to keep mum around Lord Quincy!

"Very well." But, under his breath, Blackthorn swore fluently. Quincy would not be satisfied with whatever recent on dits he could call to mind from the past week or so in London. And older gossip would not interest him. Instead, the man would want to know exactly what family business he himself had been upon, what relationships were involved, why Blackthorn had found it necessary to go himself, every last detail . . .

He did not dare allow Quincy a glimpse of Frederica and the children. Lord Quincy was a man who wanted to *know* and then, in the know, would dress up the bare bones of a story, in this case, Blackthorn's traveling with Frederica, in as many different versions as the number of times he told the tale.

Frederica would become everything from his mistress to the indigent wife of an old friend to a chance met actress befriended along the way to the children's governess to . . . Blackthorn decided his imagination must not be very good. He could think of no other possibilities, but Quincy's creativity was limitless.

Unfortunately, the stories he told were told with verve and, because they were often titillating, they were passed on.

Frederica must be protected.

Quincy's soft insinuating voice carried them into the inn where Blackthorn turned into the taproom. Quincy hesitated, but then followed. "I say, haven't you a private parlor?"

"Not today. I see a table in the corner." Blackthorn moved toward it, nodding pleasantly to the three ancients lining the bench along one wall. "Ah, sir!" he said to the host. "I've discovered an acquaintance with whom I'll dine. You may put his tab on my bill."

"Very well, but . . ."

"We'll have whatever you choose for us. We're not fussy."

"Certainly, my lord, but . . ."

"And ale. In fact, I'll treat the gentlemen along the wall there. At once, my good man." Blackthorn grimaced slightly. *After* that *performance I'll not dare stop here ever again!* he thought.

"In a good humor, are you?" asked Quincy.

"Should I *not* be?"

"Heard the coachy tell you a trace needed mending."

Blackthorn instantly wondered just exactly what else Quincy had overheard. What had they said? Had he mentioned Frederica . . . ?

"That'd make me angry," continued Quincy.

"How so?"

"Well, Coachy should have run his glims over the harness before using it. I'd fire the man."

"Even if you knew there was a perfectly good reason why something might have happened during your period of travel?"

"Oh." Quincy thought about that. "Can't think of anywhere you'd have been that would have strained the harness . . ."

"Can you not?"

"If you were on the Bath road, that'd be different . . . being in Bath with a carriage, well that's a mug's game altogether, is it not?"

"My Aunt Amelia is in Bath. She visits an old friend there each summer. Her letters are scathing about the changes which have occurred since she was a girl."

Quincy chuckled, a low, knowing sort of laugh which implied

so much but which, in actuality, meant nothing much at all. It was simply Quincy's way, always, to make something of nothing. "Doubt your aunt could top my grandmother when it comes to moaning about the degeneracy of Bath society!"

"Which grandmother would that be?"

For perhaps five minutes Quincy became lost in family genealogy.

". . . But you ain't interested in all that," he finished, abruptly. It was *other* people's genealogy which challenged Quincy now, having spent his early years learning his own inside out.

The inn's host approached with their ale. "My lord . . ." He was startled when both men looked up. "I mean my lord Blackthorn, if you would only . . ."

Blackthorn glared at him. "Later. Can't you see I'm preoccupied?"

Obviously feeling harassed, the man's lips tightened. A muscle jerked in his jaw. "Really, my lord . . ."

"It isn't your place to be offended," said Blackthorn in a lofty manner totally unlike his normal character. He groaned silently. Quincy would suspect something fishy merely because his awkward behavior would give him away. He rose to his feet. "Back in a moment," he said to the fop who disappeared into his tankard.

Blackthorn tugged the innkeeper's arm and headed for the door. The man followed. Blackthorn stood where he could keep an eye on Quincy. "Now. Quickly. What is it you want?"

"My lord, I have run out of a sweet course. I just wished to apologize and ask if stewed fruit would do!"

Blackthorn grinned. "I don't know if you've noticed, but that sprig of the ton with whom I'm forced to dine is a gabble-grinder. I'd just as soon he had no knowledge of my business here. I feared you were about to reveal something I'd no wish for him to know!"

"Yes sir. I thought it might be something of the sort. I'll pass on that information, my lord."

"Good. Stewed fruit, by the way, sounds quite satisfying."

Blackthorn forced his features into less revealing lines and returned to his table, pausing for a moment when one of the elders, spokesman for them all, expressed their thanks. His

Lordship continued to his table, grimly determined Lord Quincy would gain no food for gossip from him, no matter what he had to do to prevent it. But it meant his meal turned into a verbal sparring match.

The opening jab was Quincy's demand to know what the innkeeper had wished to tell him.

"Merely that there was still another problem with the harness." Having parried that, Blackthorn got in a leading question. "Tell, me, Quincy, have you been anywhere interesting or are you on your way now to a house party?"

That held them through another tankard and by then their meal arrived at which point Quincy got in a low blow. "Saw Rufus taken into the stables, but you've got your traveling carriage. Not alone, Blackthorn?"

Quick footwork got His Lordship out of that sticky spot: "Do you travel without your valet?"

"Valet ..." Quincy looked blank for a long moment. "Hmm. Hadn't thought of that." But the elaborately dressed gossip monger eyed Blackthorn suspiciously.

"Tell me," said Blackthorn, "is one of your brothers going to take over the vacated seat in East Anglia?"

"Seat? My brother?"

"The vacancy in the Commons, Quincy," he said patiently.

"Oh. The Commons ..." After a moment he asked, "The common what?"

"Quincy, you are not that ignorant! I refer to Parliament, of course."

"Oh, *that* Commons! How would I know what my brother intends?"

"Because you always know everything," said Blackthorn sweetly.

Quincy took the comment for a compliment and preened. "Try to," he said modestly. "One does one's poor best." Which lead him right back to the subject Blackthorn wished to avoid. "Speaking of *knowing* things, what I want to know now is where you've been. It must have been a dire need to have taken you from London just now."

Thinking half the truth was better than an outright lie, Blackthorn said, "Typhus."

His eyes widening, Quincy half rose from his place, then

settled back. "Oh. Not you, of course. Wouldn't be here . . . die?"

"Not the last I knew."

Quincy became rather goggle-eyed at that. "But should you have left?"

"What?" Blackthorn chewed thoughtfully, trying to figure that one out. "Oh! You don't think I went anywhere near infection, surely?" He glanced toward the door where he saw his son staring at him. He shook his head, a stern look on his face. "You should know I'd not put my skin into such danger!"

"No. Of course not. Who would be so foolish?" asked Quincy with a bit of fervent animation unusual to him.

Matthew, his head down and feet dragging, moved out of sight. Blast. Now he'd insulted his son. And if the boy complained to Frederica, she'd come sailing in to tell him about it in no uncertain terms! What to do? Well, there was always the excuse of needing to use the necessary! Blackthorn rose to his feet.

"Back in a moment," he said, already on the way to the door.

"Problem?" Quincy gave him an interested look.

"Just those two tankards of ale," said Blackthorn over his shoulder and matched Quincy's knowing grin with a bared-teeth grin of his own. Feeling harassed, he again entered the hall. He looked both ways, wondering which way to go . . .

Ah. He strode down the hall to where Matthew stood disconsolate. "Boy, go back to the parlor. I don't want you, *any of you*, where you can be seen until that man leaves, do you hear me?"

Matthew paled. "Yes sir. He's . . . a bad man?"

"Not in the way you mean. Just a bloody nuisance. Now, off with you."

"I told you," he heard Stewart say. "I *told* you he was a bad man."

"Maybe we could just sit in the corner in there. We could watch and warn . . ."

"And have your father complaining we didn't obey him? Come along," insisted Stewart. "He'll be all right."

"He isn't your father. You don't know . . ."

Blackthorn forced himself to return to the taproom where he

met the hopeful gaze of three pairs of eyes. He smiled and, catching the arm of the serving wench, told her to give the old men another round of heavy wet on his bill.

Then, reluctantly, he again moved on toward the table . . . and stopped, blinking. Where had Quincy gone! Had he observed the words exchanged with his son? And, worse, did he know he'd not gone where he said he gone? Blackthorn reversed himself and went off to where he'd said he was going! He could always claim he'd gotten lost! When he returned, Quincy was seated at the table, innocently carving into a huge slice of sirloin.

"Sorry," said Blackthorn as he seated himself. "I went the wrong way and got lost."

"Hmm. Of course you did."

Blackthorn didn't like the look in Quincy's eye, but he refused to rise to the bait. "What are your plans for the rest of the summer."

Blackthorn wasn't at all happy that Quincy obligingly allowed the conversation to continue along completely innocuous lines. Where had Lord Nosy-Parker been and what had he learned?

Blackthorn felt like gnashing his teeth, but waited patiently. He knew Quincy. The man couldn't possibly leave things as they were. He'd have to give a hint of what he knew. At last Blackthorn was rewarded.

"Turned into the family nanny, have you?" asked Quincy, grinning. "Was told you arrived with a flock of brats and a couple of maids in tow!"

Blackthorn cast him a bland look. "I *did* tell you typhus and family matters, did I not?"

"I can see why you'd not want it spread around that you were bear-leading brats."

"One of those brats is my son and heir, Quincy. I've a strong interest in seeing him home safe at Seymour Court."

"Your son?"

"My heir."

"I see." Quincy pushed back from the table, a disconsolate look on his face, but then brightened. He grinned that irritating grin, the insinuating tone back, and added, "Also see why you didn't wish to eat in your private parlor! Not with a swarm of tadpoles! Perhaps I'll see you in Brighton later this summer?''

"Very doubtful. It appears that we'll be stuck in London the whole of it.''

"Ah well. Thank you for my dinner.''

Blackthorn nodded and watched Quincy leave the taproom. He waited, listening hard. It seemed a long time before he finally heard the sound of hooves clattering on the cobbled yard. Then he heard Quincy's raised voice telling someone to "let them go.'' And then iron-bound wheels sang over the stones. Very soon all was quiet. Blackthorn relaxed.

Finally.

And then, feeling as if he'd spent the day in battle, Blackthorn rose to his feet. Wondering if he walked like the old man tottering out of the room ahead of him, he made his way to the parlor where his party was, he hoped, still dining.

The room was empty.

Frederica! Had Quincy set eyes on Frederica! If so, the idiot's learning of two nursery maids traveling with the children would have been for nothing. Blackthorn swung in a circle, searching the room he already knew was empty. Where had they gone?

Rushing to the entrance, he stepped into the sunshine and looked around. No one. Nothing but a gray cat warming itself in the wide sill of a taproom window. Lazily, slowly, the cat blinked big yellow eyes.

Lips compressed, Blackthorn moved through the high gate. He looked both ways along the road. *Still* no one. Where the devil had they gone?

Blackthorn returned to where his coachman was checking each trace, every inch of harness. "Better check the coach, too, the axles in particular.'' Murdoch nodded. "You haven't seen the children, have you?''

The coachman glanced up. He turned his eyes toward the back of the inn. Blackthorn swung around. There had been a bit of a garden back there, he recalled from his visit to the necessary. A small grassy plot with flower beds surrounding it and a vegetable garden beyond. He strolled around the corner, confident he'd find his party . . .

Again he was disappointed. *Where was Frederica?* And, more important, *had Quincy seen her?*

On the far side of the garden was a lynchgate. He crossed to it and opened it, discovering a path which, in one direction, led off into a spinney and, in the other, across the edge of a field of golden ripe grain. Still again he peered in each direction. Nothing. No one.

But Murdoch had indicated this was the way they'd gone. Given the sun, he guessed Frederica would opt for the spinney. He stalked off in that direction and was soon rewarded by the rather high-pitched and whiny voice of the younger girl. "I want to go *home,*" he heard.

"My dear, I wish you *could* go home. If your mother wasn't so afraid for your health, you might do so."

That was Frederica.

"I want Mama," said the child.

"Don't be a wet," said Stewart, scornfully.

"I think you'll like Seymour Court, Bitsy," said his son, much more gently. "I don't think it is too much farther now."

Oops. Wrong tactics, my boy, thought Blackthorn. Never lie, *especially* when you'll instantly be found out! No, not *that* exactly, another side of Blackthorn's mind argued. The boy shouldn't lie at all! He hurried deeper into the spinney and discovered a quiet glade just around a bend in the path.

"Frederica. Children?"

He was met by silence, his son moving a trifle closer to Frederica. Now what? He sighed.

"Bitsy," he said to the child, "I fear I must contradict Matthew. We've still a rather long journey and I'm sorry about that. On the other hand, he was quite right that you'll enjoy yourself at the Court. There is a very large doll house, for instance. It has eight rooms and an attic. And a great deal of furniture which, I fear has become badly disarranged. I hope you'll spend a trifle of your visit setting it to rights?" The child stuck her finger in her mouth and stared at him. He sighed again. "You've found a pleasant spot here."

"Yes. A rather oddly dressed young man was kind enough to point out the gate to me," said Frederica. "He thought the children might like a walk before we leave. I checked with Murdoch," she said defensively. "He said there'd be time. At least," she added a trifle doubtful, "I think that's what he said?"

Blackthorn sighed for the third time. "Lord Quincy spoke to you."

"If you mean the man with guinea gold hair and very odd clothes, then yes. Should he not have done so? Matthew would have it you didn't like him, but Stewart said you said he wasn't dangerous . . . ?"

Blackthorn felt a sinking feeling in the pit of his stomach. Quincy had spoken to Frederica! "*Physically* he is no danger to any of us. Blast and bedamned," exploded His Lordship. "Why could you not have stayed in the bloody parlor? Why leave the inn? Why did you put yourself in the way of that idiot? I suffered agonies keeping one step ahead of him and then, in one stroke you undo all the good I accomplished."

"Good?" Frederica chuckled. "Telling the man a whopper by calling me a nursemaid is *good?*"

"You don't understand." Blackthorn ran his fingers through his hair. "He'll . . . He's . . . Oh, the *devil.* You don't understand," he repeated helplessly.

Sal, seated on a log and cuddling the second MacKivern daughter, spoke. "No and why should she understand? Poor girl's never been anywhere more nasty than Cheltenham now and again. She's never, thank the good Lord, met that sort."

"You took his measure?" asked Blackthorn.

"I'm an old woman, my lord. I've met just about *every* sort in my life. That one will have your business spread all over the west country before he's done or I miss my guess."

"You've guessed *part* of it. The thing is, for Lord Quincy, the truth is never enough. Much too tame. He must embroider and embroider and embroider. Worse, every time he tells the story, he'll come up with a different notion and each will be worse then the last!"

Frederica chuckled. "Perhaps someone should suggest to him he become an author of Gothic tales."

"It is not the least bit humorous, Mrs. MacKivern! What he'll do to your reputation is something I don't care to contemplate. Now what do I do?"

"You do exactly as you planned. You continue to escort us to your home and then you leave."

He stared at her. "You really don't understand, do you?"

"Perhaps it is merely that I don't care? I will, soon enough, return to my own home. And there I am well known. No one will believe badly of me."

"No one? How very lucky you are in your neighbors."

"No one I care for," she amended with a smile .

Sal set the elder girl on her feet and carefully rose to her own. "This isn't getting us anywhere, my lord, and certainly it isn't getting us on the road. Come along children," said the woman, gathering the girls to her and starting toward the inn. She glanced back and tipped her head. "Stewart? Matthew?"

Stewart ran off, but Matthew looked at his father. "That man. He'll say bad things about Mrs. MacKivern?"

"I fear he may, Matthew."

"Can't you stop him?"

"I tried." Bitterly, he added, "I failed."

Frederica, seeing Matthew's shocked expression at the thought his father might fail at anything, insisted, *"You* didn't fail. I did that for you, if, as you insist, merely speaking to the man was sufficient to undo your good work. Now run along and catch up with the others, Matthew."

The boy, after a quick look at his father's closed expression, ran off along the path.

"You will not find it so amusing, Mrs. MacKivern, when you are pointed out by all the old tabbies as my mistress," he said when they were alone.

Frederica blushed slightly. "I insist that nothing the man says can damage my reputation amongst those who are important to me."

Blackthorn, irritated with her lack of proper feeling, snapped, "Ah. But what about mine with those important to *me?"*

She eyed him. "I see. I'd not thought of that, had I? That you'd not like it put about that, when traveling with your son, you had your mistress in tow?" She looked into the distance. "And worst of all, of course, such a long-in-the-tooth long meg of a mistress?"

He stiffened. "You are impossible, Mrs. MacKivern."

She nodded stiffly. "So I've been told."

He glared down his nose. "You truly don't understand the harm which can be done, do you?"

"If you are implying you might be forced to offer for me

in order to whitewash my reputation, then rest easy," she snapped. "I'll never remarry."

Blackthorn was startled into asking, "You won't? Why not?" He felt his ears warm. "No, never mind. It is none of my business, and we must return to the carriages. I fear we've lost so much time it will be impossible to reach the Court this evening as I'd hoped. We'll put up for the night in Winchester."

"And, in Winchester, am I to pretend I am not with your party of children?"

"Don't be a fool when I know you are not!"

"Then *you* will pretend you are not with *our* party?"

"We will neither do any such thing. In Winchester where I am known, I can tell the innkeeper the truth and be believed." After a moment's hesitation, he added, "He will see we are not disturbed in any way." Had there, he wondered, been a trifle too much of an insinuating tone to that?

When Frederica stared at him for a moment, he feared there was. Without a word, she moved ahead of him and walked down the path. For half an instant his temper boiled up again and for just a trifle longer than that he considered catching her up, pulling her into his embrace and kissing her senseless, behaving in just the manner she seemed to expect!

The thought of holding her, touching her, kissing her, had its usual discombobulating effect. With a sigh, Blackthorn moved off in the *opposite* direction, needing time to compose himself.

When he returned to the inn he discovered the carriages gone. Questions elicited the information that Sal and the girls left in his and that the hired post chaise, the boys' mares tied on behind, held Frederica, Stewart and Matthew. Damnation! He'd meant for Frederica to travel in his well-sprung coach with Murdoch driving. He'd wanted everything as comfortable as possible for her.

With still another sigh, Blackthorn settled his bill, had Rufus saddled, and, not pushing either himself or his horse, followed after. He knew he'd catch up long before the coaches reached the inn in Winchester.

Long before, but long enough? Somehow, he must discover what to say or do to put Frederica back into her usual good humor. It was distressing to be out of favor with Frederica.

How had either of them come to lose their temper in any case? What exactly had he said . . . ? Had she said . . . ?

Blackthorn had not quite determined the first cause of argument when he saw his party rounding a curve not far ahead. He slowed Rufus so that they need not breathe the dust raised by the carriage wheels. Besides, he still had to determine how he was to apologize.

It would help if he were certain what it was, exactly, for which he need apologize!

Chapter Eight

"Are you angry with my father?" asked Matthew. He'd been watching Frederica closely for some miles and could stand the suspense no longer.

Her head swung around from where she'd stared, blankly, out the window. "Am I what?"

"Are you angry? With my father," repeated Matthew.

"And why would I be angry with him?"

"I don't know, but you muttered a bit ago about boiling oil and something about a rake?"

"A dungeon and a rack. Or thumbscrews, perhaps?"

"No, you said something about punishing all rakes . . . ?"

"I mention rakes and you think of your *father?*" asked Frederica.

"No, it was when you said *that man* that I decided you weren't angry with me or Stu, that it must be my father. Please don't be angry with him."

Frederica realized, just in time, the inappropriateness of asking Blackthorn's son if his father was a rake. Back there in the spinney, Blackthorn's tone more than his words seemed to indicate he was. And the way he'd looked at her at the end—well what else was she to assume?

"*Are* you angry with my father?"

She sighed. "I don't know."

The boys looked at each other. "How," asked Stewart, "can you not know? You always know when you're angry with *me*."

"Yes, but your behavior is always clearly right or wrong, Stewart. It is easy to determine if you deserve punishment. Adults are more complicated. Sometimes you hear something and it means what you think it means. But sometimes it does *not*. I just don't know . . ."

"Could you ask him? And then be angry if you *should* be? And not be angry now?" asked Matthew, his big eyes pleading.

Frederica smiled. "A very sensible proposal, Matthew. Except, I don't think I'll ask. I'll wait and see . . . what happens." She looked from one lad to the other. "Will that suit?" They looked at each other, shrugged, and nodded. "So, how should we while away the hours?"

Stewart bounced on his seat. "I know. That game where we get points when we see something. Something on the list? We've not done that yet."

"A very good notion. I'll keep track. Matthew, you look out your window and Stewart, you look out yours. And no cheating by looking across the coach!"

She dug a short pencil and a small notebook from her reticule. Carefully she wrote each boy's name at the top of facing pages.

"There," she said, her pencil poised. "All ready."

"Five geese!" shouted Stewart instantly, just as Matthew proclaimed, "A scarecrow! I see a scarecrow!"

The game sufficed until they reached a barren stretch. When they'd seen nothing to add to their lists for a good two miles, Stewart proclaimed the game a bore.

"Then I shall get out the traveling chess set and you may play a game or two of that."

"Chess," asked Matthew doubtfully. "I don't believe I know all the rules."

"Then Stewart and I will play and we'll explain as we go along. Stewart, you may set up the board." She handed over the small highly polished wooden board with peg holes in each square. The bag for the chessmen was made of a stiff sort of material and, if one was careful, would actually stand up a bit when the sides were rolled down. Frederica put it between the boys, but very soon Matthew picked it up and began handing each piece to Stewart who would give its name and then how it was allowed to move on the board.

"Have you never played, then?" Frederica asked Matthew.

The boy blushed. "That tutor who taught me piquet? He started to, but then I had to go to school and he went away, so . . ." Matthew shrugged. He handed over another white pawn which Stewart carefully pegged into a hole in front of the white queen. Chess held them for another hour, but the boys tired of that too.

Frederica then pulled out her heavy guns: A Gothic novel, something she normally wouldn't have allowed. Stewart whooped. Matthew gave each a curious look. "We are to read?"

"Mama will read, idiot. Come on, Mama! Don't fiddle about so! Read!"

Frederica read. And read. And read some more. No one was more happy than she when they pulled onto the cobbles paving the road at the outer fringes of Winchester! As they went down the hill, she saw Blackthorn ride past the carriage and her mood shifted. *Was* she angry with the man? Should she be? Had he *really* suggested . . . ?

And if he had, wasn't it only what she herself had wished, wondered, hoped, wanted . . . ?

Her gaze shifted to her son and across to Matthew. How could she be such an idiot? Even if he held . . . interesting . . . notions about her person, he'd do nothing where it might harm his son! Her frown faded and she focused on the boys, discovering they were watching her carefully.

"It's all right," she said. "I'm not about to make a scene!"

"Good," said Stewart. In a bored tone, he added, "I abominate scenes."

It was, very obviously, in mimicry of someone and, even as she chuckled, Frederica wondered who. She was still chuckling when, his face a picture of caution, Blackthorn opened the carriage door and handed her down. "I am forgiven then?" he asked softly.

"Forgiven? Is there something for which you need forgiveness?"

"Hmm. I hadn't thought so, but you must admit you were angry when you left me there in the spinney."

"So I was." Frederica smiled. "You must know that my temper tantrums rarely last long."

"If I didn't, I do now. Boys," he said. "There is still a bit of daylight. I wondered if there was a teacher among your tutors you wished to visit. A stroll would be just the thing, I think. Frederica?"

"I should like an opportunity to rid myself of the stiffness travel induces."

"Boys?" he asked, turning to them again.

They looked at each other and grimaced. "Do we *have* to?" asked Stewart.

"You don't wish a walk?"

"We don't wish a *visit*," the boys said in chorus and then made horrid faces at each other.

"You needn't then. Where would you suggest we stroll?"

The boys looked at each other and, without conferring and without hesitation, once again spoke as one: "Up St. Catherine's Hill!"

"Hmm. I should have thought of that myself. Come along then."

"Shouldn't we settle in first?" demurred Frederica.

"That's all seen to. Your driver . . . well, I think you've had better?"

"He was a little . . . awkward getting through town traffic."

"Yes. I arrived before you and saw to everything. Also," he said gently, "Sal is with the girls who are playing in the back garden, so you needn't worry about them."

She tipped him a quick glance. Just how did he know she'd been about to suggest she'd changed her mind and would stay with Bitsy and Maria?

"Now, are we ready?" he asked.

Blackthorn watched, silent, as Frederica made up her mind. She wanted a walk. She wanted to be with her son. But most of all she wanted to be with Blackthorn—and there was the rub! She shouldn't succumb to that desire, because every time they were together it only fed her ridiculous emotions and made it harder, the next time, to resist him.

Frederica sighed and Blackthorn hid a quick grin of triumph. He offered his arm, she took it, and they turned toward the cathedral. They went around the edifice and into the cloisters,

through them, and out a gate facing the college. Very soon
they reached the old playing field where the boys, after a look
at Frederica for permission, raced off.

"They mind you very well," he said.

"I think it is because I try very hard not to give orders or
make rules unless I feel they are important."

"An excellent way to go on." He strolled on in silence, his
eyes straight ahead. Finally he spoke. "I have tried to understand why it was we fell into a . . . an . . . a . . ."

"A snit?"

He blinked. "A what?"

"Snit."

Blackthorn's laughter rumbled around them. "Such a word!
You never cease to surprise me. Very well, a snit. I still cannot
understand it."

"Must you? Understand it, I mean?"

"I would like to avoid such things in future, Frederica."

It was Frederica's turn to march along silently. It was the
second time he'd used her name in public. Should she object?
Did she wish to object? She didn't know.

"*May* I call you Frederica? It is how I think of you, you
see."

She bit her lip, cast a quick look at him and then stopped,
forcing him to stop too. Half turned toward her, he looked
down at her and she stared at him. She saw such tenderness!
How could the man look at her with such . . . affection? And
why? And what did it mean?

"My dear?"

"Now *that* I will *not* allow," she said sharply.

"What . . . oh! I think of you that way, too."

"Nonsense. You can't know me well enough."

"But I do. I don't know how, but I do."

She turned to look at the school buildings. The sun gleamed
along one of the higher roofs. "We should go back, I think."

"How have I erred this time, Frederica?"

"You . . . imply feelings I cannot believe you experience. I
don't wish to discuss it."

"Someday we must."

"Must we?"

"I think so."

Frederica carefully removed her arm from his. "I would like to go back to the inn. Please find the boys so we may return."

"You'd see them coming now, if you would look. And someone in tow . . ."

Frederica glanced down the path. A youngish master held each boy by a hand, and looked down first at one and then the other, laughing. He glanced up, saw the couple awaiting their children.

"Welcome," he called. "I never thought to see these two gentlemen until the very last moment come fall and the beginning of Short Half. Neither lad, I think, has the making of a scholar!"

Matthew cast a quick look at his father and, his cheeks red, he looked at the path. Stewart's lip thrust out and he glared at his mother.

"I found nothing wrong with Matthew's school report. The headmaster's letter was carefully complimentary, I thought," said Blackthorn calmly.

"Surely the headmaster does not lie to a parent," said Frederica. "Stewart's report was, likewise, quite adequate."

"I didn't say the boys were stupid or that they lacked discipline. They do their work and do it well," said the young man. He grinned. "But they haven't that *love* for it which would add another man to our country's roll of savants!"

"*I* want to go into the army," said Stewart. "I want to fight Boney."

Matthew didn't say anything, still looking at the path where, now, his toe scrapped arcs.

"Matthew?" said Blackthorn. His son looked up. "Have you a dream for your future?" he asked softly.

"It's stupid." He again stared at his toe and the arcs he carved in the path.

"Truly stupid or just different?" asked Frederica.

Matthew looked at her. "Different?" He grimaced. "Oh, it's different all right!"

"You aren't required to tell us," Frederica went on gently.

Having been given permission *not* to tell, Matthew's words tumbled over each other. "I-want-to-cross-the-Channel-in-a-balloon," he said it so fast it was difficult to untangle one word from another.

"That sounds like something your last tutor suggested!" said Blackthorn and one could hear a bit of reprimand in his tone.

But Matthew's eyes glowed as he said, "He took me to where a balloonist came down in our rough pasture. We talked for a very long time while they straightened the bag and folded it properly and they let me ask all the questions I wanted. The man explained about how the gas is made and how one fills the balloon and the cold when one is up high no matter how warm the sun and . . ."

"Did you discuss valves?" interrupted Frederica, curious. Matthew nodded vigorously. "Well, that is something I don't precisely understand. You may explain it to me later—" She eyed Blackthorn's growing frown. "— but I think we should return to the inn now. It all sounds very exciting. *And* very dangerous, you know."

"It isn't the *danger,*" said an outraged Matthew. "It's learning about things."

Blackthorn was about to say something when the Winchester teacher spoke, his eyes on Matthew. "Perhaps I was wrong. Now here's all the evidence of a fervent need to learn that I looked for in vain all last year. The boy has far more curiosity then I ever knew!" He looked up and, seeing Blackthorn's brow as black as his name, he said, "If I could have a word with you, my lord?" He glanced at Frederica. "Boys, take Mrs. MacKivern to the chapel and show her the fan vault which is one of finest examples in the country." He flushed slightly at Frederica's raised brow, but then grinned. "We will meet you there shortly," he finished. The boys grabbed Frederica's hands and hurried her off.

"I told you it was stupid," muttered Matthew.

"*Not* stupid. Not at *all,*" said Frederica sharply.

"Well, at the least it's not something the heir to an earldom is supposed to want," said the boy.

Matthew looked so sad Frederica wished she dared gather him to her and hug him tightly. She did tighten her hand around his.

Matthew sighed. "Let's go see the chapel's stupid ceiling!"

When the men joined them, a frown still marred Blackthorn's brow, but he had a completely different look to him when his gaze fell on his son. On the other hand, he didn't seem to know what to say. Soon the party, increased by the addition of the scholar, returned to the inn for dinner.

The evening passed in a convivial manner. *Especially* so after Sal took the tired, sad, and homesick Marian and Bitsy to their room. Not too much later, Frederica excused herself, taking the boys up and seeing them into their bed before she went to her own.

Blackthorn had encouraged her to return to the private parlor, but she feared another confrontation. As soon as the Winchester scholar left, she knew she'd come to verbal blows with Blackthorn on the subject of his son's interest in science which was her own passion and not to be despised! And, because she'd enjoyed the evening very much, she didn't want it to end in controversy.

Alternatively, she didn't wish it to end in another sort of confrontation either. She was equally unready for a discussion of the very real but barely admitted feelings which flowed between them whenever they'd a moment alone. She couldn't believe him when he implied he felt the softer emotions. They'd spent so little time together it simply didn't make sense. That her own feelings raged along unfamiliar paths was, she felt, irrelevant. She was merely a country mouse and couldn't be expected to have the experience to withstand the charm and personality, the address of an experienced man of the ton! But he . . .

He'd had years among the highest in the land. In parliament, at balls and soirees, at house parties, he'd all that experience she lacked. So how could she possibly believe that a man, who met and conversed with eminent intellects and politically powerful men and socialized with the greatest beauties of the age, would find an insignificant country-bred widow such as herself of interest? He *must* be amusing himself, playing with her emotions.

And it was wrong of him!

Fuming, Frederica fell asleep, her dreams a mishmash of nonsense in which two utterly different men, both bearing the Blackthorn face and title, competed for her favors!

Very different favors, of course!

She was not in the best of moods when she woke the next

morning. Her bedding twisted around her and her pillow fallen to the floor. She'd been driven from her sleep more than once, but, as usual, was unable to remember the details of the dreams. As a result she felt unrested and confused and unhappy.

It was all she could do to face the children with a pleasant face and assure them they would have a reasonably short ride that day and then they'd be free to run about and use up the excess energy they were storing up.

She ignored Blackthorn, much to his disgust, but with the children vying for her attention, he found it impossible to catch her eye let alone a moment of her time. Mounting and leading the way, he swore he'd have some few words with her before he rode on toward London. Knowing he must not stay any longer than necessary once the carriages arrived, he urged Rufus to a faster pace and had nearly an hour to give orders to various servants before returning to the front drive where he awaited his guests' arrival.

Sal and the girls went off with the housekeeper and a cheerful maid who was the eldest of a large family and very good with children. They would find the nursery rooms opened up and aired and could explore to their heart's content. Gruddy, his head groom, took the boys and their mares, along with Frederica's gelding, in charge, leading them off to the stables. The scene was set.

"I must leave immediately," he told Frederica quietly. "Will you walk down the drive a ways before I go?"

Frederica, bemused by the organization which had left her almost alone with his lordship. Alone except for footmen, busy unloading the carriages, the drivers waiting to pull around to the carriage house, and a shadowy figure inside the door who, she thought, must be the butler. Since servants, in the minds of many, didn't count, they really were, by convention, alone.

"Have I a choice?" she asked.

He studied her raised chin. "No, I don't believe you do," he said thoughtfully. "Come along, Frederica." He took her elbow and, unless she wished to make that scene she'd assured her son she'd *not* make, she truly had no choice.

"You, my lord, are a bully."

"I, my dear, have no time to play games and I must speak with you."

"I've a few words for you, too, my lord. And I'll have mine first. You had no right to look down your nose at your son's dreams. I was ashamed of your reaction to his ambition, my lord. *You*, of all people, who had a dream of your own, who wished to become a doctor, to lack the understanding and patience for such things in another!"

Blackthorn, who had hoped to achieve a better understanding between them before he left, stopped at the tone of her first words. He stared down at her. "I haven't a notion what you mean and what the devil has it to do with anything anyway?"

"*Do* with anything! We are discussing your *son*. Do you mean to say your son and heir is *not* important to you?"

"My son is very important, but not at this precise moment. I wish . . ."

"Your son should be the first and last thing on your mind, my lord, at *any* time. And you still have to explain why you, who experienced the blighting of your particular dreams, should react exactly as your parents must have done when it comes to *your* son's dreams!"

"My son's dreams are . . ."

Frederica interrupted still again. "They are *important.* Instead of that perfectly useless ninny you hired to tutor him this summer, you should have found the fellow who taught him piquet! Obviously *that* young man understands and has the boy's interests at heart!"

"I tried," said Blackthorn angrily. "I sent him a letter which was returned by his tutor who informed me he's in Greece with several fellow Oxford students! Blast it, Frederica, will you listen . . ."

"I said I had words. And I'll say them all. They've been boiling around in my head and if I don't get them out I'll have still another night's bad sleep." She drew in a deep breath. "You, my lor- . . . umph erg ungh! . . . ummmmm . . ."

Determined to cut off the tirade, Blackthorn pulled her into his embrace and, before she could even squeak, kissed her. At first she was rigid as a board, but, as the kiss softened so did she, enough so that her arms crept up around his neck and, with no more than the lightest of encouraging pressure from his hands, she leaned into him.

"Rickie . . . Rickie . . ." he whispered into her ear, nibbling on it. "Blast it all. I don't want to leave you."

She struggled. He loosened his hold, looking down at her with deep sadness. She stared back, stunned. With great effort, Blackthorn kept himself from kissing her again.

"No more words, Frederica?" he asked, the whimsy there again.

"Oh yes, my lord. Words and words and words. Lots of new words! But not until I get them straight in my head!"

"I shouldn't have done that, but I had to stop you talking about Matt when I needed to tell you I'll miss you, that I'll be thinking about you . . ."

"Nonsense. You, my lord, may have hidden it from your son who believes you all you should be, but you *are*, instead, the rake I thought you! Release me!"

He opened his arms. Instantly, he grasped her elbows when she teetered from the loss of support. When she found her balance, he again let her go. "I'm not a rake, Frederica. I don't understand why you'd think that."

She sighed. "My lord, I'm a simple country woman. I'm a widow of uncertain years. I'm not particularly attractive, even if I'm not an antidote. How can I believe other than that you've decided you've a captive female available and will see just how naive she is. I refuse to swallow your hook, my lord, no matter how sweetly baited."

His frown grew as she spoke. "You wrong me, Frederica."

"Do I?" She studied him. "I don't see how that can be." She thought for a moment. "No. I'm certain I've analyzed the situation accurately. And, since I'm not here for your amusement, my lord, I think you'd best be on your way to where you *can* find the more agreeable company you crave!"

"Blast it, Frederica, you are the most stubborn, most irritating, most—" Seeing the fire flash in her eyes, Blackthorn paused, relaxed, smiled. "—endearing woman I've met for a very long time. I wish you felt the same, my sweet. But you are correct in one thing. I must go on. I mean to stop a night at Timberly Manor where, with any luck at all, I'll find that agreeable company of which you spoke. *Lord* Timberwood was at Winchester with me, you see," he finished with just a touch of acid. He was not displeased when Frederica blushed slightly and spoke more gently as he went on: "You will meet him and his wife, a couple who have the bad taste to be very much in love with each other, when you come to the Court at Christmas."

He stared at her as if memorizing her features and it wasn't until he was about to turn away that he realized she was staring back with much the same intensity.

"Take care, my dear," he said softly, turning them toward his horse. He walked slowly, speaking as they went. "Write occasionally to tell me how you go on. Later, I'll arrange for my aunt to come and keep you company and perhaps I'll be able to join you here for a week or so. If there is anything at all that you need, you merely ask Jennings and he'll see to it. Jennings," he added, "I'm off now. You take very good care of Mrs. MacKivern . . . and the children as well, of course." He nodded to his butler who, although playing the part of a groom was totally beneath him, held Rufus's reins. Blackthorn turned back to Frederica. He caught her hand and lifted it, looking into her eyes. "You'll understand me eventually, my dear." He kissed her palm. "I swear it."

Jennings, staring off into the distance over a long row of copper beech, was obviously pretending to be deaf. Frederica, knowing he was *not*, blushed hotly and hoped he would also pretend to be dumb! At least where her affairs were concerned.

"My lord," she said shortly. "Have a pleasant journey."

He smiled a rather self deriding smile. "You *will* understand, Frederica. Eventually I'll have time to make certain of it."

"Good-bye, my lord."

He sighed and mounted, and then, looking down at her he shook his head. "I wonder if I am truly needed in London," he mused.

"The last time you stayed away a few short days, they sent for you. I'd guess that means they think you important to them."

"So they did." Still he hesitated. "I don't wish to go. How strange. It is only the second time ever that I'm not anxious to return to the fray."

"And the first?"

"When I met a certain fiery redhead, my dear. I was returning her son and thought to collect my own and be away. It didn't happen."

"And now you must be away again," she hinted.

"You aren't going to give an inch, are you?"

"No."

"Impossible woman." Irritation had a muscle jumping in his jaw. "Until we meet again, then," he said gruffly and reined Rufus around, urging the horse to a canter down the long drive, only to pull up after the second curve.

Blast! he thought. *I never actually got around to explaining that Matthew's tutor at Winchester outlined a course of study for the boy which would forward the lad's interest in science!*

It was no wonder he'd forgotten, perhaps. He'd been far too interested in forwarding his own interests! In discussing his feelings for her, his growing affection and the plans he was making for their future . . . He rode on, deeply regretting parting from Frederica before he'd managed to straighten out her head and convince her of his growing love for her. Now, the way things were going in London, he'd have no opportunity until late summer.

If then.

For her part, Frederica only half listened as the comfortable housekeeper, Mrs. Clapper, told her of the arrangements made for her comfort. Tentatively, of course. Assuming Mrs. Mac-Kivern had no objections?

"Hmm?"

"Poor dear. You're tired, aren't you, then," said the housekeeper, determined to think the best of the woman the whole household believed was soon to be their mistress.

And about time, too, thought the comfortably plump housekeeper. Lord Blackthorn had been remiss in waiting so long before taking another wife. Far too long. Nanny was fretting. She wanted babies in her nurseries. And, no matter how she tried, as a mere housekeeper, she could not take the place of a proper wife and mistress of the household. She hadn't the same authority to order things done. Nor had she, she admitted, a good eye for what was needed.

So went Mrs. Clapper's thoughts as she took Frederica to the suite which had been prepared for her. "I'll send a maid to you, since you didn't bring your own," she said.

"No need," said Frederica, startled out of her musings. "I've no need for a maid!"

"Ah," said Mrs. Clapper a trifle slyly, "I hoped you'd allow young Sarrie the experience. The girl has some talent to be a lady's maid and I've done what I can to train her, but there is nothing like experience, is there?"

"And I'd be conferring a boon on her if I accept her?" Frederica's eyes twinkled.

"That you would." Mrs. Clapper's smile was a trifle lop-sided. "And on me. Sarrie's my only child, you see. I'd like to see her well settled."

"Then how can I say you nay? But I'd like a rest before I must learn to deal with her! You see, I've no more notion of what to do with a personal maid, then she must have of being one!"

Mrs. Clapper nodded. This one would do. There was no pretense to her. No la-di-dah airs and graces. Yes, a proper woman for a very proper man. "You just ring then—" The housekeeper gestured toward the bell pull which hung by the high testered bed. "—and I'll see she attends to hot water for you."

"A whole bath would be welcome . . ."

Frederica offered the suggestion a trifle tentatively. Her father, contrary to common thought, had held the belief that cleanliness was important to health rather than the contrary view that too much bathing was detrimental! She longed for a bath after their several days travel.

"If it is not to be thought of . . ." she added.

"I'll see a fire is lit in your dressing room and that a tub is set up while you rest, madam. You just ring when you want Sarrie to come to you." The woman turned and left.

Instantly Frederica put the housekeeper from her mind, her thoughts returning to Blackthorn. That kiss! She must take great care or, at some point, she'd not even recognize that he'd seduced her until it was done and she'd been allowed space to think again! It wasn't fair that he could induce such fire in her veins with nothing more than a kiss.

Ah! If only she dared believe his protestations of affection. But she didn't. She truly didn't believe this man could be what her heart told her he was. Worse, she didn't believe there was anything in herself special enough to draw a man who was, himself, so very special!

And perhaps, hardest to accept, was that if she could not have it all, a wedding and proper marriage bed, then she wanted nothing. Perverse creature that she was, half a loaf was *not* better than nothing for the simple reason that all too soon *she'd* be left with nothing but pain when he, having gotten what he wanted, left her to her lonely future . . . All notion of seducing the man, assuming she might find the courage, was forgotten. What remained was a determination *she* would not be seduced by *him!*

Chapter Nine

Frederica stared out her sitting-room window at the beautiful day. From somewhere in the gardens she heard the high-pitched voices of the children who had settled in more quickly than she'd done herself. She herself still felt exceedingly *unsettled* and very much out of place.

Useless, actually.

Childish laughter caught her attention. A fluffy white cloud drifted into view. A lark, singing somewhere above Seymour Court's high roof, caroled his enjoyment of the excellent weather.

Frederica wished she were out there, too.

But she wasn't.

And she wouldn't be. At least, she wouldn't if she didn't finish this task she'd set herself. Frederica glanced down at the paper set before her. The excellent pen. She'd promised herself she'd write His Lordship, thanking him for his thought in making careful arrangements for their comfort. And she would.

But it might be easier if she were absolutely certain what *motivated* that care. Her mind wandering off at a tangent still again, Frederica's gaze wandered toward the window, wondering, thinking of every time he'd let slip that careful control, revealed what she feared was his real goal.

And yet . . . hadn't she too thought of seduction? Been unhappy she didn't know the way of it? Distressed with herself for even thinking of such a thing? Was she blaming him for her own failings, making herself seem purer by making him seem worse? Especially since she'd given up all ambition of seducing him?

Surely not . . .

Frederica sighed, bit her lip, forced her eyes back to her page and told herself she must write. Besides, she genuinely wished to reassure his lordship that the children were content. The girls, once they'd learned to trust the strange maid and had discovered the wonders in the nursery, had even forgotten to miss their mother.

Especially when they realized they needn't worry about pleasing their beloved aunt as they must their exacting parent and, also, that Frederica was not to leave them alone in this wonderfully strange place. They were more content than Frederica had ever known them to be! Even *happy.* For the first time in their lives they'd managed to get extremely dirty and *were not scolded for it.*

Frederica smiled, remembering. On that particular occasion the girls had helped the boys build a dam across a narrow rivulet down the side of the drive which appeared after a heavy rain . . . Frederica's smile widened to a grin at the memory of the four children returning to the house tired and happy and just about as dirty as it was possible for children to get.

Determined to write her letter, Frederica still again turned away from the sunny day outside her window and stared at the pristine sheet of hot pressed paper which awaited her words. The ink was best quality. The pen had the very best steel nib to it, neither splayed so that it spattered, nor so new it didn't allow the ink to run smoothly. So why couldn't she begin? She would. Because if she did not, she'd not allow herself to go out. And what a waste of a beautiful day that would be.

"Dear Lord Blackthorn," she wrote and paused before continuing . . .

"Thank you for your kind consideration. The Court is well run and your servants exceedingly kind."

How stiff and formal, she thought, and sighed aloud. But it could stand. She would not change it.

"The boys spend several hours a day with your head groom who is giving them practice in jumping. The boys love it and,

*even if my heart is in my throat each day until they return from
the paddock, I force myself to allow it. Ian would be proud of
me.''*

Too stiff and now far too revealing. Again Frederica sighed.
What else?

That is, what else which didn't betray how deeply she'd
come to admire his home. It was a wonderful house. The older
parts retained an Elizabethan charm, with odd corners and
different levels and built to a very human scale, while the clean
lines of the newer Palladian addition had been fitted on without
causing what one might have predicted would be an ugly con-
trast of styles.

Here at the Court one was left with the best of both worlds.
The snug comfort of smallish rooms running one out of the
other as well as the modern version of classic perfection which
could, if badly done, be cold and unwelcoming. At Seymour
Court it was a feast for the eyes, adding peace and tranquility
to one's surroundings.

And room. Great, wonderful, lovely space!

Frederica had often told Ian she didn't resent the size of the
Dower House, but, truth to tell, she often felt cramped and
closed in there. Especially during the coldest wettest months
of the year when it was uncomfortable to be out and around.

Which thought reminded her that she wanted to be out and
around today, too, tagging along with Blackthorn's agent. The
man had given her the politely phrased invitation the preceding
afternoon. He'd suggested, diffidently, that she might like to
come when he made his rounds of the tenant farms and that,
if she'd oblige him by agreeing, she could be a help to him.
She, he said, would have a woman's eye to what might be
needed and he'd appreciate her advice, assuming she had nothing else planned? As if she *would,* here, where she'd no responsibilities and no acquaintance!

Once again Frederica looked at her letter. It had gotten no
farther forward for her musing.

*"They spend their mornings with the tutor whom they do
not love. But it does them no harm, and I've told them that if
they do their work promptly, then they will sooner be finished
and that bit of advice seems to have taken. Then, too, I understand that at Winchester the boys work much at their own pace*

and the farther along they get this summer, the better for them there, which they know. However that may be, the tutor has a set amount of work which is to be done each day. The boys finish quickly—or so it seems to me, but the fellow tells me they do all properly.''

That was all right. Now what else . . .

"I've discovered several pleasant rides. You've exceedingly well maintained coverts, do you not? I was told quite bluntly I was to avoid certain areas and since I am punctilious in doing so, even your head gamekeeper seems not to dislike me, which, I can tell you, has set me up in my own esteem. You will note, I do not say Mr. Williams likes me since I believe the rogue is the sort of man who takes delight in disliking everyone!''

Babbling? she wondered. Perhaps . . . but acceptable babble.

Still again Frederica sighed noisily while casting a yearning glance toward the windows. The agent had said ten, give or take a bit, and she feared it must be getting on for that . . .

"I can think of nothing else to say,'' she finished abruptly. *"All goes well here and I hope with you too. Your servant, Frederica MacKivern.''*

"There!" she said aloud.

Frederica folded the sheet and wrote out his lordship's direction before reaching for the wax disks provided for sealing letters. She realized she'd not brought her personal seal and sighed—this time with exasperation. Searching the drawers of the dainty desk, she discovered one with a star on it. She heated it and pressed it against the wax. *There.* It was done.

Happily, Frederica stood up, lifted her habit skirts and left her room, anticipating a proper ride, rather than the poky little jaunts she'd so far taken. And she'd meet Blackthorn's tenants.

Halfway down the front stairs, she stopped, frowning. Would his people think she was encroaching or, alternately, had some sort of right to interfere . . . ? It was a thought which gave her pause until she once again heard the lark and noticed the bright blue sky through the doors open to the world!

Blackthorn stared, bleary-eyed, at the blank sheet of paper laying before him. He was determined to write Frederica before he allowed himself to go to bed and end what had been one of the more hectic, not to say one of the longest, most frustrating, days of his life. He picked up a pen, played with it as he thought about the series of niggling irritations which, in toto, added up to anger inducing aggravation.

Prinny, having fulfilled his ambition of becoming Regent, had grown more obdurate and unpredictable than ever. Today he'd demanded Blackthorn's presence at the abominable hour of ten in the morning; at twelve-thirty, when Blackthorn proved less malleable than His Royal Highness hoped, on the question of an increase to his allowance, he'd said outright that he'd be more than pleased if he never saw Blackthorn again.

And *then*, not more than two hours later, he'd sent a royal messenger to summon that same happily exiled peer back to the Presence.

Blackthorn had obeyed, of course. Immediately. One could do no other. But, arriving promptly, he'd then been made to kick his heels for several wasted hours while Prinny consulted with one of his Whiggish intimates who delighted in raising every possible argument to thwart the government's needs. When the prince at last remembered his urgent request that Blackthorn be summoned, he became quite angry His Lordship had not yet appeared.

Blackthorn's respectful explanation that he *had* arrived as requested, that he had waited patiently to be called into his prince's presence, had done no good. Prinny was in a capricious mood. It was impossible to do right when the next king of England decided he'd not be pleased.

A hopeless situation indeed, and Blackthorn would not have put up with it from any other living person. He'd have stalked out. But this was the Prince and future King, and there were conventions one could not break. It was impossible to leave a Royal's presence until one was given permission to do so. . . .

A candle guttered and Blackthorn glanced up from his paper on which he scrawled a last word, realized what had caught his attention and lay his pen aside. He replaced the candle with a new one. Others were little more than knubs, and, still thinking about his day, he replaced those too.

Returning to his desk, Blackthorn picked up his pen . . . and scratched away as he'd been doing before the candle misbe-haved. When he finished telling Frederica of his day, of the irritations, of his thoughts and his hopes, he lay down the pen and flexed tense fingers. He straightened the small stack of paper and then, amazed, he picked it up and counted. Six pages of his careful script. Six pages, back and front, of his neat but rather cramped penmanship!

What in Heavens name had he written?

Blackthorn settled back in his chair, twisted slightly sideways to catch the light, and read. He frowned. *Dare* he send her so much drivel? Or perhaps that was too harsh a word? Still, there was, more often than he liked to admit, a complaining tone. And there were silly questions she could not know how to answer. On top of that he'd talked of people she'd never met, both those she might like and some she'd find as pernicious as he did. He had thought to give verbal sketches of those same people, so perhaps they had some substance as well as a name.

But still . . .

Blackthorn stared toward his window, which his valet had, much earlier, covered with the drapery. He stared as if he could see all the way to Seymour Court, could see what she was doing, could actually talk to her . . . which, he realized, was exactly what his long letter was all about. He'd been talking to Frederica much as he might if she were right here in the room with him.

In his bedroom . . .

A half derisive snort emphasized his realization that, if Frederica were there in his bedroom, a neatly turned-down bed not more than six feet away, there'd be no *talking*.

At least, not for some indefinite time!

But the letter . . .

Even as he pondered the wisdom of sending it, the consequences if it fell into the wrong hands, he was folding it, writing the direction on the blank side of the last sheet. He reached for his wax and a seal and then decided he should *not* trust the thing to the Royal Mails. He'd send it down by one of his grooms. Unfolding it and turning to the end, he added a few words, crossing his lines since there was no more space.

His postscript asked that Frederica allow no one else to read his effusion, since it was just the sort of thing his enemies would like to lay into Prinny's hands! He added a further cramped note that the groom would wait a day or so for her answer.

Since the undergroom he meant to send was sweet on the second upstairs maid, whose wandering eye more often than not lit on one of the younger footmen, the lad wouldn't mind a day or two at the Court in which he could pursue his fickle love.

Blackthorn set the finished and sealed letter aside, feeling, he realized, a great deal of jealousy of the groom! As he slipped into bed, he mused, half—but only half—jokingly, that perhaps he could anger Prinny to the point he'd be told to leave London altogether? He pulled the cover up to his chin and rolled to his side, shaping his pillow into the form he preferred. Such a big bed, he thought, sleepily. And so lonely.

Strange. He'd never before noticed that it was so very lonely. . . .

Lady Amelia Morningside leaned both hands on the polished knob of her cane and glared across the music room at the barefaced intruder. How dare the impudent miss sit there demurely playing the piano? Her Ladyship's eyes bulged, more prominently even than was usual.

"It's true then," she sputtered. "I didn't believe it for a moment. Not of Spencer Seymour! What has come over my nephew to bring his doxy into his own home!"

Frederica stiffened into an ivory statue, her fingers changing from bending gently to the keys into talons. Carefully she uncurled them. Slowly she turned. Very slowly.

"I don't believe we've been introduced," she said, her tone icy. Gracefully, she rose, straightening to her full height which was above average and well above that of the angry matron facing her. "I also cavil at the term doxy or any other of the sort. I am not and have never been *that* kind of woman, whatever term you give it."

Lady Amelia relaxed very slightly, tipping her head thoughtfully. "I agree that you dress like a lady, if more than a trifle out of fashion," she mused.

"Fashion has never held much interest for me." Frederica succumbed to the temptation of ridding herself of a bit of spite for being called "doxy." "I see that, for you, it must play a great role in occupying your time."

Lady Amelia's mouth, which had begun to soften, firmed up again. "Fashion is important."

"As important as the health and welfare of one's tenants? As important as the war against Bonaparte? As important as the king's condition? As important as teaching . . ."

"Ah! That explains your lack of interest. A blue-stocking, then." Lady Amelia nodded. She turned toward Blackthorn's butler. "Why in Heaven's name do you insist on clearing your throat in that ridiculous fashion while standing so near it must irritate your betters! Go away."

"My lady . . ." He cast a harassed look toward Frederica which was both apology and a plea for help. "It's Lady Amelia, Mrs. MacKivern . . ." He cleared his throat still again.

"Ah," said Frederica, enlightened. "You are Blackthorn's aunt, then. And I believe Jennings is attempting to gain your attention in order to correct what is a misapprehension on your part. You may go, Jennings." She paused until the butler bowed and left the room. "I haven't a notion where you came by it, but you seem to think me something other than I should be. What I *actually* am is nothing more than the mother of Lord Blackthorn's son's best friend. Young Matthew was visiting us for the summer. When Blackthorn discovered there was typhus in our region, he insisted we come here, where his son is out of danger. There is Matthew, my son, my two nieces, and an old servant for the children. Now, what have you heard that has set you into such a tizzy?"

Lady Amelia grimaced. "I suppose I should have taken the source into account."

"The source."

"That scamp Lord Quincy is in Bath with friends. I fear he's told the story everywhere he's stayed this summer, so it is very likely spread all over the west country. All too soon, someone will carry it to London. I had to come see for myself that it wasn't true. And—"

The plump matron leaning on her cane, interrupted herself, looked around for the butler and called him back. She motioned Jennings closer. "Don't just stand there you idiot," she said.

"Give me your arm!" When she was gently seated across from Frederica, Lady Amelia returned to her original topic.

"—*of course,* it is not true. But Spence must be warned what the chatterers are saying. He can put around that I am here as chaperone and, whatever tales are told concerning his guests, they can be ignored. Jennings!" she called.

The butler, once again quietly leaving the room, returned to her ladyship's side. "Yes, my lady?"

"I require my lap desk and you must order a groom to make himself available. A missive must go off to his lordship. Instantly."

The butler cleared his throat.

"There you go again, making that irritating noise!"

Frederica, who had not decided that she liked this impulsive woman who jumped to conclusions and then when proved wrong jumped just as quickly in another direction, instantly arriving at some other conclusion, cleared her own throat.

"You too?" asked Lady Amelia. "Is it something in the air?"

"I suspect Jennings wishes to explain that one of His Lordship's grooms is even now preparing to leave for London," said Frederica soothingly.

Lady Amelia straightened her rounded shoulders and glared at the butler. "Then stop him!" she ordered, tapping her cane hard against the floor. "My letter must go with him."

Jennings bowed slightly and left the room, this time making his escape. A footman returned with the required lap desk and Lady Amelia, wasting no time thinking out what she wished to say, wrote three full pages for Blackthorn's perusal while Frederica, amused, watched.

"There," said Her Ladyship. "That should make all clear to him and tell him exactly what it is he must do to set things right. And *now*—" Jennings once again appeared and still again departed, this time with a sealed missive to add to Frederica's and those the boys had written his lordship. "—Now," repeated her ladyship, "I must know more of you, my dear. I didn't quite understand *why* you are here. Oh typhus, I remember that much, and I can see why Spencer would demand his son return to Seymour Court, but I don't believe that explains you or your son or, especially, your nieces?"

"Matthew and my son, Stewart, are the very best of friends. His lordship thought there was no reason they not spend the rest of summer together. We simply changed the venue, here instead of at my home as was planned."

Frederica avoided explaining exactly how those particular plans had originated and hoped she'd never have to tell this eccentric the details of the boys' exchange of homes.

"I believe," she added, "that we have still not been properly introduced? I am Mrs. Frederica MacKivern."

"We have not, have we?" said Lady Amelia, sounding surprised. "I am Lady Amelia Morningside, Spencer's aunt."

"Lord Blackthorn mentioned he hoped you'd come here from Bath once your visit ended. I don't believe he'd quite this sort of arrival in mind, however."

Lady Amelia sighed. "That gormless boy. Oh! Not Blackthorn, of course. His tales—I mean Lord Quincy's, you know—almost always prove to have inaccuracies in them—except when they are *entirely* baseless which is not at all unusual with him." She tipped her head, her eyes on some distant prospect. "I wonder why anyone ever believes him for a moment." Her gaze returned to settle on Frederica, a laughing look in her eyes. "Ah! But I do know. The silly man tells each story with such verve and elan that one cannot help but believe." Her gaze sharpened. "Have the neighbors visited?"

"No. While on the way here, we met a Mrs. Newton who lives somewhere nearby? Lord Blackthorn asked her to see that I was introduced around, but she hasn't called."

"You *are* an innocent, are you not? Surely you realize Mrs. Newton didn't believe my nephew? That she thought he meant to foist a lightskirt onto the neighborhood?"

"I don't think she thought that at all," said Frederica, choosing to be amused rather than insulted. "In my opinion she is simply one of the mean-spirited sort who enjoys making life difficult for others. Not that my life here has been at all difficult, of course. I've never objected to solitude and have, always, ways of keeping myself occupied. For instance, I've begun a class for those serving maids who wish to learn to read and write and do simple calculations."

"Bah! I do not believe in educating a girl above her station! It can only lead to trouble."

"Nonsense. It can only better a girl's life."

"It will make her discontent, unwilling to remain in the position God gave her."

Frederica realized she'd missed having someone with whom she could argue! She retorted, "It will add interest to lives which are full of responsibility but little amusement, and increase the possibility of advancement."

"Life was not meant to be amusing. It is duty and responsibility and hard work."

Even as she wondered just when Lady Amelia had last done any work, hard or otherwise, Frederica riposted, "Duty, responsibility, hard work, and, when that is finished, whatever one may find which will lighten the daily load. The ability to read will, I believe, make dalliance among the servants, which is now the chief way of alleviating their burdens, much less a problem. Instead of flirting and getting themselves into, hmm, *difficulties* with the men, the maids may sit themselves down with a story which will entertain and teach."

"Gothic romances!"

"I was thinking more along the lines of moral tales, but I've no objection to the occasional Gothic romance. The few I've read seem to insist that evil be punished and good rewarded— even if the getting from the beginning to the end is done with idiocy on the part of the heroine and unbelievable luck on the part of the hero!"

Lady Amelia chuckled. "Good girl."

Frederica, who had been enjoying herself, blinked at the change of subject. "What?"

"Indeed, it is excellent. You'll not be bullied into changing your mind when you are certain of your beliefs! I like that!"

"Thank you," said Frederica cautiously and added a soft: "I think." She watched the woman, a wary look about her.

Lady Amelia chuckled again. "You don't know what to think of me, is that it?"

"Well, since you ask, no, I do not."

"Never mind. You'll soon discover I'm on your side. And, speaking of sides, we must attack at once before the war is brought to us. No shilly-shallying, now. Tell me what you have in your wardrobe suitable for morning visits?"

"If you mean smack up to the echo—" Frederica colored

slightly at the cant phrase which slipped past her lips. "—as my son would say, then nothing."

"Ha! And something neat and clean and presentable?"

"I would hope everything I brought to the Court is that."

"Hmmm," murmured Her Ladyship, eyeing Frederica's morning gown. "Well, different standards must apply in your area of the country. Wherever that is. I wonder . . ." Her voice trailed off.

"If you wonder where that is, I come from the wold above Broadway. Lord MacKivern's manor is well known in the region."

"Broadway." Lady Amelia repeated the town's name several times. "Ah! Lord Merrick has an estate in that region . . . ?"

"Much to everyone's regret, that is true."

Again Lady Amelia chuckled. "Well, we'll not mention that particular opinion of His Lordship, shall we? In polite company, that is? Not when his lordship's estate will locate you for those among our neighbors who have an interest in such things, and for some of the others, it gives you a cachet that you live so near a marquis. Yes, I know you don't wish to make yourself something you are not, but a marquis is more than a mere baron, which I believe is all MacKivern may claim? Your husband could not come with you at this time of year? You were not worried, leaving him behind where there is illness?"

A choked laugh . . . or was it a sob . . . escaped Frederica. "You misunderstood, my lady. Lord MacKivern is my brother-in-law. My husband, his brother is . . . dead."

Once again Lady Amelia's eyes bulged as she stared at Frederica. "A widow . . . Well, that makes all the difference in the world. Oh yes," she said, rising awkwardly to her feet, "all the difference. We mustn't delay a moment! We attack this very day. If rumors *have* reached this area, they must be firmly countered. Even if they have, Spencer's guests should not be subjected to such nonsense. He is known as an upright and responsible gentleman and that should be protection enough." She was halfway to the door, leaning heavily on her cane when she muttered, "I do not see why people take it into their heads to believe the worst of a person they've never met but it seems to be human nature to do so!"

Since, on her arrival, Lady Amelia had accused Frederica of about the worst of which one could, save treason, Frederica smothered a laugh which her ladyship would not have appreciated! Frederica was shaking her head in wonder when the woman turned back.

"Well?" asked Lady Amelia.

"Well, what?"

"Are you coming?"

"Where?"

Lady Amelia heaved a great sigh of exasperation. "To change and then to begin our round of visits."

Gently, Frederica asked, "My lady, are you certain you'd not be better resting? It is not a horrendously long journey from Bath, but still . . ."

"I will suffer aches and pains whether I take myself to my bed or take myself to my neighbors. I would much rather take the neighbors who may, occasionally, be amusing which my bed is not. At least, not these days." She sighed then roused from some reverie of past intrigues and smiled. "Do come now, my dear. I'll just take a little peek at your wardrobe and choose what will do." She turned away, again muttering, but not so that Frederica could not hear: "Or what we must do *with*."

Frederica wondered if there were any way she could change Lady Amelia's obvious intention of introducing her, that very day, to every neighbor within a reasonable driving distance. "Lady Amelia, I don't see the point of this. I'll be returning to my home in a few weeks and will never again see any of these people. I couldn't care less what they think of me."

Lady Amelia straightened. She slowly turned. Again she eyed Frederica with that bug-eyed stare. "I didn't think you a fool."

"I don't believe I am."

Her ladyship rested both hands on her cane and stared. Finally she nodded. "Either a fool or an idiot and you are not the latter! You *must*, therefore, be a fool. Come along now."

Frederica sighed softly. She'd been right. Lady Amelia had the bit between her teeth and, unless she was rude, perhaps even insulting, there was no way she could avoid her ladyship's intentions!

But, despite Lady Amelia's sharp words, it was obvious to Frederica that the older woman suffered from a great deal of pain. That Her Ladyship wasn't the sort to give in to it, that she wouldn't make of herself an invalid lying about all day on a couch, that she would do whatever it was she felt she must do in spite of aching joints, was a trait Frederica admired. Or, she would if Lord Blackthorn's aunt didn't carry her determination too far.

"Perhaps," Frederica said in a coaxing tone, offering the suggestion as a compromise, "we might make only *one* visit instead of a whole round of visits?"

Again Lady Amelia stopped, turned and stared. Finally she nodded. *"Not* a *complete* fool. An excellent notion, in fact. Word will get around I'm here. On the other hand it will not look as if I were desperate to overset whatever gossip is making the rounds. It will be as if everything were exactly as it should be."

"Which," Frederica gently reminded her ladyship, "it *is.*"

"What!" shouted Lord Blackthorn, startling his valet. "Blast that pond scum! How dare he! I'll have Quincy's lights and liver!" He waved two pages of his aunt's letter in one hand, the sheets crackling, as he continued scanning the third. "I don't believe it." A few lines later he added, "I might have guessed." And still later, as he finished the last page, "Well, I suppose," he said a trifle doubtfully, "that things could be a great deal worse . . ."

Then His Lordship stared blankly toward the plain unadorned wall until his valet, a trifle concerned, cleared his throat and asked a question.

"You said something, Browning?"

"I wondered if you'd require riding clothes, my lord," repeated that much put-upon soul.

"Riding clothes. Why should I have need of riding clothes when I am to breakfast with the first minister?"

Red spots appeared on Browning's cheeks. "The last time you received an upsetting letter you were off instantly. I simply wondered if this letter had upset you in the same way?"

"Not the same way. As much as I would prefer to return

immediately to the Court, my Aunt Amelia has arrived there and is perfectly competent to sort out any difficulties in the neighborhood. Besides, I will likely be needed here to scotch the rumors which will make their way to town from Bath—'' Blackthorn's brow arched as Browning cleared his throat. ''—as I must assume, from that hesitant sound you just made, that they *have?*''

The valet nodded.

Blackthorn sighed. ''You might have warned me. What is being said?''

''Only that you've taken your doxy to the Court until the area in which she resides is clear of the danger of typhus.''

''My doxy. Only my doxy?''

''Also her son and daughters.''

''I am the sort of man to allow my son and heir to play cozily with the son and daughters of a doxy? *My* doxy?''

The valet blinked. ''I didn't think of that.''

''Then you've not contradicted what you've heard?''

''Er . . .'' Browning's eyes flicked toward his lordship and away. ''Well, hmm, in a word, no.''

''I think,'' said Blackthorn softly, ''that you might have done so *whatever* you might have believed yourself. The notion your master had taken a lightskirt to his home must have given you pause. You've known me for a very long time. I am, you think, the sort to do such a thing?''

''Well . . . no.''

''So.'' Blackthorn scowled. ''Browning, I am not pleased.''

''No, my lord.'' The valet clutched Blackthorn's robe tightly and then, quickly smoothed out the wrinkle his nerve-dampened hands caused.

His Lordship frowned, crossing his arms. ''I will be *less* pleased if you do not immediately remedy the situation.''

''At once, my lord.''

''Well?''

''Well, my lord?''

''Why do you stand there if you will instantly set about denying the gossip you've heard?''

The valet blinked. ''You haven't told me what I'm to say.''

''Ah.'' Blackthorn glared. ''I seem to remember that you knew I allowed my son to visit his friend for the summer?''

"Well . . . yes."

"And," His Lordship continued sternly, "You packed for me when I was forced to retrieve that same son from a region in which typhus was reported?"

"Er . . . yes."

"And I believe, when I returned to London, that I mentioned that I had delivered my son, my son's friend, the friend's mother and her nieces to the Court and wished that I might have stayed to see them settled? But that I did not since my responsibilities here in town called to me?"

The valet smiled. "Yes. It was just that way!"

"Then why do you ask what it is you are to say? The truth, of course."

"But," argued the valet, "she could still be your . . . er, no," he finished at Blackthorn's increasingly thunderous look. "She couldn't. She lives too far away, doesn't she?"

"To say nothing of the fact that I'd never met the woman before chasing down my son at the beginning of the summer and that, besides that, she is a woman well respected in her own region! *What is your problem?*"

"If I might be so bold, my lord," said Browning on a stubborn note, "you haven't been yourself since you met her. Couldn't help but wonder if . . ."

"You aren't paid to wonder!"

"Er, no sir."

"But you are human and you do so anyway." Blackthorn sighed. "Browning, do what you can as tactfully as you can. You may already have damaged the lady's reputation beyond repair by not jumping in to defend her, but let us see if we cannot put all right."

The valet's eyes widened. "You ain't saying you might be forced to wed the dox- . . . er, the bit of musli- . . . er, *whoever!*"

Blackthorn eyed his reddening valet. "I see you need still more convincing. Browning, Mrs. MacKivern is not and has never been a lightskirt. She is a widow, which is something you need not mention. What you *can* say is that she's as respectable as . . . as the queen!"

"But *is* she?"

"Blast you, Browning, when have I ever lied to you?"

"Then why, my lord," asked the valet, obstinate to the end, "have *you* changed, become so different?"

Blackthorn's lips compressed and his brows drew into a deep frown. "If it is any of your business, Browning, which it is not, I fear I've fallen deep in love. Since I've sworn I'll not rewed, it is unsettling, a bit of a fiasco to have done so! But Mrs. MacKivern is unaware of my feelings and will, come time for Winchester to open, return to her home *still* unaware of my lapse! Now are you completely clear on all dimensions? My aunt will see to Freder—*Mrs. MacKivern's*—reputation around the Court. It is up to you and me to see she does not suffer among those who love gossip here in town."

"Yes, my lord."

For another moment Blackthorn studied the man he'd thought completely loyal to himself. Now he wondered. Still, he hadn't time to think about it. He had to get to the first minister's house for their breakfast meeting!

"I've wasted too much time already, so I hope, Browning, you are now convinced!"

Wasted *far* too much time. He must hurry or he'd be late.

"Where's my hot water, Browning? I must shave. Quickly now . . ."

Chapter Ten

Dear Lord Blackthorn, as you are aware from her missive, your aunt, Lady Amelia, arrived this morning somewhat before lunch. Our introduction included accusations, an argument and, finally, a meeting of minds.

You must not worry about our initial discord, because you were, odious man that you are, quite correct when you predicted I'd like her. I enjoy Lady Amelia's impetuosity and admire her loyalty to you. She insists we cannot allow the present situation, which I believe she explained to you, to continue. I tell her it means nothing to me, but she says your *reputation will suffer so I've agreed to follow her lead.*

*She had been in the house not five minutes when she was
sorting through my wardrobe, tut-tutting and becoming quite
cross at its inadequacies which she deems grave, but she finally
agreed my rose day dress was not too badly out of date and,
once I'd donned it, agreed that it was, despite my carrot colored
hair, quite becoming. It has, I'll admit, always been a favorite
of mine . . .*

Was that far too informal? Should she begin again? But no.
It said only what was true, after all.

*. . . Within two hours of her arrival (I insisted we sit down
to a light luncheon or it would have been much sooner) she
was back in her carriage and we were on our way to Mrs.
Newton's which was far nearer than I'd any notion. I believe
I once rode not more than a quarter mile from the Newton
estate on an outing with the boys. In any case, Lady Amelia
rolled Mrs. Newton up foot and guns, as the military saying
is, and was in high good humor when we returned to the Court.
Which was just as well—*

Frederica experienced again an echo of the debilitating panic
she'd felt on their arrival home.

*—since we were greeted by the news my young hellion and
your son were missing which, as you may guess, sent me into
a tizzy. Lady Amelia asked what had been done to find them.
When it became clear that, except for a desultory search of the
nearer prospect* nothing *had been done, well, the dear lady
turned into such a general as Wellesley would be proud to call
his own and would much like to have under him in Spain for
his battles against the French!*

*I must immediately inform you, so that you will not worry,
that our sons are quite safe. They were found, covered in mud,
thoroughly soaked, but happy as larks, hobnobbing with a most
interesting if quite disreputable little man who was teaching
them to . . . tickle? Can that be correct? . . . fish. Why anyone
would* wish *to tickle fish, I've no notion, but the boys assure
me it is the best of good fun.*

*The man told Matthew he taught you to do the same, so
perhaps you know to whom I refer? So far as* I *am aware, the
fellow has no name! I believe the boys have taken no harm
from their afternoon's adventure, although I may not recover*

quite so quickly and I know that, if your aunt had not been here, I would have succumbed to hysterics that my son was missing and would have been of no use to anyone . . .

Once again her words were far more open than she quite approved, revealing, as they did, her inner thoughts in what she feared was an unacceptably frank fashion. But hadn't Lord Blackthorn suggested they try to get to know each other better through their letters? She bit her lip. Did she *want* him to know her better? Her weaknesses and failures? But wasn't it better that he understand sooner rather than later just how ill-suited she was to his life so that he'd cease giving out those exceedingly interesting hints that he wanted . . . more of her?

Frederica wished, once again, that she knew just exactly what "more" he had in mind. It would make her own feelings toward him clearer and her decision how to deal with him easier. How one could tell a man one would not succumb to lures when no lures had been cast was something of a difficulty. It was more difficult when one had to admit one was unsure that, under certain conditions, one would *not* succumb!

Then too, if it were *marriage* he wanted wouldn't she . . . But no! She'd not been bred to such high position. She would be as out of place as Countess of Blackthorn as Prinny would as groom to her mare. *As out of place as a hog on ice*—as Lady Amelia's maid, Berry, would say!

Frederica chuckled at this particular bit of evidence that Lady Amelia's maid had a weird way with words! Then, reminding herself that she was in an impossible position, she sighed. The sigh caught her attention. She looked at the clock and realized why she felt utterly exhausted. It was way past her bedtime and, given everything else she'd said which she probably should *not*, she decided she'd just tell him that too. As she reread her penultimate lines she grimaced at the word hysterics, however apt it might be!

And having admitted such weakness when it comes to my son, I'll also admit that it is late and I am tired. I hope your difficulties have smoothed themselves out and your days are less irritating than you've recently found them to be. Your servant, Frederica MacKivern.

* * *

Blackthorn reread Frederica's lively epistle, picked up his aunt's from a few days earlier, reread a paragraph in it, and laid both aside. He leaned back in his chair and tiny smile playing at his lips. Between them, Aunt Amelia and Frederica would have everything in order in no time at all.

He thought of his aunt's missive, which had arrived by the hand of the groom along with an earlier message from Frederica, of Amelia's admission she'd actually gone so far as to accuse Frederica of being his doxy and, once she'd straightened out that mistake, very likely insulted the poor dear once again, and unbearably, by denigrating her wardrobe.

Nevertheless, he'd been assured, they would attack the neighborhood at once and stem all adverse gossip instantly. She wrote that they'd begin with Lady Winston, go on to Lady Mapleton, then Mrs. Temple the vicar's wife, and then, if there was still time, to that awful Lady Newton's terrible house where the overabundance of gilding and scarlet hangings always gave her a headache. He would know, she said, that, in her beloved nephew's behalf, she would suffer even that.

So why, he wondered, had Frederica written that they'd gone *only* to Lady Newton's? Blackthorn put his mind to the problem and, finally remembered how very tired his aunt had been the last time she came to the Court. She'd also been, he'd thought, in great pain, but had refused to admit it and he'd decided, because of her behavior, that he was wrong.

Had the same been true again? Had Frederica, more perceptive, seen the same clues he'd seen, but come to a truer conclusion? And then, somehow, manipulated his unmanageable aunt into doing the sensible thing?

Blackthorn moved from his comfortable chair before his small fire to his desk and drew out paper. He'd find out, he decided, just what had happened.

Dear Frederica, he began, then wondered if he should change that to Mrs. MacKivern. But no. She knew it was how he thought of her. Why should he continue to pretend he did not? But to put it on paper . . . ?

Well, why not? The letter was unlikely to fall into anyone's hands but hers since he would send this, as he'd sent the last, by way of his groom.

Dear Frederica, I have just read your description of our wet and muddy young with great delight. It brought to mind long forgotten memories. The gentleman to whom you refer is known as Gray Shadow. I haven't a notion if that is his name or his sobriquet! He began the pursuit of poaching long ago, has lived by such means ever since, and, so far as I know, has never been brought to book.

Of course it could be that he took every young lad in the region in hand and trained them in his ways, believing—perhaps with reason—that if boys grew up thinking him a hero, they'd be less likely to prosecute him when in a position to be angered by his encroaching ways! I know I've turned a blind eye, even when my keeper has stormed and raged and demanded the man be brought to book for his depredations on my birds or fish. But, in my opinion, Gray does not take more than the land will bear and why should poor deprived Londoners not have access to the good things we take for granted?

Besides, I believe I've occasionally dined on my own trout when at certain tables here in town. Or off my pheasants! So why should I deprive myself, *if it comes to that? . . ."*

He grinned as he heard, in his mind, Aunt telling Frederica that they were his trout and his birds and if he wished to eat them in London, then he should have them sent up. How could he tease her a little? Ah. Tongue firmly in cheek, he added,

. . . You need not suggest I sell my own game rather than allow a poacher to make free with my holdings. You know very well I'd need to go into trade to do so and that would be outside of enough, would it not, putting me well beyond the pale in the opinion of polite society?

Would she think him serious? Or would she chuckle in that low husky way she had which caught at him and caused . . . Blackthorn grasped such thoughts firmly and put them, and the feelings aroused by them, firmly aside.

. . . I'm certain the boys enjoyed themselves immensely. And, believe me, our sons will come to no harm because of any little adventures they have with Gray.

Did that sound as if he encouraged the boys to misbehave? That wouldn't do!

. . . You might, however, inform them that if they ever again disappear without telling someone where they're off to, if they frighten you to death that way ever again, I'll drive down and personally take a rod to their behinds! That threat ought to keep them in line, but if it does not, you are to let me know. Having said I will do it, I will of course perform as promised!

Blackthorn reread that and grinned. If it weren't that Frederica was so easily frightened by her son's escapades, he'd indulge the hope their imps *would* run off, thus requiring him to fulfill his promise. Because, if he were forced to post down and give the boys a hiding, he could also see his Frederica face to face!

He picked up Frederica's letter and reread a large portion of it. Ah ha! He'd almost forgotten:

. . . I haven't a notion how you prevented Aunt Amelia from wearing herself to a thread when she'd just arrived, but I'm certain it was your doing she didn't follow through on the plan she outlined in her letter. My aunt refuses to give in to her disabilities, but I believe they've become far more of a problem then she's willing to admit. I admire her determination, but I fear for her health and well being. Thank you for seeing she didn't overdo.

Should he urge Frederica to continue watching over his favorite aunt? Well, his only aunt, but that wasn't relevant! But, Frederica would see to Amelia's comfort without prompting, so a request of that nature would, likely, be taken as an insult and bullying, if not worse. So. What else . . . ?

. . . I believe that just perhaps things are beginning to sort themselves out and have hopes that I may, before too long, leave behind the hot dirty streets of London for the fair clean air of the Court. I cannot tell how much I look forward to seeing you again . . .

Blackthorn reread that last bit and grinned. If he told her just how much he looked forward to it, she'd run away, screeching in fear and trepidation as she went!

"No she wouldn't," he muttered.

His grin widened. Not his Frederica. No, she'd very likely plan exactly how to scold him for admitting to such improper impulses. And she'd scold with all the verve and imagination of a fishwife, his beautiful termagant!

. . . When I arrive, we will take a pick-nick to the river and

I will show the boys that I myself have not forgotten how to tickle trout. Will that surprise them do you think?

Very likely it would, he thought, recalling his own childish belief his father had forgotten everything about how it was to be young! The notion of taking Frederica to lounge beside the river—even if they must take all four children and old Sal, a maid, and a footman who would see to the basket and blankets and fishing gear—put such titillating images into Blackthorn's mind that he abruptly rose from his chair and went to the window where he stared down into the open court to take his mind from such delicious visions.

Even at this late hour, people came and went. A mud-splattered coach passed the gate pulled by an obviously tired team. A sporting man who had rooms on the next floor rode in, his leathers splashed. A group of loud and boisterous young men, one of whom lived on the ground floor laid side bets on a dice game some grooms played in one corner. And, off to the side, a flower woman was seated among the remnants of her day's stock.

That poor old woman looked as tired as the sporting man's horse had looked, he thought. As tired as his aunt had likely been . . .

Impulsively, he rang for his valet. "Browning, take my purse and buy up the rest of that flower woman's stock. She is too old to be sitting there so late in the day. She should be in her bed."

Browning stared at his master. Without a word, although his expression said much, the valet stalked out of the room, only to return before he'd gotten so far as the stairs. "Just what am I to do with the flowers when I've bought them? My lord?"

Blackthorn grinned. "You may give them to that black-headed Welsh woman who works in the coffee house next door."

Two spots of color appeared in Browning's cheeks. "My lord!"

Blackthorn's smile faded instantly. "If that look implies what I think it suggests, you're a fool! *I've* no interest there! Or am I wrong that you've developed a tendre for her?"

The valet deflated. "Not to the point I'm foolish enough to give her a bouquet as big as a house!" he admitted ruefully.

"Then I suppose you must dump the flowers out behind the stable. All but the bit you give the Welsh woman!"

"Yes sir," mumbled his valet and, once again, left the room.

Blackthorn watched his man make the purchase from the bemused looking flower woman before returning to his desk. He reread his last few lines and, instantly, he was again making up dreams in which he lay beside his Frederica under a willow near the stream.

He could almost hear the buzzing of busy bees, the songs of squabbling birds, the gentle sound of moving water . . . and he could almost feel what it would be like to lean over his Freddy, to touch his lips to hers . . . and suddenly he was brought to his senses by a loud, querulous, and very young voice out in the hallway which insisted, at length, its mother was wanted!

Blackthorn's head jerked up. A child? In *this* building? If the owner had rented to a family, then it was time he opened Seymour House and moved back to the square! But, such a cry from one of her nieces was, he thought ruefully, just how *he* was likely to be interrupted if Frederica and he were, in reality, to behave in such a manner while on a picnic.

The querulous child's voice faded as a door closed and Blackthorn sighed. Perhaps he'd better open his townhouse. Or perhaps the thought was one more indication he was truly ready to marry and settle down? But how was he to court his lady if he were never to be alone with her? Discovering the means to be alone with his Frederica was, he thought, going to be a very large problem indeed, but one to which he'd find a solution. Or else!

At least, he would if only he could leave London and go to her where he'd have the opportunity of doing so!

"Lady Amelia, I did not expect you down so early. Will you check this week's menus with Mrs. Clapper?" Frederica tried to hand over the sheet of paper with the neatly listed menus. "For reasons I've not understood, she's insisted, ever since my arrival, that I do so, but now that you are here . . . ?"

"Menus?"

Frederica gestured toward the waiting housekeeper who stood stiffly to one side, her expression unrevealing.

Lady Amelia stared first at the paper and then at the housekeeper. After a moment during which some sort of information seemed to pass between them, she said, "Ah! The *menus. I've* no interest in such things, my dear. If you'd oblige our dear Mrs. Clapper, I'm quite certain she'd feel just as she ought and thank you kindly for your help."

Frederica didn't want to ignore the further speculative glance Lady Amelia cast toward the housekeeper, but she'd no opportunity to probe the matter just then because all four children, neatly dressed and brushed marched into the breakfast parlor. They stood in a row awaiting Frederica's attention, Sal to one side, a stern look on her face warning the youngsters to be quiet and to be patient.

Frederica turned to them. "Well, children. What plans have you today. You first, Maria."

Her niece stepped forward and, very softly and still with a trifle of trepidation, said that she and her sister were planning a tea party for the dolls under the wisteria vine.

"An excellent notion, but a word of warning." Frederica caught the girls' eyes, looking from one to the other and back again. "You are *not* to pretend the seeds of the wisteria are food for your party. You must, *under no circumstances whatsoever,* eat them because they will make you ill. Do you understand?"

"We won't Aunt Freddy," piped up the younger child. Showing a missing tooth and, revealing her awe by her hushed voice, she added, "Mrs. Clapper—" She cast a smile in the direction of the housekeeper. "—has said we may have a *proper* tea from the kitchen and a maid to help so we won't need to pretend, will we?"

"That sounds lovely. Boys?"

"The usual," said her son with a sigh. "Mr. Simpson has set us an essay on Ciceronianism and then—"

"Ciceronianism?" interrupted Lady Amelia.

"Cicero's style. We're to compare him to someone else." He shrugged. His frown disappeared, animation returning to his expression. "Gruddy says we may raise the bars today!"

Frederica felt wobbly at the mere thought. "Very nice I'm sure," she forced herself to say. "Run along now."

The girls went instantly to Sal and, each taking a hand, they walked out in a demure fashion. Stewart headed toward the door, but Matthew's few quiet words stopped him. When the door closed behind Sal and the girls, Lord Blackthorn's son approached Frederica.

"It is all right, Mrs. MacKivern. Truly it is. Gruddy would not allow us a higher jump if we were not ready for it."

"I know that, Matthew, and I try very hard not to worry, but I cannot help it. You are not to allow my concern to stop your practice, however. I am informed by an expert that most falls are due to the rider being poorly trained and I fear *that* still more, you see." She smiled. "It is not sensible of me, but there it is."

Matthew frowned, giving her a thoughtful look. "Perhaps it is that you are like other women after all?"

"And how is that, young Matthew?"

"Skitterwitted?"

"You think most women skitterwitted?" Frederica frowned when the boy nodded solemnly. "Some are, of course, just as some men are dolts, but I don't believe many woman are particularly shatterbrained. Where did you get such a notion?"

"From Cook. A long time ago I overheard her telling a maid my father would not remarry because he'd been put off women by my mother's skitterwitted ways!"

Frederica heard Lady Amelia muffle a chuckle and couldn't quite repress a smile herself. "Perhaps she was exaggerating, Matthew, but even if she was not, you mustn't believe all women are that way. It would not be true, you see."

"Ah, then perhaps I was wrong and it isn't that women are skitterwitted that they . . . Stu, let go!" he said when Stewart pulled urgently at his arm. "Perhaps—" He jerked his sleeve from Stewart's grasp. "—Do let go, Stu! Perhaps—" He turned on his friend who had once again grasped his arm. "—Why do you . . ." His brows rose at Stewart's grimace and he nodded. "Oh. Yes, of course . . ."

"Boys?" asked Frederica, looking with curiosity from one to the other.

"Hmm. Nothing." Matthew, red around the ears, looked at his feet.

"May we go?" asked her son, a wary eye on his friend. "We've that essay . . ."

After a moment's hesitation during which she decided against probing into the boys' secrets, she said, "You may go." She waited for the door to close. Turning on Lady Amelia, she tipped her head. "I wonder what that was all about."

"I haven't a notion, but skitterwitted certainly fits Spencer's dead wife to a cow's thumb . . . to quote my maid still again! I know one should not speak ill of the dead, and I wondered for a moment if Matthew felt insulted his mother was referred to in such a way, but you cannot *know* . . ." Lady Amelia's chuckles broke out and stopped her flow of words. "If only you knew . . ."

"I will have words with Cook," said Mrs. Clapper sternly. "She should not speak of such things to the maids!"

"Ah. Mrs. Clapper!" exclaimed Lady Amelia. "I'd forgotten you were here. Frederica, do look at the menus and then we'll get on with our breakfast. Now that I'm rested, I've a full day planned for us. We'll leave cards on all and sundry and visit with a few old friends. Besides that, I'll stop in the village to see what, if anything, is available in the shop which might be made up into a gown or two . . ."

The door closed behind Mrs. Clapper and her menus, which Frederica had checked as her ladyship rambled on, crossing out two items she felt too elaborate for a simple country meal and adding a new dish to another. "I cannot and will not buy a new gown, Lady Amelia," she said sternly.

Lady Amelia's brows climbed toward her well groomed hair. "Now did I say the gowns were for you?"

Frederica felt her skin warming. "I apologize if . . ."

"Well, they are," interrupted Lady Amelia. "My gift to you."

"No."

"Mrs. MacKivern, you cannot go about in rags!"

"Lady Amelia, my dresses are not in rags."

"They might as well be," said an exasperated Lady Amelia sharply. "So out of style as they are!"

"I will not pretend to be other than I am," retorted Frederica with some heat. *"Which is a not-impoverished but not-wealthy widow!"*

Amelia sighed. "Surely you could afford an Irish muslin for a day dress? Mrs. Clapper has a surprisingly good hand at cutting a sleeve and I'm sure she's trained that daughter of hers to be a more than adequate seamstress since she has such ambition for the girl!"

"Sarrie is very good with a needle. She mended a rent in Bitsy's gown I thought impossible to fix and, once, when I stepped on a flounce, she fixed it so you'd never know I'd torn it."

"Then she can sew up one or two gowns for you," said Lady Amelia, her expression set in rather belligerent lines.

Frederica thought of her slender funds. She'd set aside what would be necessary for vails for the servants here and on her way home at the end of the summer. She'd also decided how much she'd give the local vicar before she left. And what did that leave her? Enough for their transport home and very little left over.

"I can see you are thinking carefully. What have you in the way of expenses, that you hesitate?"

Frederica promptly told her.

"Oh, my dear, surely you know you'll have no expenses getting home! Spencer will send you behind his own coachman and, if he does not go himself, will send a well-trained groom to see to your comfort. Which must leave you well to do, given the cost of travel these days! Just two dresses?" she coaxed.

"I do not believe I should allow Lord Blackthorn to pay my way."

"But he will allow nothing else, so there you have it!"

"I will," said Frederica after a moment, "buy enough dimity for one day gown."

"Only one?"

Frederica nodded firmly.

"Better than nothing I suppose," grumbled Lady Amelia and applied herself to her egg.

An hour later they arrived at the Winston manor where Lady Amelia was warmly welcomed by Lady Winston who then turned a smiling face toward Frederica.

"I am very glad to have the opportunity, finally, of meeting you," said that plump matron. "I'd thought to leave cards on you, but you've shown no interest in meeting any of your neighbors and I concluded you were, as is now proven true, awaiting Amelia, who would introduce you around!" She smiled widely. "And none too soon, Amelia! It would have been far better if you'd come sooner. *Before* the tales began circulating. Alfred and I laughed merrily, I assure you, at the latest!"

Thinking of their awkward introduction upon her arrival at the Court, Lady Amelia cast a very slightly shamefaced glance toward Frederica and then turned back to her friend. "Just what *is* being said?"

"The most common report is that Mrs. MacKivern is governess to the little girls staying at the Court. All but a few agree that Blackthorn would, under no circumstances whatsoever bring his light o' love to his own home, especially when his son is under his roof, so that particular speculation is noised only by those few who wish him ill. Then there is the version in which he has taken a destitute relative into his home along with her children until he can arrange something more permanent for her, a notion which some actually believe and, finally, there is a tale whispered to the effect that she knows something to Lord Blackthorn's detriment and is blackmailing him into allowing her and her brats houseroom!" finished an obviously delighted Lady Winston.

"What a mishmash of nonsense!"

"Of course. And now—" Lady Winston smiled broadly, a cat eating cream smile. "—I shall be *the very first* to hear the truth!"

"Actually you won't," said Lady Amelia bluntly. "I decided to begin with the worst offender and we visited Mrs. Newton the day I arrived. I enjoyed setting that sharp-tongued gossip straight!"

"You've yet to set *me* straight," said Lady Winston encouragingly, looking expectantly from one to the other.

Still again explanations were made. Lady Amelia ended her tale by explaining why they couldn't stay, that they meant to stop at as many homes as possible, leaving cards and making one or two brief visits.

"My very dearest of old friends," said Lady Winston, her

wistful look an obvious sham, "I don't suppose you've room in your carriage for a third?"

Lady Amelia and Frederica looked at each other and each broke into a broad smile. "I'm quite certain we *do*," said Frederica dryly "That is, we do if you mean to come with us, letting the local ladies know that you too approve of me!"

"Ah! Such a bright mind our new friend has," said Lady Winston, beaming. "Now if you'll just settle yourselves here while I change, I promise I'll not take more than one or two moments."

"You'll be back before the cat can lick his whiskers," said Amelia in a sly tone.

"What?" In her confusion Lady Winston blinked.

Amelia grinned. "I've a new maid. I've had such fun learning all sorts of new expressions from her. That, I assure you, is one of the milder ones!"

Shaking her head, Lady Winston left the room and Frederica turned to Blackthorn's aunt. "Have you other friends as nice as this one?"

"One or two. Unfortunately, you'll discover several you'll wish to avoid like the plague. Unfortunately, you'll also discover they stick to you like plaster! We'll be very circumspect in *their* company, I assure you!"

"They are like Lord Quincy, and would make up a tale if the truth is uninteresting?"

"I know of no one who comes close to Lord Quincy's versatility in such matters," said Amelia with just a touch of acid. "Unfortunately there are *other* ways of making a nuisance of oneself. One lady is encroaching. She'll put herself forward, telling you how much she can do for you, but in truth will be on the watch for anything *you* may do for *her*. There's one who has her eye on my nephew, not that he's ever given her a bit of encouragement. She won't like you at all and another who, I believe, briefly had Blackthorn's eye. She's another who will not love you, though she's a married lady and had no hope of catching more than his eye!"

"They sound like perfectly normal human beings. I must admit I've wondered about Lord Quincy!"

"He's a blot on creation, but is, I fear, all too human. Ah—"

she added as Lady Winston returned, ''—that *was* quick. Shall we go?''

They went. And it was just as boring a day as Frederica had feared. She'd never enjoyed keeping to the careful rules governing morning visits and hoped they'd not have to do it again any time soon. She was looking forward to reaching home and seeing all was well with the children when the carriage pulled into the village inn's small yard.

''Lady Amelia? Is something wrong?''

''Wrong?''

''Why have we stopped?''

Lady Amelia grinned. ''You've forgotten you are to choose a new gown!''

Frederica, who *had* forgotten, sighed. ''I did, but that's not a problem is it, as you've remembered it for me. And I was *so* looking forward to putting up my feet and hiding my nose in a book!''

Lady Amelia merely chuckled as she led the way to the shops.

Chapter Eleven

Frederica found that the days passed surprisingly pleasantly after Lady Amelia arrived. She was the first compatible female acquaintance she'd had about her for any length of time and Frederica discovered that her fears that a female companion would interfere in her life unbearably were not necessarily true. Lady Amelia joined in her interests, which doubled her pleasure in them ... except for her teaching the maids to read and write. There she and Her Ladyship disagreed strongly and never ceased to find a great deal of enjoyment in their ongoing, on-the-whole-friendly argument.

They were discussing it when Stewart and Matthew raced into the drawing room to inform them that Lord Blackthorn's valet had arrived with boxes and trunks and the word that Lord Blackthorn himself would appear well before dinner.

"Oh dear. And we've nothing more interesting planned than a roast chicken!" exclaimed Lady Amelia.

"Should I go at once to ask Cook what might be contrived at such short notice?" She rose to her feet. "Does Lord Blackthorn prefer several courses to his dinner?"

"We'll both go. I will make his favorite onion pie and you, my dear may fix that compote you contrived last Sunday when I impulsively invited Lord and Lady Winston and the vicar and his wife to dine with us. With another side dish or two that will be sufficient. Or, if the man does want more, I will inform him it is his own fault for not sending ahead any warning."

As she spoke, Lady Amelia struggled to rise, grasped her cane firmly, and started for the door. Halfway there she tripped over nothing at all and fell, letting out a muffled shriek.

Instantly Frederica knelt beside the older woman. "Lady Amelia. You are hurt!"

"I fear I am, my dear." Her Ladyship had a white look around the mouth. "My arm . . ."

"Don't move it. Stewart, find Mrs. Clapper at once. And Jennings, Stewart." As she spoke Frederica examined Amelia. "Tell Jennings to send a footman for the doctor. I fear Lady Amelia's arm is broken." She soothed her friend's objections to calling the leech. "Ah, Mrs. Clapper. Ice, if you will. I find that when there is swelling, as there most often is with a broken bone, that ice helps to reduce it and, also, eases the pain one feels. Jennings, you have sent for the doctor? Good. Now I believe we must contrive to take Lady Amelia to her room. What would you suggest?"

Jennings ordered the largest and strongest footman to carry her ladyship up to her room, although Lady Amelia protested that as well. "It is not my legs which are hurt! I can walk."

"But you might jar the break," soothed Frederica. "The less movement, the less damage, you know."

"I am totally chagrined, my dear," complained Lady Amelia as she allowed herself to be picked up, "that this has happened."

"You must rest and not worry. I watched closely as you made that onion pie just last week. I believe I can do something similar if you will trust me to try. And the compote is so simple it can be made by anyone. I will set one of the kitchen maids to that as soon as I'm certain you are settled.''

"You will order the extra side dishes?'' asked Her Ladyship, anxiously.

"I'll not forget.''

Frederica followed the men who carried Lady Amelia upstairs and watched while Her Ladyship's maid removed her clothing, ripping seams open on both dress and chemise. That Her Ladyship was in far more pain than she would admit was proven when she didn't object to this desecration of one of her favorite gowns.

Ice was packed around the arm, towel wrapped, and a waxed cloth spread to catch the dampness as it melted. Frederica could see her friend relax as the cold eased the pain.

"I'll do, my dear. Berry will sit with me so *you* get yourself along to the kitchen!''

Knowing Lady Amelia would only fret if she did not, Frederica reluctantly took herself off. She was nearly down the stairs when Jennings hurried to throw open the doors. Lord Blackthorn had arrived.

Frederica couldn't take her eyes from him. His, meeting hers, never wavered. Removing his gloves, he approached her. "Rickie,'' he said softly.

"My lord?''

"It is good to see you. You and my aunt are well?''

His question roused her from her preoccupation with this man who took up far too much of her thoughts, Frederica bit her lip. "Actually . . . no.''

"My aunt?'' His tone sharpened, that warmth she hadn't known she craved leaching from his gaze.

"She fell not half an hour ago and her arm is broken. I've sent for the doctor and packed it in ice. I should be with her now,'' she said a trifle defensively, but rallying, added, "if it were not for you!''

"And how am I at fault?'' he asked, the trace of a smile returning.

"You, my lord, require an onion pie for dinner and she demands I see to it at once.''

"And how well I know my aunt! She'll not rest easily if

you do *not* tend to it, will she. You, on the other hand, will fret that you are not with her. I see a solution.''

"You will see to the pie?'' asked Frederica innocently.

"Tease! I can just see the results of *my* endeavors in such a cause! You, my dear, will do the pie, while I go to my aunt. Or do you not trust me to keep her as quiet as may be?''

"I've proof you do very well in a sickroom, my lord," said Frederica, sobering. "I do not forget that you sat with my son."

"Speaking of your son," he said, glancing around, "just where are the scions of our respective houses?''

"For once I neither know nor care. Concern for your aunt has driven all other matters from my mind! You will oblige me, my lord, by giving your gloves to Jennings who has been waiting for them and you will then take yourself upstairs to your aunt while—" She sighed. "—I make a pie.''

He handed over not only the gloves and hat but his crop as well. "You need not, you know." Free to do so, he moved nearer and took her hand between his. "Not if it will distress you."

"And you, of course—" Her eyes on their clasped hands, she forced a light tone. "—will explain how that came about when your aunt asks for a sliver and then perhaps a second serving with her supper?''

He grinned. "She'll not admit to a liking for such a plebeian dish but uses any excuse to make it." As if he could not prevent himself, he reached to touch her cheek. "I, however, freely admit it is a favorite with me as well.''

"Then I'll get on with it although I doubt it will be the same as hers. Jennings, take the doctor up the moment he arrives, please.''

Jennings nodded, but Frederica didn't notice. She was already on her way to the green baize-covered door which led to the butler's pantry and from there to the servant's dining room and, beyond that, into the kitchen. There she discovered Cook already elbow-deep in flour, spewing orders right and left to her helpers.

"I see you have things well in hand, Cook," said Frederica, quietly finding what she needed for her pie.

"Browning came down as soon as he saw His Lordship's boxes to his rooms. Said His Lordship told him to tell us not to concern ourselves with his unexpected arrival. He said he was quite willing to take pot luck.'' Cook sniffed. ''As if we would allow such a mean meal to be set before His Lordship as you and Her Ladyship persist in thinking sufficient!''

Frederica wondered if that hadn't been a rather royal 'we.' ''I'm very glad to see you know what is proper.'' She asked which kitchen maid could most easily be spared to see to the compote which Lady Amelia had requested and watched only a moment before she sensed the girl knew what she was about.

The room settled down some then. Frederica soon had a crust ready for the deep flat dish in which the onions and custard would be poured and, not long after she'd removed the partially baked crust from the oven she put it back complete with the filling.

''I'll see it comes out at the proper time,'' said Cook complacently from where she checked that a fricassee would not scorch. ''I do regret there will not be a joint, but one cannot *make* time for things which *take* time when there *is* no time.''

''No, it would require waiting forever to serve dinner, would it not? His lordship rather likes a rabbit pot pie, but even that simple dish requires long cooking for the flavors to marry properly.'' Frederica lifted a lid, wandered to where the maid was pouring wine over peeled and chopped fruit and came back to check on her pie.

Cook stepped between her and the oven. ''You are fretting to return to her ladyship. You needn't fear I'll not set a proper meal before His Lordship! Maybe not just in the style to which he is accustomed but the ham is particularly good. Jennings may slice it at the sideboard and we've fish, thanks to your son and our lordling.''

''Matthew and Stewart have certainly been putting their new skill into practice, have they not?'' asked Frederica, smiling. ''Yes, a nice platter of trout along with the ham and chicken should be more than sufficient. And you are correct. I am fretting about Lady Amelia.''

She thanked the maid who had helped her and left the kitchen by way of the back stairs. Soon she knocked softly and entered Lady Amelia's sitting room where she found Lord Blackthorn walking the floor, stopping to look at the bedroom door whenever he turned that way.

"The doctor is with her?"

"Yes. He told me to take myself away."

"He will not tell me to go," said Frederica and determinedly entered the bedroom where she found Lady Amelia in tears. "What is this?"

"Merely that the bone will not come into place," said the doctor. "Leave. I cannot have distractions."

Frederica watched, her temper rising, for perhaps two minutes before she turned on her heel and exited the room. "Lord Blackthorn, tell that man to leave this instant. He is mauling her! I believe you and I can do better without him."

Blackthorn frowned. "I have watched bones set before, but have never done it. Are you certain?"

A vein throbbed in her forehead. "We can certainly do no worse!"

The doctor, protesting wildly, was forcibly ejected from Her Ladyship's side. Then Frederica watched anxiously as Lord Blackthorn, perspiration dotting his forehead, gently went about the delicate task of setting the bone. All three were relieved when it was done and the arm bound against a board. Frederica insisted Lady Amelia take a dose of laudanum, which Her Ladyship much disliked doing, but the arm was badly swollen thanks to the doctor's incompetent handling and she allowed that it hurt like the very devil.

"If you had not taken a dose the pain would keep you awake all night," soothed Frederica and added, "I believe sleep is healing, my lady."

"It does feel better," admitted Her Ladyship, her eyes growing heavy.

"Why did you not call me in?" asked Lord Blackthorn.

"He said it would hurt and that I must accept it."

"He hadn't a notion what he was doing. How does someone like that have the nerve to call himself a doctor?" asked Frederica.

"He is all we have," said Lady Amelia, her words slurring as the opiate did its work, her eyelids drooping, lifting, drooping slowly once again.

Her maid was again set to watching her and Lord Blackthorn led Frederica from the room. "That tired you," he said.

"Whenever it is necessary that I make a decision of that sort

I always worry that I do the *wrong* thing, but that man was impossible! Someone had to try to do it right and you did very well. You had just the right touch, gentle but firm, not at all tentative or hesitant. Now I know why you wished to be a doctor!''

"Now I've done that bit, I don't know that I would like it. That was *work,* worrying the whole time that I would only make things worse. And what if I did? Make it worse, I mean?'' he asked, still worried.

"You set it properly. You did just as you should," insisted Frederica and then frowned. "Did we tell her maid the ice packs must be replaced all evening and perhaps on into the night? I can't remember . . ."

"We did and they will be. But I'd best check that we are not low on ice in our ice house. If we are, I'll send to Lord Winston for more. Come now," he coaxed. "Have a glass of wine with me. You need it and for at least the last two or three miles I looked forward to something to slake my thirst—and that was, at the very least, an hour ago!''

Lord Blackthorn took Frederica to his library where, after she sipped her wine and leaned back for a bit in one of the chairs pulled up near the empty fireplace, she raised her lids to discover Blackthorn's gaze on her.

"Dimity, Dorcas or Damask?"

"What?"

"Your middle name."

She smiled. "You've not yet guessed, my lord."

He pretended to sigh. "I'll get it yet. Now, tell me what has been happening. Have our boys had any more adventures?"

"They are still practicing what they learned on their last one. You'll enjoy the fruits of their labors with your dinner, but I believe you'd better have a word with them if you wish to have any trout left in your stream for fishing! They are most assiduous."

"Where are they now?"

She frowned. "They ran in to tell us of your valet's arrival, but then Amelia fell and, well, frankly, I've no more notion than a babe. I'll just . . ." She started to get up.

He gently pushed her back. "They'll keep. You rest." He relaxed only when she, after a moment's dithering, did so. Then he talked about his last few days in London. ". . . I couldn't believe it when Prinny finally signed the full agreement. Not a one of us had thought to get home before Christmas!"

"The boys, I think, had about decided you'd not be able to take Matthew to London this fall after all. Matthew is disappointed, but I believe they've been planning for Christmas instead. Actually, I think Stewart was pleased. If you and Matthew do not go up to London, then Stewart will have several more days here at the Court and, frankly, he likes it here, being put through his paces by Gruddy and having a friend to play with."

"I'd not forgotten my promise concerning Astley's." Elbow on the arms of his chair, Blackthorn toyed with his empty wineglass, watching her over the top of it. "I'd a notion to take *all* of you up to town for a week or so. Before sending you and the girls back to your home, you know. Dr. Milltown wrote me, by the way, and says it is safe again. But now—" He frowned. "—with my aunt in bed . . ."

Frederica nodded. "Lady Amelia will not feel like travel for some time, I fear. Actually, I, too, had a letter only yesterday. From Ian. He says he thinks it time I return. He admits he misses his daughters and wants them home again."

"But you *will* go by way of London?" asked Blackthorn a trifle sharply.

"I had thought to go back through Oxford and Burford rather than the way we came," she said. "But we need not go all the way to London to do that."

"Only a few days?" he coaxed.

"I think not."

"I thought to take *all* the children to Astley's, you see." He watched her purse her lips, the faintest hint of a frown between her eyes. "They would enjoy it," he added.

"And you will not?" asked Frederica, her eyes suddenly gleaming with humor.

"Do you think less of me that I admit I'll enjoy the show nearly as much as the children will?"

"I think *more* of you, my lord, that you will own to it!"

"You would enjoy it too."

Frederica thought of her inadequate wardrobe and her dislike of crowds. "I might . . ."

"It is a long drive whichever way you go. I arranged that you, my aunt, and the girls stay with a lady who is Aunt Amelia's very good friend. Now Amelia will not wish to travel, but you and the girls may do so even if she does not. I do not believe you should try to reach home in only two days. It would leave the children, in particular, exceedingly tired and Sal is not young. It would be hard on her. A day's drive to London where they may rest and then two days more . . . ?"

He eyed her, the sort of hopeful expression she'd occasionally seen on his son's face when the lad was wheedling a favor from her. "I will agree to two nights in London," said Frederica, capitulating.

"Three?" he instantly asked. "I had thought to take you and Lady Amelia to a concert . . ."

"You are forgetting that Lady Amelia will be unable to go. Two."

"We'll discuss it again. Now I'm sure that you're recovered, I believe I must change from all the dirt of traveling." He rose to his feet and started for the door, saying as he reached it, "I will see you again at dinner, my dear."

Frederica's head came up sharply. But he was gone. "I really must," she muttered, "have a word with His Lordship about those endearments he tosses around so casually. It is not at all proper."

Hidden behind curtains covering a bowed window, the two boys grinned at each other. Later that night, when they were supposed to go to sleep, they talked it over and decided that if Lord Blackthorn were calling Mrs. MacKivern "my dear," then surely that meant their plan was moving along quite nicely.

"Now," said Stewart a day or two later, "if we can just figure out how to keep Mama in London for several extra days . . . ?"

"If you were to get sick," suggested Matthew, "she'd have to stay to care for you."

"I was sick once this summer. It's your turn. She'd be as likely to stay for you as me."

"How about if one of the *girls* were to get sick . . ." asked Matthew, ignoring what he didn't wish to hear.

"Much better," agreed Stewart admiringly. "That way you

wouldn't have to stay in bed. How does one make someone sick?''

They thought about it for a bit and finally, reluctantly, Stewart admitted, ''I don't think Mama would like it if we were to make one of them *really* sick ...'' he said doubtfully, ''but Maria, particularly, isn't a good traveler. If we convince her she'll feel better if she rests longer, maybe she'd pretend?''

''But she couldn't be sick when she first gets there or she'd miss Astley's!''

''She wouldn't like that, would she?'' asked Stewart thoughtfully. ''So maybe she could say she ate too many sweets and had a tummy ache?''

''I don't know if she can tell a good lie and she'd have to, wouldn't she?'' Matthew sighed. ''It's difficult, getting them married, isn't it?''

''I didn't think it would take so long,'' agreed Stewart. ''I thought they'd just *know* it was a good notion. Or something.'' He yawned. ''How *do* people decide to get married?''

''Well—'' Matthew's forehead creased. ''—sometimes it is needing heirs, I think, but we're the heirs so they won't be worrying about that.''

Stewart yawned again. ''Property, then? I remember my aunt saying my father was pleased when my mother inherited from her father. But he couldn't have been too pleased since he sold that estate and bought another one which will be mine someday.'' Stewart yawned still more widely. ''It is supposed to be in a better location or something. Or so my aunt, who is always talking about such things, says ... although I do not understand why anyone would wish to be closer to London which is what *she* meant. I mean, except for Astley's and a few things like that, why would one want to live in the middle of busy streets with nowhere to play?''

This time Matthew couldn't respond. He'd succumbed near the beginning of Stewart's comment to the arms of Morpheus. After all, thinking about marriage was exceedingly boring.

The next morning, after checking on his aunt, Frederica joined Lord Blackthorn in the breakfast room. ''Most of the swelling is down,'' she said by way of greeting.

"I stopped by myself before coming down. She insisted everything was just fine."

"Yes," objected Frederica, "but she does that. She can ache in every joint but will not admit it. I checked for myself. I do wish I'd had the sense to discover whether your local doctor was any good before calling him in. You would have thought I'd have heard gossip about the man or some stray comment here or there. Something."

"Do not feel guilty. You are so used to Dr. Milltown that you are not aware just how inadequate many medical men are. They are not required to take courses in medicine, you know. It is merely that they must pass tests in Latin and Greek."

"It is believed they must say incantations in an antique language while dancing around the ill, perhaps?" asked Frederica scathingly. "Why are men sometimes so utterly absurd about the truly important things?"

Blackthorn recalled the absurdity of the political backing and forthing which had gone on from the moment the king's condition was admitted to be incurable and that a Regency must be established. "Perhaps we are simply made that way?"

"Absurd!"

He laughed at her response.

"Besides," she said primly, "I have known *several* perfectly sensible gentlemen."

"So many as that?" he asked, keeping his features sober with effort.

"And I believe many more *might* be sensible if only they would make the attempt."

He grinned. "I cannot top you, can I? By the way, Deborah, Dinah, Dorothy?"

"Not even close."

"I begin to think you were named for a city. Damascus perhaps, or Delhi? Were your parents traveling when you were born?"

"To my knowledge, they never went anywhere farther than Bath in the whole of their lives. Or is Oxford farther away?" She frowned. "I must look at a map."

"Your father was an Oxford man?"

"He attended Christ Church, my lord."

"I am a Baileiol man myself."

"Have you enrolled Matthew there?"

"Yes. It is the thing to do, is it not?"

They discussed their sons' futures in a light and bantering fashion until the boys themselves entered the breakfast room. "You wished to see us, my lord Father?" asked Matthew when the adults noticed them and motioned them forward.

"I do believe I did." Blackthorn pretended to frown. "The thing is, I can't just off hand, recall exactly why it was I demanded your presence."

Frederica chuckled. "You, my lord, are a Banbury man. You know very well you wished to ascertain with your own eyes that your son was in good health."

"Ah yes. Perhaps that was it. And I see that you are. Do you ride later?"

"When we have finished with our tutor, Grubby will continue schooling us over the jumps."

"Then I had best allow you to remove to the schoolroom, had I not? The sooner you finish there, the sooner you will enjoy Grubby's interminably telling you you can—" His voice became more guttural and a scolding tone entered into it. "—do better nor *that.*"

The boys chuckled, looked at each other, sobered, nodded, and, as one, turned on their heels to leave.

"Boys!" Frederica called after them in a *truly* scolding tone.

They turned back, their cheeks red. "Sorry," said Matthew, his eyes flying briefly toward his father. "We wish you both a pleasant day," he added, bowing.

"Sorry, Mother," said Stewart. "Oh! We forgot to ask about Lady Amelia. Is her arm better?" he asked politely.

"Considerably better, thank you. Now the pain is lessened she will be bored. She would like you to come to her this afternoon for a few minutes. I suggest you ask the gardener to pick you a nice bouquet to take in to her."

The boys sighed in unison, nodded, looked from one to the other and waited, obviously impatiently.

"You may go," said Frederica after a moment, when she realized why they did not.

They were gone in an instant.

"My son appears to have found his tongue," said Blackthorn approvingly. "Do I have you to thank for that?"

"Perhaps. I have been teaching them to answer promptly, fully, but without excess. Matthew feels far more comfortable now he has some notion of what is proper and what is not. And he also begins to believe you have some feeling for him, which he did *not* only months ago."

Blackthorn picked up his half-empty cup and, unconsciously, held it like a shield before him. "You would scold me. And with reason. I felt guilty when my wife died," he mused, "because I'd felt so little of *anything* for her for far too long. I threw myself into my political work so I need not think of how relieved I was that the foolish woman was no longer a millstone around my neck. Because he reminded me of her, I suppose I avoided my son. I am sorry for it." He frowned. "Surely no permanent damage has been done him?"

Frederica was not put off by his chill tone. She knew how difficult it must be for him to admit so much. Warmly, she said, "He is a good boy and I do not believe he has been badly scarred—" She paused. "—providing . . .

"Providing," he interrupted, "that I do not in future once again forget I've a son." After a short pause during which he touched his tongue to the center of his upper lip as he eyed her. "I believe I need *you* to keep me to the proper road, my dear."

Frederica rose abruptly to her feet. "You must not."

More slowly, Blackthorn rose, holding his napkin in one hand. "Must not what?"

"Must not say . . . such things."

He frowned. "What did I say? I cannot think what could possibly cause such heat. That I need you? But I do. Your good sense and easy humor are just what is needed here, by me and by all of us."

Had he not even noticed that he'd called her his dear? Frederica's lips thinned. Her eyes darted from one thing to another. Should she or should she not make a more specific objection? But if he did not even notice what he'd done, would it not be rather forward to point it out to him? Perhaps even hint to him that she liked it, that she wished for even more from him?

"Frederica?"

"I . . . must check the flowers, my lord."

She left the breakfast room, her plate still half full, a steaming cup of tea which she'd just poured for herself at her place. Lord Blackthorn looked from one to the other. He sighed. Why must his Rickie be so prickly? It had only been the simplest of endearments, had it not? Well, he'd just have to be more careful in future.

"It would seem," he muttered, his hand touching the outside surface of the pocket hidden beneath his jacket, "that I was a trifle premature when I bought the license?"

"My lord?" asked Jennings, who was patiently waiting in one corner to serve whatever was required.

"You there, Jennings? Sorry. I was talking to myself, I fear. A very bad habit I acquired in London and one of which I'd best rid myself."

He eyed his tea, blowing on it softly to cool it, and wondered if the man had heard his words. "And very quickly too!" he muttered. Especially here, he thought, where everyone has known me forever.

"Jennings," he added once he'd finished his meal, "I will be with my aunt if needed. I brought a new book down from town which I'd thought to give her, but perhaps it would be more distracting if I were to read it to her. Do not, please, disturb us for a trifle—only if the house is on fire or some such?"

"Yes sir," said Jennings—and wondered if he dared tell even Mrs. Clapper that His Lordship was so desirous of wedding Mrs. MacKivern he'd bought a license! Reluctantly, he decided he'd better not. His Lordship would not approve his passing on information he was not supposed to have.

Stewart and Matthew lay hidden in their favorite spot in hay stored above the cow barn where, with a window flung open, they could lie back and see for miles. They each nibbled an apple inveigled from Cook and stared at the countryside laid before them.

"It isn't the same as what I know at home, but I like this country," said Stewart, thinking of the wold and comparing the two.

"My father once said Kent is the Garden of England."

"Yes. I had that from my tutor when we studied the globes,"

agreed Stewart. "Did you hear Mama order Sal to begin packing for the girls?" he continued, abruptly changing the subject. "That she's changed her mind and decided we go home and *not* up to London?"

"Yes." Matthew sighed. "You are going home and nothing is settled. Did she say you'd come back at Christmas?"

"She didn't say and if we are not to go to London, our plan to ask one of the girls to pretend to be ill won't fadge." Stewart scowled. "There must be *something* we can do to keep them together!"

"I agree, but what? I thought when Father arrived, your mother was glad to see him—but perhaps that was because of Aunt Amelia?"

Stewart set his teeth just a trifle off center, a habit he had when thinking. "I wondered if that were it, but I think she *does* like having him here. You know. Just because it's him. You've heard how they tease, and you don't tease where you don't like! Matt, we *must* keep them together a little longer."

Only the crunch of apple could be heard for some time. Idly, Matthew said, "I suppose I was foolish, but I wondered, when we heard he was coming, what we'd done that he must post down to beat us. Remember your mother reading that bit from one of his letters? It was silly, was it not? We *hadn't* done anything. Well—" He turned to meet Stewart's eyes and grinned quickly. "—nothing they know about anyway!"

The boys had spent a delightful few hours tickling fish in the Newton trout stream some days previously. It was definitely something the adults would not approve, but old Newton was such a screw and had been so mean when they'd strayed completely by accident, not meaning to at all, onto his land one day. He deserved to have his fish stolen!

"But maybe he does know?" said Stewart slowly.

"Don't be silly."

"No. Really. Or at least, maybe we *think* he knows? And are afraid of him? And don't want a beating? And maybe—" Stewart lowered his voice to a mere thread of sound. "—we run away?"

"Why would we do that? Even if he does discover—"

Matthew's words, spoken in a normal tone, were cut off by

Stewart's hand over his lips. When released, he continued, but more softly.

"—our adventure, it's only a beating. He'd not be too hard on us."

"You're a stupe! We want to get them married, don't we?"

"Yes, but I guess we'll have to wait until your Christmas visit."

"If we come! Besides, that's us and a whole lot of other people!"

Matthew stared across the countryside. "You mean we need to get them married now, before a lot of strangers are around to interfere and distract them?"

Stewart nodded. "So, you see if we were to run away, then they'll stay together until we're found and surely they'll decide they should stay together forever!"

Again Matthew was silent, thinking. "I don't know, Stu. Your mother would be upset. You know the way she gets. Would she be thinking about marrying my father if she were worrying the whole time about you?"

"I don't think he'd let her worry. I think he'd help her and she *needs* help. She's only a woman, you know, even if she is better than most—as women go, that is."

"I thought your Uncle Ian helped her."

"Yes, but Aunt Tilda wishes he wouldn't, I think, although I don't see why."

Again they stared in silence out the window.

Finally Stewart asked, "Can you think of another plan?"

"No."

"Then should we do it?"

The boys were silent for another stretch. "I guess we'd better," said Matthew, finally.

"Then the quicker the better since we're to go any day now. It's too late to leave today, so maybe tomorrow?"

Matthew nodded hesitant agreement.

"We'll write notes," Stewart continued, the plan forming even as he spoke. "One for our parents and one for our tutor telling him your father is taking us off for a treat and we won't be in for lessons."

"That's a good thought."

"Yes. He won't check on whether it's the truth since he'll

be able to get straight into his books which he'll like! No one will look for us until we *don't* go to Gruddy.''

They spoke more slowly after that, each adding a bit here and there to the plan.

''We'll have to leave very early, Matt. Maybe before it's light . . .''

''Do you suppose we could have our mares left out in the pasture so we wouldn't have to get them out of the barn?''

''Good thinking. That way we wouldn't have to open their stalls.''

''Only the tack room door. It squeaks, Stu.''

''Good thing you remembered that. We'll rub some candle wax on it before we go in. Now, the next thing. *Where* are we going?''

''Winchester, maybe? Would we be allowed to stay if we say we'd been sent back early?''

''Coming by ourselves? Someone would write your father and very likely take us to the headmaster,'' said Stewart scornfully. ''No, we need somewhere better than that . . . You know, Matt, I'd rather like to go home, I think.''

''But that's . . . That's *days*.''

''Not really. Riding, we'd go faster than coaches, you know. Oh, we might have to sleep out *one* night, but it's warm and maybe we can find a shed or a barn or something. We can catch fish to eat and steal apples from trees. It won't be a lot but—'' He pulled Matthew's fingers from his sleeve. ''—What is it?''

''Apples aren't ripe yet,'' said Matthew with a trifle of Stewart's occasionally scornful tone. Then he added. ''We can *catch* fish, you know, but I don't know how to cook them. Do you?''

The boys eyed each other and then grinned.

Matthew suggested, ''Maybe we'd better take a loaf and some ham and cheese or something from the larder.''

''Won't Cook notice?'' objected Stewart.

''Have you ever been in there?'' asked Matthew. ''There's so much I don't see how she can possibly know every bit she's laid by.''

''Then we'll do that. And extra clothes for if it rains?''

The boys continued their plotting, decided they'd thought of every possible point, and left the barn to begin implementing their adventure. The first thing on their list was to put wax on the tack-room hinges during some moment when no one watched!

With the boys gone, an apparition rose from the hay in one corner, his hair every which way. He shook off the loose bits sticking to his clothes and grinned, white teeth gleaming in the shadowy, mote-filled light.

"So!" said the little man. "Little boys want big adventure, do they?" He lay back, grinning and picked up a straw on which he chewed thoughtfully. "Well, then, we'll just have to see they *have* adventure, won't we!"

Chapter Twelve

Dawn was just putting the faintest of rosy touches to the eastern horizon when the boys were sneaking out of the tack room, each carrying a saddle, bridle, and saddle blanket. After very carefully shutting the door, they waited, listening. Nothing. Not a sound. Except for the occasional stamping of a hoof or the sound of a horse chewing a morsel of hay. Even the cat, curled up on the box by the door, merely looked at them and blinked, much too lazy to meow.

When certain no one was going to come, they stole out of the barn and, carefully, afraid each step would bring an angry Gruddy down upon their heads, they moved toward the farthest paddock where they'd left their mares the night before, earnestly explaining to Gruddy that the horses really wanted to stay out and that there wasn't a bit of cloud or wind or any reason why they should not. Gruddy, after exchanging a grin with his second-in-command, allowed that it did look like the mares wanted to stay out.

"I brought an apple to catch them with," whispered Matthew as he lay his tack over the top of the fence.

"Good thinking. But we better go get our saddlebags first."

"Right."

The boys hadn't been able to carry bags and gear and everything but only five minutes later they'd returned, the badly packed saddlebags lay on the ground nearby. Stewart whistled softly and his mare lifted her head from where she'd been browsing idly at the meadow grass.

Matthew called, "Come along, girl!" and held out the apple.

Both boys were right by the fence, leaning over it, watching their mares and hoping they'd not have to go chase them down when, suddenly, with no warning, a rough sack fell over each head, an arm coming around from behind to hold them tight. They were lifted and carried away, kicking wildly . . .

Clutching the note she'd discovered on the table beside her son's pillow, Frederica did her best to control the shaky feeling in her limbs. She closed her eyes tightly, steadied herself, and counted to ten. To a hundred. It did no good. But she must move. She must *not* fall to pieces . . .

She must find Blackthorn. At once.

Frederica turned on her heel and ran from the boys' room where she'd gone when she discovered the boys had not been with their tutor that morning. Her heart pounded as she wondered how long it might have been before they learned of this escapade if Gruddy had not sent a groom up to see why they were late for their lesson.

Frederica clutched the bannister tightly, hoping her legs would not give way before she reached the hall below. It looked so very far away. Her limbs trembled and she closed her eyes briefly before forcing herself to go on. It seemed to take forever to reach the entrance hall, to go along the corridor to Blackthorn's study, where he was closeted with his man of business. Unceremoniously, she thrust open the door and then, her eyes huge with fear, simply stood there.

Spencer James Matthew Seymour, Earl of Blackthorn, turned a frown of irritation toward the intruder, took one look, and almost instantly was at Frederica's side. "My dear. What is it!" His arms closed around her, his hand pulling her head to his chest. "Rickie, my girl . . ." he said soothingly. "Come now, my love . . ."

Frederica raised one fist and pounded lightly at his shoulder. "I never cry," she said.

"Then you must have good reason," he soothed. "Tell me."

Instead she thrust the note at him. Still holding her, he flipped the paper open with only one hand, twisted his elbow up so the page was at an angle he could read it, and then, swearing fluently, helped Frederica to a chair.

Mr. Green, his agent, had risen to his feet when he'd first seen Frederica. Embarrassed by the little scene, he'd wondered how he might, properly, remove himself from it. Blackthorn's swearing, however, made him wonder if it were something with which he could help.

"My lord?" he asked.

Blackthorn swung around. "Ah! Green. Yes. Find out everything you can. I want to know who last saw the boys, whether their mares are in the stable, if they took anything with them . . ."

"The boys have . . . have . . ."

"The little idiots have run away!"

"My lord . . . !"

"Go quickly. There is no hope of keeping this secret and I don't know that I would if I could. Someone somewhere will have seen them. We must discover where they've gone, how they are traveling and *get them back.*" Blackthorn turned on his heel and looked, rather helplessly, at the woman he loved. "Rickie, we *will* get them back."

"Yes. Oh yes, of course. But they are so little, they know so little of the world. The dangers . . ."

"Yes there are dangers. But the boys are not stupid." The door closed behind the agent and Spencer went to Frederica, pulling her up and back into his embrace. "My love, they will be all right. I promise."

"Don't pretend you can make such a promise. Don't try to soothe me with lies!" She struggled to release herself.

"That was stupid, was it not?" he admitted. "What I can and do promise is that absolutely everything possible will be done to recover them. Frederica?" He tipped her face up and stared down at her tear wet lashes, at the determined chin, at the woman he'd recently discovered he loved with a depth of emotion he'd not known he could feel. "That I do promise," he repeated softly. "And, having promised, I must begin organizing to cover every possible contingency. Will you be all right?"

"No." A watery, wavering smile tipped her lips briefly. "Which you knew was the case, my lord. Until my boy . . . our boys! . . . are returned, I'll not begin to be all right. Why did they do it?"

"Their note says they feared my wrath." He frowned. "You know, Rickie, I can't help thinking that's nonsense. They were perfectly sensible when I saw them last. So there must be another reason. Just why, do you think, *did* they run off?"

"I kin tell you that," said a voiced filled with humor. The words came from the open window.

Frederica broke away from Blackthorn and turned. His Lordship's hands settled on her shoulders and she was glad of the support when she saw the dirty-looking man leaning his elbows on the sill. The perky-faced fellow grinned at her, a broken tooth revealed among white fangs.

"Mr. Gray!" exclaimed Blackthorn.

"Jist Gray will do. But about those scamps o'your'n, I heard them planning, you see."

"When? Where?"

"Don't make no nevermind when nor where. But what I heard, well decided to take a hand myself. You see?"

"No, I don't see. Where are our sons?"

"Safe as houses. Not that I ever thought much of houses, o'course, so safe as a babe in its mother's arms?"

"Mr. Gray, please . . . ," Frederica began, but stopped when the man scowled.

"Jist *Gray*. Or Gray Shadow. Translated from my real name which you gorgios have trouble getting your tongue around."

"You're a Gypsy?" asked Blackthorn. He added "Why did I never know that?" just as Frederica asked, "What's a gorge-o?"

"Gorgio. Someone who isn't a gypsy," explained Blackthorn. "But Gray," he continued, frowning," you've lived here forever, so far as I know. I didn't think Gypsies did that."

"Can't help it if'n I'm a fool, can I?" the man drawled. "Fell in love with a gorgio miss." The man sighed deeply. "Married her, too. Then found she wouldn't leave her family. So—" He shrugged, lifting his hands briefly."—I stayed. She's buried near here . . ." His eyes got a faraway look and then seemed to focus on them again. He grinned, showing his teeth. "But that's neither here nor there, is it?"

"No it isn't," said Frederica, snappishly and then she blushed at her rudeness. "As sorry as I am that your wife died," she said more softly, "I'm too worried about my son to have a proper concern for your grief."

"Herself died more'n twenty years ago so don't worrit yourself about that, lady. The boys are safe. And on their way home. *Your* home," he added, shifting his look toward Frederica.

"But how can they be safe, out there all on their own! They don't know . . ." She frowned. "Why do you grin like that?"

"Boys won't go running off again." White teeth flashed in a leathery face. "I promise you *that.*"

"Gray," said Blackthorn sternly, "tell us a round tale or let me get on with organizing a search."

The teeth flashed again. "Boys think they've been kidnapped by Gypsies. Think they're being taken to be sold to a slaver. When they get near your home, lady, they'll be allowed to 'escape' and I don't think they'll ever again want to take off on adventures of this sort!"

"You arranged this, Gray?" asked Blackthorn, relaxing a great deal once he knew where his son could be found.

"My kin were camped on that land they've a right to." Again the shrug. "Headed out anyway, so jist did it to oblige me."

"They earned the right to that land many generations ago," said Blackthorn softly.

Gray nodded, but Frederica scowled up over her shoulder. His Lordship realized his love hadn't relaxed one smidgen.

"The tribe saved the life of an heir to this house back in the mid-1600s, Frederica. I think they are doing the current heir a favor by not only teaching him a lesson he'll not forget, but by allowing him to believe he gets himself out of the tangle he thinks he's in, which will leave him with self-respect intact! Gray, I'll owe your people a further debt."

He stared thoughtfully at the bland-faced Gypsy man leaning at his window who, at that comment, quirked one brow.

"I will," said Blackthorn finally, "tie a mare out in that glade once each year. My son will do likewise, but I cannot promise beyond that."

"Good carriage stock'd be better," was the laconic reply, no pretense made that a reward wouldn't be welcome. "The princess's old horse ain't good for much any longer. Getting old. Horse trained to pulling or even a good ass?"

"You believe our boys are safe?" asked Frederica softly, tugging at Blackthorn's sleeve.

"If Gray says they're safe, then they are."

"But you said he's a poacher," she whispered, casting wary a look at the man still standing outside the window.

"It will be just as he says," soothed Blackthorn, also looking at the Gypsy who nodded. Blackthorn frowned. "On the other hand, if the boys truly think they've been kidnapped to be sold, then they'll tell that tale when they get free. It might be a good idea Frederica, if you and I manage to reach Ian and your local magistrate *before* they escape and tell their tale. Hadn't thought of that, had you, Gray?"

"Oh didn't I then? Told them not to hurry, I did," said Gray, his grin once more in evidence. "Thought you'd head off reprisals!"

"They boys . . . are they . . . will they . . . how . . ." Frederica bit her lip and drew in her breath. "Will they be hurt in any way?"

Gray eyed her a trifle warily. "Can't have adventures and not get hurt a *little.*"

Blackthorn's hands tightened on her shoulders. "My dear, if Gray says a little than he means only a little. They've been tied?"

The grin flashed. "At the ankle, one to t'other. Have to learn to walk together."

"They'll stumble. Fall." Frederica's skin, already pale from worry, whitened still more. "They might break a bone!"

"If'n they do, then it'll be set proper. Not like that gorgio who says he's a doctor!"

"You know about Lady Amelia's arm?"

Gray gave her a pitying look. " 'Course I know . I know everything around and about."

"But I don't want either of them to have a broken bone!"

"Can't have adventures without a little hurt," repeated Gray. "Jist wanted you to know where they were. Know they be all

right. Just scared, maybe and, right now, that's good for 'em!''
Once again that perky grin and the face disappeared.

That suddenly the window was empty. Frederica rushed forward and leaned out. She saw no sign of the poacher. He was simply gone! Frederica turned back. "Spencer," she urged, "shouldn't we hold on to him? What if it's all a lie to keep us quiet? What if his tribe really does mean to sell the boys?''

"I believe Gray is to be trusted and the boys will be released. But, given what *they'll* believe, we've a duty to do our part. Frederica—'' He slightly emphasized her name since she'd just, unconsciously, he thought, used his. "—we must be on our way as soon as possible. How quickly can you pack a portmanteau? I'll order a carriage for the girls and Sal, since you and I will go by curricle." Then, as an afterthought he asked, "If you think you're up to it?''

The impropriety of driving such a distance alone with Blackthorn didn't even cross Frederica's mind. She merely calculated what she would need and how quickly she could throw it into a box which could be strapped to the back of his rig.

"Twenty minutes. Half an hour at the outside," she said.

He chuckled. "I should have realized you'd be unlike other women in this respect as well as all the other wonderful things you are. You've more time than that, my dear We'll have an early lunch after you've given orders to Sal about getting the girls home. I'll talk to Murdock who will drive them and I'll send Mr. Green with them to see they are safe and well cared for, and speaking of Mr. Green, here he is. What have you to report?''

The agent bowed to Frederica, but turned instantly to Lord Blackthorn. "The boys' mares are still in the pasture where they were put last night at the boys' urging. Their saddles were found on the railing there this morning and Gruddy has had words to say about the bloom the dew caused in the leather! There's also a couple of saddlebags with a change of clothes apiece. Mrs. Clapper says a cottage loaf, a chunk of cheese and a few slices of ham are missing from the larder and, perhaps, some apples as well. Those we didn't find near the saddles.''

"Who saw them last? Their tutor?''

"No. Boys left him a note as well. Said they'd be with you today and wouldn't be having lessons. So," said Green disparagingly, "that one stuck his nose in a book and hasn't given them another thought. The best I can figure, no one has seen the br- . . . er . . . *boys* since last evening when Sal went in to check they'd washed properly."

"Last evening!" exclaimed Frederica.

"Yes'm. After you'd heard their prayers and tucked them in. The boys rarely went right off to sleep, Sal says, so she'd gotten into the habit of waiting until the girls had gone off before checking the boys."

"So very likely they either left *then* or waited until sometime early this morning," mused Lord Blackthorn. "If it were me and I didn't know exactly where I was going, I'd want a bit of light. There was no moon last night? At least not until very late?"

"Moon rose about four, my lord," said Mr. Green.

"So, very likely not before four. They'd have been captured by the Rom right there by the fence rather than after they'd gone off, or the mares and saddles would also be missing . . ."

"Are you thinking of trying to catch up with the Gypsies, my lord?" asked Frederica.

"Gypsies!" Mr. Green cleared his throat. "*Our* Gypsies, my lord?"

Blackthorn smiled a quick sharp smile. "Yes, Green, our Gypsies. I owe them a new favor, which I've already negotiated, for this bit of business."

"I don't understand, my lord."

Blackthorn explained what they'd learned from Gray. "You may tell everyone the boys have gone off for an adventure with our Gypsies but not that the original notion for that was not their own! I believe all will be well, but if it is *not,* I want to handle what turns up as it turns up! We've had no trouble with that tribe. Not in the nearly two centuries they've used that glade for their camp. And I know personally from that year . . ." A tinge of red-colored his ears and he waved a hand. "Well, never mind *that.* But I don't want to get on their bad side if it isn't necessary!"

He gave Green a well-filled purse and orders for getting Sal and the girls home, telling him to leave first thing in the morning. He then called in Jennings, telling him the abbreviated tale and said he'd be going with Mrs. MacKivern to her home, leaving just as soon as they could be ready. He asked that a light meal be set out and then headed up the stairs to his aunt's room.

"My dear! I've just heard," she exclaimed, leaning forward, her good arm extended to him. "You must be worried out of your mind!"

"I was, but only briefly." This time he told a round tale. "Since the boys are not to know they weren't kidnapped, then it behooves me to get to the authorities before they do! Our Gypsies will be trusting me to see them safe." He paused. "You frown. Why?"

"Spencer, you are very sure the boys will be all right? I mean, Gray is to be trusted? A *poacher?*"

Blackthorn hesitated. "My dear, I must believe him. Because if I waver at all, then Rickie will fall into a state of nerves which . . . well, I do not know what might happen. You didn't see her when she came to me with the boys' note. She was white as your sheets there, and trembled so badly she could barely stay upright and yet she could not give into her fears."

"Could not?"

"I believe so. She's been responsible for young MacKivern for years. She cannot let someone else take that responsibility from her. Where any normal woman would be having hysterics and taking to her bed and letting *anyone* else see to things, Rickie must do *herself* what she feels must be done."

"Blackthorn, not all women behave as did that ninny you married!"

"I know. Especially not my Rickie."

"*Your* Rickie? Amelia brightened. "Oh, then she has agreed . . ." She trailed off when he raised a hand, shaking his head.

"I've not yet asked her, Aunt. I will, but I can hardly do so when her every effort, all her senses, are trained on that blasted boy of hers! I had hoped, I'll admit, to do a bit of wooing while here and then in London, but then she decided she'd not go to London. Which reminds me!"

He asked that Lady Amelia write her friend and tell her they'd not be coming, using her broken arm as an excuse, rather than spreading the tale of the boys' escapade.

Frederica, hearing only the words "that blasted boy" turned

on her heel and, instead of entering Amelia's room, moved quickly down the hall. Blackthorn had said that. He'd been exceedingly irritated, not worried. And she had thought he *liked* Stewart, had almost been willing to believe he might be falling in love with her however strange it seemed to her, and she'd almost, if not quite, admitted she'd fallen in love with him. But not now.

She would have nothing to do with a man who could think so badly of Stewart. Stewart must come first. Besides to call him a "blasted boy"! What of his own son, then!?

Their sons were trudging along, ankles tied firmly one to the others, each swinging his leg in time with his friend's. At first they'd stumbled and tumbled and had to pick themselves up, to the obvious amusement of the Gypsy children, but, spurred on by the youngsters' laughter, they'd soon gotten the knack of walking together.

"Do you think they really mean to sell us?" Matthew asked Stewart quietly, glancing fearfully at the Rom who walked only a little ahead of them.

"I don't know," murmured Stewart. "We'll just have to watch our chance and escape when we can. At least we're going in the right direction, you know," he added still more softly. "I mean, if they keep on this way until we're close to my home then we'd have somewhere we could escape *to,* if you know what I mean?"

Matthew nodded and cast a quick glance at his friend. "Thank you for telling that old woman they'd make more ransoming me than by selling me. You know, I've always been rather proud of our Gypsies. Now I'm not certain what to think."

"What do you mean, our Gypsies?"

Matthew told the tale of the rescue of his ancestor from a flooding stream with far more drama than his father had used when telling Frederica. He also explained about the rights given to the tribe in perpetuity, allowing them to camp in a particular glade on Seymour property.

"But wouldn't your father take away that right if your Gypsies did something like this?"

"I'd *think* he would. If he ever finds it out. I mean why would he think them involved? He trusts them; he'd never guess it's our Gypsies."

"Which brings up a good question, Matt," said Stewart earnestly. "*Are* these your Gypsies? Would you know? Maybe it's another tribe trying to do the first one a bad turn?"

Matthew blinked. Blinked again. "I . . . don't know. Not for sure. The lady's caravan, well, it looks like one I remember . . . but . . . well . . . The devil! I just can't be sure." Awkwardly, he tried out a few of the swear words he'd learned from Gruddy that summer.

Stewart added a few of the more colorful phrases which he'd long ago learned from Ian's grooms while playing in and around his uncle's stables and getting underfoot as often as not. "You haven't made friends with any of the gypsy children?" he asked when they'd run out of words which didn't take long.

Matthew stared straight ahead. "I suppose it is the sort of thing *you'd* have done, but you forget how fussed about and supervised I was. Until you came. Now I think maybe I was watched so closely because there was no one to be responsible for me. I mean, like your mother."

Stewart stifled the first laugh he'd felt since they been captured as they'd stood by the fence, calling to their mares in the moonlight early that morning. "You mean she worries enough for all of them?"

"That too."

Matthew smiled and Stewart grinned.

"But what I *really* meant is that I think servants shouldn't be given more responsibility than need be. They . . . They . . ." He frowned.

Stewart, quick to catch his friend's meaning, also tried to think how to phrase it. "Maybe what you mean is that they're *too* responsible. Is that it?"

"If you mean they'd lose their place or maybe be sent to gaol or something if something were to happen to the heir, me, I mean, then I guess that's what I mean," Matthew said, still trying to think it through. "It really *isn't* fair, is it? Asking them to put their very lives on the line?"

"Is that was your father did?"

"I think it is. I wonder if he ever realized it."

"Probably not. He seems a fair sort of man."

"He *is*." Matthew swiped a sleeve across his face.

"Baby!" When another tear slipped down Matthew's cheek, Stewart added, "Don't cry. We'll escape. Really. Or they'll come to their senses and ransom us. You at least."

Stewart shivered at the thought of what *he* might suffer. To be *sold*. Like an animal! He set his teeth. Never. He'd escape if he had to chew through his bonds with his teeth!

"What if I never see him again?" asked Matthew in a small voice, his eyes still wet and glistening.

"Your father? Of course you will," said Stewart encouragingly. "He'll not stop looking for you until he finds you. And my mother will help him. She's a pretty intelligent woman, you know," said Frederica's son judiciously. "She'll think of something if he doesn't."

What she was thinking at that moment was that she'd been a fool to agree to travel, alone, with Blackthorn. They'd just stopped for refreshment at a neat looking well cared for country inn when, of all people they knew, Lord Quincy exited just as they were about to enter.

"Well, well, well, well, well!"

"A very deep subject, is a well," said Blackthorn, coldly to the grinning Quincy. "Mrs. MacKivern, if you'll just step inside, I've a few words to say to this—" He eyed Quincy. "—excuse for a gentleman. Quincy, your misdeeds have caught you up!"

Frederica, staying right where she was, watched Blackthorn take Quincy by the arm. Firmly. His Lordship led the still grinning man off to the other side of the road where, gradually, the grin faded. After another long tirade which Frederica wished she could hear, a drop of sweat ran down the side of Quincy's face. Another. A stream of sweat. What in heaven's name was Blackthorn saying to him? she wondered.

A hand still firmly around Quincy's arm, Blackthorn strode back, stopping just in front of Frederica. "Well?" he asked his captive.

"Er. Apologies, my lady. Er, Mrs. . . . Hmmm . . ." He glanced at Blackthorn whose brow was turning as black as his name. "Don't know *how* to apologize," he muttered, his grin flashing, but fading quickly at Blackthorn's expression. "Never have," he added, sullen.

"You don't know how to make a sincere apology for the damage you've done this lady's reputation? Then I know how to teach you." Quincy looked alarmed. Very coldly, Blackthorn asked, "Just where are you to be found, my lord, when I've finished the business I'm now on?"

"Er . . . Jamaica!" Quincy nodded several times in a row very quickly. "Just on my way out of the country. Pater's urged me forever to see to our plantation there!" He swiped at the newly budded sweat popping out all over his head at the thought of a duel with Blackthorn.

"I see," said His Lordship judiciously. "Just on your way out of the country. *For how long?*"

"Er . . ." Quincy looked to Frederica for advice, but got none. He tugged at his collar. "Years? Likely?"

"Hmmm. Maybe the gossip you started, not only about Mrs. MacKivern but all your other targets, will have been forgotten. I would suggest, Quincy, that you mind your tongue while in Jamaica. I've heard the people there are hot-blooded. You think *me* dangerous and I am. But I'm nothing at all so dangerous as a Jamaican who believes he or his have suffered insult!"

". . . er . . . well, hmmm!"

Blackthorn, who had felt it necessary to warn the bumbling idiot, now wondered if the fool would change his mind about going. "Quincy, if you are to be found, I'll find you. I suggest you not put off your journey despite the danger at the other end. After all, *there* you haven't insulted anyone. Have you? Yet?"

Quincy tugged again at his already mangled neckcloth, saw that Mrs. MacKivern watched him with an interested eye and, swallowed. "I truly didn't mean to . . . to . . . make you mad," he said.

"Mad? More sad than mad. You've no notion how your tales harm people, do you?" she asked.

"But why?" He looked startled, casting his eyes from Frederica to Blackthorn and back. "They're just, well, *tales.*"

"Which others believe, or pretend to believe, and then repeat. Lord Quincy, have you ever thought to put your talent to use in making up stories for publication? If you're making them up about *pretend* people, you won't need to make them up about *real* people."

His eyes grew huge. "You think I could write a novel?"

"Why not?"

A thoughtful look settled across his somewhat bovine countenance. "Maybe I will, then."

"Remember to pack up a goodly supply of paper with you and your pencils, for your sea journey," said Blackthorn, his gaze warm where it rested on Frederica.

"Pencils?" he muttered. "No, no, no. Only the best pens and a very clear ink will do . . ."

Quincy continued mumbling to himself as he wandered off to where his curricle awaited him, it never occurring to him to say good-bye. Instead, he was wondering if the couple with whom he'd been staying had decent ink or only the muddy sort of stuff too many households used. And paper. He needed good paper. Maybe he should pack up and go home? Would his father be there just now? Quincy, about to pick up his reins, looked up. "Say, Blackthorn, what's the date?"

After a moment's thought Blackthorn told him.

"Ah! Then the pater's in Scotland. I'll go home."

"And then to Jamaica."

"Jamaica?" Quincy looked completely blank. "Why would I want to go to Jamaica?"

Frederica put her hand on Blackthorn's arm. "You might learn something for your stories there. Byron learned a lot when traveling in the East, did he not?"

"Travel . . . ? Well . . . hmm . . . Maybe." A stubborn look took up residence in his face. "But not just yet. Gotta go home . . ."

They watched the dust rise behind him as his team trotted down the road. "Do you think he will?"

"Go to Jamaica?" asked Blackthorn. "He would have if you hadn't put it into his head he could be an author! Now I'm going to have to find him and—" He glanced at Frederica. "—hmmm, order him out of the country all over again."

"You mean to call him out. Please don't. He truly doesn't understand, you know. It would be like punishing a puppy long after the act. There is no point to it if you can't catch him chewing on your slipper or making a puddle where he shouldn't!''

"You believe I should wait until he's gossiping about someone and *then* call him out? I think not."

"I believe we should simply forget the whole thing. Who knows? Perhaps he *will* become an author!" She took Blackthorn's arm and tugged him toward the Inn door. "He hasn't a notion how much work is involved, of course, so perhaps he'll give it up after a short time and return to his usual haunts among the ton."

Blackthorn patted her hand. "And *then* I'll find him and—er—order him off to Jamaica?"

She chuckled at his satisfied tone. "You, my lord, appear to be at least as stubborn as *he* is."

"I don't know about stubborn, but I'm dry as beda- . . . er . . . as dust."

"I, on the other hand, am dry as bedamned," she said, her features perfectly bland.

It was his turn to chuckle. "I am glad that idiot was nowhere near when you said that. He'd not see the humor. Only the flouting of propriety. Ah, my dear, I haven't had so much fun in years as I've had since meeting you! Shall we go in?" he asked, holding the door for her.

Since the host had appeared just inside it, she could not, as she should, berate him for the use of the endearment. So, shutting her mouth tightly, she went. Besides, she had, also, just recalled what he'd said about her son. That blasted boy, he'd said!

Once again she determined to treat His Lordship as coldly as one would a mere acquaintance. It was the only way she knew to contain the pain growing in her breast, her only means of hiding the hurt. It was truly unfortunate she'd begun to suspect he felt more for her than she'd ever expected he might but, even if it true, it was irrelevant. Irrelevant, yes, but it hurt, the thought of what *might* have been if he'd proved to be, without any doubt, the man she'd thought he was.

But he wasn't.

Besides, why, she wondered, was she so foolish as to think a man so far above her socially would feel anything for someone like her but a moment's lust? That he felt that, she *did* believe, and also that he'd be very happy if she'd agree to join him in his bed. For a time, anyway.

Until he tired of her or until another woman caught his eye. *Deluded, my girl,* she told herself. *You deluded yourself right royally and now you'll pay for it ...''*

Chapter Thirteen

Some little time later Blackthorn set down his wineglass with a snap. "No, I will *not* promise that I'll not call that idiot out at some future date for some future offense. Someone needs to teach the blockhead a lesson."

"Why are men such fools?"

"Why do women take pity on those who do them wrong?"

"I hope that's a rhetorical question, my lord." Frederica, too, set down her glass, but she did so with meticulous care. "Because if you cannot answer it yourself, then I pity *you.*"

Baffled he stared at her. "I don't understand you."

"Is it necessary that you understand me?"

"You know it is!" He grasped the edge of the table with both hands, his knuckles white. "Surely you know it is!"

"Then I guess you'll just have to think about it, won't you?"

"Rickie," he said after a moment, "we're fighting. Why are we fighting? I don't want to fight with you."

"Do you not? Perhaps it is that you cannot fight with the idiot, so you are easing your temper on me?" Even as he shook his head she went on. "Too, we are both upset and worried about our sons. However much you protest your tribe of Gypsies won't hurt our boys, you cannot *know* and that concern leaves us both on edge. And on top of that, we are very definitely going against all rules of proper society by traveling together with nary a chaperone in sight. That knowledge, too, must have you a trifle out of curl."

"That," he said blandly, "is the one thing which worries me not at all."

"It doesn't? Well, my lord," said Frederica, rising from her place, "perhaps it should." When he automatically moved to rise, as any gentleman would, she waved him back to his seat. "Please remain comfortably in your chair, my lord. What we do, traveling together, is not proper, so why worry about such a minor transgression? Blackthorn," she went on, her tone altering from biting scorn to sincere concern, "you are a very important man in London. If gossip is spread about our little journey it will do your reputation no good."

"It would do yours far more harm—" He fiddled with his glass, twirling it back and forth between his fingers. "—but there's a solution," he said, casually and settled back, seemingly relaxed.

Frederica, however, noted that his other hand, half hidden, was a tightly clenched fist. "Solution?" she asked, turning away.

"We could wed. There will be no talk about either of us if we are married."

Frederica moved closer to the window. Hoping her voice wouldn't reveal her emotions, she said, musingly, "I don't believe I wish to be married for that reason."

"Then—" His voice took on a harsh note. "—marry me because I love you and think, *hope,* you love me."

She swung around. *"Love—"* All emotion was erased from her expression except that her lips formed a tight line. Silently, in her mind, words whirled. *"—In a pig's eye you love me!"* was one of the least vicious of her rampaging thoughts. That he would use words which should be spoken only in tenderness merely to get his own way was despicable!

Eyeing him, she heaved an exasperated sigh before saying, "You, my lord, have the tact of a . . . a . . . What is that odd creature that looks like a pig with horns on its nose? Rhino . . . ocerous? Rhino is the Latin which has to do with the nose, is it not, so perhaps that is the creature I have in mind?"

For a moment she tried to remember, then, looking up, she noted his lips twitching and his eyes sparkling and those nice laugh lines one always found so intriguing forming at his temples.

"I cannot see where our situation is at all humorous, my lord," she complained. "We must travel together for some way yet. It will be embarrassing when I tell you I will not wed you. You should *not* have asked me now when we cannot say the proper polite words, a brief good-bye, and then part!''

All signs of humor faded. ''You are correct, my dear. I should not have asked you now. You are in no state to be thinking of our future when you worry about the future of your son.''

''And yours.''

''And mine.''

They each stared at nothing in particular, anything . . . so long as it was not each other.

Finally Blackthorn, in turn, sighed, but his expression was one of sadness. ''We will, if you'll agree, put this scene from our minds. It will be as if it never happened. You must not feel embarrassed in my presence, Frederica. Not ever. Not for any reason. I am sorry you have not said me yea, but I will assume it is because of the situation and will not despair.''

Frederica stared. She opened her mouth to reply and closed it. Finally, still exasperated, she said, ''I do not understand you!''

''Then, since I've already admitted I don't understand you, we are both groping in the dark, are we not?''

The whimsy in his voice brought a choke of laughter to hers.

He smiled. ''That's better.'' He rose to his feet, a tall straight commanding figure that held Frederica's gaze even as she wished it did not. ''I suppose we must continue on our way. I'll have the team harnessed. Ten, perhaps fifteen minutes?''

''Ten will do,'' she said.

Seated on either side of the old woman who gave the orders, the boys squeezed each other's arms behind her back. Instead of their ankles, their wrists were now tied, the bindings attached to a ring set into the wood behind the seat.

''Such silent boys,'' said the woman in guttural English. ''Silent boys?'' Her bulk shook with silent laughter. ''That is nonsense, is it not? Boys are never silent.''

Matthew looked to where several older boys swung along beside the carriage ahead. They hadn't, so far as he knew, spoken a word in miles. Stewart, less reticent, pointed that fact out.

"But those are not boys," objected the woman. "Those are young men."

They could not possibly be more than fourteen, Matthew thought, and leaned forward to look across the woman's ample front at Stewart, but his friend was hidden on the far side of the big woman.

"You don't agree?" she asked looking down at him and, when Matthew didn't respond, nudged him with her elbow. "They are not men, you think?"

"They are very young, are they not?" asked Matthew diffidently. "I do not think I'll be a man at that age."

"Ah! But you are gorgio and they are Rom. There is the difference, you see."

"I think there must be," said Matthew politely. "Thank you for taking us up with you. My legs ache. A lot."

"Won't do," said the old woman cheerfully, "to have you worn to a thread when we get where we're going."

Matthew shuddered. He felt Stewart's hand squeeze him gently and squeezed back. He felt a little better for that encouragement, but not much. The thought of what was to happen to them made him feel sick. Very sick.

The train of wagons pulled from one of the narrow hidden lanes, on which they'd so far traveled, out onto a main road. The boys, one to either side of the woman, straightened, looking around. Disappointed at seeing no one, not even the smoke from a distant house, they leaned back.

The woman chuckled. "We don't use the big roads much. And never where we might run into trouble. I think you boys might be trouble so . . ." She raised her voice and the procession stopped, several people who were on foot, drifting nearer the old lady. She spoke briefly, sharply, in the Gypsy's own tongue. A swarthy man disappeared toward the back.

The boys felt the caravan dip and sway and suddenly, behind them, a door slid open. Their bounds were detached from the ring and, a hand in the collar of each boy's jacket, they were lifted with much the same ease as if they'd been nothing more than feather filled bolsters. But, jerked into the interior, the door closed, the bright light of the sunlit day disappearing, they were suddenly, if temporarily, blind.

Their arms were untied and the boys forced to lay on a cot

built into the sidewall where, once again, they were bound, their mouths covered this time with rough gags. Stewart glared and the man laughed.

"Won't be for long," he said softly. "We'll be back on our sort of roads in a mile or two."

For an instant there was light again and then the wagon bounced as the Rom jumped from the back. With a jerk they started forward. It was actually not unpleasant in the dim warmth, lying on the softly padded bed. The boys, worn out by their early rising that morning and the long trek, were almost asleep when the rocking motion caused when the wagon stopped startled them awake. They turned their heads, looking at each other, their eyes glistening in the mote filled dusky light.

"Give ye good day, my lord," said the old woman seated not far beyond their heads. "Ye be far from your ken."

"From home? Not all that far."

Matthew jerked, tipping his head as far up as he could. He struggled to get up. Stewart also recognized Blackthorn's voice and he too squirmed and fought his bonds, trying to get free but only tightening the ropes until the pain brought tears to his eyes.

"And ye travel far?" asked the Gypsy politely, the sound of laughter to be heard in her voice if one listened carefully.

"We are headed for my home, madame," said a second well-known and much-beloved voice.

Stewart's yell was muffled by the gag. Matthew, giving up, flopped down. He turned away from Stewart to hide the tears, not of pain, but of loss, running freely down his face.

"Have ye good journey then."

"You too," said Blackthorn, politely.

Blackthorn had driven fast after leaving the inn, concentrating on the road and his horses. Suddenly, ahead of them, Frederica saw a line of slow moving Gypsy wagons. Her heart beating hard, she wondered, hoped. . . . feared . . . that these were the people who held her son captive. She glanced at Blackthorn when, slowing slightly, he eased by them, pulling the curricle to a stop at the side of the road. Slowly, ever so slowly, the first two wagons passed. The third stopped.

"Give ye good day, my lord," said the old woman, grinning. She pointed over her shoulder at the inside of her caravan. *"Ye be far from your ken."*

"From home? Not all that far," said Blackthorn. Silently, he mouthed, "They are well?"

The woman, her eyes twinkling, nodded. *"And ye travel far?"* she asked.

"We are headed for my home, madame," said Frederica, her voice unsteady.

"Have ye good journey, then," said the Gypsy.

"You too," said Blackthorn. He watched as the woman lifted the reins and the old horse responded by setting off again. As she passed, he handed Frederica the reins and dropped to the road, a raised hand keeping the next wagon from moving.

"Are they truly well?" he asked the Rom driving it.

"They don't enjoy themselves," said the man, his tone dry as the dust of the road they traveled. "They are frightened. A bit." He turned dark eyes onto Frederica, back to Blackthorn. "You will tell that one her son is honorable and as brave in his way as a Rom. He told us you would ransom your son for a great deal more than we could get selling them. He admitted he didn't think he was worth so much."

"The boys are good boys."

"For gorgios." The Rom shrugged, a sardonic expression hooding his eyes.

"I've made an agreement with Gray Shadow. Annually, a horse will be tied in your glade during my lifetime and that of my son. Beyond that I make no promises."

"Not long beyond that we'll have no need of horses. Anthea foresees a new form of transport. One which goes without horses."

Blackthorn blinked. "A horseless carriage? Is that possible?"

The Rom shrugged. "I should not have said so much." He too lifted his reins and his horse started forward, the wagon behind following, the driver averting his face so that he need not acknowledge Blackthorn. When the procession turned down a narrow lane some half mile beyond His Lordship sighed and returned to his curricle.

"I am to inform you, Frederica, that your son is very nearly worthy of being a Rom. To save Matthew he informed the tribe I'd ransom my son for far more than they could make selling him. He admitted he didn't think he was worth so much!''

Half laughing and half crying, Frederica searched her reticule for a handkerchief. Silently, Blackthorn handed her his.

"You trust them?" she asked when she could speak.

"I have said so, have I not?—" He grinned, a quick flash of white teeth. "—Actually, I'll admit I feel better now we've spoken with them. Did you see the incredulity on the face of that first driver when I pulled over and he passed us? He was not only startled to see us, I think he felt a touch of fear as well."

"But that woman did not."

"That woman is a princess, Frederica. Her mother was queen. One of her sisters is now queen."

"They have that sort of structure to their life? I've always thought of them as wanderers without culture or society."

"You would be very wrong to believe that. They have a language and culture far older than ours. We are mere upstarts in the world, my dear! The Rom believe they were an ancient people when the Egyptian Pharaohs sat their thrones."

"They have records?"

"They have . . . traditions."

"How have you learned so much? I thought they were a secret people."

He glanced at her, back at his horses. "The man with whom I spoke? He is the princess's son. I traveled with him for several months after I came down from university and my father would not allow me to go up to Edinburgh where I wished to study medicine." He chuckled. "I thought I was punishing him, running away with the Gypsies, but given Gray's prompt appearance at my study window this morning, I wonder, now, if he didn't tell my father where I was and that he needn't worry! Now I come to think of it, I believe it was Zall's off-hand offer to take me with him that gave me the notion to go."

"Were you punished when you returned?"

Blackthorn set his horses in motion. "My father never seemed all that interested in my doings. When I returned he merely said that it was only fair that I spend an equivalent amount of time with his steward, traveling around our estates, meeting our people and learning the extent of my future obligations and duties. Since I had tired of travel I was not best pleased, but I'd expected some form of punishment and his decision seemed fairly mild. Besides, I'd given him a blistering tirade, insisting I was fully adult and he could no longer tell me what to do. He merely stared under his brows and suggested learning the extent of my future duties was the adult thing to do.'' Blackthorn chuckled. ''I remember I opened my mouth to argue, realized just in time that he was correct and didn't. Argue, that is. And, as I learned more and more from the agent, I began to understand *why* my father would not let me become a doctor!''

''I think I might have liked him.''

''Would you?'' He was silent for a moment. ''I don't know that you would. That decision was a wise one, although I doubt he'd a notion the result would be so good. I mean, I doubt he realized I'd grown up enough to see that I could not forget who I was and what was required of me.'' Blackthorn mused on that, then sighed. ''He and I were never close, I'm sorry to say. When I returned we didn't discuss what I'd learned. He wasn't at all interested in my helping him, you see. Eventually I asked if he'd introduce me to someone in the political world where I might make myself useful. He wasn't a political man himself but he knew people and was relieved, I think, that I didn't, again, importune him to continue my studies. He set my feet on that first rung and then, far more important from *his* point of view, found me a wife who I dutifully but foolishly wed, and here I am today, very nearly unable to find time for *anything* of a personal nature.'' He gave her a quick glance. ''I must change that . . .''

The glance told him her lips were compressed and her chin raised. Receiving no encouragement to continue along those lines, he sighed and fell into a silence which lasted for several miles. In fact it wasn't broken until, the sun far down toward the horizon, they pulled into Burford.

And there, just as they came down over the hill into the market town, the off-side horse threw a shoe. Blackthorn remembered it had been Burford where his Rufus lost a shoe the last time he was on this road.

He swore softly, then, glancing at Frederica apologized. "I'll have to lead them to the blacksmith's," he said.

"How far is it from here to my home, my lord?"

"Something between three and four hours," he responded promptly. "Assuming the smith has his forge up and working, we can still make it although it will be very late."

It wasn't to be. Once again the smith was visiting his sister, his forge cold and black.

Blackthorn glanced at the westering sun. "Shall I see if I can hire a team?" he asked.

"Please."

But that too was impossible. Nothing was available. Every team was out and none would be available until the next day.

"I'm sorry if it distresses you, Frederica, but I don't know what I can do except hire rooms at the inn."

She sighed. "Produce me your inn. I only hope the smith is up and about early so that we can get away. I'm tired. I will, I think, go straight to my room."

"Just as soon as you've eaten a light supper," Blackthorn said, seemingly agreeable. But he held his breath, letting it out silently after she reluctantly agreed. The last thing he wanted was another argument with his skittish love.

The wagons pulled into a rough circle in a valley hidden on the southern rim of the Cotswolds. The boys had been allowed back onto the woman's seat once they were again traveling the rarely used lanes and by-ways. Their arms were, as before, tied behind her. Now, in camp, they were tied at their ankles as they'd been when they walked, and pushed down on a rocky outcrop not far from the fire where two women worked preparing the evening meal. Young and incapable of constant worry, they watched what went on with a great deal of interest.

A boy not much older then themselves dropped to the ground just beyond Matthew. He had a small sharp knife with which he deftly carved pegs for hanging a washing, an item Gypsies offered for sale when they stopped in a village or at a farm. The boys watched the lad finish the first and begin a second. Before their meal was ready he'd completed a small pile.

The good smells coming from the stew pot had Stewart's

mouth watering. "I hope they mean to feed us," he whispered to Matthew.

Matthew turned a startled look his way. "Surely . . ."

"We're prisoners," hissed Stewart. "Who *knows* what they'll do."

"The lady said she wanted us in good condition," said Matthew after a moment. "I don't think they'll starve us."

"But they've fed the men so why not us?"

"I think that's the way they do it." Matthew searched his memory for something Gray had said about his tribe during their hours of rambling when learning to see the world around them in a new way though the eyes of the old man who loved it very much. A silent woman finally brought them each a bowl and spoon. Matthew thanked her politely and Stewart, a trifle belatedly, did so as well. A flickering smile and a nod were their only answer.

They finished their food in record time and looked longingly at the pot still simmering over glowing coals. The hint they wanted more was ignored, assuming anyone noticed and, as they later admitted to each other, each discovered he was too proud to ask. Much to his surprise!

Mugs were brought when the woman returned for the bowls. Matthew, thirsty, took a big swallow and then found himself coughing so violently he wondered if he'd embarrass himself by emptying his stomach. Stewart, about to drink, helped his friend as well as he could and was more cautious how he sipped.

Cider, he decided, but stronger than any he'd ever tasted. "We mustn't drink this," muttered Stewart. "Maybe pretend and then spill it?"

"I don't think we should do that." A woman walked by and Matthew held out his mug. "I'd prefer water, please," he said in his polite way.

Only then did the boys look around. There were big grins on the men's faces and some of the younger children were hiding giggles behind hands. Perhaps it had been a test? Or a jest? Or even something worse? Had they hoped to get the boys drunk on hard cider so they'd make fools of themselves?

He looked at the young man—a boy really—who was again seated quite close to Matthew and back to work on his pegs.

Off to the far side, someone played a fiddle softly. Soon, drowsy, the boys nodded.

"Do you suppose we'll have to sleep right here?" asked Matthew. He looked around, yawning widely.

The idea of sleeping on the ground didn't appeal to Stewart at all although, when they'd planned this journey, they'd assumed that's what they'd do. "I don't know." He thought about it and added, "If I were them I'd lock us into one of those caravans so we wouldn't get away during the night."

"Hmmm."

The youngest children had fallen asleep, leaning into their mothers or each other. Finally two women collected the raga-muffins, taking them to one of the caravans and putting them inside. So. Very likely they'd do the same with their prisoners. Stewart saw the boy gather up his finished pins and put them into a rough bag. The lad slipped his knife into a scabbard at his waist . . .

Or thought he did. It fell to the ground as he rose to his feet. Stewart bit his lip, trying hard to remain perfectly natural when his heart pounded so hard he thought it must be heard be everyone in the glade. He also held his breath. Would the boy notice the knife was gone . . . ?

He didn't. He handed the bag of pins to one of the women and joined the men around the fiddler who was playing livelier music now. One of the men, fire-lit, stood a little away from the others and stamped his foot. He stamped it again. Everyone still awake drifted nearer and suddenly the man was dancing a wild sort of dance that had Matthew's eyes wide with wonder.

Stewart, however, didn't forget the knife. He nudged Matthew who pushed back, never taking his eyes from the dancer.

"Stop staring at them and look to your left," hissed Stewart.

"Left . . . ?" Matthew briefly turned his head to the right, looking at Stewart instead.

"The Rom boy dropped his knife," whispered Stewart urgently when Matthew looked back toward the dancers. "We need to get it, hide it."

This news filtered through Matthew's bemusement with the dancing. He looked all around and found the knife which lay not too far from his foot.

"Can you reach it?"

"I think so," said Matthew. He glanced across the glade to where a woman had joined the man, the two facing each other as they danced, checked that everyone's attention was on the performers, and stretched out his foot. With some difficulty, he scraped the knife nearer. Finally it was just beside the rock on which they sat and, after another check to see it was safe, he reached down and picked it up.

Matthew immediately shoved the blade into his pocket, but it didn't fit. Not only did the handle cause a bulge, the blade poked through the material. "What shall I do with it?" he asked.

"Here. Give it to me."

Anther check on those watching the dancing and they exchanged the knife. Stewart shoved it up his sleeve, pulling his cuff down so it would hold the handle.

"It'll cut you," whispered Matthew, worried.

"When everyone's asleep I'll fix my stocking so I can shove it inside my boot somehow. Now be still, I think that old woman's coming to get us."

She was. She lifted them by the collars and pushed them ahead of her toward her caravan. Inside she put them in one bunk, head to feet, and securely tied them in. "And just in case you think to escape, I sleep like a cat. Besides, the doors and windows will be locked. We've plans for you two, you know."

And then, pulling a blanket across the front of the bunk for modesty's sake, she got herself ready for bed.

When they heard her snoring softly, Matthew whispered, "Should we try to get away now?"

Stewart thought about what the woman had said about sleeping lightly. Then he heard feet outside the caravan, pacing. "Shh. Better not. Tomorrow sometime."

"I'm afraid," admitted Matthew softly.

"So am I. But we'll get away. If they keep going north, then by evening we shouldn't be far from my home. And you heard my mother. She'll be there and your father and at least that part of our plan has worked!"

"You mean that they will have been together."

"Yes. Maybe they'll get married before we go back to school. What do you think?"

Matthew almost pointed out that they might not be going back to school and then thought better of it. "I don't know . . ." he said. He was silent for a moment. "I've a cousin who got married last year. It took *forever.* There were balls and parties and she had to buy what she called her bride clothes and then . . . well, it just took forever. I don't think it's possible. Not that fast," he said.

The snores from the other bunk changed to snorts, which, if they hadn't known she was asleep, they might have thought was muffled laughter. But the Gypsy woman was asleep and they'd no wish to wake her. After murmured orders to each other to be quiet, they settled down themselves and were soon sleeping the deep restful sleep of the young.

Neither Blackthorn in his room at the inn nor Frederica in hers fell to sleep with anything like the innocent freedom of tired youth as their sons managed, in spite of their fearful situation.

Blackthorn cursed himself roundly for bungling his first real proposal of marriage, since the farce which was his first didn't count. Staring at the dark ceiling, he remembered that long ago day. When he'd proposed to Matthew's mother it had been a conventional fiction, the awkward scene the performance of amateur actors playing roles. The marriage, settlements and all, was already arranged by her father and his own. The principals, the bride and groom, had only to go through the motions. So he'd said conventional words to which she'd given a conventional response and, after a quick conventional kiss to her cheek, he'd exited.

It had taken considerably less than an hour out of his busy day, ten minutes of which he'd actually spent with his bride, and he'd forgotten all about it when he'd returned to the office where he was secretary to one of the first minister's more important advisers.

He chuckled wryly as it occurred to him today's bungling had been Frederica's fault. At least in part. She'd given him such an excellent opening for a proposal. Except her words hadn't meant what they seemed to mean, *hadn't* been a hint he should ask! He frowned thoughtfully. To the contrary, he thought. She'd felt . . . insulted, had she not? But *why?*

He grimaced, knowing very well why. He'd used her suggestion their escapade would harm their reputations as an excuse for asking rather than doing as he should have done.

What he *should* have done, instantly, was expose the depth of his feeling for her, his need for her, his desire to care for her and Stewart, to have both of them close forever more.

And why hadn't he? It was obvious why he'd not. He'd feared she'd scorn his love. So, because he'd not told her the truth immediately, she'd not believed him when he *did* speak of it. Nor had he told it all. He hadn't told her he feared he'd merely exist, go through the motions of living, for the rest of his life if she told him no. And why? *Because he'd feared she'd laugh.*

In other words, because he was a coward, he'd lost her. Possibly forever. Soft curses drifted into the dark night.

In *her* room Frederica might have felt better, if only she'd known such words. A few of those curses might have relieved her tensions! She'd berated herself off and on all afternoon for forcing that proposal from him. How could she have been so stupid? He'd so very obviously asked *only* because it was the proper thing to do.

And how utterly absurd his claim he loved her. Especially when he'd already revealed how little he wished to wed her. That bunched up, half hidden, fist was the true indication of his feelings, of course, and she'd had no choice but to turn him down. Not that she wouldn't have turned him down in any case, of course, she firmly reminded herself.

But, oh! It *hurt.* Even though she'd already come to the decision that his attitude toward her son precluded having anything to do with him, that she must say no if by some odd chance he proposed! It wasn't until he'd actually *asked,* she realized, feeling a blow directly to the heart, just how much she wished to say *yes!*

Frederica scolded herself again. This time for allowing tears to flow freely down her cheeks and into her pillow. Tears were stupid and useless and something in which she *never* indulged.

But perhaps just this once? And then, never again. She'd put this interlude behind her, return to her active and satisfying life in the home Ian provided for her and her son and she'd forget she'd ever met his irritating lordship.

She turned onto her other side and stared out her window at moon-waxed clouds which scudded along on a rather brisk breeze. Clouds. She sighed at the thought it might rain tomorrow. Wouldn't that put the seal on their discomfort! An open carriage and too many miles to go . . . and then how long to wait until the boys were allowed to escape? How much longer before she could clasp Stewart to her bosom, hold him tight, never ever let him out of her sight again . . .

Another sigh escaped her and this time she flopped onto her back. However enticing that particular image might be, she could not do it. Stewart would hate her for treating him like a baby. Actually, she wouldn't like herself very well either if she didn't continue to learn how to allow him the freedom to grow and change and become the man he would become. Despite what Ian seemed to believe, she no more wanted a lapdog for a son than she wanted a lapdog of any other sort!

Which thought brought her thoughts back to Blackthorn who, whatever else he was, was *not* a lapdog! Why had she been so foolish as to lose her heart to him? Now, after that scene between them at the inn, she couldn't even indulge her daydreams that she might find the nerve to become his lover! That would never do.

Not now. If they had come to such a relationship naturally, then, perhaps . . . But probably not. Very likely she would never have overcome her upbringing and never allowed herself to go to his bed unwed. So. She should, should she not, feel relief that the embarrassment they endured did not make that which was already impossible more impossible? Unfortunately the thought didn't seem to help one bit!

Besides, how was she to discipline her mind, make it give up those delicious dreams that left her, of a morning, so needy and wanting and . . . curious? Somehow she must! Because she wouldn't put him from her mind if he continued to haunt her sleep! Frederica turned again, this time putting her back to the window and the glow of moonlight that kept her awake.

At least, she *told* herself it was the *moon* which kept sleep at bay. Nothing else . . .

Chapter Fourteen

The smith remembered Blackthorn and, only his twinkling blue eyes giving away the joke, he solemnly told His Lordship that he'd paid a witch to put a curse on travelers so that their horses would cast a shoe as they went through town.

"You must pay her extra for this one," said Blackthorn politely. "I was barely over the hill when that benighted animal—" He gestured. "—lost his. How long will you be, then?"

"Takes a bit o'time to get a fire hot. But not long then. Not long at all."

Blackthorn nodded and strolled back to the inn where he found Frederica sitting in the garden in which he'd once sat. But then it had been high summer and the plantings lush, the scent high. Now, the summer ending, the plants looked tired, dusty, and what scent remained was less sweet, tangier.

He strolled forward, drawing her attention, pulling her from obviously dark thoughts which had almost seemed to form a cloud around her. She looked up at him, looked away. Seating himself beside her, he nodded when she silently offered him a cup of coffee from the pot set on the low table between them.

"How much longer?" she asked after a moment.

"Once the fire is up, I'm informed it won't be long at all." She merely nodded, falling back into whatever reverie had had such hold on her when he arrived. Although he hadn't found the smithy's jest particularly amusing himself, she might. "I discovered why it happened," he said in as solemn a voice as he could manage.

"Oh?" She stared at the rough brick wall which backed the garden and over which a morning glory vine crawled.

"Yes. The smith informs me he pays a witch to put a curse on travelers."

She swiveled in her seat, staring at him. Settling back, her disbelief evident, she said, "A witch, you say."

"Yes. I told him she was well worth whatever he paid. This is the second horse of mine to throw a shoe in Burford."

He shifted his eyes to the side, looking to see how she took that and discovered she was looking sideways at him. He grinned. She did, too. He chuckled. She laughed.

And, with laughter, came ease. For the moment, at least, they were back to the banter which had, although neither was about to admit it to the other, enriched their friendship almost from their introduction, only slightly less quickly turning instant friendship into love.

A boy arrived as Frederica poured their second cup of coffee. The shoe was just as good as new and did my lord want the team brought up to the inn?

"We'll walk down in a few minutes," he said and tossed the boy a small coin. As the lad disappeared he cast a guilty glance toward Frederica. "I should have asked. You would like the walk, would you not? We'll be jounced about for several hours yet and, I for one, find a walk now and again helps so that I'm not so stiff at the end of it."

"I agree." She rose to her feet and he followed suit. "Shall we go, my lord?"

He'd paid their shot and, since he'd had their boxes put in the curricle before seeing the smith earlier, there was nothing they need do but stroll down the street.

"You haven't looked in any of the windows we've passed," he mused half to her and half to himself.

She looked up at him. "Should I?"

He grinned, a slanting teasing grin. "In *my* experience women are incapable of passing a shop without wondering if there might not be a special something they'd regret leaving behind."

"But if one does not look, then one does not know."

"Ah, but how does a woman *not* look?"

"You suggest, my lord, that I am not a woman?"

"Heaven forbid! You, my dear, are very much a woman, and one I think highly of—" He glanced sideways. "*—as you know.*"

"Don't."

"Don't flirt with you? Tease you?" Again he glanced at her and, softly, added, "Love you? I cannot help myself."

Her chin rose a notch. "I'll not have you pretending simply because you fear you've compromised me," she said a trifle grimly. "You live a life you prize, one you've carefully contrived to suit you right down to the ground. You are mistaken to think that you are forced to marry me and change it all around."

"Blunt. May I be equally blunt?"

"Of course you may! I cannot take a liberty which I do not allow others."

"Then I'll inform you that although I was precipitate yesterday, when I asked you to wed me I have, for some little time now, had every intention of doing just that. I had meant, however, to wait until I thought you knew me better, until your feelings had perhaps come to match mine for you. I'd hoped that by no later than Christmas, at the latest, you'd have reached that point. If we'd not been thrown together, now, I'd have waited, but, Frederica, my love, I would, eventually, have asked."

"I do not believe you. You are simply trying your best to put a good face on it all. Please cease to press me, my lord."

Blackthorn sighed. "You are merely stubborn. You've taken a notion into your head and I must ponder how I am to shake it out." He pressed her arm, where it lay through his, to his side and she looked at him, only to be disconcerted by the tenderness she saw in his eyes. "Never fear," he said, smiling. "I'll figure it out!"

They arrived just then at the smithy and Blackthorn released her, moving forward to pay the smith for his work. ". . . And here," added His Lordship, tongue in cheek, "is a bit extra for your witch! Such expertise should be rewarded."

The smith grinned. "I'll see you when you next pass this way, my lord."

"Perhaps I'll go *around* Burford."

"Hmm." The smith scratched his head. "Mayhap I'll have to see if my witch can't curse the *roads* so this one is the only one open?"

"Your neighbors might object."

The huge muscular man grinned. "So they might." The smithy stood back, hands splayed against his hips, and watched Blackthorn lift Frederica to the curricle's seat. "If you've far

to go, you better move them along, my lord,'' he warned.
"There's a storm blowing in from the west."

Blackthorn glanced that way, where, for the first time, he
noticed that roiling clouds, low on the horizon, threatened to
loom larger very quickly. "Ask your witch to hold that storm
back a few hours, will you?" he asked, a grim note to his voice
and around his mouth. "Frederica, hold tight. As soon as I'm
across the bridge, I'm going to spring them."

"The boys . . ."

"The boys will be fine, but I'm afraid they'll not make it
home tonight. The tribe won't travel in really bad weather. Not
if they don't have to." He laid a hand on her thigh for just a
moment. "Don't worry, my love. But do hold on!"

Frederica couldn't have spoken if she'd wanted to. The
warmth from his palm burned into her flesh long after the brief
touch was gone. How dare he touch her *there?* And how,
she wondered, despairing, would she ever manage to convince
herself she must cease wishing he'd the right to do so!

One Gypsy after another cast worried glances toward the
west. Whenever there was a break in the trees, or as they passed
alongside a stone-fenced field, the boys, too, looked at the
slowly approaching storm. Would it, they wondered, whispering, be a help or would it make escape impossible?

"Where, exactly, are we, Stu?"

"We came up onto the wold just after daylight. And it must
be getting on for noon. Say we've been moving at four miles
per hour . . ."

"Better say three."

"All right. Three miles per hour, which is pretty slow, you
know . . . ?"

"For horses, but we're walking."

"Oh. Of course. All right. Six hours?"

"We stopped for breakfast, remember . . . ?"

"Oh. Five then. Three times five is . . . ?"

"Fifteen. So?"

"So maybe . . . another fifteen?"

Matthew bit his lip. "Stewart, I don't think I *can* walk
another fifteen miles. Not today."

"I don't think I can either."

They moved along, swinging their tied legs in the manner they'd learned from hard experience.

"Maybe," suggested Stewart after a bit, "you should pretend to limp and maybe that woman would take us up beside her again?"

"I don't have to pretend," said Matthew grimly. "There's a hole in one stocking and I've a blister, I think, and I *am* sort of limping."

"Maybe I could pretend to faint? They'd have to take us up then."

"You maybe, but not me."

"Oh. Maybe *you* should faint. You've got the blister . . . wait, why are they turning into that field?"

"To stop and eat, maybe? I hope!" Matthew rubbed his stomach. "I'm starving."

Stewart glanced toward the approaching storm. "Maybe they've decided to stop altogether. Maybe we'll be here for the night."

They eyed each other.

"We'd have all afternoon then, to try and get away . . ." suggested Matthew.

The boys stared at the clouds.

"Should we, do you think?" asked Stewart, hesitating. "I thought we'd be closer to home when we tried it. If we got away *now* and then they catch us, well, they'd see we didn't escape again, wouldn't they?"

"So—" Matthew bit his lip. "—we should wait?"

"What do you think?"

"I don't know. You know the area better than I. Could we get away?"

"I don't know *this* area at all. We're miles from home yet!"

"Oh. Well . . ."

"Shh. They're forming a camp."

"Let's wait til we're closer to your home," said Matt, urgently whispering. "I don't think I could bear to be caught again . . ."

"Me either . . ." Stewart, his eyes narrowed, set his teeth slightly off center. "All right," he decided. "Tomorrow, then, if we don't go on today."

A few moments later the big man they'd learned was the old woman's son came to them, grasped them by their shoulders and pushed them forward into the center of the camp, seating them near where a small fire already burned. They were surrounded by men and women working and milling children and the dogs that got in everyone's way but were, as usual, ignored.

The boys eyed each other and grinned weakly. Without speaking each knew the other was thinking it was just as well they'd decided to wait: In this crowd they'd never have been able to sneak away even if they managed, secretly, to cut the bonds holding their ankles together.

"That church tower means we're approaching Stow-on-the-Wold," said Blackthorn. We'll stop and I'll hire a closed carriage for you. The storm is *not* going to hold off until we get you home." He pulled around a curve which then reversed itself and turned back north. They drove up the wide street to where the ancient Royalist Inn stood, its front door wide open. The low hall beyond was a dim but welcoming sight as was the groom who came running to stand to the head of the horses. Blackthorn climbed down and came around to lift Frederica down.

Pushing from her mind the effect his hands had on her body, she said, "You must rest your horses."

"I'll leave them. If they'd not worked hard all yesterday, I'd take them on, but I can't push them any further. Certainly not at the speed they've been going. This is a good inn. I'll not fear for them here."

Frederica bit her lip, then drew in a deep breath. "You could ride with me, my lord. I don't like to think of you getting soaked merely because it is conventional that we not ride together in a closed carriage."

Blackthorn hesitated, the temptation almost too much to bear. "If it begins to rain, I'll join you," he promised quietly, wishing the skies would open right then and there.

Frederica glanced at him and nodded. "I'll just be a moment, my lord," she said and entered the inn where she was met by the landlady who showed her through the maze of rooms and out the back where, as she'd promised him, Frederica spent a very brief time. So brief, in fact, that when she returned, the post chaise and his curricle were not quite hitched up.

She waited in the doorway, sipping the mild cider the landlady handed her and looked over the roofs of the row of houses across the street. The storm loomed, the black bottoms of the clouds heavy with moisture and the tops billowing. Here and there a quick flash of lightning lit them from the inside out.

Where was her son? she wondered. Blackthorn's son? Would they be soaked to the skin when the rain came? Would they be chilled, come down ill, catch pneumonia . . .

Blackthorn finished inspecting the team he'd hired for his curricle and came over to her. "What is it, Frederica?" he asked, breaking into her thoughts.

"What? Oh, nothing . . ."

"It isn't nothing. Not when your skin is pale and you've actually bitten through your lip so that it bleeds." He handed her his handkerchief but, when she just looked at it blankly, lifted it to touch the side of her lip himself. He held it away so she could see the small spot of red. "Now, tell me, my love!"

His love? If only . . .

Frederica pushed away that fruitless wish while only half formed. Now, what had he asked?

"It *was* nothing, my lord. Or nothing *new.* I am concerned for our sons, worrying they'll get wet and chilled when that storm breaks, that they'll be ill."

"They'll be cared for, Frederica. Please don't let your imagination run away with you."

"But Gypsies . . . will they know that our boys are unused to living out in all weathers? Will they know our sons are not . . . not hardened to rough travel? Will they . . ."

"They *will.* I assure you. Frederica, have you forgotten I traveled all one summer with them? That I know their ways? It's my guess that just about now they've formed a camp somewhere to the west of us and will, as soon as they've eaten, put the children inside a caravan. They'll remain where they are until the storm passes. If it clears they may travel on into the night and, in that case, we could have the boys home before noon tomorrow. They've their own life, Frederica. They cannot spend days and days caring for a pair of runaway gorgio brats."

"Blackthorn," she asked the thought which had been teasing her mind off and on ever since she'd found and disbelieved the boys' note, "has it occurred to you to wonder *why* the boys ran away."

"Why they've *really* run away?"

She nodded. "That letter they left. I didn't believe it. You didn't either, if you'll remember."

"Their letter was a red herring. So it is a mystery, is it not?"

Frederica winced at a brighter flash of lightning but Blackthorn ignored it.

"Perhaps," he suggested, "when we have them back again, we can discover the truth of it?"

"I don't know that I'll try," mused Frederica. "Not right away, anyway."

"Perhaps you're right in not pressing them. Then—" He grinned a quick, rather devilish, grin. "—when they think we've forgotten and are off their guard, *then* we'll pounce!"

Frederica chuckled. "I'd not thought of doing that, but a very good notion, my lord."

Blackthorn grimaced. "I wonder if you'll ever stop milording me!" His voice softened. "I would much prefer it if you were to use my name, Frederica."

Call him Spencer as his aunt did? All humor faded from her expression. "I don't think *that's* a good notion at all. My lord."

He sighed. "Well, since we're speaking of names, would Diana, Damaris or Daphne do?"

"None of those," she said, relaxing. "I very much dislike my middle name, so please stop trying to discover it, my lord."

"But it has become a challenge! I must discover it."

A challenge. Was that what she was? Was he the sort of man who could not bear to be turned down, whose image of himself was such he couldn't conceive of any woman saying no to him? By refusing him, had she actually made his determination to wed her stronger? No matter what a disaster that might be?

Or, for him, would it be a calamity? Although he did not love her, he was, for reasons she didn't understand, attracted to her. He'd have no difficulty coming to her bed even without love. But then men were strange that way. They didn't seem to need love in the way most woman did. She sighed softly.

If only, she thought, I could say yes, could *make* love with him without *loving* him.

"Frederica?"

"What?" Startled out of her cogitation, she glanced around, then at him. "Did you want something?"

"Only to discover what is going on under that beautiful hair, inside your head, my dear. You've been lost in thought for ever so long now." When she didn't respond, he sighed softly and, more brusquely, added, "Long enough your carriage awaits you. Come along."

Blackthorn drove off ahead of the heavier carriage, the hood of his curricle up, just in case the heavens opened. They had well over an hour, at the very best estimate, before they reached her home. He hoped she wouldn't be chilled in the carriage if the weather changed. He'd asked that hot bricks be put in and a robe, so surely she'd be all right . . .

But what *had* she been thinking that she'd had such a sad look when he'd called her name, drawing her from her thoughts. Was it again the boys? Somehow Blackthorn didn't think so. So he tried to come up with two or three things it *might* have been, but failing and pretty much allowing his horses their heads, his mind slid into inventing scenarios for the *next* time he proposed to his stubborn love.

Such dreams held him until, suddenly, a wild gust of wind, coming from nowhere and pushing hard at the hood to his curricle, very nearly shoved his rig off the side of the road. He was forced, then, to pay attention to the team. Luckily they were well beyond a long stretch of road where there was no sign of life, and approaching the crossroads of Bourton-Downs where a thatch-roofed inn catered to coaches going north toward Broadway, east toward Moreton-in-Marsh, or south toward Stow-on-Wold, the town from which they'd just come.

Blackthorn pulled into the inn yard, jumping down and telling a groom to see to the team, that they'd be stopping to see if the storm would blow through in a reasonable time. He ran back out into the road just in time to flag down Frederica's coach, motioning the driver to turn in.

The coachman was pleased to do so, not at all eager to drive through the pouring rain he expected to fall any moment.

Frederica, however, was not so happy. "Why have we stopped?" she asked, leaning out the window.

Blackthorn, holding on to his hat, motioned toward the skies. Not allowing her to argue, he opened her door and, lifting her from her carriage, practically carried her inside. They were no sooner through the door then a horrendous clap of thunder rolled overhead and, almost at the same instant, rain teemed down, splashing from the cobbles paving the yard and off the front of the inn. More thunder rolled. More lightning flashed.

"Stewart!"

"Is most likely under cover in one of the tribe's wagons! Don't worry so much, my dear. Trust Zall's people to have a little common sense!"

"I wish I were *home.*"

"And what, my love, would you do at home?"

She smiled a wry smile. "Probably pace the floor, worrying."

"If you *must* pace, I will have the host move the tables so you might do so in his dining room. In this weather I doubt he'll need the use of it! Or, upstairs? There might be a suitable hall?"

"The hall sounds delightful."

"Probably dark and the floor uneven," he warned. "Not good for proper pacing."

"Then why did you suggest it?"

"Perhaps to hint how absurd the whole notion. Pacing and worry will do no one, including yourself, a bit of good. Instead . . . oh perhaps our host has a deck of playing cards and we might play piquet? I've gained ownership of Ursa Major, my love, and you might win it along with the milky way which you lost all those years ago?" She didn't respond to his teasing. "Perhaps some other game, if you'd prefer?" he asked politely.

Frederica, realizing she was making a nuisance of herself, sighed hugely and dug down into her large travel reticule. At the bottom—she wondered why whatever she wanted always seemed to be at the bottom—she found the traveling chess set with which she'd beguiled some of the boys' journey early that summer. Freeing it from the clinging material, she handed it over.

"I don't know if I'll recognize a knight from a bishop, my lord, but I'd prefer chess to cards, I think."

"Chess it is."

Wondering if Frederica would object, Blackthorn ordered a private parlor and asked that warm drinks be served. She didn't, docilely following him down the hall and into the cozy room where the host immediately bent to light the fire.

The day had darkened considerably so he also lit a pair of lamps, one of which he set on the round table at which Frederica seated herself. Before leaving the room, he also pulled the curtains across the small windows in an attempt to hide the storm, but nothing would keep out the flashes of lightning or the sound of thunder, to say nothing of the sound of windswept rain rattling against the small bottle glass panes.

"You were right to stop, my lord," she admitted, once the landlady brought in mugs of mulled wine and set a pitcher of the same near the fire to stay warm. "The horses would very likely have bolted in this and neither you nor my driver could have avoided a drenching. I'm sorry I behaved badly on our arrival."

"There have been too many upsets, Frederica. Too many delays. I understand and you've no need to apologize."

Matthew shivered as another burst of lightning slashed across the small window across from the bunk to which he and Stewart had been tied, but this time with enough of a tether they could move a bit. He cringed at the thunder which rolled in great booming waves almost instantly after.

"I don't like storms," he said through gritted teeth.

"*Neither do I,*" agreed Stewart.

"I'm . . . scared."

Stewart winced at another crashing drum roll of thunder. "*Me too.*" A sharp bark of unfunny laughter broke from him. "Do you know I've never said that before. I've always thought it was only me. That only babies were scared of storms."

"Gruddy says thunder won't hurt. It's only the lightning that can kill." Matthew cringed as another bolt briefly lit the inside of the wagon, faded to nothing only to be followed by rolling sound which literally shook the little house-on-wheels. "Maybe it won't hurt one, but it . . . it startles one so."

"That's it probably," agreed Stewart. "You don't expect it,

you know?'' After a moment, he added, ''My uncle says that the longer between the lightning and the thunder the farther away the storm. I wonder why that is.''

''That last must have been pretty close then!''

But Matthew wondered why, too, and tucked the question into a pocket of his mind where he kept for such mysteries, things he liked to think about when he'd a moment or two. Right now he could think of nothing at all. Not when still another blue-bright bolt was followed instantly by thunder and then a cracking sound which was *not* thunder: A crashing-crackling-crunching sound that could only be the noise of an ancient tree falling.

Next came a scream, followed by swearing, and orders shouted from one to another.

Matthew looked at Stewart and Stewart back. ''Do you suppose . . . ?''

Just as Matthew spoke, so did Stewart: ''I wouldn't wonder if . . . You first,'' he urged.

''Do you think the tree hit one of the wagons?''

''From the sound of things, I'd guess it did. I wish we could *see*. That's the worst, isn't it? Not knowing what's going on . . .''

His words trailed off as the back door opened and a man, ducking his head, entered, gently placing an unconscious boy on the bunk opposite. He knelt beside the pallet and touched limbs. Soft swearing indicated something was wrong.

''What is it? Sir?'' asked Stewart.

''His head,'' growled the man. ''He's got a big knot.''

''Concussion!''

The man glanced around. ''What is that, gorgio boy?'' he growled. ''This concussion thing?''

''It's when the brain is hurt and you have to stay in bed forever and be quiet and have the room dark and your head aches to beat the devil and—'' Stewart paused trying to remember. ''—something about the eyes, I think . . .''

''Oh. That. We call it something else. Boy—'' The man stood, his head and shoulders bent beneath the low roof. ''—we need help. If you'll promise not to try to escape I'll release you so you can take care of my son. You seem to know what to do?''

''Stewart had a concussion early this summer,'' offered Matthew.

''We'll honor a parole. For *tonight,*'' said Stewart.

A lightning bolt again lit up the wagon just in time to reveal a white-toothed grin in the dark face turned toward the boys. ''Very well. Until sunup. Watch my son closely!'' He quickly untied their knots and then disappeared out the back.

''He trusts us with his son?''

''Yes. We offered and we've promised to stay until sun up. Now we'd better see about *him.*'' This time Stewart knelt beside the other bed, gently touching the lad's face and moving his fingers around to the back. ''It's a pretty bad bump, Matt.''

''They put ice on your head, Stewart.''

''We don't have ice, but I'll bet that rain is pretty cold. Here's my handkerchief. Open the back door just a little and hold it out until it's wet and cold. While I hold it to the bump, you can be wetting yours and we'll trade off that way, all right?''

The old woman, water dripping from her shawl covered hair, her nose, and her skirts, arrived when they were exchanging rags for the third time. She watched for a moment, grunted that she had other, more needy, patients and that they were to keep on doing what they were doing for this one.

The night seemed to go on forever and both boys, by the time someone came to see about the lad who had awakened once and then drifted away again, were dropping with fatigue. They hadn't even noticed when the storm moved on, the noise and light fading into the distance. It was a younger woman who came, her hair hidden under a brightly colored scarf, who finally relieved them. She pointed toward the other cot, tightly tied the ropes and then, a pan of water beside her, began soaking rags and holding them to the boy's bump.

Stewart and Matthew, after a moment to assure themselves she knew what to do, turned their heads to the wall and fell deeply asleep. They didn't notice when, the storm completely over, the wagons were hitched and, leaving the ruined one, pulled away from the glade and back onto the lanes and byways gradually taking them farther north. Camp, formed as the east paled, was on the Earl of Conventry's land nearly in the shadow of the Broadway Beacon built on the edge of the escarpment near Fish Hill above Broadway.

The sun was high in the sky when, yawning and rubbing his eyes, Stewart rolled to a sitting position. He looked first to the young man lying quietly on the opposite cot, awake, but a certain tension about the eyes and mouth revealing he was in pain, and then out the small window.

He swallowed a gasp when he saw and recognized the two round towers at opposite corners of the crenelated square structure which was not much larger around than one of the towers. It was unmistakable. There was nothing else anywhere that would look like it. The sun turned the Cotswold stone from which the towers were built to a honey-gold and, at the sight, he had to fight back tears: He was *home*.

Well. Almost.

His uncle's estate was only a few miles distant. And, except for the sick boy, they were alone. At least, he could hear none of the sounds he associated with the Gypsies' camp. Not even a dog.

They were *alone*—at least almost alone—and it was time to go home! Stewart shook Matthew awake, covering his friend's mouth when he'd have objected.

"It's time . . ." he whispered, glancing warily at the sick lad.

Chapter Fifteen

"Here you are, my dear, home again," said Blackthorn, opening the carriage door and peering at Frederica who sat in one dim corner, back from the sun which, after the storm, poured down on them.

"Home." She looked beyond him across the wrought-iron gate to the dower house.

Why, she wondered, had she never realized how small the house was? She almost despaired at the thought of living in such restricted quarters after a summer's freedom in the ample space at Seymour Court. Then, silently, she berated herself for such selfish and ungenerous thoughts.

"Frederica?"

"What?" She drew her gaze back to Blackthorn and noted his waiting hand. "Oh!" Quickly, she grasped it and stepped down from the coach. The sound of hooves brought her head around and she smiled. "Ian!"

"Rickie! You've come home!" He dismounted and drew near. "But, were we expecting you and where are the children?"

"There's a problem, Ian. Come on in. While I take off my bonnet, Lord Blackthorn can explain."

Frederica moved between the men and through the gate, noted the hinges needed oiling and the gravel on the path renewed but, after a passing thought to what else might need doing inside and out, she ignored the fact that her handful of weeks away had resulted in such deterioration.

After a few minutes in her musty-smelling bedroom she returned to the parlor where Ian immediately came to her, taking her hands, and pressing them. "You poor dear. How worried you must be."

"Not at all. Blackthorn assures me, as I'm certain he has you, that the boys are safe and will arrive here eventually."

"You are more calm than I could be if it were my son," accused Ian. "In fact, I can't feel at all calm. Stewart is my heir! Even if he were not, he is my nephew and important to me. I cannot understand you!"

"Peace, Ian. I've had time to adjust, to accept, to learn patience. And I must believe Lord Blackthorn *knows.* It will be all right. They will come home safely."

Ian rounded on his heel, glaring at Blackthorn. "You *cannot* be certain. You have merely soothed Rickie's feminine fears by *seeming* certain! Do not, I beg, lie to me as well."

"I have not lied," said Blackthorn quickly. "I know this family. I lived with them one whole summer. Besides that the Seymours, for generations, have had a good relationship with them. It has occurred to me that for reasons I don't understand, they watch over the sons in my family, doing what they can, when they can, to see to their, hmm—" His teeth flashed in a quick grin. "—education? Our boys will be returned to us in due course and you'll find they've matured a great deal. The lessons taught are sometimes subtle, and rarely does one realize at the time what one is learning, but one *does*. Learn, I mean. Believe me.''

A muscle jumped in Ian's jaw. He looked from one calm face to the other and had no notion just how dearly bought that calm was for Frederica. She dared not allow Ian know how worried she was. He would instantly set forth to organize a search party, which would frighten the tribe. He would, perhaps, prosecute them—and Blackthorn would not like that.

In fact, their plan to reach here *before* the boys returned, was to tell their story and prevent that very thing.

''I will wait until this evening.''

Ian made the decision after more dithering than Frederica remembered him indulging in the past. Or was it that she'd become accustomed to Blackthorn's decisive ways?

''If the boys have not appeared, then I'll set in motion the means of finding them.''

Blackthorn frowned. ''The storm will have slowed them. I believe the boys will arrive today, but I do not *know* they will. Give us until *tomorrow* evening.''

''Us?'' asked Ian with a coldness foreign to his nature. ''You think of yourself as a Gypsy, Lord Blackthorn?''

This time it was Blackthorn's jaw in which the muscle jumped. ''I am an adopted member of the tribe. I feel loyalty to those who helped me grow up at a time I badly needed shaking up and my feet set on the right path. I will not see harm come to them when they are doing the same for the next generation.''

''I do not trust Gypsies.''

''Some are not to be trusted. In any group, any nationality, people are good and bad or, for that matter, simply different. You cannot judge all by one or two anymore than you can judge any given family by a single member.''

Frederica choked back a laugh. ''Lord Quincy!''

Blackthorn bent an approving expression her way. ''Exactly.''

''Just who is Lord Quincy and why do you use him as an example? What has he done?'' asked Ian.

''He's beneath contempt,'' said Blackthorn promptly.

"He's . . . got an overly developed imagination," said Frederica more slowly. "It is something of a problem . . ."

"Oh?"

Ian's belligerent expression caused Frederica to sigh.

"Ian," she said, "please, stop acting like a stern and suspicious father stalking around the stage in a farce? I should never have mentioned His Lordship, except that he is a prime example of not judging a family by one member. I've been assured by more than one person that the *rest* of the family is in no way exceptionable." She tipped her head. "Is that your teeth I hear? Ian, you really should not grit them that way."

MacKivern's lips compressed. "I don't know what is going on, but I'll find out. However that may be, Frederica, you'll discover this house is unprepared for your return. You must come along with Lord Blackthorn up to the manor and stay there for a day or two until your servants put into shape for you."

"I had noticed and wondered about it." She wiped a finger through the dust on the table and looked at it. "Where *are* Betsy and Martin?"

Ian's expression shifted from stern determination to faintly defensive. "Matilda thought it foolish to leave them idle. She ordered them up to the manor where they've made themselves useful. We'll send them down and when they've done whatever it is servants do, *then* you may return."

"I think not, Ian. Stewart is, I believe, more likely to come here than to the manor. If he does go there, you and Lord Blackthorn will be there for him. But someone must be here. *And,*" she added, when she saw that Ian would argue, "I am tired. I would be pleased if the two of you were to leave now so that I may rest."

"But it is very nearly noon and I know you usually eat something . . ." objected Ian.

"I mean to take a nap." She glanced down her length and grimaced: The good eating at the Court along with less exercise than usual had added an unnecessary inch or so. "In any case, it will not hurt me to do without!"

Blackthorn cleared his throat. "I think I'll take myself off to the inn in the village. Lady MacKivern would prefer to be warned of my arrival rather than have me suddenly thrust upon her. Besides, you may inform her that her daughters are coming along behind us and should arrive today as well.''

"You did not think it proper to escort them?" asked Ian with a dangerous edge to his voice.

Blackthorn's voice hinted at still greater danger. "I did what I thought proper, MacKivern, and reaching this place before my son and your heir was more important than following along at the slow pace my agent must take, especially given your elder daughter's, hmm, *aversion* to travel. If it hadn't been for the storm, we'd have arrived yesterday." His Lordship turned to Frederica and grasped the hand she automatically held out to him. Holding it in both his own he stared down at her. "You'll be all right?"

"Of course."

"I'll return when I think you've rested. Remember. The boys are fine. They'll look back on this as a great adventure."

"I know."

"Soon, then."

"Yes."

They continued standing there, staring into each other's eyes.

Ian cleared his throat and Blackthorn realized he still held Frederica's hand. He released it and, nodding to Ian, immediately left the room.

Frederica remained silent until she heard the front door close and then rounded on her brother-in-law.

"What is wrong with you?" she demanded.

"I don't know what you mean."

"From the look on your face, you know exactly what I mean!"

"I don't want you alone with that man ever again, Rickie. I'll send him a message he is to come to the house, *not here.*"

"You will do no such thing."

"My dear, you don't understand. There has been . . . talk."

"Who? What sort of talk?"

"Merrick passed it on when he arrived for a short, er, *visit* earlier this summer. You are thought to be Lord Blackthorn's mistress, Rickie. Such talk must be scotched."

"*Quincy.* Blast and bedamned to the man!"

"Your language seems to have deteriorated over the summer as well," said Ian coldly.

"As well?" Frederica glowered. "You, who have known me all your life, *believed* such idle rumor?"

An abashed look crossed Ian's face but soon faded. The grim expression returned. "It is not relevant what I believe or do not believe. What is important is what our neighbors believe."

Her brows arched. "I must remember to thank Matilda who has, of course, done her best to contradict the talk?"

Ian's ears reddened. "Rickie . . ."

"Do not do your feelings damage by trying to explain, Ian. I understand everything. But do you?"

"Do I what?"

"Understand?"

"I . . . don't know. He's a very attractive man and he was attracted by you from the first—" Ian's expression revealed he couldn't quite understand why. "—and you are . . . you've reached an age when . . . Well, women . . . hmmm . . ."

"That's what Tildy told you? That when a woman fears she has lost her looks she grabs at any chance to prove otherwise? And just when was this great affair supposed to have taken place? While we traveled with four children and two servants, perhaps? Or when we reached Seymour Court, I suppose, with those same children all over the place *and Blackthorn instantly gone off to London?* Oh, go away, Ian. You disgust me. I do not know you. I don't want to see your face again until I come to terms with the fact you could ever, for a moment, have thought I'd behave in such a manner!"

"Rickie!"

"I am hurt, Ian. Deeply hurt. And I haven't the time for it. Until Stewart is back, I haven't the energy to waste wondering what I ever did that you could think such a thing." She swung around, putting her back to him. "Go away, Ian. Now."

"Rickie, I'm sorry. You know I wouldn't hurt you for the world. But you weren't here and, well . . . Oh, I don't know."

"And your precious Matilda, who was perfectly willing to allow me to take her children and be responsible for them, convinced you I was the sort to, at the same time, indulge my passions with a man I barely knew!"

"Don't insult my wife!"

"Ian," she said turning, her eyes flashing "will you leave

before we have a fight which results in a permanent fissure in our relationship?''

He stared at her, baffled. ''I don't want to fight with you, but you mustn't insult Tildy.''

''No, of course I mustn't,'' said Frederica on a sigh, wondering if he would ever realize he allowed that same Matilda to insult her. ''Please leave me alone. I just want to be *alone.*''

''You mustn't allow Blackthorn entry when he returns,'' warned Ian.

''Must I not? We'll see.''

Ian hesitated. ''I'll give Martin his orders. And I'll return when you are rested and less twitty.''

''Twitty!'' Frederica glared.

''I'll send Betsy down with a tray from our kitchens. Perhaps you are merely hungry,'' he mused, eying her warily.

''Go away Ian,'' said Frederica through gritted teeth, her eyes again flashing the fires of an aroused temper.

Ian smiled indulgently and, completely certain in his own mind that he'd discovered the problem, he left. Frederica wished with all her heart that he were not quite so good at rationalizing things which bothered him so that, having done so, he no longer had to think about them.

''Hurry,'' urged Stewart, pushing Matthew out the wagon's door.

''Let me look around. We don't want to walk right into someone, do we?''

Stewart realized the justice of that. As Matthew looked out, he looked behind him at the boy on the bed, wondering if they should gag him so he'd not raise the alarm. The lad had his eyes closed and appeared to be asleep and he *was* sick. Stewart remembered how he'd hated remaining quietly in bed while he recovered from the bump on his head. Stewart couldn't bring himself to add to the boy's discomfort by tying and gagging him.

''Well?'' he asked, turning back to Matthew.

''It looks all right.''

''We can't stand here forever. They might come back.''

''Yes, you're right about that.''

But even so Matthew hesitated another moment before he hopped down, Stewart following.

Stewart grabbed Matt's hand, racing off toward folly, a more substantial structure then most, since this one had living quarters in the central tower. The boys were soon hidden from the sight of anyone on the other side and there they paused while Stewart looked over the terrain, remembering the terrain and plotting their best way home.

They'd gone maybe half a mile and finally felt they were probably free and clear when Matthew asked, "How far is it?"

"Just a few more miles. We'll be safe and Uncle Ian will have those gypsies brought up before the magistrate! They won't be taking any other boys off somewhere to sell them!"

"You know, Stewart," said Matthew after a moment, "I've begun to wonder if they ever really meant to do so."

"Meant to what? Sell us? But they said . . ." Stewart looked baffled when Matthew just stared at him. "What do you mean?"

"I don't think they would have really done it."

"They *said* they would. They kept us tied up." Stewart glanced at Matthew. "Worst of all, they didn't let on we were there when your father and my mother were talking to them . . ."

"Yes, and that's another thing," said Matthew sounding slightly outraged. *"Why didn't my father ask them if they'd seen us!* He didn't even ask if they'd watch out for us, help him find us. He *should* have asked. And he *didn't."* More quietly Matthew added, "That tribe is our tribe, don't you know?"

"No, I don't know." But Stewart slowed down, a frown creasing his brow. "You think it was all a hum, their saying they meant to sell us? Because now you mention it, just how did they know we'd be running away that morning? They didn't usually came up that close to the house, did they? At least I never saw them . . ."

"I think it's all a bit of mystery and *I* think my father knew all the time we were with the Gypsies and I think he let us stay there because it would teach us a lesson!"

Stewart thought about it. He felt chagrined when he concluded that not only had the knife been dropped on purpose, but the Rom had left them alone today just so they could get away. "That Rom boy never did come looking for his knife, did he?" He walked on a bit further. "Do *you* suppose the camp was deserted on purpose just to give us our chance?"

"*I* think so," said Matthew, limping along beside his friend. "What do you think?"

"Well," Stewart grumbled, "even if that's what they did, *we* did what we set out to do, didn't we? Your father and my mother were together. We managed *that*. Even if they *knew* we were *safe*?" He glanced at Matthew. "If they did, of course!"

"They were together, all right."

The boys stalked on another hundred yards or so.

"Do you suppose he asked her?" asked Matthew.

Stewart stopped, stared straight ahead. "I can't even guess," he finally admitted, stepping out again. "I guess we'll have to wait and see . . . find out when we get home."

"I *hope* it worked." Matthew sighed. "I don't know what we might try next if it didn't."

"I suppose I could refuse to go back to school," said Stewart, after a moment's thought.

"What good would that do?" asked Matthew, a touch of scorn in his voice. "You'd be stuck at home with her worrying you to death. Or, at least, that's what you always say she does."

"There's that." They walked on for another hundred yards or so. "You think of anything?"

"No."

Stewart sighed. "Then I suppose we'll just have to wait for Christmas."

"*If* you come . . ."

"What?" Stewart stopped again and grabbed his friend's shirt when Matthew didn't stop as well. "What do you mean, *if* we come?"

"Well, your mother may be mad at us, you know?"

"She'll be mad, but I don't think she'll try to keep us apart . . ."

"Keep us apart!" This was a concern which hadn't crossed Matthew's mind. "She couldn't be so cruel. She isn't such a meanie as that . . . !"

"Maybe not. But she's *female* so who can know?"

"There's that." Matthew now had something new to worry about.

For a very long way the boys remained silent, just trudging along side by side and hoping for the best.

Behind them, like a shadow, a young Rom followed. He'd volunteered to see that the boys reached home safely. He'd found it easy to trail them since they never looked back. Now and again he smiled at the sight of the two, walking apart, but exactly as they'd done when tied at the ankle, swinging first their inside legs forward and then the outside legs. He grinned as he wondered how long they'd continue that habit . . .

"Martin, I do not care what Ian ordered you to do. I pay your wages and you will obey me or you'll find yourself and your bundle in the middle of the road with nowhere to go!"

Martin grinned. "Yes, Mrs. MacKivern. I hear you. I'll admit Lord Blackthorn when he comes." He bowed, not quite far enough to hide the grin which he managed to wipe from his face as he straightened.

Frederica did a more adequate job of stifling a groan as she watched him leave the parlor. Would he admit Blackthorn? Or would he agree to do so, but obey Ian's orders after all? Frederica paced the room once, found it far too small and over-full of furniture for the maneuver, and stalked upstairs for her pelisse. The front walk would be more adequate to the task . . . or, even better, the road out front of the dower house!

It was just as well she was in the road, because, when he appeared, it was obvious Blackthorn was a trifle upset at seeing her. "Frederica?" he asked. "Has something happened?"

"Only that my idiotic brother-in-law has decided I may not invite whomever I please into my home." She opened the gate and walked through. "Will you come in for a moment, my lord?"

He didn't move, merely asking, "Is something wrong?"

The thought running through Frederica's mind was that suddenly *everything* seemed wrong. However, all she *said,* was, "Nothing new." Her knuckles turned white where she grasped one of the spikes at the top of the gate.

"My dear . . ."

"No, I understand," she interrupted, speaking so fast her words ran together. "That ghastly Quincy's tales have reached even this corner of the world and you must be careful, of course, not to add to the rumors which can only hurt your career. I will await word of the arrival of our sons or, if they come here, I'll immediately send word to the Hall.''

"You do understand then," he said a trifle hesitantly.

"Of course I understand." She almost spit the words at him and, turning on her heel, stalked up the path and into the house.

Blackthorn stared after her. "No, my lemon-tart love, you don't understand at all or you wouldn't act the shrew," he murmured. He winced as her door slammed behind her. "It is for your protection, my love, that I'll not come in, not my own!"

Clasping his hands behind his back and bowing his head, he meandered his way on up to MacKivern's manor. He was in no hurry to arrive, because he feared that when he did he'd be required to do the pretty by Lady MacKivern and he'd never in his life felt less like playing the part of a proper guest!

His torture lasted only half an hour before the carriage arrived with the MacKivern girls. They burst into the house, racing up to hug their father and, more slowly, to their mother where, not quite certain, they stood before her looking up with identical hopeful looks.

Tears running down her face, her ladyship opened her arms and her daughters went gladly into her embrace. "I have missed you so." She held them away and shook her head. "But what ragamuffins you are! You must come along with me up to the nursery. At once. I'll help you change out of those travel-stained clothes and—" She frowned down at one and then the other. "—you may tell me all about your summer with your aunt."

Ian cleared his throat and Matilda glanced his way. He gave her a stern glance. Blushing slightly, she nodded before, taking each girl by a hand, she drew them away up the stairs, Sal following behind.

Ian waited until they were beyond hearing before turning to Blackthorn. "I do not know why it is, but she's been muttering and fuming and worrying that Rickie will have ruined them, allowing them to run wild. I've told her she is not to scold, that the girls have been on vacation and if, for a few days, they are a little rambunctious, she's to understand and gently hint them back into proper form. She's not to blame them for it.''

"She is to blame Mrs. MacKivern, perhaps?''

Ian glanced at Blackthorn, was rather surprised by the grimness revealed in clenched jaw and frown. "Well, she *will* be to blame, will she not? If the girls have forgotten how to behave?''

"You mean if they have learned how to behave as children instead of like small adults?'' asked Blackthorn politely.

Ian felt his ears heat up at hearing the same sort of false sweetness that Frederica used when wishing to tell one one was a fool. From Frederica Ian could accept such criticism. From Lord Blackthorn it was intolerable.

"I apologize,'' said Blackthorn before Ian could frame a properly scathing retort. "I am on edge. Until the boys have actually appeared, I cannot relax. *Not,''* he added, "because I fear the Gypsies, but because there is always the possibility of accident.'' He sighed. "Perhaps if you do not dislike the notion, we might have a game or two of billiards which would distract me?''

The offer of a game instantly distracted *Ian* who loved to play but had few opportunities to do so. He nodded, turning toward the game room. Blackthorn, rolling his eyes upward in a silent prayer of thanks that he'd managed to defuse what had almost become a serious argument, followed.

If Blackthorn's game was not quite so good as usual, Ian very kindly put it down to the fact they were awaiting the arrival of the runaways, instead of where it actually lay: His Lordship's worry about Frederica and also the fact he was busily scheming, planning his next assault on her determination to say him nay!

Chapter Sixteen

Startled awake, Frederica sat perfectly still, her eyes closed, not quite certain where she was or why she'd awakened. Then she remembered: She was home.

Frederica swung her neck in circles, yawning. *A stiff neck, she thought, is the least I deserve! How could I have fallen asleep in my chair?*

And for how long? She cracked open one eye. The sunlight, which in the morning shown brightly into the little parlor, had faded to the point she decided it must on into midafternoon. She yawned again and stretched.

"I think she's awake," whispered a young voice.

"Maybe," said another doubtfully, "but you don't want to wake Mama too quickly. She snaps when she's only half awake."

Frederica grinned to herself. She turned toward the sound, snapping her teeth. "Grrr," she said.

And then the sight of the boys brought it all back. They'd run away. They'd been gone forever it seemed. And they were back.

"Just how long have you been there," she demanded.

Stewart sighed. "Long enough I'm really hungry. Where's Betsy? Why isn't there anything to eat? There isn't *anything* in the larder," he added accusingly, "not even an apple."

Frederica slowed the flow of her son's words with a raised hand. "It doesn't help me that you're hungry. You are *always* hungry. I still haven't a notion how long you've been here."

She stood as she spoke and went to the mantle where the clock gave her no help either. Very obviously the thing hadn't been wound for days. Weeks. Perhaps the whole time she'd been at Seymour Court? Turning back she noticed Matthew was taking off his shoe. She dropped to her knees and picked up his foot.

"Blisters," she exclaimed. "Blast it! Blackthorn swore the Gypsies wouldn't allow you to be hurt!"

"They didn't know," responded Matthew quickly in the same breath as, disgusted, Stewart said, "So, you did guess where we were!"

Frederica looked from one boy to the other. "Guessed where you were?" she asked.

"Matt thought you had. That time you stopped to talk to the gypsy princess? He said you'd have asked them to watch out for us if you truly thought us lost."

"Matt was correct that we knew," she said, looking from one boy to the other, "except we weren't required to guess. Your Gray Shadow was kind enough to tell us where you were."

"Gray Shadow? *He* knew?" Matt's eyes rounded. "But how could he know?"

"I've no notion. And at the moment it isn't important. We must get that heel cleaned up, bandaged, and go up to the manor where your uncle, Stewart, is very likely organizing a search party!"

"Search party?" Stewart looked at Matthew who shrugged. "Why would he do that if you knew where we were?"

"He decided to give you until this afternoon to come home, as your father, Matthew, said you'd do, but if you didn't, then Ian meant to run down your Gypsies and wrest you from them."

"I told you we should have gone to the manor," accused Stewart.

"You only wanted something to eat," said Matthew with a touch of scorn. "Ouch!" he added, twisting around to find out what Frederica did to his foot.

Very soon, a boy on either side, Frederica set out for the manor. They explained about being tied up, about how frightened they'd been, thinking they were on the way to some northern port where they were to be sold.

"But then we got that knife . . ." Stewart's voice trailed off. "Matt, he did drop it on purpose, didn't he?"

"Of course he did. We were meant to escape."

Stewart was silent for a long moment. "You know, Matt. Now I think it over, it wasn't really much of an adventure, was it?"

"Well, it was scary enough while we were doing it," said Matthew a trifle hesitantly. "Does that count, do you suppose?"

Stewart trudged along another few yards. "Do you think then, we could call it an adventure even if we were safe as houses?"

Frederica smiled. She waited to hear what Matthew would reply and he didn't disappoint her:

"For my part it's more adventure than I want for a long time to come!"

Again Stewart was silent for a moment. They he sighed hugely. "I guess for me too." After another silence, he asked, "Can we go around to the kitchen?"

"No," said Frederica. "You deserve to suffer, after the nightmares I've had because of what you did. You two can just wait to eat until after you've apologized to Matthew's father and to your uncle for worrying us so!"

"But if you knew . . ."

"The trouble is, Stewart, we only *hoped* we knew. We could not be certain your Gypsies wouldn't disappear and you'd be lost and gone forever. We couldn't truly *know*."

This time Matthew broke the ensuing silence. "Did you enjoy your journey with my father?" he asked politely.

"Enjoy feeling anxious every foot of the way? Wondering where you were and how you were being treated? I should say not!"

Frederica didn't know why the boys sighed huge exasperated sighs, but she wasn't in a mood just then to ask. She turned off the drive and into the gardens, heading around the side of the house to where she thought the men might be whiling away the time in the games room. She'd no desire to see her sister-in-law just now. Not until the worst of the brouhaha was over and the boys off to the kitchen to beg an early supper from Cook . . .

". . . And I tell you you'll marry her!"

Ian's voice, loud with anger, broke into Frederica's thoughts. The fact the window was open was very likely not relevant to her overhearing him. In fact, she wondered if they couldn't hear him roaring all the way down in the village.

"You'll remain here," insisted Ian only slightly more quietly, "while the banns are called. I'll see you at the altar with my sister-in-law if I have to hold a gun to your head . . . !''

Frederica stopped, her eyes closing, her teeth clenching, and her head falling back. But only for half an instant. She stopped the boys, who were grinning at each other in a fashion she didn't wish to think about.

Later. Later she'd find out why they looked so pleased with themselves. Not now. Not when she had to deal with Ian.

Pointing the boys toward the back of the house, she whispered, "I've changed my mind. You run along and eat. And don't come until you're called."

Matthew winked at Stewart. Stewart winked back. They ran off and Frederica set herself another reminder that she was to discover what went on in their heads. Then she moved nearer the open windows.

". . . gun to her head, too?" Blackthorn was saying. "And what will you do when the vicar asks the crucial question and she says no? Pull the trigger?"

"She wouldn't be so foolish."

"She's *already* said me no," said Blackthorn wearily. "I admit it was not the most adroit of proposals, but she caught me off guard and I misinterpreted something she said. I suppose it was wishful thinking, actually. I'd hoped to propose before the boys left for school, but what I planned included time together in London during which I could woo her properly."

Frederica blinked. Was he making that up? He *must* be. Surely it was just something he'd thought up which would soothe Ian's outrage? But pretending didn't really sound like the Blackthorn she knew, did it?

"Ah!" There was satisfaction in Ian's tone when he asked, "Then you'd heard the gossip and meant to do the proper thing all along?"

"The gossip is not relevant. It wasn't then and it isn't now. I wish I could get it through your thick skull that I *want* to wed your sister-in-law!"

Frederica bit her lip. A telling point, Ian's. Still, Blackthorn *sounded* sincere. *But why,* she wondered, *would he want to marry me?*

"Why?" asked Ian.

Oh Ian! Blunt to a fault. But, even as the wry thought crossed her mind, Frederica strained to hear the answer.

"If it is any of your damn business—"

She could envision Blackthorn running fingers through his hair and wished she dared peer into the room, could see *him.*

"—I've fallen in love with her. She's magnificent. I don't know how I could have helped myself."

"I guessed you found her attractive, but . . . love?"

Must Ian sound so astounded? She wasn't so unlovable as all that! Frederica made a wry face, sticking out her tongue much as she'd have done when a child and mad at Ian or Stu!

"Are you certain?" added her skeptical brother-in-law.

Which made her still more angry! She was *not* unworthy of a man's love! *Not!*

"I'm so certain," said Blackthorn grimly, "that I purchased a special license and carried it with me to Seymour Court. Just in case. Then the boys upset my plans and we're here. Now, will you let this drop? I must woo my elusive love my own way. She's the most skitterish woman I've ever met."

"Skitterish? Rickie?"

"When it comes to love, she's wary. Very wary." Blackthorn sighed. "I don't know if your brother was less than loving, a less than skillful lover so she's afraid of a physical relationship, or whether she's still so deep in love with him she cannot look at another man. Whatever it is, I want her and I'll have her, but I must deal with whatever is holding her back."

Her heart beating more rapidly and a distinct warmth infusing her emotions Frederica turned away, moving deep into the rose garden. Before she saw Blackthorn again she had to rearrange her thinking. For so long she'd been sure he could not love her the notion he *did* took some believing!

But he did. He *did!*

Frederica wrested a blossom heavy with scent from a bush and strolled on, leaving a trail of petals behind. He loved her.

Or did he? Did she *dare* believe Blackthorn? Or was he merely trying to convince Ian? But then, why should he bother?

Unless it were true?

And a special license . . . *he bought a special license.* The warmth raced up her body, coloring, she was sure, her cheeks and her ears, which tingled. Surely it meant he'd seriously considered wedding her even before he left London. But, however much he protested, whatever he *said, wasn't* it more than likely he'd done it because of the gossip?

On the other hand, Lady Amelia had insisted the gossip was a nine days wonder. Surely his aunt had convinced him, too, that there was no need to marry for that reason. They'd scotched the rumors around the Court, even among her most virulent ill-wishers. But, in London? Such talk would have currency only so long as nothing new came along over which the gossips could chew.

And, when she herself had suggested the rumors might do his political career no good, he'd insisted they would not harm it . . . Frederica plucked another rose before turning into the shrubbery which had been designed to protect one wishing mild exercise in blustery weather.

Blackthorn wanted to marry her.

The thought ran through her mind over and over again. For whatever reason, he wanted to marry her. And he'd wanted it for some time. It had *not* been their equivocal situation, traveling together unchaperoned, or her awkward choice of words which, wrongly, hinted she thought they should wed. Neither of those had led to his offer there in the inn.

So why, then, the clenched fist? Could it possibly have been that he'd feared she say him nay, and *not,* as she thought, that she say him yea?

"The boys said you were out here somewhere," said his well loved voice from some paces behind her. "Thank you for leaving a trail for me to follow."

Frederica swung around. "You."

He glanced down his length, back at her. "It was the last I looked," Blackthorn admitted, rueful.

She smiled. "Trail?"

"The rose petals." One of his brows arched. "Were they not to guide me to you?"

She looked down, back the way she'd come and realized the pink petals lay bright and colorful against the green sward. "Sorry. The roses were an accident."

"I'll thank Heaven for accidents, then. I might have searched forever if you'd not left me that clue."

"You wanted to talk to me?"

"Among other things." Again that rueful note and this time with an added suggestive twinkle in his eyes, his gaze resting for a moment on her lips.

Frederica ignored his flirting. "You know I heard you and Ian talking?"

"Talking? Arguing, more like, and yes, the boys said you overheard some part of it." He looked at his fingers and, very casually, asked, "Did you hear anything which worried you?"

She gazed over his shoulder at nothing at all. "Only that you might be forced to do something you don't want to do."

"And if it were something I wished very much to do?"

She looked at him, hesitated. "I'd hate to see you disappointed or unhappy."

He sighed. "I can read that answer both ways, Fredcrica. Please? a yes or a no? *Will* you wed me?"

She bit her lip.

"Now none of that! I don't like wiping blood from your tempting lips! I've other, far more interesting plans for them!"

She knew she blushed rosily at that. "I wish I knew how to answer you. I wish I knew what was for the best."

He reached for her, holding her shoulders, his gaze serious. "If you will not do it because we love each other, and I think we do. At least—" He tipped his forehead until it rested against hers "—I know I'm deep in love with you." He sighed when she didn't respond. "If not because we love each other, will you do it for the boys? They did tell you what they told me, did they not?"

"Why they really ran away?"

He nodded.

"I didn't ask. But what explanation could they give that would make any sense at all?"

"They had a notion it would keep you and me together for a few more days. You'll recall I'd told you it was safe to return to your home and you mentioned a letter from Ian asking that you bring the girls home at once?"

"But we ... London ... ?"

"You changed your mind about London, remember?" said Blackthorn brusquely, then smiled. "I think the boys have more sense than you or I, my dear."

"How so?"

"It seems they decided as long ago as when I brought your son home to you early this summer that we should be married. It seems that not only—"

His face settled into lines of a false sobriety and Frederica instantly felt both wary and curious as to how he'd finish that sentence.

"—will they then be brothers, but since they are exactly the same age, almost, they'd be *twins*. Do we dare stand in the way of such ambition, my love?"

There it was again, that whimsy she loved.

"I love you," he said softly.

But no humor in *that*. And she loved him.

"I hear the Lake District is lovely this time of year . . ." he said, thoughtfully.

"I've always wished to visit the lakes . . ."

They eyed each other.

"Then you will?" he asked.

Frederica drew in a deep breath. Before a single other thought could come into her head to confuse her all over again, she nodded. One firm nod of her head.

With that admission any thought at all became impossible. She was drawn into his embrace, his mouth finding hers and passion such as she'd never experienced rose within her. She was not happy when, breathing a trifle hard, his heart pounding under her hand, he set her away.

"This will never do, my love," he scolded, "Ian will be back with that gun he threatened to hold to our heads and he'll not even give us time to tell him it's unnecessary! Not if he finds you as compromised as I'd like to compromise you. Much more of this and he would, too!"

Frederica silently berated herself for wishing Blackthorn hadn't thought of Ian. She'd been so close to discovering what it was she dreamed! At least she was pretty certain the feelings she felt when he reluctantly released her were identical to the ones with which she awoke each morning.

Matilda, told at dinner that her sister-in-law was to marry Blackthorn was torn between conflicting emotions. She'd finally be rid of Frederica who, without even wanting to, upset her peace. But that same sister-in-law . . . now she was merely an untitled widow and of little consequence. Married to Blackthorn, she'd become something far above what Matilda herself had achieved. *Frederica would be a countess,* a notion which didn't sit well with Matilda. Not at all.

When the women removed from the table to the drawing room Frederica said the only thing she could think of which might set Matilda's mind in better frame. ''Just think what fun we'll have when your girls are old enough for their presentation, Tilda! By then, surely, I'll have met all sorts of people who can help put the girls feet on the proper path! They'll have a wonderful season, will they not?''

Reminded that there might be advantages to having an earl in the family, Tilda set aside her jealousy and offered to help Frederica plan the simple wedding she and Blackthorn agreed was all they wanted. More, she threw herself into the planning heart and soul!

A short week later Frederica stood in the back of the village church. Her new gown was a prime example of Matilda's meddling in the wedding. It was the best the village seamstress could manage in the time available and was far too ornate and far more girlish than Frederica thought suitable. But Matilda and the seamstress had chosen the frilly style over Frederica's objections which were, by both Matilda and seamstress, considered missish in the extreme. Whoever heard of such a plain gown for a wedding dress as Frederica requested? Not even a single flounce! They agreed it wouldn't do.

Matilda had been difficult ever since the betrothal was announced and letting her have her way in such things as the design of the gown maintained a precarious peace. So, badly dressed in her own opinion, Frederica held her son's hand with her right and, with her left, Matthew's. The boys were feeling exceedingly anxious about the responsibility they'd accepted: They, after all, were to give away the bride!

With great care the boys led Frederica to the altar where Blackthorn awaited them, Ian and Dr. Milltown at his side. The church was filled with neighbors, servants and villagers. Somewhere at the back, the sweet voices of the children's choir rose in glorious song and, facing her, smiling, the vicar who had wed her to Stewart held open his book to wed her to her new love.

The wedding was, according to the Misses Fraymark, the most moving they'd ever attended and, since Rose and Violet had attended every wedding held in the region since they were old enough to go to such things, that was felt a compliment indeed. Matilda, they said, did the couple proud. Everyone who attended praised the wedding breakfast which was everyone who could scramble for an invitation.

Frederica was happiest, however, when, finally, she went to change from the wedding dress.

"Much better," agreed Blackthorn when she joined him in the hall before going in to say their good-byes. He touched her cheek gently. "It was generous of you, my love, to give in to Matilda and allow her her way, but I am very glad to see you looking yourself again! My Delilah."

He grinned as she blushed rosily, eying him askance.

"So. I finally guess."

"And, having guessed, you may instantly forget!"

"Ah, but I was hoping you'd be *my* Delilah? I'm perfectly willing that you cut my hair, you know. Not that I'll be your Samson in any other way, but I *want* to be caught in your toils!"

Frederica merely gave him a look and turned to make her goodbyes to neighbors and friends. The boys accompanied them out to their carriage, promising to behave and not get into mischief and that, yes, they would also be good when Uncle Ian took them back to school, and no they'd not cause Aunt Matilda any trouble and . . .

"Isn't it everything great!" exclaimed Stewart to his friend, as Blackthorn helped Frederica into the coach.

"Absolutely the best!" agreed Matthew.

"What do you mean?" asked His Lordship.

"Why, that we finally managed to get you two married, of course!" they said more or less in chorus.

Blackthorn squeezed Frederica's hand and winked at her. "So you did," he agreed. "The very best idea you've ever had!"

Epilogue

No one was ever able to convince Stewart and Matthew they'd not contrived the whole. Nor would they admit they were not twins, even though their birthdays were several days apart.

Or perhaps it was merely they didn't wish to be convinced?

In any case, they went through the rest of their lives smugly telling their younger siblings, two sets of *real* twins, that *they* were the best pair, because *they got to choose each other,* while the others had no choice at all, each having to take his or her twin, will-he nill-he, just as he or she happened to be!

Dear Readers,

My next regency, *Lord Galveston and the Ghost,* has a romantic ghost in it. Not only does she get her way, marrying off our heroine, Lady Winifred Alistair, to a proper rake, Lord Marcus Galveston, but she finds the perfect bride for a young man some of you may recall from *A Lady's Deception.* Grenville Somerwell, a gentleman who is plagued by seeing ghosts, discovers that Miss Clare Tillingford, Winifred's cousin, is another such. Not satisfied with two weddings, our ghost, Lady Gwenfrewi, also promotes a match between Winifred's widowed father, Lord Wickingham, and Lady Westerwood, a widow. All in all, Lady Gwenfrewi is a very busy lady . . . er, ghost.

I hope you enjoyed *A Lady's Lesson* which I took great delight in writing. The story was conceived as I toured the boys' school in Winchester, England, an ancient place which has occupied the same buildings without a break for nearly six hundred years!

I enjoy hearing from my readers and enclosing a self-addressed stamped envelope will ensure a reply. All the best to all of you,

Cheerfully,

Jeanne Savery

Jeanne Savery
P.O. Box 1771
Rochester, MI 48308

LOOK FOR THESE REGENCY ROMANCES